# Eternal Hunter

**Also By Cynthia Eden**

Angel of Darkness

Angel Betrayed

Angel in Chains

Avenging Angel

Immortal Danger

Never Cry Wolf

The Wolf Within

Eternal Hunter

I'll Be Slaying You

Eternal Flame

Hotter After Midnight

Midnight Sins

Midnight's Master

**And read more from Cynthia Eden in these collections:**

Howl For It

The Naughty List

Belong to the Night

When He Was Bad

Everlasting Bad Boys

# Eternal Hunter

CYNTHIA EDEN

KENSINGTON PUBLISHING CORP.
http://www.kensingtonbooks.com

KENSINGTON BOOKS are published by

Kensington Publishing Corp.
119 West 40th Street
New York, NY 10018



All Kensington Titles, Imprints, and Distributed Lines are available at special quantity discounts for bulk purchases for sales promotions, premiums, fund-raising, and educational or institutional use. Special book excerpts or customized printings can also be created to fit specific needs. For details, write or phone the office of the Kensington special sales manager: Kensington Publishing Corp., 119 West 40th Street, New York, NY 10018, attn: Special Sales Department, Phone: 1-800-221-2647.



ISBN-13: 978-0-7582-3429-2
ISBN-10: 0-7582-3429-5
First Kensington Trade Paperback Printing: January 2010
First Mass Market Printing: January 2014

eISBN-13: 978-1-61773-035-1
eISBN-10: 1-61773-035-1
Kensington Electronic Edition: January 2014

10 9 8 7 6 5 4 3 2 1

Printed in the United States of America

*Megan—thanks for being a fabulous editor and an amazing lady.*

*And for my mom . . . thanks for always supporting me and for reading my stories!*
*(And you* know *I think you're amazing, too!)*

# Chapter 1

Jude Donovan was used to hunting killers—used to running them down like the damn dogs they were and caging the bastards.

So when he followed his latest prey into the swamps of Louisiana, an area that looked like it had been home to nothing but beasts for the last few centuries, he wasn't nervous.

Until a bullet thudded into him.

*Sonofabitch.* The fiery pain blasted in his shoulder even as the retort of the rifle echoed in his ears.

"You're not taking me back, you bastard!" The snarl came from up ahead, to the right. The tip of the barrel jutted over a fallen log.

Jude gritted his teeth, but didn't bother glancing down at the wound. No time for that, not now. "Bobby Burrows!" He called out the man's name. Voice loud and hard, as if he weren't bleeding like a freaking stuck pig. "There are two ways we can handle this . . ." He stalked forward. Drops of blood littered the ground around him. *Great*. Blood would attract the gators and hell knew what else. *The bastard would pay.* "First way's easy, as in . . . you drop that rifle and come out with your hands up."

"I'm not giving up! I won't go to jail! I won't!" The tip of the weapon began to move. *Fuck.*

"Then we do it the hard way." Jude inhaled and caught the cloying scent of the swamp, the rich flavor of his own blood, and the man's scent of fear and sweat. "I come and get you—*and I rip you apart.*" Simple enough. His eyes narrowed on his target. The ground disappeared beneath Jude's feet as he sprang forward.

A man darted out from behind the log, eyes wild, rifle clutched tight to him. *With a big-ass scope on it, of course.* He lifted, aimed—

Jude growled, a deep, inhuman sound, and he swiped out with his right hand. He caught the wanted man in the right shoulder, and saw the spatter of blood in the air. Bobby's this time, not his.

Wound for wound. Blood for blood. The way of his kind.

He grabbed the weapon, wrenching it out of Bobby's hand. Bobby, a guy in his forties, balding and with big fists, stared up at him, terror on his face. "You—you're not—"

Jude smiled. Held up his hands. Blood stained the claws that seemed to burst out of his fingertips. "Human?"

A whimper.

The smile stretched even more. His shoulder ached like a bitch, pulsing every few seconds, but Jude ignored the pain. An old habit. He leaned forward, ran his claws over the squirming man's stubbled face. "No, I'm not. What I am, Bobby, is the worst nightmare you've ever had." He let his claws dig into skin. "Tell me, did you enjoy cutting those women?"

Bobby's screams pierced the night.

* * *

The first time she saw him, Jude Donovan was covered in blood. Erin Jerome recognized him instantly—she'd seen his picture in the local paper just days before. She watched as Jude handed the wanted man he'd apprehended over to the local cops. Watched as Bobby Burrows, a man who'd cruelly sliced up the faces of his ex-wife, his two ex-girlfriends, and some unlucky woman he'd stumbled across in Baton Rouge, was shoved into the backseat of a squad car.

She could hear Bobby's shouts from across the street. His yells of "Monster!" And his ravings about claws and killers.

Disgust tightened her lips. Jerk was probably already preparing for his defense. An insanity plea. Erin would bet a month's salary on it.

Not that she was going to let the freak get away with something like that.

Oh, no, as an assistant district attorney, it was her job to make sure that old Bobby got to see the inside of an eight by twelve foot cell, preferably for the rest of his miserable life. Angola prison was waiting for him.

Straightening her jacket, because this was only her second week on the job and she needed to be professional—or, at least try to be—Erin crossed the street. Her eyes were drawn to Jude.

The bounty hunter.

He worked for Night Watch, a huge, multi-state operation that had a main base in Baton Rouge. Night Watch was reputed to be one of the best, if not *the* best, bounty hunting agencies in the country. No matter what it took, their hunters caught their prey.

A fact that, right then, made her enormously grateful. Her job would get a whole lot easier now that she had the defendant in custody.

Her heels tapped on the pavement. Time to—

Jude's head shot up. His eyes, the bluest she'd ever seen, lazered in on her.

Erin stumbled. No, oh, hell, no—

She caught his scent then. The wild scent of her kind.

*Other.* Shifter.

Erin wasn't human, well, not completely anyway. And she knew the truth about the world around her.

She knew that humans weren't the only killers out on the streets.

Sucking in a sharp breath, she straightened her shoulders and kept walking. The animal scent of the hunter teased her, as did the thick fragrance of blood in the air.

*Dammit, this is the last thing I need.* She'd tried so hard, for so long, to be normal.

Then this guy had literally landed in her path.

His nostrils widened as she came closer. She knew he was drinking in her scent, knew too by the faint line that appeared between his brows that he couldn't quite understand what she was.

*Story of my life.*

"Ms. Jerome." One of the uniforms stepped toward her, a wide smile on his face. His partner slammed the car door, effectively isolating Bobby and ending his claws rant.

*Maybe that hadn't been an insanity plea in the making after all.*

She crouched down, gazing at Bobby through the window. Her breath rushed out. "What happened to him?" But she knew.

The uniforms looked at Jude.

Jaw clenched, so did she.

And Erin realized she'd made a serious mistake. His eyes held hers. Saw too much.

*Danger.*

Oh, yeah, this guy was a serious threat. To her.

Not good-looking, not really, at least not in that classic, magazine way. A mane of thick blond hair teased his shirt collar. Framed a face that was hard, a little cruel. High cheeks. Sharp nose. Square jaw.

No, not a GQ face. But still . . .

Sexy. Somehow, he was still sexy. Maybe it was those lips. That scar that slipped right over the edge of his top lip. Shouldn't have been sexy, but it was.

He was.

Freaking animal attraction, *that's* what it was.

The guy had an air about him, one of those I-don't-give-a-damn attitudes. A wildness in his eyes and in the curl of his lips.

Erin swallowed. She couldn't help taking an uneasy step back.

His eyes followed the movement, and one golden brow rose. After a moment, he shrugged. His gaze raked over her body. "And you are . . . ?"

"Assistant District Attorney Erin Jerome." Gritted out. Why was there blood all over Bobby? If something happened and this case got thrown out—

"Not the question I was asking." Bland as you please. That brow was still up.

Her lips parted. "What?" No way could he have meant—

His eyes swept over her again, and a smile lifted his lips. "Interesting."

Right then, the only interesting thing she saw was Bobby. *A lie.* But she'd always been good at lying to herself. And about herself. "What. Happened?"

Another shrug. "He slipped in the swamp. Fell on some branches."

It was Erin's turn to let her eyes drift over him. Drift over his too-wide shoulders and muscled chest. "Is that your blood?" she asked quietly. "Or his?"

"Little of both."

A headache began to pound behind her left eye. Erin grabbed on to her patience and held tight.

What was the guy's deal? Was *he* the crazy one?

"Uh, Ms. Jerome?" It was the uniform to her right. "You want us to go ahead and take Burrows to processing?"

Erin shook her head. She'd been listening to the police radio, hoping for some word on Bobby. The guy had vanished less than an hour after posting bail—she still didn't know what the idiot judge had been thinking. She'd been desperate for some word on the sadistic jerk, and then, like a sweet gift from Fate, she'd caught the news of his capture.

She'd almost flown down to Burns Swamp. "Take him to the hospital. Get him patched up." She pointed at the cop. "Do *not* let him leave your sight for even a second, understand? Bail's revoked. Once the docs give the ok, haul his ass back to jail." Hopefully, he'd stay locked up for the rest of his miserable days.

The uniform, Ray Neal—she'd met him twice before—gave a nod. He and his partner climbed into the car, then drove away, taking her criminal with them.

And leaving her alone with the hunter.

"Wanna answer my question?" His voice was deep, rumbling.

Goosebumps rose on her bare arms, and it was far too warm for her to have a chill from the weather.

"Just what question was that?" She tilted her head to the right.

"*Who* are you?" A pause. "What are you?"

She let her brow furrow. She'd fooled *Other* before, she

could do it again. "I'm really not sure I understand. I told you, I'm Assistant District Attorney—"

"You don't smell human."

Her breath caught on a gasp. No, he hadn't just said—

He stepped toward her, a fast move that brought their bodies too close. Jude leaned in, lowering his head over the curve of her throat. And inhaled.

"Stop!" She shoved him, hard, and watched with no small satisfaction as he stumbled back.

*Oh, yeah, big guy, I'm much, much stronger than I appear.* He wasn't the first one to learn that little lesson.

She almost bared her teeth at him. Almost.

After all, she wasn't an animal. No matter what the whispers back home said.

"I don't know just what you *think* you were doing," she snapped, glaring at him as she narrowed her eyes. "But you'd better watch what you do and what you say around me." Was the guy crazy? *You don't smell human.* He couldn't say things like that.

The words were too dangerous.

She reached into her purse. Dug out her card. "Call my office. My assistant will take care of any paperwork you've got."

He stared at her a moment longer. Then, slowly, his tanned fingers rose. Long fingers, callused. Strong. He took the card, and his fingertips brushed over her hand.

Erin didn't flinch and she was extremely proud of that fact.

"Good work, Donovan." After giving him that grudging token of appreciation, she nodded and began to march back toward her car.

She'd taken all of five steps when she heard his whistle. Long, loud, and very appreciative.

Erin stilled.

*I really don't need this shit.*

"I've got your scent." Hard words. Scary words. Because she knew what they meant.

If Jude Donovan truly was a shifter, and every instinct she had screamed that he was, then having her scent, well, it meant he had *her.* He'd be able to follow her, to find her, almost anywhere.

*A shifter*. What were the odds she'd stumble onto him?

One of the little perks in the *Other* world—the world full of supernaturals and nightmares, the world that, rather unfortunately, was her life—was that like recognized like. Demons, because, yeah, those conniving bastards were real, could "see" others of their breed. They could look right past the magic glamour and peer into the darkness inside.

Witches felt the power pull from their brethren.

And shifters, well, they could smell each other—a distinct scent. One that carried the wisp of power and the scent of the beast.

Jude Donovan smelled of power. Of wild, strong man. Of savagery. No denying that scent.

As for the beast . . . she didn't need the marks on Bobby's face to know Donovan had claws.

Erin began to walk again. One determined step after another.

And even when she climbed into her car, she could feel his eyes on her. Watching and seeing too much.

Now, she'd have to be extra careful to stay on her guard and not let the hunter discover the secrets she kept so carefully hidden.

"What the hell happened to you?" Dee Daniels asked the minute Jude strode past the rather unassuming entrance of

Night Watch's Louisiana branch. She stood quickly, her blond hair cut brutally short around her elfin face. There was envy in her eyes as she stared at him with her lips slightly parted. "You lucky bastard, you took prey down, didn't you?"

Jude grunted and rolled his shoulder. He'd shifted before coming into the agency. A fast, hard shift to speed up the healing process. His kind were blessed with a freaking phenomenal recovery system. Some shifters were lucky, they could heal almost instantly from their wounds. Others took a few days for a full recovery. It all depended on the power of the beast inside.

Because he was a very rare shifter breed, Jude was on the luckier end of the spectrum. He could heal fully in hours.

Yeah, he'd have a scar because the system wasn't that perfect. More like he had his own little micro surgeon inside, stitching him back up. Soon, all that would remain of the jagged hole would be a slim line of raised flesh—once the skin melded itself back together.

He dropped his bag near his desk. Damn but he was tired. He hurt.

And he was horny.

All because of a little human.

No, not a human. He'd stake his life on it.

"You tracked the bastard down in twelve hours." Dee gave a faint *hmmm*, kind of like a revving motor. "Jerk, you've just broken my record."

The disgruntlement in her voice had a reluctant smile tugging at his lips. "Don't worry, babe, there's always next time." Dee was a bloodthirsty one. She was the toughest and sneakiest fighter he'd ever come across.

And she was one hundred percent human.

A human with a serious attitude.

"I couldn't let that asshole stay on the streets." Because

he'd seen the pictures. Seen just what good old Bobby had done to the women who'd "wronged" him.

Poor Sheila Gentry had gotten seventeen stitches in her face because she'd made the mistake of saying no when the guy asked her out for dinner. She'd taken a pit stop at a gas station and found one hell of a Romeo who wanted to pick her up.

Psycho.

*Caged* psycho now.

The little ADA had better do her job and keep him there.

He eased into his chair. Heard the grunt of the leather. "Dee, what do you know about Erin Jerome?"

She blinked her chocolate eyes. The lady was all of five-foot-three. One hundred and fifteen pounds. She looked like a hard wind would blow her over.

But he'd seen her take down demons twice her size.

Dee knew the score about the *Other* world. Knew it, and often hated it.

A frown had her brows pulling low. "The new ADA? She just started."

Yeah, he knew that. He would have known about her if she'd been around for more than a few weeks.

*Her scent.* He'd never smelled anything like it. Roses. Soft, subtle. And . . . more. An alluring, haunting scent of woman.

She didn't smell like an animal. Didn't give off the wild, rich scent of female shifters.

But the minute he'd seen her, the minute he'd caught her fragrance in the air, his whole body had stiffened.

And he'd gotten the biggest hard-on of his life. There was something there. He *knew* it.

"Oh, hell, she's *Other.*" Dee curled her lip. "I swear, you guys are taking over the city."

Yeah, they were.

"What is she? Witch? Djinn? One of those charmers?"

Jude didn't speak. Because he didn't know.

"A vampire?" Ice dripped from her voice. Dee *hated* the vamps. Her mission in life was to exterminate as many of them as she could.

Not that he blamed her, really. A vampire master had slaughtered her family years ago.

Dee was real big on the "eye for an eye" mentality.

"I don't . . . think so." Erin's skin had been flushed with color. Kissed by the sun. Vamps were usually paler than, well, death.

The lady had been a real looker. Coal black hair, thick, spilling to her shoulders. Red lips. Cheeks almost brutally sharp. Eyes wide and gold. And a little black mole near the corner of her left eye.

Great body. High breasts. Round hips. Long, long legs.

Sexy.

Tall, slender, she'd walked with confidence, grace.

Until she'd seen him.

Then he'd watched her stumble, for just a moment.

*Because she'd sensed what I am.*

Only another shifter should have been able to sense him.

"She didn't smell like a shifter," he muttered, rubbing his hand over his face. Hell, he shouldn't even be worrying about this now. He should be sleeping. Drinking. Congratulating himself on another job well done.

Not obsessing over a woman who clearly wasn't interested in him.

*Yeah, 'cause smelling a woman, sniffing her like a freaking dog—that was the way to get a date.*

"Just let me know if you hear anything about her, okay?" he finally said.

A cautious nod.

"Thanks, Dee." He closed his eyes . . . and saw Erin.

Shit. He needed to get a life.

He needed to take a life. Needed to kill. Needed to feel the sweet trickle of life being washed away.

The Slasher, Bobby Burrows, waited just behind the bars. There he stood, stalking around and muttering about evil and devils and hell.

And annoying the hell out of him.

That bastard had been on the news for the last two nights.

Bobby's fat, ugly face had been splashed across the screen—making him sick.

Bobby Burrows didn't deserve fifteen minutes of fame. He deserved a trip to the grave.

Bobby grabbed the bars of his cell. Tightened his thick hands into straining fists around the metal and screamed, "*The fuckin' devil marked me*! I want reporters in here, I want my lawyer, I want—"

"Relax." He sidled closer to Bobby, finally stepping out of the shadows he loved so much and smiling. He jerked his thumb toward the group of guards who were watching television near the entrance to the cages.

Cages. That's what he called 'em. *To keep the animals inside.*

But sometimes, the cages couldn't hold the animals.

He drew in a deep breath and caught the scent of the man's sweat and blood. "They're not gonna help you." They were too busy huddling up and watching a game to give a shit about the guy left in holding. He smiled and hoped he didn't look too hungry. "But I will."

Bobby squinted at him. The left side of his face was covered by a large, white bandage. "What? Who are you?"

His hands rose to the bars, reached for Bobby's—

The Slasher jumped back.

*Ah . . . not as stupid as he looked.* "Why don't you tell me who hurt you, Bobby?"

"I-I did. The devil—"

"The devil's not real." He'd never seen him. Judgment wasn't for the afterlife. It was for here and now, to be delivered by the strong.

"Yes, he is." Absolute certainty. "Found me in the swamp. Changed before me. I *shot* the bastard, but he still came after me." He licked his lips. "Then he cut me."

The bars were so thin. Not nearly strong enough to keep him out.

But strong enough to trap the human inside.

"He let you live, didn't he? I don't think the devil would do that."

"*He's a monster!*" Spittle flew from Bobby's mouth. "Hiding behind the face of a man. That fuckin' hunter! Pretendin', he's pretendin'!"

"We all pretend," he told him softly, aware of the excitement burning through his gut. He didn't have any more time to waste. "It's how we live." His hands flew through the gap in the bars. His right hand locked around the Slasher's throat.

A wheeze slipped past Bobby's lips.

Smiling, he jerked the human's head to the right. He heard the sharp snap of bones.

And felt a rush of power as the man sagged in his grip.

Slowly, his left hand rose. He cast a glance back toward the guards. They were still glued to their TV.

Fucking oblivious humans.

Claws pushed from the ends of his fingertips. He raised his left hand and plunged the claws into Bobby's heart.

As the blood flowed, a soft sigh escaped his lips.

*No way was the media going to be able to overlook this kill.*

He'd be taking over the news now.

Jude got the call from the police station forty-five minutes later. A cop who owed him a favor tipped him off.

The call was brief, and the details came fast. Burrows was dead. The ADA was on her way.

And, oh, yeah, it looked like an animal had attacked the guy—while he was locked up. Of course, the cops hadn't seen a thing. Bobby had been all alone in holding one minute, then sliced and diced the next.

Jude grabbed his jacket. Slung it over his shoulder—almost healed now. He ran for the door.

And ignored Dee's shout behind him.

# Chapter 2

"You don't want to see the body."

His voice, even deeper now, stopped her as Erin began to climb the steps leading to the police station and to the dead man.

She glanced back over her shoulder. She'd caught his scent seconds before he'd spoken. "How do you even know there's a body here, Donovan?" The District Attorney's office had received the call less than fifteen minutes ago. Just how had the hunter learned about the death?

Suspicion had her eyes narrowing. "You didn't—"

He jumped up the steps. Grabbed her arms. "I didn't kill the bastard, no. If I'd killed him, well, he would've been left in the swamp and been gator bait by now."

Erin swallowed. *Nice, to, ah, know*. "Then why are you here?"

"Same as you. I want to know what happened to the Slasher."

Her eyes narrowed. *You don't want to see the body.* "Sounds to me like you already know." Which meant she had a leak in the department. Not surprising. Not particularly good news, either.

His wide shoulders lifted in a shrug. "Trust me on this, you don't want to see Bobby Burrows right now."

She licked her lips. "And, trust me, I'm a big girl. I can handle it." Not like it was her first murder scene. Not by a long shot. She was twenty-nine years old, and she'd been working the rough cases since she'd passed the bar years ago.

To make a difference, sometimes you had to get your hands dirty.

Erin turned and continued stalking up the stone steps. Jude shadowed her moves, his body a ripple of muscle.

His scent filled the air around them.

Her heart raced, too fast. Was the frantic beat from the dread filling her at the thought of a dead man waiting in what should have been a secure cell?

Or was it from something more?

*No.*

She shoved open the glass doors. A guard near the front rushed forward. "Ms. Jerome—"

Her thumb jerked toward her hulking shadow. "Keep Donovan up here. I don't want him anywhere near my crime scene."

Her sensitive ears picked up the hunter's swift inhalation and the nearly soundless . . . "You'll need me on this one, sweetheart."

*Sweetheart.* She slanted him a scathing glance. "Doubt it, hunter. Doubt it." Then she stalked down the tiled hallway, heading for lockup, and wondering just what sort of sight waited for her.

*You don't want to see the body.*

* * *

The lady had one fine ass.

Even as anger tightened his body, Jude couldn't help but admire that beautiful sway.

His nostrils were full of her scent. Woman, roses, and just a hint of rich, wild forest. Yeah, that wildness—that fragrance had slipped into the air when those gorgeous eyes had narrowed and rage coated her voice.

Erin Jerome was so much more than she pretended to be.

The beast within him roared when she got close, *and* when she got too far away.

"Sorry, man, you heard the orders." Jamison McGee, a good cop and a good human, frowned at him. "You're gonna have to stay—"

"It's all right, James." Jude rocked back on his heels. He could smell the blood from here. "She'll be changing her mind." Because he hadn't been kidding when he told the pretty ADA that she'd need him.

Jude glanced toward the vinyl chairs near the entrance. "When she comes looking for me, I'll be waiting."

Five minutes, ten tops, and he'd wager his ADA would be running her sexy ass right back to him.

Because it seemed that another monster was out hunting. One that had killed right under the noses of the Baton Rouge PD.

Talk about a bold asshole.

Jude almost could admire that. Almost.

The scent of the blood burned her nostrils. Most of her kind liked that smell. She *hated* it.

Erin straightened her shoulders and strode forward. Four uniformed cops stood just in front of the entrance to the pen. They glanced up at the clicking of her heels. One of them, an older guy with rich coffee skin, graying hair and a strong chin, stepped toward her. "Ms. Jerome, you'd better brace yourself."

He looked worried. Looked like he thought she was going to pass out after one glance at the stiff.

She really wasn't the passing out kind of girl.

"Thanks for the warning." The second one she'd gotten in less than three minutes. But Grant Tyler wasn't being an ass with his warning. The young cop next to him was stark white and shaking. He looked like *he* might be doing some fainting at any moment.

*Oh, hell.* A cop ready to hit the floor was never a good sign.

Erin pointed toward the door. "Show him to me."

Grant pushed open the door.

The stench nearly made her gag. Then she saw him.

Bobby's arms had been yanked through the bars, left to hang over the edges of his prison. His wrists had been cut, long, thick slices, and his blood pooled on the floor. His eyes were open, wide, and his face had been slashed. A bloodred smile stretched from one ear to the next.

Positioned. Styled. His body had been arranged for the ultimate shock value.

Erin's lips pressed together.

"You okay?" Grant whispered.

There was a flash of light as the crime scene guy snapped a photo.

She flinched. "Fine." No, no, she wasn't *fine.* What the hell had happened? Her gaze jerked to the left, then the right. The other cells were empty. Transfer had been made just hours before, and she knew Bobby had been the only prisoner in holding.

She'd *planned* for him to be the only one there—all the better for the cops to keep an eye on him.

This was so not good.

A killer, murdered while he was surrounded by cops.

*Murdered by cops?* Her stomach knotted.

Erin turned away from the body. Goosebumps rose on her flesh. "Who was here?"

"I was." Admitted quietly. "Burns, Grimes, and Hyde."

Her fingers pressed into her right temple. *The blood.* "And you didn't see a thing?" Doubt had her voice rising. No way, *no way* was that possible.

"We were up front." His lips tightened. "Didn't see what happened and didn't hear a peep."

Oh, shit. This was a nightmare.

Captain Antonio Young strolled in then. Wearing a perfect suit, not so much as a wrinkle anywhere to be found.

Erin growled at him. He wasn't on her top ten list. Over the last week, she'd gotten a pretty up close look at the captain, and came away thinking the guy was a bit of a prick. He was secretive, he didn't share his case files with the rest of the PD, and the guy was given to disappearing for long periods of time. Hardly upfront police behavior.

Erin had no idea how the man had ever been promoted through the ranks.

He must've had some serious connections somewhere or else he'd known where some bodies were buried. Maybe he'd helped to *bury* those bodies.

"Your men have to be cleared." Her voice was sharp. The captain knew this, and he still had Grant and the others less than ten feet away from the victim. "What the *hell* are you thinking?"

His dark eyes narrowed. "I don't need you to tell me how to do my job."

"Uh, yeah, obviously, you do." The press would go wild with this story. *Wild.* "Four cops. One dead perp. You do the math, Young." Okay, so she sounded like a bitch. Screw the polite chitchat. *The man knew better.*

Bobby Burrows was dead—not just dead—slaughtered. *Aw, hell.*

Young's handsome face—cause, yeah, no denying he was a pretty boy with those elegant planes and hollows on his face—tightened. No sign of his flashing dimple. He glared at her, and she glared right back.

"We didn't do it." From Grant. Strong, steady Grant. She'd had a good feeling about the guy from the beginning, from the first moment she'd met him at the courthouse. A real upfront kind of guy.

Now this.

"We're going to have to prove that," she said. *Not going to be easy.*

Another flash of light.

Erin licked her lips and knew what she had to do. "Excuse me." Much as she hated it . . .

She was going to have to get close to that body. She spun and headed for the perp. Um, victim now. Her steps slowed as she approached the body. "Give me a minute, Mark," she said to the crime scene analyst, and he moved back.

Less than a foot away, she stopped. She didn't touch Bobby or the bars, no way was she going to risk contaminating evidence. But . . .

But her eyes touched him. Her gaze scanned every inch of him, paying careful attention to the wounds and—

*Shit.*

Her heart slammed into her chest.

Those weren't knife wounds. No, she *knew* the shape of those wounds.

Intimately.

Those slices had been made by claws. She'd seen marks like that too many times in the past.

Her nostrils twitched and she stared at Bobby's bloody form.

The cops there—the captain, the three men, and the woman—they were human. So were the crime scene guys.

No shifters.

But a shifter *had* been here. He'd killed.

And she knew there was a shifter close by, one who didn't mind a little blood and who sure had a hard-on for Bobby.

*Jude.*

Her steps were very precise as she turned and left the holding area. Once she was clear, her fingers knotted into fists, and she stormed down the hallway, racing back to face the hunter.

Jude stretched his legs out, letting the heels of his boots press into the old floor. He didn't glance at his watch, but he figured Erin had been with the body about eight minutes or so now and—

*Click. Click. Click.*

The sound of fast-approaching high heels.

He glanced up.

And saw Erin bearing down on him, her face tight with fury and her eyes blazing.

*Glowing?*

She stalked right up to him, put her hands on the hips he'd like to touch and demanded, "What did you do?"

*Whoa.* Jude stood up, slowly, aware that he towered over her slender figure and using that to his advantage. "I think you've got the wrong idea here, sweetheart."

"I am *not* your sweetheart." She jabbed a finger into his chest. "You think I don't know what got a hold of that bastard?" Her voice was fierce, but pitched low enough that only he would be able to hear her. "I recognize the work of claws when I see 'em, Donovan."

"Not *my* claws." The words came out more growl than anything else. He cleared his throat, tried again. It was hard to speak normally, with her so close, with that sweet scent filling his nose, and with the beast roaring. "I told you, if I wanted him dead, he wouldn't have made it out of that swamp."

"You knew what I'd find in that cell." A pause, just for a beat of time. "How'd you know, hunter? Because you'd been the one to send Bobby to hell? Just had to put a smile on his face, didn't you? A grin for him to greet the devil with?"

He grabbed her hand, tired of her fingernail digging into his chest. "I didn't do it, *sweetheart.* I've got an alibi. I was at Night Watch and at least four other agents can attest to that." Good thing, too. He rotated his shoulders. No more pain. Not even a twinge.

"*How did you know*?" Gritted from between her teeth. Teeth that were starting to look a bit sharper than before.

He almost smiled. Would have, if they weren't talking about a dead body and if they hadn't been surrounded by cops. "I've got a friend in the department. He called me." *Because he owed me and because the sly bastard knew he'd need my help*. Just like she would.

Erin just didn't want to admit it yet.

"What. Friend?"

"Aw, now, you can't expect me to—"

*"What. Friend!"* Her voice wasn't soft anymore, and a couple of cops glanced their way. "Tell me, because I'm sure as hell thinking you're—"

"It was me, ma'am." A slow-drawling southern voice said.

Erin's head whipped to the left and her mouth dropped open as she stared at Antonio. "Bullshit."

He smiled at her, flashing his perfectly capped, too-white teeth. The teeth looked even whiter next to his caramel skin—coloring Jude knew the guy had gotten courtesy of his very lovely Mexican mother. " 'Fraid so, Ms. Jerome. 'Fraid so."

"*Why?*"

"Because I'm not quite as clueless as you seem to think I am." His voice was low but fierce. "And one look at that body told me the cops in that room weren't suspects." He jerked his thumb toward Jude. "But one of his kind sure as hell was."

She froze. Then, it was as if a veil fell over her face. Erin's expression cleared, until only a false mask remained. "His kind? What's that supposed to mean?"

Jude blinked. The lady was good. If she hadn't just been snarling at him about claw marks, he might have bought her confused act.

Or maybe not.

Because apparently even Tony wasn't buying it. The captain snorted and said, "If you really don't know, ma'am, then you're gonna have one hell of a time survivin' in *this* town."

She was living a nightmare. An absolute somebody-please-wake-me-up screaming nightmare.

Antonio knew about the *Other.*

Yeah, that was a problem, but the *big* deal was that she had a shifter gone bad who was slicing up killers *right under the noses of the PD.*

The news headlines would be brutal.

"I hate to break this to you, Ms. Jerome—"

"Erin," she choked out because the captain drawled her surname out in a way that was like nails grating on her nerves.

"But the world you live in, well, only half of what you see

is real." Antonio paced the small confines of his office, looking very much like a caged cat.

He wasn't. The guy didn't so much as give off one whiff of shifter scent.

But then, her smell was pretty damn hard to detect, too.

"Really?" She kept her voice mild with an effort. After the captain's big revelation, he'd herded her and Jude into his office. She was playing the innocent human, for now. And for as long as necessary.

"Two years ago, I was out in the swamps. A vampire tried to drain me and leave my body for gator bait."

Nice visual. "A vampire?" Erin shook her head. "Sorry, captain, but vampires aren't real." Yeah, right. Those bastards were as real as she was.

Jude rolled his shoulders beside her. He'd been doing that every few moments. What was up with that?

"They're real." Antonio stopped his pacing. "Get used to the idea."

She had, about twenty-five years ago, when she'd watched her mother go claw to teeth with a vamp. "Um . . . tell me, captain, have you been in for an evaluation recently? Perhaps a trip to the police shrink is in order." Erin braced her hands on the armrests of her chair and pushed to her feet. "Now, unless you want to tell me a few fairy tales about some trolls running loose in the city, I've got a murder to solve. I don't have time for this crap." A good exit line. She headed for the door, chin up, shoulders back.

And heard clapping behind her. Glancing over her shoulder, Erin saw Jude smiling at her.

"Nice." He pointed one long finger at her. "But why don't *you* cut the crap, ADA? We both know you understand all about the monsters in the dark, and playing the innocent isn't gonna work with me."

*We both know you understand all about the monsters in the dark.* Her lips parted.

He rose slowly and stalked toward her. Yeah, *stalked*, his movements slow and steady, strangely graceful, his eyes predatory. His bright gaze dropped to her mouth. Seemed to heat.

*Trouble.* Oh, but the man was going to be dangerous to her. She'd known it from that first glance. Erin licked her lips. "I, uh . . ." No, that wouldn't work at all. She cleared her throat. "I don't know what you're talking about, Donovan." One fast glance toward Antonio. "I'm not going to jump on this insanity parade—"

"Gloves are off, lady. You know what I am."

*Shifter.*

He leaned in close and she watched the flare of his nostrils. "And I know what you're *not*."

*Human.*

Asshole.

"So let's cut to the chase, here, okay? No pretending's necessary when the door's closed." And the door was closed. Closed and locked. She'd heard the soft *snick* after Antonio shut the door. "You saw the body. You said yourself—those were claw marks, right?"

Her gaze darted once more to the left. Antonio stared at her with his wide eyes. Denial was still an option. She didn't have to blow her cover, the cover she'd worked so hard to get. Four months. It had taken her four months to find this job and to escape from her past.

A past that had come calling today—memories stirred up by the cloying scent of blood and death.

Running from monsters was hard work, because they were everywhere.

Silence hung in the room, too thick.

Jude swore. "Fine. I'll take a look at the body and see what I—"

Erin grabbed his hand when he tried to push past her, and she kissed her new life good-bye. "It was a shifter."

Antonio exhaled. "Damn woman."

Jude's skin felt warm beneath her fingertips. His eyes bored into hers, and she watched his pupils flare.

*Dangerous.*

She pulled her hand back and smoothed her fingers over the soft cotton of her pants. "It was a shifter, and, *how convenient*—there's a shifter standing right in front of me." Towering over her. Surrounding her with his heat and scent.

"I didn't kill him—"

"Jude wouldn't—"

Their words twisted and blurred in her mind. She waited for the denials to finish, then raised a brow. "You said you could prove your innocence."

His eyes narrowed, but Jude nodded. "Good," she muttered. " 'Cause you'll have to do that." And she believed he could. After that whole alibi business was taken care of, it would be time to get down to business.

"Call Night Watch," Jude said. "You can verify my whereabouts in less than two minutes."

She'd do that, but first . . . "Are you up for another case, hunter?" She knew just how hard it was to catch a shifter, especially one who hungered for the sweet thrill of human prey.

"You trying to hire me?"

Yeah, she was. She knew that Jude Donovan would be her best bet for catching this killer. The cops wouldn't be able to track a shifter.

*It takes a beast to catch a beast.*

Oh, the games the *Other* played.

"The DA gonna be up for this?" Antonio asked, inching closer.

Erin didn't glance his way. "He'll go for it." She'd make absolutely certain he did. "But will *you*?" she asked Jude.

His hard face was unreadable. Jeez but the man was *big*. She topped out at just under six feet, but he towered over her by several inches.

Just what kind of beast did Jude carry? Shifters—the beings that most said carried two souls.

The soul of a man.

The soul of an animal.

Most shifters were pretty harmless. They could transform into foxes, birds, or snakes.

Others were more dangerous. Bears, panthers, wolves.

*Wolves.* Some believed—with good reason—that those were the most dangerous of the shifters. Fierce, bloodthirsty, and, just for fun, every now and then . . . psychotic.

"I'll hunt for you." His gaze never left her face. "For a price."

"The city will pay you." She'd talk to the mayor and the DA. She wasn't planning a big reveal about the *Other* world with them; at least, not unless she wasn't given a choice. But Gus and Clark were smart guys. They'd wise up real fast to the benefits of having this case handled as quietly and quickly as possible.

If Jude could contain the guy, they'd be more than willing to pay his price. A price she expected to be *very* high.

Jude shook his head. "Not talking about the city."

Antonio stopped his inching closer routine.

Her heart slammed into her ribs but she kept her voice quiet and silky when she asked, "Then just who are you talking about?"

A slow smile. One that whispered across his face, lifted his upper lip and had her thighs clenching.

"You, sweetheart. *You*."

Erin gulped. Dammit—that scar on his top lip—*sexy.* She could see the hunger in his eyes. The man's hunger and the beast's.

And she felt the hot rise of her own need.

*Not going to happen.* She took a moment to let her heart rate ease back to normal. This wasn't the first time she'd had a strong physical reaction to a shifter.

*Okay, a really sexy shifter.*

And it wouldn't be her last. She couldn't stop the rush of sensual awareness, but Erin controlled the wild instincts inside. She always had. "The city will pay you," she said again and let the ice chill her words. "And pay you well." Because hunting a killer like the one who'd slaughtered Bobby wouldn't be easy.

He snorted. "They'd better." Jude didn't look away from her. "But, sweetheart, you'll pay, too."

The words were a definite threat.

Shifters always thought they were the baddest assholes on earth.

Because some of them were.

The local news carried the Burrows story that night at ten. A bright, perky blonde appeared at the top of the hour announcing, "Bobby Burrows, the suspect in the so-called Slasher Crimes, was found dead in his holding cell today. Police aren't releasing any information on this case yet, although sources say foul play is suspected . . ."

*What?*

He stared at the screen and felt the rage boil in his blood.

*Foul play was suspected?* Fuck, yes, he'd carved up that bastard.

And he'd done it for *her.*

The image on the screen flickered and a close-up shot of the mayor and the DA appeared. The DA was running his fat mouth about the security at the station.

Blah. Blah. Blah

The camera angle altered, just a bit, and his prey appeared.

*So perfect.*

Erin stood a bit behind the mayor. Looking all calm and lovely in her button-down shirt and pants. Controlled and elegant.

Such a beautiful lie.

He knew who she was, what she was, down deep, past the skin.

She was just like him. She liked the blood, the screams, the pleas for mercy.

He knew all about the real Erin. Flawed, broken, and wild for death.

Just like him.

He hoped that she'd liked her little present. Hoped she enjoyed *all* of the presents he would give to her. Soon.

He rose and went to the TV. He touched the spot just over her image.

Sweet, sweet Erin.

"No more running, love, you're mine."

She should have known escape wasn't possible.

*She should have known.*

# Chapter 3

She went to him. When the press conference was over, when the freak-out in the mayor's office had finally subsided, Erin went straight to Jude.

She knew where he lived. She'd gotten that information from Night Watch when she called to verify his alibi.

Jude's lair was at the edge of the city, skirting the swamps. More of a cabin than a house, and one that didn't look overly inviting.

Raising her hand, Erin banged on the door. So, sure, it was close to midnight. And, okay, granted, the swamp looked dark and dangerous and the call of the crickets and who-the-hell knew what else had her ears ringing.

The mayor had sent her to Jude. The DA had sent her.

And she'd come because she needed to see him.

The door opened with a creak. Jude stared down at her, stubble on his cheeks, his blond hair tousled and his eyes hooded.

No shirt. His chest was bare and too close. *The man had*

*serious muscles. Damn.* His jeans hung low on his body, wrapping around his hips and clinging to his strong, hard thighs.

*Hunter.*

"Took you long enough," he said, voice so deep it was nearly a growl.

Light surrounded him and spilled onto the porch. She shifted, her high heels scraping over the old wood. "Didn't realize you were waiting for me."

*Lie.* She'd known that he wanted to talk to her, *alone*, just as she'd wanted to talk to him.

Erin had to find out what he knew about her—and *how* he knew it. *So I won't slip up and make the same mistake with someone else next time.* "Do I get to come inside or do I have to stay out here all night?"

His mouth hitched into a half-smile. Erin inhaled.

Then Jude stepped back, motioning for her to enter.

The fingers of her right hand tightened around her purse strap and she walked forward, hesitating for only the briefest of seconds when she caught sight of the deep gouges along the doorframe.

Claw marks.

Some shifters sure did like to mark their territory. Her jaw tightened and she brushed past him, all too aware of the heat and strength of his body.

The interior of his place was Spartan bare. A couch. A giant TV. A paperwork-covered desk shoved into the corner. A big, scarred wooden table, two chairs around it, a small lamp on its surface. Erin caught a glimpse of the kitchen—or was that a closet?

"Not here much," he said with a shrug, following her gaze. "Too busy—"

"Hunting." She knew exactly how he spent his days. In the hours since they'd parted, she'd done her homework.

Jude Donovan. Age thirty-five. College graduate, with a degree in criminal justice. He'd been recruited to work for Night Watch when he'd barely been twenty-two. His reputation for hunting was vicious, and so were the criminals he captured. The vilest of criminals.

Humans . . . and she'd be willing to bet *Other*, too.

She reached into her bag and pulled out a check. Not the usual way things were handled in the DA's office, but . . . "I've been authorized to acquire your services." He didn't glance at the check, just kept those blue eyes trained on hers. Her fingers were steady as she held the check in the air between them. "This check is for ten thousand dollars."

No change of expression. From the looks of his cabin, the guy shouldn't have been hesitating to snatch up the money.

"Give the check to Night Watch."

At that, her lips firmed. "I already gave them one." A hefty one, at that. "This one's for you. A bonus from the Mayor. He wants this guy caught, fast." Before word about the true nature of the crime leaked too far.

"So old Gus doesn't think his cops can handle this guy?"

Gus LaCroix. Hard-talking, ex-hard-drinking mayor. No nonsense, deceptively smart, and demanding. "He's got the cops on this, but he said he knew you, and that you'd be the best one to handle this job."

Erin strongly suspected that Gus belonged in the *Other* world. She hadn't caught any unusual scent drifting from him, but his agreement to bring in Night Watch and his almost desperate demands to the DA had sure indicated the guy knew more than he was letting on about the situation.

Could be he was a demon. Low-level. Many politicians were.

Jude took the check. Finally. She dropped her fingers, not wanting the flesh on flesh contact with him. Not then.

He folded the check and tucked it into the back pocket of his jeans. "Guess you just got yourself a bounty hunter."

"And I guess you've got yourself one sick shifter to catch."

He closed the distance between them, moving fast and catching her arms in a strong grip.

*Aw, hell.* It was just like before. The heat of his touch swept through her, waking hungers she'd deliberately denied for so long.

Jude was sexual. From his knowing eyes, his curving, kiss-me lips, to the hard lines and muscles of his body.

Deep inside, in the dark, secret places of her soul that she fought to keep hidden, there was a part of her just like that.

Wild. Hot.

Sexual.

"Why are you afraid of me?"

Not the question she'd expected, but one she could answer. "I know what you are. What sane woman wouldn't be afraid of a man who becomes an animal?"

"Some women like a little bit of the animal in their men."

"Not me." *Liar.*

His eyes said the same thing.

"Do your job, Donovan. Catch the freak who cut up my prisoner—"

"Like Bobby had been slashing his victims?"

*Hit.* Yeah, there'd been no way to miss that significance.

"When word gets out about what really happened, some folks will say Bobby deserved what he got." His fingers pressed into her arms. Erin wore a light, silk shirt—and even that seemed too hot for the humid Louisiana spring night. His touch burned through the blouse and seemed to singe her flesh.

"Some will say that," she allowed. Okay, a hell of a lot would say that. "But his killer still has to be caught." Stopped, because she had the feeling this could be just the beginning.

Her feelings about death weren't often wrong.

She was a lot like her dad that way.

And, unfortunately, like her mother, too.

"What do you think? Did he deserve to be clawed to death?"

An image of Bobby's ex-wife, Pat, flashed before her eyes. The doctors had put over one hundred and fifty stitches into her face. She'd been his most brutal attack.

Erin swallowed. "His punishment was for the court to decide." She stepped back, but he didn't let her go. "Uh, do you mind?"

"Yeah, I do." His eyes glittered down at her. "If we're gonna be working together, we need honesty between us."

"We need *you* to find the killer."

"Oh, I will. Don't worry about that. I always catch my prey."

So the rumors claimed. The hunters from Night Watch were known throughout the U.S.

"You're shivering, Erin."

"No, no, I'm not." She was.

"I make you nervous. I scare you." A pause. His gaze dropped to her lips, lingered, then slowly rose back to meet her stare. "Is it because I know what you are?"

She wanted his mouth on hers. A foolish desire. Ridiculous. Not something the controlled woman wanted, but what the wild thing inside craved. "You don't know anything about me."

"Don't I?"

Erin jerked free of his hold and glared at him. "Few things in this world scare me. You should know that." There was one thing, one person, who terrified her but now wasn't the time for that disclosure. No, she didn't tell anyone about *him*.

If she could just get around Jude and march out that door—

"Maybe you're not scared of me, then. Maybe you're scared of yourself."

She froze.

"Not human," he murmured, shaking his head. "Not vamp."

Vamp? Thankfully, no.

"Djinn? Nah, you don't have that look." His right hand lifted and he rubbed his chin. "Tell me your secrets, sweetheart, and I'll tell you mine."

"Sorry, not the sharing type." She'd wasted enough time here. Erin pushed past him, ignoring the press of his arm against her side. Her body ached and the whispers of hunger within her grew more demanding every moment she stayed with him.

*Weak.*

She hated her weakness.

Just like her mother's.

"You're a shifter." His words stopped her near the door. She stared blankly at the faded wood. Heard the dull thud of her heart echoing in her ears.

Then the soft squeak of the old floorboards as he closed the distance between them.

Erin turned to him, tilted her head back—

He kissed her.

She heard a growl. Not from him—no, from her own throat.

*The hunger.*

Sure, he made the first move, he brought his lips crashing down on hers, but . . . she kissed him right back.

Her hands locked around his shoulders, her nails dug into his flesh. Oh, damn, but his flesh . . . Strong, hot.

Her mouth was open, lips parted for the thrust of his tongue. She'd tried to play the good girl and walk away, but there was no denying she wanted this—*wanted him.*

Tongues met. Took. Tasted.

And he tasted *good.* Even better than the chocolate she craved in the middle of the day. Erin realized she wanted more. So much more.

She rose on her tiptoes. Widened her mouth, and this time, the growl that she heard came from him.

His hands clenched around her hips, and he jerked her even closer to him. The hard bulge of his arousal pressed against her. Long and hard and promising such fierce pleasure. She could have him, thrusting deep and hard into her, and Erin knew the ride would be fantastic. The sex great.

She *could* have him.

His fingers cupped her ass.

*Take him. Take him.*

He ripped his mouth from hers. She sucked in a sharp breath and tried to clear the lust from her mind. She needed—

His mouth pressed against her neck. Right over her pulse.

Her weak spot.

His tongue laved her and her knees trembled. Then Jude bit her, a light, teasing bite.

A marking, nonetheless. She knew the way of shifters.

But that didn't stop the heat that swept through her. Erin's nipples swelled against him, her sex moistened.

Freaking animal response.

*So much need.*

"You want me, Erin, just as much as I want you." The words rumbled against her flesh.

She wouldn't deny it. She wouldn't give in to the furious desire, either. With one serious effort, Erin made her hands stop clutching him and she pushed against his chest instead.

*Nice* chest.

He didn't move.

She pushed harder, letting some of her enhanced strength flex. "Let me go."

His head rose and he stared down at her with eyes shining brightly. So blue it almost hurt to look into them.

"Shifter." He said this again, but it wasn't so much a question. Too certain. "I can see it in your eyes."

No, no that couldn't be possible. She *always* controlled her body. No claws. No glowing eyes. No too-sharp teeth. The guy was guessing, trying to trip her up.

"Sweet little shifter. You can't hide your beast from me."

There was no beast. "Let. Me. Go." Her voice was huskier than she would have liked, but she meant the words. Being near him right then, not really an option.

Running, yeah, that was the best option. Not because she was afraid, but—

Shit, okay, she was afraid.

So there *were* a few things that scared her.

Jude dropped his hold.

Erin spun around and fumbled with the door. Her purse, all but forgotten, banged against her hip. Then she was outside, stumbling onto the porch and putting some much needed space between them.

Now if her heart would just slow its frantic beat.

"This isn't over." His voice followed her down the steps.

"Damn right." She tossed him a glare over her shoulder. "You've got to find my killer—"

"Not that." His steps were slow and heavy on the porch. "Us. We're not over. We're just getting started." He licked his lips. "I can still taste you."

She could taste him. And her panties were wet. Just from a kiss.

What would happen when they were both naked?

She would *not* find out.

"We're gonna happen, sweetheart. Deal with it."

Arrogant asshole.

Sexy beast.

"No, we're not." Some temptations had to be denied. "You deal with *that*." She opened her car door and climbed inside.

"Why do you hide your animal side?" He raised a hand to his shoulder and ran his fingertips over the small wounds that she could see even in the dim light from the porch.

Because some of her senses were enhanced, too.

*Thanks, Mother.*

She'd marked him. The way of the beast.

"I have no animal side," she said quietly.

"Bullshit. There's an animal in you, just growling to get out." He motioned to the wild land around them. "Wanna shift and run with me?"

Ice froze her blood. "You're mistaken about me, Donovan." *Flawed. Broken.* "There's no animal inside for you to play with—sorry." Then she slammed her door. Seconds later, she shoved the gear shift into reverse and spun out of his drive.

*Some temptations had to be denied.*

No matter how much pleasure they promised.

He was dreaming about her when the phone rang. A hot, sexy dream that had him aching. Erin wore two thin strips of black lace. Her eyes were shining. Her lips moist.

She wanted him.

His hands couldn't touch her enough. Couldn't enjoy the feel of that satiny skin enough and—

And then the phone rang.

Jude reached for the receiver near his bed, ready to give someone a serious ass-chewing. "What the hell do you—"

"Jude." Erin's voice.

Not breathy with desire like in his fading dream. Sharper, tinged with fear.

The lady had said she didn't fear much.

Jude sat up in an instant and his fingers tightened around the phone. "What's wrong?" A call in the middle of the night was never a good thing.

"I need you."

Okay, she'd said *that* in his dream, but not quite the same way.

"408 St. Charles Avenue. Come as fast as you can, okay?"

*Click.*

For one second, two, he stared down at the phone.

Then he ran for the door.

*Because Erin was afraid.*

There weren't any police cars in front of the old house on St. Charles. No swirling blue lights.

Jude had expected to see them, or at least some sign of trouble.

The antebellum house sat quietly, time having ravaged the once beautiful frame. Azaleas did their part to hide the house, nestling it in perfumed security from curious eyes. But the beauty of the place had faded and only a whisper of glory remained.

A fixer-upper. There were plenty of old houses like it in the city.

But only one that had his Erin inside.

Jude's gaze scanned the yard. His nostrils twitched. There was another scent in the air. Heavy. Drifting just under the azaleas and their sweet fragrance.

Blood.

He bounded up the steps and shoved open the door.

And slammed into Erin.

They fell to the floor in a tangle of limbs and a cloud of curses. He tried to spin to protect her from the fall—and his weight—but it was too late.

They hit hard.

She didn't even flinch.

Her golden eyes met his and Jude tried not to notice just how incredibly good she felt beneath him. Tried, failed.

Her breasts were crushed beneath his chest. Her thighs were spread, cradling his hips in just the, *oh yeah*, right way.

If the scent of blood weren't clogging up his nostrils, he sure as all hell would've enjoyed the moment.

Later.

He levered up onto his forearms. "What the fuck is going on, Erin?"

She licked her lips. "Get up."

No. Dammit. He wanted to stay exactly where he was.

And he wanted to find out why there were shadows in her eyes.

He got up.

Erin exhaled. "I—this has to stay between us, okay?"

Jude blinked. "*What* has to stay between us?" He had a real bad feeling about this situation, and much as he liked the sexy ADA and wanted to get her naked, he wasn't about to break the law for her.

Well, he wouldn't break it *much* for her. A little bending, he'd do that.

His nostrils twitched again.

*That was human blood.*

Shit. Wary now, he kept a close watch on Erin as she rose to her feet. She still wore the sexy blouse from earlier. Her makeup was gone. Faint brown smudges were under her eyes.

He could all but smell the fear dripping off her.

"I thought you didn't scare."

She gave a rough laugh at that, kind of a desperate sound. Her fingers raked through her black hair. "No, hunter, I said there wasn't much that scares me. *He* does."

Jude tensed. "Someone else is here?" He didn't smell him. Just that thick blood, coating every breath he took.

The animal inside loved the scent of blood. It was a response Jude couldn't control. Primal.

Like the response he felt for Erin.

But the man knew the coppery scent was bad. Trouble.

"Not anymore," she whispered. "He's . . . gone."

Jude's hands fisted. His gaze swept the room. Caught sight of the old staircase, twisting up to the next level. To the left, he saw the gleaming wooden floors and the oversized doors that led out of the parlor. Doors that were firmly shut.

"I-I went back to the police station after I left your place. I needed to talk to Antonio and find out what the ME had to say about Burrows." The words came out fast. "I was tired when I got back and didn't even notice the smell until—" Her gaze darted to the left, to the white doors.

He crossed the room, body alert. His fingers curled over the old door knobs—two doors, French style. He wrenched them open, ready for any threat.

*Sonofabitch.*

The lights were on in the other room. Bright and stark. Shining perfectly on the bloody message that had been left on the far wall.

***Missed you.***

The blood had trickled down, blurring some of the letters a bit, but the message was clear.

*What the fuck?* His growl filled the room.

This shit was twisted. "You searched the house?" Sprawling places like this one had too many rooms and far too many places for someone to hide.

With his nose . . . no one would hide from him.

He spun around, ready to stalk from top to bottom and—

She caught his arm. "I told you, no one else is here." Plump lips tightened. "The bastard delivered his message and ran."

"Some message." Not every day a woman got a love letter in blood.

Her fingers tightened around him. "I need your help."

"You need the cops. What the hell? You've got some psycho ex-lover stalking you—" With freaking blood.

"Not my lover." She shook her head. "Never that."

"Call. The. Cops."

"Some jobs aren't meant for the cops."

"And some are, sweetheart. You're an ADA—you know this shit." She should. But he'd worked with victims before, and he knew that even the professionals would forget the rules when the deadly games became personal. "Erin, when someone breaks into your house and leaves—"

"He's *Other.*"

He'd figured that. Well, either *Other* or seriously fucked up human.

Seriously fucked up *Other.*

"The cops can still track him."

"No one can track him. The bastard's too good at hiding." She exhaled, and, for a moment, he thought he saw . . . calculation in her gaze.

He tensed.

*Be careful with the ladies, Jude. You can't always trust a pretty face.*

His grandfather's warning. Given right before his senior prom, the night Susie Jo Hill had left him on the dance floor to make out with the quarterback.

He'd pounded the quarterback and come away with the scar on his lip, courtesy of a big-ass class ring and a lucky punch. Then he'd left a furious Susie Jo shouting on her doorstep.

Erin was no Susie Jo. She was something much, much more dangerous.

Her hand fell away from him and damn if he didn't miss her touch.

Not. Good.

"I've got a stalker, Jude. A guy who has been trailing me and making my life hell for the last year." Her eyes held his.

A stab of pain in his palms made him realize that his claws were out. He unfisted his hands and the claws sprang to their full length.

Erin didn't so much as blink.

"I came here to get away from him," she said. Her shoulders were straight, her chin up, but she still looked vulnerable.

And that made him want to roar with fury.

"*He* scares me. I've caught his scent before. This isn't the first time he's come inside my home. He's a shifter, I know that much."

A shifter. *Like me.*

No wonder the lady hadn't been so wild about gettin' down and dirty with him.

"I-I don't know where he got the blood." She glanced over her shoulder at the painted wall and shuddered. "What if he hurt someone? What if . . ."

Oh, the odds were good that he had. "We've got to bring Antonio in on this." That much blood, yeah, someone had been *hurt.* "It's human blood."

Her gaze darted back to his. "I know." Whispered. And she looked like she was going to be sick right then. Her hand rose to her mouth and she paled.

"Erin . . ."

She shook her head, sending silky locks tossing back and forth. After a moment, her hand dropped. "He thinks he's giving me a present, don't you see? A gift. But I'm—I'm not like him." *You.* Her eyes said it, even if her mouth didn't. "The blood sickens me."

A human reaction.

But he could have sworn she was a shifter.

No, no, dammit, he *knew* she was a shifter. The beast inside recognized her.

But shifters loved blood.

"I can't stand the smell," she whispered and stormed back into the parlor. "*I hate it.*"

Pretty unusual shifter reaction.

He followed her, closing the doors with a quiet squeak. He needed to get a blood analyst in there, right away. Because he was getting a really dark, sick suspicion.

Human blood.

*Who'd bled out so nicely less than twelve hours before?*

Burrows.

Antonio had taken Jude back to the crime scene at the station, after Erin had hightailed it to the DA's office.

He'd seen Burrows. Seen the pooled blood on the floor.

But maybe, just maybe, some of that dark blood had left the holding area.

Judging by the way the letters had dripped on the wall, the killer would have needed to come straight to Erin's house after the murder. The blood must have been used when it was fresh.

The Slasher's blood?

Possible.

Not likely, of course. Could be from some other poor bastard. Then they'd have two sick shifters on the loose.

But he couldn't discount the connection. This whole mess was too screwed up. And it set his teeth on edge.

The stalker bastard had frightened Erin, had *been* frightening her. Not an acceptable situation.

The guy had broken into her house. He could have so easily gotten to her—*hurt* her.

Jude's teeth began to burn and lengthen. The claws were already out, time for the fangs.

And time to rip a shifter asshole apart.

# Chapter 4

At least the police had come quietly. No screaming sirens. No flashing lights. Just two silent black vans. One patrol car. And Antonio, in a red sports car.

Flashy.

Figured.

Erin paced the length of her porch as she watched the crime scene team file into her house. The night was hot, humid as all hell, but goosebumps covered her arms.

*Missed you.*

Dammit. She'd flushed her old life down the toilet for some freedom, but he'd found her.

Now he was back to playing his sickass games with her.

"What the hell were you thinking?" A hard bark of fury.

She raised a brow and turned to find Antonio glaring at her, the lights of the porch shining behind him. His hands were crossed over his chest, his eyes narrowed. He shook his head. "You called in a civilian before you called the cops—"

"He's the same civilian *you* called earlier, too," she reminded him. There hadn't been a lot of options for her. With the creep on her tail, there never were. Back when she'd lived in Lillian, there sure as hell hadn't been a choice. As far as she'd known, the police hadn't known about the *Other.*

So they certainly wouldn't have been able to handle a supernatural who'd slipped over the line and gone straight psychotic.

"This is different! This is—"

"My life," she fired back at him. "I *know* this isn't protocol, okay, but this isn't your average situation." Her voice lowered to a hard whisper, "Not average at all."

A grunt. "Trust me, blood on the walls is *never* average."

True. Erin sucked in a breath and tried to push her fear and anger aside. Antonio was catching the brunt of her fury, but the guy had already done her a favor by pulling in his team so softly.

The porch boards groaned as he stepped forward. "How long has this guy been after you?"

She swallowed. "A year." Maybe longer. Hard to say. She'd gotten her first "gift" almost twelve months before. But she'd read up on stalkers and their behavior. She knew they often watched their prey for months or even years before making a real move.

"Did you think running was going to stop him?"

Jude had briefed him on her situation. Well, Jude had told the cop as much as *she'd* told the shifter. Erin hadn't revealed everything. Not yet.

She couldn't.

"I'd hoped it would," she said.

He took another step toward her. The scent of his cologne filled her nostrils. The guy always wore his cologne. Not too heavy but—

Another scent. Richer. Filling the air, surrounding her.

Shifter's scent.

Erin looked to the right, just over Antonio's shoulder, and she found Jude watching her, his big frame filling her doorway.

There was something in his eyes. A heat. *Anger?*

Desire.

"Your crew's working hard," Jude said as he stalked toward them.

Antonio stiffened just a bit, then eased away from her. "They're the best I've got, and they all know when we need . . . delicacy."

So they knew about the *Other?* Or were they *Other?*

Jude came to stand beside her, his arm brushing hers and sending some of the chill dissipating from her body. Handy talent, that.

"It's human blood." Flat.

The cop nodded. "You'd know."

Yeah, he would.

"This guy has a real hard-on for our ADA."

Antonio wasn't exactly high on the tact scale. Erin lifted a brow and managed not to grind her back teeth.

"He's chased you across the state," Antonio continued. "The guy isn't backing off."

"We're gonna *make* him back off." The words were little more than a growl from Jude.

Antonio's dark eyes locked on the shifter. "This gettin' personal for you, man?"

Jude didn't bother answering. "Send patrols out, have them keep an extra watch on the neighborhood."

Erin gave a laugh at that, and she knew the sound held a desperate edge. "A patrol car isn't going to stop this guy. He's *Other,* and he's damn strong." Sometimes she worried that nothing could stop him.

She hadn't been able to. Not that night, that cold night

when he'd caught her in her bedroom and dug his claws into her arms as he pinned her to the bed—

*No.*

Not going back there. Never again.

"Tell us everything you know about him," Jude said. The crime scene unit was still inside. Gathering their evidence. Walking through her life. They couldn't hear this. Only Jude and the cop he seemed to trust.

If only she were the trusting kind. But, other than her father, she'd never really trusted anyone fully before.

When you had a lot to lose, trusting was a foolish mistake. Way too easy to get burned.

"Not much to say." A shrug. *He found me. I tried to be so careful and he found me.* "He's a shifter."

*I don't want to run again.*

"You've seen him?" From Antonio.

Careful. "I-I caught his scent once."

Antonio just looked blank.

Jude's fingers snaked down her arm and the heat burned through her shirt. "Shifters carry a distinct scent. It marks us."

The cop sniffed. "I don't smell a damn thing, well . . . those azaleas but—"

"It's the way shifters recognize each other," Jude told him. "Like to like."

"*Oh, shit.*" Antonio's eyes widened as he stared at Erin, his jaw dropping. "*You're a shifter?*"

*Way to go, hunter.* "No, I most certainly am *not.*" Her nostrils flared. "I just have very . . . acute senses." That part was absolutely true. It felt good to be honest right then.

His gaze raked her. "You holding out on me again, ADA Jerome?"

*Yes.* "What I am or what I am *not* really isn't the issue here." No, the issue was the psychopath who'd painted blood on her wall. "We could have a victim out there, someone who needs help."

"That's why my crime scene gang is here. They're the best." Simple. "If the bastard left behind any clues, they'll find 'em."

"Good." Erin realized she was leaning toward Jude. *What?* She snapped straight back up.

She was tired, that was it. Hell of a day. Even worse of a night. So she'd gotten tired and she'd sagged a bit. That was okay.

But the tight feeling in her gut, the fierce urge to turn and push against him, that was *not* okay.

She needed to get in bed. Needed to forget the blood and the fear.

But the idea of walking into that house again . . . "I loved this house," she muttered, shoving back the hair that had fallen over the side of her face. There had been no ghosts in this house.

Until now.

Antonio frowned at her and after a moment of silence, he said, "So you've never seen the guy." Ah, trying delicacy now.

"I can't give you a description. Sorry. I *wish* that I could." Her shoulders lifted then fell. "Male, big, strong." She'd caught that much in the darkness. "But I can't tell you a single thing about his face." Not much help at all.

"You got all that from a scent?" Antonio scratched his chin. "One fine nose you got there, lady."

He didn't understand. Maybe the guy didn't know as much about the *Other* world as she'd thought.

One of the crime scene techs walked out. She had four evidence bags in her hands. Antonio waited for her to pass them, then he leaned forward and said, "You're gonna need protection."

She was stronger than any human he'd send to protect her.

A human wouldn't be strong enough to help her this time. She needed—

"She's got protection."

Jude's words had her head jerking toward him. She stared into his eyes. So deep and wild. "She's got protection," he repeated, the words fierce.

Protection . . . but at what price?

She could sure use his power and strength, but—

But Jude was a danger to her, too. Every moment she spent with him, Erin could feel the thing inside her tensing.

Hungering.

*Like to like.*

Wasn't that always the damn way?

"Maybe you should think about moving to a hotel room for the night. The team's gonna be here for a long while longer," Antonio said.

"I-I will." *Great idea.* The sooner she got out of there, the better.

*Missed you.*

*Dammit. No.*

She couldn't let him do this to her. Not again.

The hotel room was small. The air conditioner buzzed with a steady whir of sound, and the bed, a queen that looked like a double, waited with perfectly smooth covers.

Jude scanned the room, hands on his hips. "You don't have to stay here. You can come to my place and—"

"I'll be fine here," Erin said, her voice smooth as silk. No more fear. No worry. No anger.

Nothing.

The lady had frozen on him. Jude didn't like that. Not one bit.

She tossed a small overnight bag onto the foot of the bed. "Thanks for bringing me over, but it really wasn't necessary. I could have driven myself."

"I wanted to bring you." He'd wanted to make certain she was safe.

*Blood on her walls.* What kind of sick freak was after her?

And why was she so calm now? His fingers clenched. "Tony will send a unit around here, just in case."

"Nothing else is going to happen tonight." She kicked off her heels. Suddenly became two inches shorter.

The lady had nice feet. Red toenails. Kinda pretty.

"That's not the way this guy works."

She would know.

Erin lifted her hands above her head as she stretched and he really tried—*for about three seconds anyway*—not to look at her chest. But her breasts stretched the front of the blouse and those buttons looked like they might pop at any moment.

*Get a grip.* The lust was gonna have to take a backseat for the time being.

Romeo from hell was stalking her. She didn't need him jumping her then, too.

Her hair brushed over her shoulders. Such a dark, thick curtain.

*Focus.* "I can . . . stay here." Hell, yeah. "Um, to keep an eye out in case—"

Her arms dropped and the stretching show ended. "Not necessary." Clipped. She marched toward him, eyes glinting. "Look, hunter, I appreciate all of your help." Her steps halted, a foot away from him. Her head tilted up, just a bit. "I-I know I shouldn't have called you. I don't know why I did."

He knew. Jude caught her hands, closing that space between them. "Don't you?" Oh, yeah, she felt the connection, exactly like he did. The hard hunger. The need.

Her lips parted.

Jude wanted those lips. Wanted the soft body that pressed against him. The bed was so close. He could ruin those perfect covers real fast.

He took a breath, tasted her, and said, bluntly, "You need me, sweetheart."

Jude watched the flare of her golden eyes. Flecks of emerald circled her pupils. So beautiful. He knew the protest was coming even before she sputtered, "Look, you— You might think you're God's gift to the ladies, but I don't *need—"*

"Not talking about sex right now." That would come, later. "You've got a shifter on your tail, and as good as Tony and his team members are, I'm better."

Her mouth snapped closed. No argument, because she knew he was telling the truth.

"*That's* why you called me." Her breasts pushed against his chest, the nipples pebbled. He'd always been a breast man, and the lady had some *fine* breasts.

But business came first.

"I'm the best hunter in the area. You called me, before you called the cops, because you wanted my help."

Still no denial.

"You want this guy stopped? Let me handle him."

Secrets were in her eyes. Fair enough, he had his own hard stories to keep, too.

"You really think you can catch him?" Erin asked quietly.

A shrug. "I'm your best bet." He believed that, one hundred percent.

"What will I . . ." Her gaze dropped even as her hands rose to push against his chest. Small hands with red nails to match her toes. "What will I have to pay for your services?"

He didn't answer, not until that stare of hers rose slowly

once more. And he didn't back away from her either. "One hell of a lot," Jude told her and enjoyed the widening of her eyes. "I don't come cheap."

Then he kissed her because he had to taste her. Her lips were parted and he drove his tongue deep.

Damn but she was sweet. He'd been a sucker for sweets as long as he could remember.

She didn't fight him. Didn't dig her nails into his chest or twist her head away. No, her tongue swiped against his and she gave a little rumble in her throat, a cross between a growl and a moan—and then he just stopped thinking.

And started feeling.

Lush female curves. Soft skin. Lips. Tongue.

His hands snaked down her spine, caught her hips—squeezed.

*Nice ass.*

His cock rose toward her, swelling and hungering.

Her scent teased him. Those roses . . . and woman. The rich scent of her need, a fragrance that only made his arousal stronger.

And . . . something more. Earthier. Subtle, simmering just below the surface, but something familiar in the air.

Her hands shoved against his chest and Jude stumbled back.

*Forgot the punch the lady packed.*

Her lips, red and wet, tightened. "Is sex with me part of the deal?"

"No," he told her truthfully. "It's a bonus."

Jude knew he'd said the wrong thing even as Erin sucked in a sharp breath. "Listen, shifter—"

He held up his hands and tried to ignore the hard-on that stretched the front of his jeans. "Easy. What I meant"—okay, so he'd never been real good with women and words—"was that the case and us—they're separate."

But he did plan on moving into her house, if not her bed, right away.

She'd be the most vulnerable at night. During the day, she'd be surrounded by lawyers and cops. Sharks and the police—they had to keep her pretty safe. But at night, when she went back to that big old house all by herself, she'd be a target.

Jude would make sure she wasn't alone. Not until the freak was caught.

"You're so cocky." She shook her head. "You really think you can get any woman you want?"

He lifted a shoulder. "I don't want *any* woman." *Just you.* The need had been like a fist in the gut and a stroke to the groin from that first moment.

*Like to like.*

Maybe.

He'd heard about some shifter couples who were combustible in the sack. With sex and shifters, the human rules were ripped away and only the basic needs of the animals remained.

And the animals sure had a lot of needs.

But Erin claimed she wasn't like him.

A good liar, his Erin. Just not good enough.

She crossed her arms over her chest. "I can't deal with this now, Jude."

Hmmm. He liked the way she said his name. Soft. Husky.

"I'm dead on my feet and I just—I can't deal with this," she said again.

*Can't deal with you.*

Fair enough. The lady had been through one wild night. She needed to rest, and he wasn't a jerk enough to deny her.

Tomorrow would be soon enough to get their partnership started.

"Lock the door behind me," he told her.

Her eyes lifted toward the ceiling. "Yeah, because I was just gonna leave it open so every creep in the city could sneak in."

Smart-ass. He liked that. Even rundown, she still had spirit.

A tough lady.

She'd have to be, in order to face what was coming.

He'd seen his share of psychopaths while working with Night Watch. The agency had earned its reputation for going after the scum of the earth for a reason.

They hunted those criminals that others wouldn't, or couldn't.

So he'd seen freaks, come upon scenes that had caused bile to rise in his throat and sweat to bead his upper lip.

The beast within had roared at the carnage, but the man had leashed him and gotten the job done.

Shadows lingered under her eyes. The woman was all but swaying on her feet. "Get in bed." *Next time, with me.* "I'll see you first thing tomorrow."

He brushed by her, locking his eyes on the door. *Don't look back. The woman will make you weak.*

With the freak shifter on the loose, he couldn't afford to be weak.

"Thank you." The whisper froze him at the door. Then, dammit, he looked back.

"I owe you, Donovan." *Back to Donovan, huh*? "I won't forget that you came for me." She rocked on her heels. "I can't remember anyone ever coming to my side so quickly."

*Leave or toss her on the bed.* Jude sucked in a desperate gulp of air. The lady had no idea what she was doing to him. That husky voice. Those deep eyes.

That scent.

Had the other men in her life been worthless idiots?

Nothing could have stopped him from getting to her side.

His head jerked in what he hoped was a nod. He yanked the door open. "See you . . . in the morning."

The door slammed closed behind him. He waited a minute, two, then heard the *snick* of the deadbolt being thrown.

Good.

Jude took the steps three at a time and was down in the lobby, leaning over the registration desk, in less than a minute's time. He slapped his hand on the counter, letting the twenties peak through his fingertips.

"Give me the room that connects to the lady's." No way was he leaving her alone. Jude planned to be close enough to hear even the whisper of fear from her.

The clerk, a teen with a bad case of acne on the left side of his face, eyed the money with a narrowed gaze. "You're not some kind of perv . . . are ya?"

Jude growled.

The kid hopped back.

"I'm her boyfriend. We're having a fight." He smiled, showing teeth he knew to be a bit too sharp. "It'll be over long before dawn, so *just give me the damn key.*"

His fingers shaking, the kid tossed him the key.

"Good." Jude caught the key card in his left fist. His right hand lifted, revealing the money. "The extra forty is for you. If anyone comes around sniffing after my lady, you let me know ASAP, got it?"

The money disappeared in a blink. "Uh, got . . . it."

"Good."

The room card bit into his palm, and Jude forced himself to ease the grip.

Just to make sure the place was clear, he scanned the lobby. Then, satisfied, he headed back upstairs.

The hunt would start tomorrow.

The beast inside jerked against his leash.

*Tomorrow.*

* * *

Jude woke, his heart racing and his eyelids flying open.

He strained, struggling to hear. *What had woken him?*

A whimper. Muffled.

He jumped out of bed and lunged across the room. One yank and the lock on the connecting door broke. "*Erin!*"

She screamed and sat up, her eyes wide open.

*Alone.* His heart was about to burst from his chest. "Sweetheart, you scared the hell out of—"

She flew at him, snarling, hands out, claws extended.

Swearing, he stumbled back, but not before those claws raked a trail of fire across his chest.

*Not a shifter, my ass.* "Erin!" He grabbed her. No choice. Self-preservation instincts were strong in him. His fingers locked tight around her wrists and he jerked her arms down. "Calm—"

She broke his hold. In about half a second.

She. Broke. His. Hold.

And came at him again with those razor sharp claws shooting from her fingertips.

He snarled and she froze.

Then she blinked and shook her head. "Jude?" Her claws retracted. "What are you—"

He saw the flare of her nostrils. She'd left a lamp on near the bathroom, and the light spilled in a soft circle, giving him a perfect view of her. Even without that light, he would have been able to see.

"Your chest!" Horror broke across her face. Her gaze dropped to her hands. She turned them over, staring at her palms, her fingertips. Looking like she'd never seen the things before.

"I heard you cry out," he said, pushing his right hand against the throbbing wound. He'd had a hell of a lot worse before. No big deal, but—

But he hadn't expected such a fierce attack from her. "Thought you might need me."

Her shoulders dropped. "I-I don't remember. I guess I was . . . dreaming."

"Had to be one hell of a dream." The scent of his blood seemed too thick in the air.

"I . . . guess so." She reached for him and Jude held his ground. Erin bit her lip. "I should wash this, bandage you." She caught his arm and led him to the bathroom.

He could have stopped her. Told her it was just a flesh wound and that even without shifting, it would be gone by dawn.

But he liked the way her hands felt against him.

He'd ditched his shirt before he'd crashed in the bed. Kept his jeans on, just in case.

Good thing he'd had the denim on. He'd have to make sure he kept her claws away from *that* part of his anatomy.

The bathroom was the size of a closet, a miniscule one. After flipping on the lights, Erin turned from him and wrenched on the water. She snagged a cloth, held it under the flow of water, soaped it up, and then eased it across his bare chest.

The lady didn't meet his gaze. Just kept one small hand over his heart while the other swiped the cloth over the five long claw marks.

No denying what they were.

She turned from him, her hip and shoulder brushing against him as she rinsed the blood from the cloth.

"Want to talk about it?" He inched closer, the better to trap her against the sink.

Erin's face was pale. "I have occasional night terrors, okay? Had 'em for years, even before the creep got attached to me." Her lips pressed together. "I don't remember the dreams."

"Don't you?"

She flinched.

His hands rose slowly and curled over her shoulders. "If you don't want to talk about the dream, then how about you try telling me one more time that you *aren't* like me. Because I know a shifter's claws when I see them." *And feel them.*

Her gaze held his in the mirror. Her hair was a dark curtain around her face, and despite her height, she still looked fragile, delicate, against him.

Looks could be so deceiving.

"Having claws . . . doesn't make me a shifter." Her chin lifted and color finally began to drift back into her cheeks. "Any number of *Other* have claws."

True enough. His head lowered over her shoulder. She'd finally ditched her business clothes and slipped on a loose pair of pajama pants and a white top. The neckline was low and scooped, showing off that perfect cleavage.

Jude bent over her. Really, he was in the best position. That sweet ass before him. Her neck, all but bared so close to his mouth.

A faint tremble shook her.

He lowered his head, setting his mouth right over her throat. Just an inch separated him from that sweet flesh.

Vamps weren't the only ones who liked to bite.

"Jude . . ."

His lips closed over her skin. Kissed. Sucked. Her head fell back, exposing even more of that tempting flesh.

His mouth eased over her. Found that sweet spot where neck and shoulder met. A favorite for his kind.

His fangs burned.

He bit her.

Not too hard. Not a marking.

Just a taste.

That firm ass rocked back against him as she moaned.

His heart thudded, the drumming filling his ears. The dream—night terror, whatever the hell it had been—was gone.

Now it was just the two of them. He was ready, *more* than ready, his cock hard and thick with lust, and she wanted him, he knew that.

Erin lunged forward, her palms slapping against the counter. "*No.*"

His teeth snapped together as he fought to rein in his hunger.

Her hair fell over her face, shielding her from his view. Erin's shoulders heaved as she pulled in several deep breaths.

Jude glanced toward the shower and thought about hopping in, then cranking on the ice cold water.

"I'm not what you think," she whispered, still with her head down.

Not gonna have that. "*Look at me.*" Guttural. The need was too stark for anything else.

Her head lifted and the coal black strands slid back. Her eyes held his in the mirror.

She said, "I-I've got shifter blood."

No doubt.

Her head moved to the left, then right. "But I can't shift. *I can't.*" Anger, no, fury in her voice.

Well, hell.

He'd heard of a few others like her. Hybrids. From the matings of shifters and humans. Or shifters and charmers or even demons. Some hybrids came out even stronger than the purebloods. The strength of both parents, the weaknesses of neither.

But then there were tales of other hybrids . . .

Those who got the weaknesses, but not the strengths.

*No, I've felt her strength. Erin sure as shit isn't weak.*

"I'm . . . flawed, okay? The beast in me—hell, she may as well be dead."

He leaned over her, grabbed her hands and trapped them against the countertop. "She's not dead." Erin felt so good against him.

Right.

"Look," he ordered. Across the top of the counter, etched in deep, were claw marks. Just like the ones on his chest.

"You've got a beast all right, sweetheart. And whether you can shift to let her play or not, doesn't make a bit of difference." He turned his head, rubbed his nose against her throat.

Some cats really were all alike.

"I want you, and I don't fucking care what you are—or what you aren't."

Then, before the last of his control splintered, he shoved away from her.

Erin twisted, staring up at him with those eyes that he knew could easily see right through him. *In too deep.*

"And you're fucking not *flawed.*"

He stormed for the connecting door. So the lock was broken. He needed space right then. Or else he was gonna pounce on her.

"You don't know, hunter." She'd followed him from the bathroom. Her voice sounded hollow and when he looked back, her face could have been a blank mask. "*You don't know me.*" Her chin lifted. "And trust me, you're better off that way."

Jude had left her. Good. She didn't need things to get sexual between them. It would just make the situation worse.

*Like it could really get much worse.*

He didn't understand. When she'd told the guy she was

flawed, she hadn't been talking about her inability to shift. No, she'd always thought not shifting was a blessing.

"*You don't understand.*" A whisper directed at the closed white door.

No one did.

Well, just one person . . . the bastard who'd left her the bloody love letter. He knew too well what she was like on the inside. That knowledge was why he was after her.

Damn him.

*Flawed.*

*Broken.*

# Chapter 5

"We've got a new case." Jude kicked the conference room door closed and eyed the man who'd first recruited him.

Jason Pak. Half-Korean, half-Choctaw—and one hundred percent charmer. A tough asshole, one who liked to wear three piece suits and go gator hunting on the weekend.

Well, not so much hunting, since his gift allowed him to *talk* with the gators.

Pak lifted a brow. The guy was pushing fifty, maybe sixty, but there wasn't a single line on his face. "I'm aware of the situation with Bobby Burrows. I talked to the ADA myself last night."

"Not just about Burrows." Jude had come to Jason right away, because he wanted the backup of the agency. "It's about Erin."

"Our ADA is much more than she seems." Pak eased back in his chair, steepling his fingers beneath his chin. "Isn't she, Jude?"

No shifter senses, but Pak always seemed to *know* everything about the *Other.*

"Gus is sure she's not demon, and I don't take her for a witch." Pak's black stare didn't leave Jude's face. "You stayed with her in a hotel last night. Does that mean she's one of yours?"

*Mine.* If only. "It means she's my client."

Pak didn't blink.

"She's got an asshole stalking her. He's *Other*. Last night, he left a bloody message on her wall."

"I know."

Of course he did. "She needs protection, the kind of protection the cops can't give her."

A slow nod. "But we can."

Damn straight. "I want this guy." Well, mostly he just wanted to kill him. "Give me Daniels and Wynter." They were the best, well, after him.

As far as Jude knew, Pak *was* Night Watch. The agency was his baby. If there were superiors to him, Jude had never seen them or caught even a whisper of their names. So if he was going to pull in the other two agents, he'd need Pak's go-ahead.

And if he didn't get permission—screw it. He'd find another way to protect Erin and to nab the bastard.

"All right." Pak's long, bony fingers reached for the phone. The speaker clicked on and he ordered, "Send in Dee and Zane."

*Yes.*

Normally, Jude hunted alone. He liked it that way. But this time, he wanted extra eyes. Not eyes for his own back, but for Erin. The better to keep her safe.

Pak rose from the chair. Straightened his jacket. "Careful, shifter. If you let the case get personal, you could find yourself in dangerous waters."

*Too late.* He watched silently as Pak left the room. When the door shut, he muttered, "It's already personal."

One beat of time. Two, then . . .

The door shoved open. Dee came in first, her small body moving fast. "Hey, Jude! What's up?"

Zane strolled in after her. The guy always seemed to take things at a stroll. When the door shut behind him, he lifted a brow and just . . . waited.

Jude's gaze drifted between them, the two agents he trusted the most at Night Watch.

Dee. *Ms. Sandra Dee Daniels.* But if any fool made the mistake of calling her Sandra Dee, she kicked his ass.

Dee was small but deadly. She could track a man across three states and barely break a sweat.

And Zane Wynter. Tall and lean, the guy knew how to hunt and how to catch prey. Dark hair, green eyes—a lie that, because Jude knew the cagey bastard really had demon black eyes—and a knack for tagging supernatural killers. The guy loved playing on the dark side and playing with his prey.

Dee stared, one golden brow arched. "This got anything to do with all the action that went down at the ADA's place last night?"

Now, with Pak, Jude never knew where the guy got his info. But with Dee, he knew the source. Tony told that woman too much. Jude was about twenty percent sure the two of them had been lovers at one time.

"The ADA?" Zane stretched slowly, the floor creaking beneath him. "What's Prichard doing now?"

"Not him." Dee sighed. "The new woman—Jude's lady."

"She's not *mine.*" Yet.

"Huh." Zane's lips curved down. "She human?"

Generally Zane's first question on every case. The guy

preferred to hunt *Other*, and he had a real deadly hunger for the demons who'd crossed the line.

The guy liked to kill his own. Whatever. Not Jude's issue.

Erin was his issue. "The fuckup who is after her isn't." *Missed you.*

Zane's gaze snapped to him. Now he'd gotten the demon's attention.

"Just what went down there last night?" Dee asked, rubbing a hand over the back of her neck.

"Erin's got a stalker. Some asshole who has been trailing her for months."

"The guy tracked her to a new town?" Zane whistled. "Persistent, I'll give him that."

"Psychotic," Jude fired back. "I'll give him *that.*" He tossed the file he'd been compiling onto the conference table. "Crime scene photos from last night. The guy broke in, wrote a message on her wall—in blood."

Dee rifled through the folder and picked out the image of the words MISSED YOU. "Animal blood?"

"No."

Her fingers tightened around the photo. "This asshole a vampire?"

Dee's one weakness—she let the vamp cases get to her, every time. One day, that could come back to bite her in the ass.

"No, a shifter." He rubbed his thumb across the scar on his lip. After a moment, he dropped his hand and said, "Least that's what Erin thinks."

"She's seen him?" Zane jumped on that.

Now Jude hesitated. "The lady says no, but . . ." But he didn't believe her.

And he didn't trust her, either.

*You don't know me.*

Could be there was a lot more to this game than he realized. "Let's go carefully on this one, okay?" These two knew the score, and they understood what he was saying and what he wasn't.

"Where do you want to start?" Dee asked.

"With Erin." Because everything was about her. "We need to dig into her past—"

"And tear her life apart." From Zane. Never one for tact.

But he was right. "Yeah. Yeah, we do, but only her *past* life." The lady had worked hard for a new start, and he didn't want her secrets spread. "Don't talk with anyone she works with yet. Let's just find out everything we can about Erin before she came to Baton Rouge."

*Flawed.*

He'd find out exactly what she'd meant by that.

And he'd stop the asshole on her trail, too.

"Bail is set for the defendant at two hundred thousand dollars."

"*Your Honor!*" Erin jumped to her feet. *Two hundred grand?* That was spare change to Lorenzo Coleman. Why not just give the guy a ticket out of town? "The defendant is a flight risk!"

"He's a pillar of the community," Lee Givens, the snake of a defense attorney fired, on his feet now, too. "Despite the ADA's attempt to slander my client, there is barely any evidence—"

"*Enough for an indictment,*" she snapped. When it came to drugs in Baton Rouge, good old Lorenzo was a definite leader. The guy had been running his operation for years, but the vice cops had finally gotten lucky and busted his ass when there had been a shit load of cocaine stocked in the back of his office.

And the judge wanted to let him out with a two hundred grand bail?

First Burrows, now this guy. Were the judges insane? She'd had one judge almost this bad back in Lillian. *Judge Lance Harper.* The guy had been a nightmare for her in the courtroom. Every time she'd been forced to appear before him, her stomach had knotted with dread because she *knew* the guy would do something crazy.

"An indictment, yeah, but not enough for a conviction!" Lee's face flushed. "My client will walk on this, he will—"

The gavel slammed down. "Enough!" Judge Julia Went pointed the gavel at the defendant. "Surrender your passport, Mr. Coleman."

Better than nothing, but . . . "Your Honor—"

"Bail is set at two hundred thousand." Another hit of that gavel. "We're done here, Ms. Jerome."

*Hell.*

Erin gave a hard nod and tried to ignore the throbbing in her temples. She'd been in court for most of the morning, and with all the hell that had happened last night, she hadn't gotten much sleep.

Dead on her feet—yeah, that old term fit right then.

She grabbed her briefcase and shoved her files and notes inside. She'd snag lunch from one of the vendors outside, then call Jude and see what he'd found out about the blood at her house.

With one hand, she pushed open the courtroom doors. A quick nod to the guard outside and then—

"Why are you chewing my ass, Jerome?"

*Givens.*

She looked heavenward, but didn't find inspiration. Just a cracked ceiling.

"You don't need to push this case so hard. Lorenzo is a

good man, established in the community, with a family, a wife, two sons—"

Erin marched past him.

He followed.

She stabbed the elevator button and spared him a glance. "He's a drug dealer."

Givens smiled. An oily, used car salesman kind of smile. "Just because drugs were found on the premises doesn't mean he's a dealer . . . or that those drugs were even his." His southern drawl was smooth as honey. He swept back his light brown hair and gazed at her with his falsely sincere blue eyes. "He's a victim, he's—"

She snorted. "I don't have time to listen to this bull right now." Another case waited, and she still had to check in for a report on the Burrows killing.

The elevator doors slid open. A rush of people pushed by her, then Erin hurried inside.

The doors began to close. *Bye, Givens.*

He flung out his hand and had the doors easing back. "You're new in town, Erin. Don't go making too many enemies, too quickly."

Her brows lifted. "That a threat?" Her voice dripped ice. Lee Givens was an attractive guy, with one of those clean-cut faces that juries loved.

She had the feeling that inside, he could be a real snake.

She'd always hated snakes. Back home in Lillian, she'd cut the head off more than her fair share with a handy shovel.

"No." His hand didn't move. "Just some friendly advice." He smiled at her.

Used car salesman.

No, she'd met some really nice used car salesmen in her time.

*Snake.*

Another woman stepped into the elevator. She glanced at Givens. "Going down?"

He shook his head and finally removed his hand. "See you soon, ADA."

Unfortunately, he would.

*Fucking bastard.*

Rage filled him as he watched the men and women in suits drift by.

He'd seen the way the lawyer looked at Erin. Greedy eyes. Knowing smile.

*Fucking. Bastard.*

Defending that piece of crap drug dealer. Standing all high and mighty in the courtroom like he was doing something special by being in front of the judge.

Like *he* was something special.

Then the guy had followed Erin. Whispered to her.

He'd caught a glimpse of Erin's face. Seen the barely restrained anger. He knew his Erin well. She'd wanted to go after the dumb dick, claws out and teeth snapping, but she'd held back.

*Because she knows I'm here and I'll take care of things for her.*

He loved to make his Erin happy.

Loved to see her smile . . . and the hint of her deceptively delicate fangs.

*Finally.* Home.

A yellow line of police tape barred her door, but Antonio had called Erin right before she left the office and said the place had the all clear.

Erin stared at the tape. She wanted nothing more than to go inside, kick off her shoes, and fall into bed.

Little problem, though. Going inside meant she'd have to see the blood.

Cleanup was not really part of the cops' usual routine.

So she'd be the scrubber who got to remove the dry blood from her wall.

And she'd have to stay in the house, knowing *he'd* been there. Maybe another night in the hotel wouldn't be such a bad idea.

"Gonna stand out here all night, sweetheart?"

*Jude's voice.* That deep voice packed a powerful sensual punch, one that had her yearning for things best forgotten right then.

"I was strongly considering it," she murmured, not glancing back at him. Her track record with the opposite sex wasn't so great.

Gravel crunched beneath his shoes. She'd known he was there, of course. She'd caught his scent on the wind.

He brushed by her and vaulted to her porch. His fingers curled around the tape and ripped it down with one tug. "No sense staying out here in the dark."

She'd always rather liked the dark. "Where's your truck?" She hadn't seen it on the street.

His lips hitched into a half-smile, stretching that scar. Shouldn't have been sexy. Really shouldn't. "Somewhere it can't be seen."

Her brows rose at that.

"You and I are gonna be roomies until this situation is resolved."

Erin could only stare at him while crickets chirped around her and lightning bugs flashed in the distance.

A muscle flexed along his jaw. "I'll keep my hands to myself, okay? But I'm not leaving you alone, not at night. You're safe enough during the day. You usually have cops around you then, but at night—no, not 'til this freak is caught."

Hmm. She walked forward, taking the steps much slower than he had. The yellow tape dangled from his fingertips. "Nighttime protection. Is this part of the package I get for that big-ass fee I paid Night Watch?" *Drained* her savings, but she couldn't think of a better way to spend the last of her blood money. She'd sent the check to the agency this morning. Right to the big boss, Pak.

A shrug. "We aim to please."

She stopped before him. The guy was *big.* Since she was tall and loved to wear her high heels, she didn't have to look up at many men.

But her head tipped back a bit for him. "Good."

He blinked. "Good? That's it? No argument . . . *from the ADA?"*

She pulled out her keys and was happy her hands didn't tremble. "I'm not stupid, Donovan."

*"Jude."*

Erin had to swallow at that. *Too personal. Be careful, can't let him too close.* "Jude." Grudging. "Having someone here with me until this jerk is caught sounds like a good idea." If only she hadn't been alone the last time he'd caught her.

*No.* If Jude wanted to stay, yeah, that'd be more than fine with her.

Her hand twisted and she shoved the key into the lock.

"One thing." His breath blew against her hair.

Erin licked her lips.

"That whole keeping-my-hands-to-myself thing, if you want to change that rule, all you have to do is say so."

A quick push and the door creaked open. Glancing over her shoulder, she found his eyes blazing at her. "I'll keep that in mind."

His gaze dropped to her lips. "Good. 'Cause like I said, at Night Watch, we aim to please."

She just bet he knew exactly how to please a woman.

*He's a shifter. He can handle anything I throw at him.*

The knowledge burned in her mind. It wouldn't be like it had been with the others. First Jon, with his shaking hands and sweaty palms. She'd almost broken his wrists because she got a little too carried away.

*It wouldn't be like that.*

And it wouldn't be like when she'd tried a bit of bondage in college, thinking the ropes would hold her down and keep Lyle safe.

They'd snapped in an instant and she'd drawn blood seconds later with her claws.

*Wouldn't be like that.* Not with another shifter.

"Thinking about it, are you?"

Her cheeks burned. "No." Easy lie. "I'm thinking I don't want to see the blood inside." Okay, true enough.

He nudged her into the house. "You don't have to. I sent a team by for cleanup before I told Tony to give you the all clear."

"You did?"

"Umm . . ." His nostrils flared. "I swear, you have the sexiest scent. Woman, roses, and . . . wild."

*Wild*—animal scent.

He dropped the bag she hadn't even noticed until that moment—*way too busy focusing on the man*—and it hit the floor with a thud. "I also took the liberty of upgrading your security system."

She glanced toward the flashing light on the right. "Upgrade? But I already paid for a top of the line system!" One that hadn't done a bit of good.

A quick smile. Shark strong. "This one's better. It's not on the market yet."

He'd gotten rid of the blood, upgraded her protection, *and* he was there to stay the night. Erin could only shake her head. "You're not what I expected, Jude Donovan." Not at all.

"Sweetheart, you ain't seen nothing yet."

The radio blared, rocking the car. Not the classic, easy listening crap that Lee Givens listened to when clients or coworkers were around.

No, *his* music. Country, through and through. His thumbs pounded out a beat on the steering wheel as he snaked down the winding roads leading to his house.

Another damn day done. He'd get home, shower the stench of his clients off his skin, then put in a call to his ex-wife. This weekend was his son Tommy's fifth birthday, and he *would* be at that party. He'd missed the last three weekends with Tommy because of work.

No more.

He'd finally gotten the all clear. They were making him partner at his firm. No more busting his ass to prove himself. Now he'd take the plush office and easy street.

He had Tommy's new bike all nice and ready, just sitting in the garage, waiting for the kid.

Yeah, he'd call Melissa, even though it was late, because he missed that boy, and *her*, but—

Blindingly bright lights flashed in his rearview mirror.

"Shit!" Lee jerked the wheel and the tires screeched. "Asshole, turn off the brights!" He steadied the car and thought about throwing up a prominent finger. The shitass behind him sure would be able to see the gesture. His headlights were making the whole county glow.

Lee shoved his foot down on the gas. He'd lose the jerk. Couple more bends and he'd be turning off the old road and making the last stretch for home and he'd be—

The bright lights shot closer.

He stiffened. "If you want to pass, move the fuck around!" He rolled down his window and shoved his arm out, waving his hand forward. "Come around!" *Don't need this shit.* He should have moved closer to the office, but he'd kept the house. Melissa liked it. Tommy had a tree house in the back. If they came home, they'd need a place to—

The other vehicle slammed into him, sending his car jerking forward. *"What the fuck!"* Fear dried his throat. *Shit. Shit. Shit.*

An attack.

He'd handled too many criminal cases, made too many enemies, gotten too many threats.

Threats he'd never taken seriously. Until now.

He pinned the gas pedal flat against the floorboard but the other vehicle was closing in on him again. All he could see in his rearview mirror were those shining lights, making stars dance before his eyes.

What the hell did that guy have under his fucking hood?

*Jesus!* He swiped the sweat off his forehead. No, no way—

The car slammed into him again.

Lee's car jerked and his head snapped back. The seatbelt bit into his shoulder and chest and he tasted blood on his tongue. His teeth had snapped closed on it. Lee spit, snarling as—

The car flew up on the left. Lee finally caught a glimpse of it. Big, black SUV. Tinted windows. What the hell?

Too close.

His knuckles whitened around the wheel.

The black bitch slammed into the side of his car.

His secondhand BMW couldn't take the impact. The car

flew to the edge of the road, trembled. Lee yanked the steering wheel, praying.

*Not like this.* He couldn't go out like this!

His breath heaved out. His heartbeat slammed so loudly in his ears he could barely hear the radio anymore.

The SUV plowed into him once more.

The BMW lost the fight.

The car tumbled off the road, rolled, again, again.

Glass shattered. The air bag exploded before him, a white cloud that surrounded him.

The radio died.

Metal crunched. Twisted. The top of the car thudded into the earth.

*Oh, God, Tommy—*

*Sorry, son.*

Too easy. He smiled as he watched the blue car fly into the tree. Steam exploded from the hood.

Humans were so weak.

Hardly worth his time.

But if the bastard had survived the crash, maybe he could have a bit of fun with the lawyer.

Maybe a lot of fun.

Smiling, he started down the ravine.

Headlights flashed in the distance.

*Dammit.*

The roar of the truck's engine reached his ears. One of those big, souped-up trucks that the hicks in this area seemed to love.

His jaw clenched. This kill wasn't over.

But the truck was coming closer, and he was in the open.

He cast one more glance down at the twisted metal. Odds were good that the asshole was dead.

And if he wasn't, there was always next time.

*Next time.*

He turned from the ravine and hurried back to his idling SUV. If he got his butt out of there, the other driver probably wouldn't even notice the wreck.

Humans were like that. So self-involved. Never seeing the danger and death until it was too late.

Fools.

He jumped into the vehicle. The night was still young. If he hurried, he might even be able to catch his lady.

Another hunt—this one, the most important of them all.

# Chapter 6

She couldn't sleep. Erin stared up at the ceiling as the soft patter of rain began to fall onto the house. The storm that had been threatening since late afternoon had finally come.

The patter quickened as the rain strengthened, falling harder, *harder*.

She squeezed her eyes shut.

But saw Jude.

The shifter had played the gentleman. He'd walked her through the new security system. Done a top to bottom search of her house.

They'd eaten together. Hell, he'd even cooked.

Then he'd walked her to her bedroom door.

And left her.

Without even one touch.

Should have been what she wanted.

But, no, *he* was what she wanted. She wanted him so much that she was aching.

The need was like that for her. Had been, since she was

sixteen. When she wanted someone, she *wanted.* Craved. Needed so badly that her body throbbed.

For most shifters, puberty was the time when real power kicked in. The first shift.

Not for her.

The beast—or whatever the thing inside her was—had awakened, and with it, so much hunger and need.

*Control.*

It had become the center of her life. Maintaining control. *Always* having control.

Then the stalker asshole had come along and ripped all of her careful control away.

Her hands knotted beneath the sheet.

Where was Jude? When she'd offered him the room beside hers, he'd shaken his head and stared at her with blue eyes that burned with hunger. "Too close," had been his growled response.

Not close enough.

She was so screwed up.

Wanting him.

Fearing herself.

*He can handle me.*

Shifters were strong, she *knew* that. He'd be able to handle anything she threw at him.

His steps had echoed when he'd headed downstairs. Maybe he was in the little guest room she'd set up. Maybe he'd stripped off his shirt again, like last night.

*Last night.*

Her mouth dried. Oh, my. The man's chest had rippled with muscles. Beneath the jeans, his thighs bunched with power. And when he'd put his mouth on her . . .

Erin's nipples pebbled.

She turned over and buried her face into the pillow. Maybe she needed another cold shower. Maybe she—

Thunder shook the house. Erin flinched. That had been a strong blast, loud, too, shaking her bed, shaking the—

She bolted up, realization hitting hard. The thunder hadn't come from outside.

It sounded again, but it *wasn't* thunder.

Erin climbed out of bed, nearly falling flat on her ass as she hurried. That was a roar!

An animal's roar of fury, and it was coming from downstairs.

She ran for the door.

The change swept over him, hard and fast, fueled by fury, the black rage that boiled his blood and sucked the man back inside the beast.

He'd heard the rattle at the door. The scrape of claws, and Jude hadn't needed the shrill beep of the alarm to sound. He'd known the intruder was there.

Now he was going to destroy the bastard.

Bones snapped. Twisted. White fur burst from his flesh even as his claws tore from his fingertips. The snarl on Jude's lips became a roar of rage as the beast took over.

The pain didn't bother him, not anymore. But the power thrilled him.

His vision sharpened. His hearing grew more acute. In those swift moments of transformation, a new world appeared. A world where he ruled.

His mouth opened and another roar burst from him.

The bastard was running. He could hear his thudding footsteps. His favorite part . . . chasing prey.

Muscles bunching, he prepared for the hunt.

"Jude, what's going on? *Jude!*"

His head jerked toward her. Long bare limbs, sexy silk over her flesh. Her eyes were wide, her mouth open. She stood on the stairs, just steps away from the bottom, and her fingers had a white-knuckled grip around the banister. "Jude?"

He growled at her. That better not be fear on her face. He wouldn't hurt her. Not ever. No matter what form he took.

The beast wouldn't so much as scratch the woman that the man craved.

She stepped toward him, eyes too big. "I-it's you. Why d-did you shift? What's—"

No time. He whirled away from her and launched toward the open door.

Her footfalls rushed behind him. He glanced back and roared at her to stay put. In human form, she'd just be a target.

And he wouldn't risk her. Not now. Not ever.

He bounded into the night.

*Oh, shit.*

Erin stared after Jude, her heart racing so fast her chest hurt.

Jude—*a tiger.* A white tiger. Big and beautiful and deadly.

*Tiger, tiger, burning bright* . . . The words from the William Blake poem whispered through her mind as she watched him jump off her porch and disappear into the darkness.

Such grace and power.

So very, very dangerous.

*A white tiger.*

Thick fur, pale as snow, and lined with coal black stripes. The tiger was huge. The length of his body had been at least nine feet, plus that long, thick tail. His mouth—when he'd opened his mouth in that roar, his teeth had been—*hell.* He could have ripped her throat open with those razor-sharp teeth in less than a second.

But he hadn't attacked her. In his blue eyes, she'd seen the man staring back at her. Jude had full control over his beast. Not all shifters did.

"A white tiger," she whispered to the night. Jude was out there, hunting, for her.

There was a reason the white tigers bore the Chinese symbol for king on their heads. Some said the rare white tigers were among the strongest of the shifters, second only to the dragons. But the dragons, well, no one was really sure those guys even existed anymore.

Tiger versus wolf. Both strong, fierce killing machines. But the tiger—she'd lay odds he could take the wolf. He'd still better be careful, and he'd better come back to her.

Erin strode to the edge of the porch. Going after them would be foolish. She'd just get in Jude's way, and she couldn't hunt with him. No shifting, no hunting.

As much as she hated to stay behind, she wouldn't risk his safety.

Besides, a white tiger could take down just about anything.

So strong.

Strong enough to handle even her.

The rain pelted him and did its damnedest to wipe away the stench of his prey. But he caught a faint scent, one heavy with musk, smelling of the forest.

Shifter scent.

He took off after his prey, splashing through the puddles and sticking to the cover of the thick bushes and blooming azaleas as much as possible. The last thing he wanted was for a neighbor to wake up and see him running through the neighborhood in this form.

His ears twitched. His prey was fast. *Damn* fast. Had he shifted, too? Good. He'd like to see just what he was dealing with in the bastard.

Bushes slapped into his face and tickled his whiskers as he ran. *Catch him. Got to stop him.*

The thudding of the prey's steps grew weaker—because the guy was pulling away.

Faster? No way could the bastard be faster. No. Way.

But the asshole was getting away.

*Should have let the bastard come inside*. When the lock on the door had clicked open, his roar of fury had given the guy too much warning and too much time to flee.

But Jude hadn't been able to hold back the rage, or the change. The shift had burst over him with the rush of adrenaline that spiked his heartbeat. One thought—*he's coming after her.*

The beast had kicked into high gear.

The rumble of a motor growled up ahead. A car door slammed. *No, he couldn't have shifted. He wouldn't have been able to jump in the car like that if he'd shifted.*

So if he hadn't shifted, then how the hell had he run so fast?

Jude rounded the corner just in time to see the taillights of a black SUV speed away.

Dammit!

His teeth snapped together. *Give chase.*

The demand from the beast.

But a light had flickered on in the house behind him. Whoever was inside must have been alerted by the squeal of tires. The last thing he needed was to keep hunting on the road in his current body.

*Next time, bastard*. Next time.

He returned to her as a man. Naked, dripping wet. Erin met him at the door, an oversized towel in her hands. Her gaze darted over him. Thick muscles, eat-me abs, thick curling hair at his groin—

*Oh, wow.*

"Got away." Dark and rumbling. Still more beast than man.

Her gaze snapped back to his face. To those electric eyes. She held out her towel, licked her lips and swore she tasted him. "Was it . . . him?"

Stupid question. Who the hell else would have decided to come in her house at close to three a.m.?

Erin cleared her throat. She'd finally managed to stop the beeping of the security system, but she couldn't get the image of Jude's shift out of her mind.

*A tiger. A white, beautiful, scary-as-hell tiger.*

She hadn't guessed, hadn't even considered . . .

*A white tiger.*

Different shifters had different reputations in the *Other* world. You knew not to trust a hyena or a coyote. Those bastards would turn on anyone.

Wolves—dangerous. Sometimes psychotic. Great killers.

Bears were pretty easygoing, unless you got between them and a meal.

But white tigers were the rarest of the shifter breeds. Bloodthirsty. Relentless. Incredibly powerful.

*Perfect.* Yes, the more she thought about it, the more perfect Jude became for her.

*He can match me. I won't hurt him.*

Maybe she should be afraid. When she'd seen him in tiger form, perhaps she should have been scared. He could rip her body open with a swipe of his claws. Use those razor-sharp teeth on her.

But she wasn't afraid.

Seeing his power and his strength—*no,* she didn't fear him at all.

But she did want him.

Jude kicked the door closed. Water dripped from his hair and trailed over his face. "Yeah, I caught his stench." He flipped the locks into place.

Her breath jerked out. If he'd caught the scent, it had only been because the bastard out there *let* him catch the smell. She knew the other shifter could manage to control his scent. He'd sure masked the scent before.

But for the stalker to come after her like this . . . *two nights in a row.* He'd never come after her so quickly before. Not back to back.

"He got away, *this* time."

He was good at getting away, every time. "Did you see him?"

A shake of his head sent water droplets flying. "He was too fast. Don't know what beast that asshole carries, but he's *fast.*"

And strong.

And out there, waiting in the darkness. Planning his next move.

Why wouldn't he just leave her alone?

*"You're mine, Erin. Blood, bones, and beast—all mine."* Words he'd spoken to her that terrible night. Growled in the darkness.

Erin shook her head, trying to drive the voice from her mind.

"You okay?"

She licked her lips. Stared at him. *You're mine.* The asshole's voice rang in her head.

His? The hell she was.

The towel dangled in her hand.

Blue eyes glowing with need swept over her body. Jude wanted her.

She wanted him. Why fight it anymore? She wouldn't hurt him.

He couldn't hurt her.

Her heart shoved against her chest. She dropped the towel and went straight to him.

"Erin, what are you—"

She stood up on her toes and grabbed the back of his head, sinking her fingers into that wet mane and pulling his mouth down to hers. Then she kissed him. Mouth open, tongue seeking, hunger pounding through her.

His cock pushed against her. The rain hadn't done a thing to cool his arousal. The ridge was long and thick, straining, and she rubbed against him.

Tonight, she'd get wild.

A growl rumbled in his throat. His tongue swiped against hers, and his hands wrapped around her. Big and strong.

Her nipples tightened into stiff points. Her panties grew damp. And Erin knew she needed a bed.

With an effort, Erin managed to tear her mouth from his. *Hard* to do, because the guy's tongue was freaking magic. "Come upstairs with me." She didn't want to take him down there. Not with the memory of blood just a few feet away.

Upstairs. Safety.

And a big bed they could wreck.

They *would* wreck.

The beast stared out from his eyes. "Don't tease me, sweetheart. I'm not the kind of guy you can screw around with."

He was exactly the kind of guy she *wanted* to screw around with. Erin caught his hands. "I want these on me, everywhere."

*Mine.*

Hell, no. Not that sick bastard's. Her body was her own, and tonight, she'd give it to Jude, and she'd take the pleasure he gave her.

*I can't hurt him.* A reassurance that played again. *He's strong.*

*Not human.*

*Tiger.*

"Come upstairs," she repeated, her voice soft. She took his right hand and trailed the fingers between her breasts. "Come to bed with me."

She felt the tension in his hand. The leashed strength. "I can't . . . do soft and easy. Not tonight, not after a shift."

The beast still coursed through him.

Erin smiled. The beast within was exactly what she wanted. "Good." She turned from him and stalked toward the stairs. Silence thickened the air behind her.

"One minute you're telling me to keep my hands off, now you—"

She jerked off her camisole and tossed it behind her, not bothering to look back. *Can't.* "Now I want them on me."

The wood of the stairs seemed cold beneath her feet. Clad only in a pair of white bikini panties, Erin climbed the steps. Almost to the top. He hadn't moved. He wanted her, she'd felt his lust rising against her, but he hadn't moved.

*I need you.* Tonight, she needed him more than she'd ever needed another.

Erin glanced down. Her claws were out, sharpened points. She could smell the scent of her own arousal in the air and knew he had to catch the scent, too. For a male shifter, the fragrance of a female shifter's need was rumored to be nearly impossible to resist. While she wasn't fully a shifter, she'd still thought—

The stairs shook when Jude raced up them.

A smile curved her lips.

Erin reached the landing. Her bedroom waited. Inside, the lamp on the nightstand poured out soft light. Her curtains were drawn over the windows. The bed sheets were rumpled.

She took one more step forward.

Jude pounced.

His arms caught her, lifting her off her feet, and spinning her around. His eyes, blazing, too brilliant, trapped her. His mouth took hers.

*Yes.*

Fear wasn't in her mind, not then. No memories. No nightmares. Just him.

She wrapped her legs around his waist and felt that thick cock push against the crotch of her panties. He had to feel the wet touch of the silk, and she wanted him to know how much she ached.

Four steps, and they fell onto the bed. Kissing, touching, stroking.

She loved his mouth. Her tongue swiped over the sexy scar that drove her crazy.

His fingers curled over her breasts and Erin nearly shot off the bed. Her nipples were so sensitive, desperate for more.

His head lifted and, past those delicious lips, she could see the glinting edge of his teeth.

A faint memory stirred in her mind. Fear whispered to her.

*No.*

She rolled with him, twisting so that she was on top and in control.

*Jude can handle me.*

The tip of her nails—claws—raked down his chest. Over the firm, brown nipples. Down those sculpted muscles. He sucked in a sharp breath when she reached his abs.

Erin licked her lips and eased back. Her legs straddled his thighs, such hard and strong thighs, and a quiver stirred in her belly. Her hands shook when she reached for his cock, the length standing up, veins bulging the sides. Thicker than her wrist. Long enough to give her one hell of a ride.

Beautiful.

Her fingers closed around him. Pumped. Stroked. She'd like to taste him. Like to lick from root to tip and see just how long his control would last with her.

His hands locked around her waist and he shot up. His mouth closed over her right breast. Sucking, licking, tasting. Her head fell back on a moan.

"Jude!"

The edge of his teeth pressed against her flesh.

*Shouldn't enjoy that, shouldn't like it so much.*

Her sex trembled.

*Empty. Need him inside.*

Only the thin fabric of her panties was between them.

She leaned toward him and put her mouth on his throat. She teased him with her lips—and then gave him her own bite.

Every muscle in his body stiffened. Not a growl in his throat this time. Hell, that was more a roar from the tiger.

In half a second, Erin found herself on her back again, looking up at him. Jude's face was fierce, etched with savagery and lust.

His claws ripped her panties away and in the next breath, he'd shoved open her thighs.

*Fury. Strength.*

He could handle her. But could she handle him?

"Jude, I . . ."

She expected the hard thrust of his flesh in her.

But instead he pushed down her body, lifted her hips up and took her with his mouth.

Her heels dug into the mattress. "*Jude!*" Her claws slashed the sheets.

His tongue swirled over her clit. His lips locked around the center of her need. He sucked. He took.

Tasted.

Then drove that wicked tongue deep inside her.

Her climax erupted, sending spasms through her sex as she came in a fury of pleasure.

"Fucking delicious . . . nothing like you before . . ."

She could barely hear his words over her drumming heartbeat.

But she felt him, the wide, round head of his cock, lodging at her straining entrance.

*Yes.*

The wisps of memory had vanished with those sensual licks. Not like—

"I'm . . . clean." The words were deep, guttural. "Can't catch any . . ."

She strained against him. Erin wanted that cock in her *now.* She knew what he was telling her. Shifters couldn't catch the diseases humans could pass so easily during sex. Yeah, he was clean. "So am I," she whispered, and dug her heels into his ass as she lifted against him.

And shifters could only produce children with their mates. She didn't have to worry about that with Jude. Hell, not with anyone but—

He drove into her. Filled every inch of her in a powerful thrust that had her hips arching and her hands flying to wrap around his shoulders.

"Erin . . ." Gritted from behind clenched teeth. "Are you . . ."

"Fantastic." Her hands released the strips of sheets and curled around his shoulders. "Just don't stop!"

A strangled laugh. "Don't . . . worry. Too . . . good!"

Then it began. Withdraw. Thrust. Withdraw.

*Thrust.*

Her fingers dug into him, and her legs clenched around his hips. Her strength flowed, full force, as she held tight and arched up to meet him as he plunged in a fast, desperate rhythm.

He didn't tell her to stop. Didn't tell her to loosen her grip.

Jude just drove into her. Again and again and her inner muscles stretched for him, eager for more pleasure.

For more of him.

The thud of flesh hitting flesh filled the air. The scent of sex drifted around them. Her bed was sturdy. It didn't move with the powerful thrusts, but the bed springs squeaked.

She clenched her sex around him, and her breath panted out. "Harder!" Erin wanted so much more.

He could give it to her.

Jude jerked her up, rising on his knees. She stared into his blazing eyes and wondered if her own glowed as bright.

The coil of release began deep within her.

Her mouth opened on a scream.

*Flesh so close. Taste. Take.*

The thing inside would have her way.

*Mine.*

His throat was so close. She bit down on him, muffling her scream and tasting his flesh as pleasure ripped through her.

He stiffened against her, his hold grew even harder, and then he erupted inside her, shaking with his own release.

A drumbeat echoed in her ears.

Aftershocks rippled over her body.

Slowly, so slowly, her head lifted and she swiped her tongue over her lips.

And she tasted blood.

Horrified, Erin shoved against him. "Oh, hell, Jude, I didn't mean—"

He kissed her. Kept his cock buried deep inside and kissed her.

When his head rose, she stared up at him, hoping, scared, and so confused. "I didn't mean to hurt you."

That half smile made her melt. "You didn't. You couldn't." His index finger trailed down her chest. "I could fucking eat you alive, sweetheart."

*Not running away.* Not freaking out because she'd gotten a little . . . overzealous there at the end.

Tiger.

His gaze dropped to her chest. "Such sweet breasts with their pretty pink nipples." He frowned, his head lowering. "What the hell?"

Her scar.

How had she forgotten? Shit, shit! How had she forgotten that?

She should have turned off the light.

*Shifters can see in the dark.* She *knew* that!

His fingers rubbed lightly over the raised flesh just below her left breast.

A claw mark.

Jude withdrew from her, a long, slow glide, and Erin had to bite back the plea for him to stay, to thrust deep again.

*Again.*

The passion was gone, at least for him. He was looking at her now with intense eyes and a hard face.

Looking at her like she was a victim, dammit.

Not a woman.

Before, she'd been a woman with him.

Now—

Erin spun away from him. She ripped what was left of the sheet loose as she moved, using it to cover her body.

*How could I have forgotten? I see the thing every day.*

"Who marked you?" Fury there, boiling beneath the surface of his voice.

She rose from the bed, careful not to move too fast. Didn't want it to look like she was running.

Even if she was.

Erin clenched her thighs, feeling a quiver in her sex.

*So good.* But good things didn't last long in her life.

At least Jude hadn't gone running from her, even when she'd used her claws and teeth.

"*Who fucking marked you?*"

She turned back to face him.

Jude jumped from the bed, naked and damn sexy still, and grabbed her arms.

The sheet slipped to the floor.

"That bastard did it, didn't he? You said you'd never seen him, you said he hadn't got close to you!"

Time for some truth. "I lied."

At first, the wound had bled like a bitch. She'd left a trail of her blood on the street when she'd fled. But, lucky for her, she could heal without shifting. So her skin had mended, well, *as close to mending as it could*, and though her bleeding had stopped by the time she'd reached safety, she'd been left with his mark on her flesh. The wound had been too deep and long to heal perfectly.

"What happened?"

From wild sex back to business. Not the way she would have liked to spend the afterglow moments. Erin swallowed. "Not tonight, Jude, okay? I don't want to talk about this now." Not while her body still vibrated with the pleasure he'd given her. Not while she could still taste him.

Not while she could almost feel him inside.

She didn't want to go back to that other night right then.

*Not now.*

He stared down at her, a muscle flexing along his jaw.

"Not tonight," she repeated.

Silence. Then, when her heart was squeezing because she didn't want to go back there, he gave a grim nod. "But we *will* talk about it, Erin. I'm working this case for you. I need to know everything that's happened."

She licked her lips. "Tomorrow, okay? Tomorrow."

His hands dropped. She bent and scooped up the sheet. He'd go back to his room downstairs now, she'd go back to bed and try to sleep, *try*.

Erin brushed by him. "In the morning, we'll talk." A dismissal. Not sexy. Not subtle.

She'd never really been the subtle sort.

She climbed into the bed. Eased onto the mattress and tried not to notice the way his scent surrounded her.

"Scoot over, sweetheart."

Her breath caught. "You're not going downstairs?"

Jude shook his head. "Not the way things work. Not for me."

He eased in beside her and wrapped his arms around her body.

Erin tensed.

"Relax. I'm just going to hold you. Hold you and sleep."

Sounded good to her.

His right hand curved around her stomach. The fingers drifted lightly over her scar.

"Something you should know." His voice was soft.

She waited.

"When I find him, I'm gonna kill him."

If only the bastard out there were easy to kill. If he'd been easy prey, she would have killed him herself, long ago.

* * *

It took a while for Erin's breathing to ease into the slow, natural rhythm of sleep.

Jude held her, keeping his hold nice and easy, and he waited.

And he choked back his rage.

*The bastard marked her.*

Close enough to mark. Close enough to kill.

Why the hell had Erin kept the truth from him?

She stirred in her sleep, moving lightly, and her nose rubbed against his neck.

In sleep, she was soft and beautiful. Delicate. A woman who needed protection.

In passion, she'd been something else. Oh, still beautiful. With her shining eyes and hungry lips, Erin had been the most beautiful thing he'd ever seen.

But not delicate. Her hold on him had been too strong, too fierce. And her hunger had been as wild as his own.

The beast in him had been very, very hungry.

For her.

His cock was still erect, still ready—because he wanted more. But when the ghost of fear had appeared in her eyes, he'd known the passion was over. For now.

He'd had her once. He'd have her again. And he'd make sure that fear never showed again.

Jude would stop the asshole out there. No doubt.

The beast inside couldn't wait to taste the blood.

*The rain was falling again. Dripping through the broken glass.*

*Drip.*

*Drip.*

*The scent of gasoline was in the air. Thick, cloying gasoline, and the coppery stench of blood.*

*Drip.*

*Drip.*

*Erin stared at the mound of twisted metal. Her feet crunched glass on the ground beneath her, but she didn't feel any pain. "Hello?"*

*Thunder rumbled.*

*She wet her lips and inched forward. The broken car looked like hell. The roof had been smashed. The front four feet of the car had been crumbled to pretty much nothing by the tree.*

*The scent of blood grew stronger.*

*Shadows filled the interior of the car, but she knew someone was inside.*

*Living or dead?*

*Her hand reached out and touched the icy door handle. She yanked, but the thing wouldn't open.*

*Someone was inside.*

*Blood.*

*Another hard pull, this time, with both hands.*

*Nothing.*

*Her palms were wet, from the rain, from her own sweat.*

*She should get help.*

*Yeah, yeah, that was a good idea, she'd go, get help.*

*Erin stepped back, almost falling in the slick mud.*

*She'd find help, then she'd come back as fast as she could.*

*Turning, she ran for the—*

*"D-don't . . . l-leave . . . m-me . . ."*

*The voice stopped her cold.*

*"P-please . . ."*

* * *

Erin woke, breath heaving.

*"D-don't . . . l-leave . . . m-me . . ."*

The voice echoed in her head, and, dammit, it was a voice she knew.

"Erin?" Jude's growl. Sleep-roughened and deep. "Sweetheart, you must've had a bad dream."

If only.

Never that simple for her.

Death dreams. The only thing, other than her black hair, that she'd gotten from her father.

She'd had her first one when she was twelve years old. Her mother had told her it was just a nightmare, nothing to worry about.

Then the body had been found.

The damn dreams. Sometimes they came to her right before a death, teasing her and making her believe that there was something she could do. Some way to change fate.

Other times, to torment her, they came too late. Minutes, hours after the death.

Too late to do anything but mourn the dead.

*"D-don't . . . l-leave . . . m-me . . ."*

Too late. No, she still had to try.

Erin leapt out of bed. She ran for her closet and snagged the first pair of sweats she saw.

"Uh, Erin?"

Shimmying, she jerked them up. Then shoved her hands through the sleeves of a T-shirt.

"Little early for a jog."

Erin spun around. "I have to leave."

He blinked. The man looked sleep tousled. Blond hair mussed, eyes heavy-lidded, faint stubble lining his jaw.

She swallowed. *Don't mind waking up to that.*

His gaze sharpened. "Where." Demand, not question.

*How to explain this?* The long version? The one with all

the twisted shit in her past and the roots of her father's vision gifts—courtesy of her great-grandfather, a Choctaw shaman.

Screw it. Better to just cut to the chase. "I'm psychic, okay? Just like my dad." Not exactly. "Look, if I don't get to Old Dobbin's Bend soon, a man's going to die." Could already be dead.

*Old Dobbin's Bend.* When she'd turned away from the wrecked car, she'd known that road. She'd been on that winding track once, just last week. She'd ridden with a uniform out to question a witness. No mistaking that long, curving bend.

Jude stared at her for about five seconds, then gave a nod. "Right, then let's get the hell to Dobbin's Bend."

Her jaw dropped. That was it? No questions, just go? "You believe me?"

He swung his legs over the edge of the bed. "Woman, you're talking to a man who can shift into a tiger. Hell, yeah, I believe you." He jerked on his pants. *When had he brought those upstairs?* "Now let's get our asses over to Dobbin's Bend."

*Hold on, Lee.* The whisper slipped through her mind. The voice in her dream had belonged to Lee Givens, the attorney who usually pissed her off. But now, she was just scared for him.

Sure, Lee could be a real jerkoff, but he didn't deserve to die alone.

No one did.

# Chapter 7

Jude's hands clenched around the steering wheel. "You sure this is the right place?"

His voice was cool, calm, but Erin's shoulders tensed. "It's the right place."

She'd seen this exact road in her dream. Those trees. The broken pine.

*This was the place.*

"How long you been having dreams like this?"

Erin wet her lips. "Close to seventeen years now, but I don't—I don't have them that often." If she had them every night, she'd go crazy. No question. "I only have them when . . . when I know someone—" Didn't have to be an intimate knowledge, but it had to be someone she'd connected with in some way. The dreams were only about people who'd stirred her emotions, good or bad.

When her emotions were stirred, then the link, or whatever the hell it was inside of her, just clicked on. When it was time for someone she'd connected with to die, the death dreams came.

Her dad told her it was a gift. One passed through generations of his blood by the gods.

Gift? More like curse.

Her dreams sure hadn't been enough to save him.

"So if you know somebody and—"

"They have to be close to death." For the dreams to come calling, they had to hear death's sweet whisper.

"Huh."

Her brows pulled together. She didn't know quite what that sound meant. *Told him I was flawed. This death dream madness is just the tip of the iceberg.*

She felt the glance he gave her. Questioning. Weighing.

She couldn't worry about that now, not when— "Stop!"

He slammed on the brakes.

Erin shoved open her door and jumped out of the truck. This was the spot from her vision, she knew it. Her body hummed with energy. *Here.*

"Erin, wait!" The grind of the tires crunched as he pulled off the road behind her. A door slammed.

Her gaze raked the road. The rain had fallen so hard during the night, it would have washed away any signs—

"*Sonofabitch.*"

Jude saw the markings first. Figured, his senses were better than hers.

Ten feet up the road, then right over the edge . . .

They ran together, then they went over that edge.

The mud sucked at her tennis shoes, making gulping sounds like it wanted to eat her, but Erin powered on through the falling mist. The broken car was in her sights now.

*How can he be alive?*

The car had been smashed, crumbled as if by giant hands, then thrown away.

In the distance, the shriek of a siren sounded. Help was coming. The ambulance she'd called before she left her house was getting closer, fast.

Jude reached the car door first. The window was broken, shattered, and inside, Erin could see Lee's bloody form.

"Lee!" He didn't move.

"He's breathing," Jude said. "But I don't know for how much longer." His fingers curled over the side of the door, and he yanked.

The door broke loose and fell to the ground.

Erin crawled inside the car. "Lee! It's okay. Help's coming!" *Still alive.* Finally, she'd reached someone in time.

He flinched and gave a moan.

"It's okay," she said again. Voices floated to her. The EMTs. They were running down the ravine now, having the same trouble with the thick mud. But they'd get him out. They'd be able to save him. They could stop the bleeding.

Because his shirt was drenched with blood.

*Too much blood.* And it trickled from his forehead. From the gash that went too deep.

She swallowed. "You'll be all right." Lie.

His eyes opened. "T-Tommy?" Rusty, weak.

"What?" Erin swallowed, fighting to stay calm. "Lee, who—"

"L-love y-you, s-son . . ." His eyes fell closed. His breath came out in a soft rush.

"Lee? Lee!"

"His heart's stopped!" Jude's snarl. He stepped back and yelled, "Get your asses over here, now! He needs help!"

"Lee?" Her whisper.

Then Jude's arms were around her and he hauled her

back. A woman in a blue EMT uniform pushed by her, followed immediately by two men.

But Lee still wasn't moving.

Wasn't breathing.

Too late.

Again.

Story of her life.

And Lee's death.

Erin watched the swirl of red lights fade away. The EMTs had gotten Lee's heart started again, but they'd been grim about his chances for survival.

"How the hell did you two even know he was down there?" Antonio's fierce voice. He'd arrived on the scene less than ten minutes ago.

Erin shook her head. The ambulance had vanished around a curve. "We . . . saw the car when we were passing through." She'd called 911 on her cell phone. Antonio wouldn't be able to prove her story wasn't legit. Provided, of course, that Jude backed her up.

Antonio grunted. "Uh-huh. What, the two of you decided to go for an early morning drive on this shit-forsaken road?"

"Something like that," Jude murmured.

*Thank you.* He wasn't going to tell Antonio about her dream. Good. The fewer people who knew, the better.

*When am I gonna die, Erin? You know, right? You can see everything.*

*When am I gonna die?* She'd been a freak show when she lived with her mother's people.

The voices from her past needed to learn how to shut the hell up sometimes.

"Um . . ." Antonio scratched his chin. "These damn

winding roads. Recipe for fucking disaster, especially with the rains we had."

Erin stiffened. No, no, that wasn't right.

*Flawed.*

Her father had been able to see all sorts of deaths. Those easy passings that came in sleep. Those tearful last moments surrounded by family and friends.

Not her.

Erin only saw the brutal deaths. Those caused by the hand of another. Blood-soaked.

Murders.

"I think you better check the scene." *Not an accident.* No way. Not if she'd dreamed it.

"Why?" His gaze snapped to her. "What do you know, Jerome?"

She held his stare. "Check the scene." If she was right, and Erin knew she was, there would be signs. Skid marks on the road. Paint from another vehicle on Lee's car. *Something.*

Lee had been forced off the road. Left to die.

Not an accident. Not some bad slip of fate.

Deliberate. Cold.

The man had enemies, everyone knew that. But Antonio would have to find out just who hated the lawyer enough to kill him.

Antonio raised one dark eyebrow. "Rumor is . . . you and old Lee got into one hell of an argument in front of Judge Went yesterday."

Erin tensed. Word traveled too fast in this town. "We're lawyers. That's we do. *Argue.*"

"Umm . . ."

Now what was that supposed to mean?

"Just strikes me as odd. First the perp you're after winds up slashed and smiling, and now the attorney who pissed you off in court is barely breathing."

Her own breath caught. "You think I'm involved in this?"

"She was with me," Jude said, voice dark and menacing. "All night."

Antonio's eyes widened, just a bit. But the guy didn't look intimidated. More like impressed. His gaze darted over her. "Like that, huh? Hunter, you work fast."

Her face flamed. "You're an asshole, Antonio."

He lifted a brow. "Got to question things, ma'am, especially considering the report that landed on my desk right before I got the call about this accident."

Jude stepped toward him. "The blood from her house?"

"Uh-huh. It was a match, just like you thought."

She glanced back and forth between the two men. "A match?" Oh, this wasn't going to be good. She didn't need the fist knotting in her gut to tell her that. Damn, damn, damn.

"The blood on your walls belonged to Bobby Burrows."

Her eyes closed.

"Now why the hell would the stalker—you *said* you had a stalker after you—kill old Bobby and leave his blood dripping onto your pretty hardwood floors?"

"Because he's a sick freak!" *And he was giving Bobby to me as a present.*

She'd gotten enough of his presents to know his routine. If someone pissed her off, if someone hurt her, he stepped in.

*I keep you safe, when you don't even know it.*

Bile rose in her throat. She *had* argued with Lee. Antonio had that part right. Had the stalker asshole been there, watching? And she hadn't even known it?

And, oh, hell, had he gone after Lee, too? Because of her?

"Has to be a reason the guy killed Bobby," Antonio continued. "This shit's never random."

No, it wasn't. She opened her eyes to find the captain watching her.

Weighing her.

"Think you might know that reason, Jerome?"

Her lips parted.

"*Back off, Tony.*" Jude shook his head and stepped forward. "This isn't the time for this conversation and you know it. I'll come to the station, check the report—"

"It's *her* story I want," Antonio said. "There's a murderer out there, ADA. One who seems to have killed for you."

Not the first time, either.

"There something else about this case you need to tell me?"

Jude glanced at her.

Erin shook her head. They were starting to attract attention. The other cops who'd arrived on the scene were eyeing them with outright curiosity, and, once the news about Bobby's blood leaked—and it would leak—she'd be kissing her new life good-bye.

And she'd barely had time to unpack.

He'd found her too fast.

Or maybe he'd never lost her. Goosebumps rose on her arms.

Antonio's eyes tightened to slits. "I want to know everything about this bastard, you got me?"

"*Fucking ease up, Tony.*" Jude's hands fisted. "Don't push this now. We'll both come to the station, but not now."

Not when they had such an eager audience.

Antonio gave a grim nod and spun on his heel, calling out to the uniforms, "Rake the scene! Every damn inch."

After a beat of time, Jude turned to face her. "More secrets, huh, sweetheart?"

Her heart almost broke, but her chin lifted. "We can't be sure that jerk after me had anything to do with Lee's accident." But her instincts said he did. "Lee's a defense attorney. Victims, criminals—they can all get pissed at him."

"Pissed enough to try killing him?"

Maybe.

Or maybe her Romeo was out there, grinning his ass off. "Let's get out of here." She couldn't stand out there with the cops and the wreckage any longer. She marched away, or tried to in the muck and mud, not waiting for him.

"Erin! Erin, shit!" The rustle of his clothes and the slog of his footsteps behind her. He grabbed her arm. "Wait."

His hold jerked her toward him and Erin glared up at his face. "Not now, hunter."

"Yeah, you keep saying that." His nose nearly brushed against hers as he brought his face in close. "Newsflash, sweetheart, the asshole after you *killed* a man. This isn't some game!"

"I *never* thought it was!"

"I'm gonna bring the bastard down, but everything you know about him, every single thing that has happened to you because of him—I have to know."

Erin exhaled on a hard breath and knew there was no choice. "Okay."

How would he look at her, she wondered, when he learned the truth?

*At least I had one night with him.*

One wild night.

Just how many secrets was the woman keeping?

Jude sat at his desk, eyes on the computer screen before him, but not really seeing the damned thing.

*Erin.*

The woman was fire in his hands. The hottest, sexiest thing in bed he'd ever seen.

And she was dangerous. So dangerous.

Because she'd been lying to him.

The woman had a freaking twisted killer on her trail. One

the cops couldn't catch or stop, so yeah, maybe she had a reason for the skittishness he saw.

But there was more. He *knew* it.

"So, stayed at the girlfriend's last night, huh?" Zane asked as he strode into Jude's office. The guy always made himself right at home. Boundaries didn't exist so much for Zane.

Jude grunted and rubbed a hand over his bleary eyes. He'd stayed at the crash site, keeping an eye on the uniforms and the crime scene guys, and sure enough, they'd found black paint on the side of Lee Givens's car.

He'd been forced off the road. No doubt in Jude's mind.

But was the hit tied to Erin?

"Don't blame ya." Zane crossed his arms and leaned back against the window frame. "That's one hot woman."

Jude's hand dropped. "Don't." A snarl built in his throat. Zane played free and easy with the women in the city, *Other* and human.

But Erin was off limits.

"Oooh . . ." Zane smiled. "Sore spot, huh?"

Jude considered planting his fist in the demon's face. Not like it would do permanent damage, and wiping that smug-ass grin off Zane's face would sure make him feel better.

"You found out yet just what she is?"

*A woman.* That's what she was. Zane was a good hunter, but he could also be one Grade A Asshole.

"I think I'll stop by the courthouse later. Get a good look at her." Zane nodded. "I'll see what she is."

Right. Jude just bet the guy would "get a good look" at her. "She doesn't use glamour." Glamour was the magic demons used to hide their true selves from the world.

Demons really did look a lot like humans. The only physical difference was generally their eyes. A demon's real eyes were pitch black—not just the iris, but the whole eye, even the sclera. When it came to demons, there was never any waiting until you saw the "whites of their eyes."

Only darkness was in their eyes.

Glamour hid that darkness. The magic let the demons blend right in with everyone else.

Sure, the ancient demons were rumored to have a few more . . . obvious physical differences. But Jude had never encountered one of the horned and tailed bastards that some whispered about late at night. He figured they weren't real.

Hard to tell in this world, though.

"You don't know, Donovan." Zane shrugged. "Let me get a look at her, *I'll* know."

Erin was a hybrid. He *knew* that. She'd said her father was psychic. Not a demon, just psychic.

*But she'd been lying*. Shadows had appeared in her golden eyes.

Tonight, he'd get the truth from her.

"You turn up anything on her background yet?" he asked the demon.

The smile dimmed. "You know I hate doing the grunt work."

True. Zane liked to be out on the streets, kicking the shit out of the deserving. "Yeah, but I got seniority." Life could be a bitch.

"Asshole." Zane shook his head. "Her mom abandoned her, dropped her off on her father's doorstep when she was fifteen."

Jude tensed. Abandoned? Not really the shifter way. Even the damn coyotes kept their kids close.

Why would her mother leave her?

Fifteen. Right at puberty. The time of the first shift.

"The dad took her in, but he passed away during her first year of college."

Talk about getting a hard punch in the face. Abandoned by one, and death took the other. "Any other family?"

"Not that I can tell. But with the mom? Could be."

Jude's fingers tapped against the desk top. "Track the mom, see what you can find out." A shifter mother? And a shifter stalker. No way could he overlook that lead.

"Will do."

Jude frowned. "Where's Dee?" He hadn't seen her all morning.

"Pak called her on a vamp case." Zane looked down at his watch. "Right now, I'd say she's . . . oh, cutting the head off some poor undead asshole."

Probably. Dee did love her work. And if she was hunting during the day, she had the advantage.

Vamps were weak during the day. Almost human.

Dee always said that weakness leveled up the playing field. Of course, Jude figured the woman didn't really need any leveling up. She could take the vamps down just as easily when they were running at full power. A talented woman.

Jude rose to his feet. Time for him to do some hunting. No sense in Dee having all the fun.

"Where you going?" Zane asked, straightening from the window.

"To rattle some cages." And see just what the hell shook loose.

When Jude wanted, he could play the nice guy. *Play.*

But he could also be a real bastard.

He held his prey pinned against the wall, his forearm lodged against Michael McQueen's throat. "Now we're gonna go over this one more time, Mickey." He smiled, and let the hyena shifter see his teeth. "I'm looking for the new shifter in town."

Mickey spat at him.

Oh, wrong move. Jude threw the idiot across the room and swiped the back of his hand over his face. "Are you trying to piss me off?"

"You're not takin' me in!" Mickey jumped to his feet. Quick little prick.

"Yeah, I am." Mickey liked to get a bit rough with his girlfriends. And he only dated humans. Guess beating the hell out of them was more fun for him than going up against someone with his own strength. "But before I drag your ass off to jail, you *will* answer my questions."

Mickey's red-rimmed eyes darted for the door. The guy reeked of alcohol. The tequila drifted off him in waves. It was barely one o'clock, and Jude had found the shifter knocking them back in Delaney's bar.

*Delaney's*. On the surface, it seemed like a regular place, but the owner was one real witch.

Mickey picked up a table and threw it at Jude. He swore and leapt to the side, swiping out with his claws.

"Dammit, you jerks are gonna pay for everything you break!" Catalina's furious voice.

Noted. But no big deal because mostly, he just planned on breaking that idiot hyena's face.

Mickey screamed, a high, shrill animal cry, and hoisted up another table.

Jude sprang across the room and knocked the table out of the hyena's hands. Then he shoved the jerk up against the wall and pinned Mickey there with his claws.

Another desperate cry, one that had Jude's ears ringing. Damn hyenas. They had the shrillest voices.

Jude twisted his claws and Mickey whimpered. "Who's the new shifter, Mickey?" The guy was scum, but he knew every bit of shifter business that passed in the city. Hyenas and foxes always knew. They picked up every bit of gossip, every whisper.

Mickey shook his head. "No . . . new shifter."

Not the answer he wanted. Jude sighed. "Ah, Mickey, why do we have to do this the hard way?"

The hyena flinched, and a soft, familiar scent teased Jude's nostrils.

No, no way. She wouldn't be there. *Couldn't* be there.

But that scent—his cock began to swell.

Had to be her.

"*Jude*?"

*Ah, hell.* Talk about piss-ass-poor timing.

"Jude—what are you doing?"

Pretty much just what it looked like. Pinning prey.

"Help!" Mickey the idiot shouted. "This freak's trying to kill me!"

Jude twisted his claws, because he could.

The hyena's words choked off.

High heels slapped on the wooden floor. "You're in a public bar, you can't just—"

Sighing, he glanced back at Erin. Flushed face. Kiss-me red lips, and an are-you-crazy expression in her eyes. "Relax. The chick behind the bar's a witch, the half-asleep asshole in the corner's a charmer, and this jerkoff is a—"

"Shifter." A whisper from her sexy lips. Her nostrils flared, just a bit.

Of course she'd know. Like to like.

Mickey whimpered and tried to appear pitiful. Jude had to give the guy credit—he *looked* pitiful. But he always did.

"You can't do this." Erin's voice was still hushed. Maybe she wasn't buying the whole the-bartender-is-a-witch story. "No matter what he *is,* you can't just—"

A growl built in his throat. The rich scent of Mickey's

blood teased him. Maybe it was time Erin figured out just who, *what*, she was dealing with.

And sleeping with at night.

"Not a cop, sweetheart. Their rules don't apply to me." And what was she doing in the bar, anyway? Delaney's wasn't exactly well advertised in this city. More of a paranormals only club.

Catalina's magic kept the humans out. They didn't know why, but they just always walked right past the faded blue building with the white French doors on Louis Street.

"*Lady!*" Mickey's squeak. "You gotta help me! This ass-asshole's crazy. You need—"

He heard the inhalation of her breath. "Mickey McQueen."

The hyena blinked.

"You're wanted for three charges of assault and battery, McQueen."

Yeah, and Jude would be collecting that bounty soon enough. "I want the name, Mickey," Jude snapped, barreling right over Erin's words. She wasn't about to haul his prey away, not yet.

Mickey shook his head, a frantic move. "L-lady—"

"Have it your way." The burn of his lengthening canines filled Jude's mouth. His gaze narrowed on the hyena's throat, on the pulse that thudded faster, faster. Jude lowered his head, teeth barred, almost tasting—

"No new shifters—*none!*" Mickey's scream. Frantic. Mickey liked giving pain, but he wasn't so much for taking it.

Jude stilled. The little asshole had to be telling the truth. Mickey had never been good at playing chicken.

*No new shifters.* But one new shifter was right beside him. How come Mickey didn't realize that?

Erin grabbed Jude's shoulder, jerked him back, and sent him hurling across the room.

Jude fell into a table. The wood gave way, smashing beneath him and sending his ass right to the floor. Hard.

"You'll pay for that one, too," Catalina said. The witch was just stating a fact. She didn't sound too interested in the chaos.

Then, silence.

His gaze tracked to Erin. The lady wasn't even breathing hard.

"*Hot damn.*" An impressed voice, an *annoying* voice. Zane. He stood in the doorway, hands on his hips, and watched Erin with narrowed eyes and pursed lips.

Well, at least now he knew why Erin had showed up at Delaney's.

Mickey rushed toward the door, his claws out as he lunged at Zane.

The demon hit him hard and fast, and Mickey went down with a sigh shuddering out of him and his eyes closing.

Problem one solved.

Jude shoved up to his feet. Erin rounded on him, her hands fisted. "You can't attack suspects!"

He lunged across the room. Caught one of those deceptively delicate fists in his hands. Kissed it. The woman had just tossed his ass ten feet and he wanted her. She was sexy and strong and her eyes were so dark and gold. Perfect.

Flawed? Not fucking likely.

The tiger inside was all but licking his lips.

"Mickey is guilty as sin," he told her. "We both know it."

"Yeah, he is," Zane said, stepping over the prone shifter and straightening his shoulders. His gaze swept over Erin, from her head to her toes. The asshole lingered a bit too long on her breasts. He came close to getting a jab in the face then.

She ignored the demon, keeping her attention on Jude. "There are *laws*, you know."

"Human laws don't always apply to us." She should know that.

Her jaw worked. "You were going for his throat."

And she'd protected the little prick. Mickey sure owed her. "I wouldn't have bitten, sweetheart." He dropped her hand and missed the touch of her skin almost at once. But Zane was watching with those too-sharp demon eyes of his. And Catalina was pretending to clean a glass, but he knew the witch caught every word, every look. "Just trying to push some information out of him." It was the way he worked. He wouldn't apologize for threatening the hyena. Wasn't like Mickey was one of the "good" guys, not any day of the week.

Her arms crossed over her chest. "Doesn't seem like your push worked to me."

Maybe. Maybe not. "Why didn't he catch your scent?"

A furrow appeared between her brows. "What?"

Jude glared at Zane, but the guy just crept closer.

Finally, Erin glanced over at the other hunter.

"Some arm you got there, lady." Zane offered her a smile. The same flirtatious grin he tossed at every female he saw, and one that usually gave him good results. Smiles back, phone numbers, even a couple pairs of panties.

"*You*." She exhaled on a hard breath. "I recognize your voice." She would. Shifters were great at recognizing tones and cadences in voice patterns. Came from their acute hearing. "You're the one who called and told me to come down here."

Yeah, Jude had figured as much. Glaring, he said, "I

thought the plan was for you to stop at the courthouse." And not bring Erin into his hunt.

The demon shrugged. "She wasn't scheduled for court today. Had to improvise."

*Improvise.* Right. Zane had sent her right after his ass, and Erin had seen him at the worst moment.

Well, technically, it *could* have been worse. Mickey had still been breathing, after all.

"You said Jude needed me," Erin's voice heated. "That it was *urgent*, that I had to get down to this Delaney's place—"

"We're the best bar in town." A murmur from Catalina.

Erin blinked.

"He did need you," Zane defended. "Why, you stopped the guy from crossing the line, from letting that wild beast out to attack and kill."

Jude didn't speak at that. He'd had control of his beast. He'd had control for years.

'Cause the tiger had gotten loose once. He could still hear the screams sometimes. His prey hadn't gone down easy.

He crept closer to Erin.

Zane's head titled to the right, and he stared hard at Erin's face. "You don't seem too worried, lady." A pause. "You've *already* seen the beast, haven't you, Ms. Jerome?"

Her gaze darted to Jude.

"And you weren't even a little afraid of him, were you?" Zane pressed.

No, she hadn't been. Not when she'd seen him in tiger form. Erin hadn't so much as backed up a step. No, no, she hadn't looked afraid, she'd looked—

Thrilled.

Excited.

Not like a woman who was terrified of shifters.

And when he'd come back to her after the hunt, she'd done her one-eighty and seduced him.

*Hands off* to—

*Hands most definitely on.*

Not afraid.

Considering the shifter asshole after her, her attitude was a bit . . . surprising, to say the least.

"I'm not afraid of a little cat," Erin said, voice soft and husky.

Little?

Zane's loud laughter shook the room.

Jude was pretty sure he heard Catalina snort.

More laughter came from the demon. Then, after a couple of deep breaths, he managed to say, "Yeah, I guess if I were strong enough to throw him across the room, I wouldn't be scared, either."

The guy *could* throw him across the room. And had. At least three times sprang to mind. Two of those instances had happened right there in Delaney's. Some nights, the place could get good and wild.

Erin cast a glance toward Mickey's body. The hyena was still out cold. "I need to call the precinct and get a squad car out here for him—" She broke off, shaking her head. "I-I need . . ." Her voice thickened a bit and she lifted her hand, pushing her fingers against her right temple. "Th-that h-hurts . . ."

Jude stiffened and his stare jerked to Zane. The demon's laughter was completely gone now and he was focused totally on Erin.

*Bastard.* He'd been waiting, biding his time to catch her off guard.

With a demon, one big-ass portion of his strength was psychic in nature. Demons could slip right into the minds of humans.

Erin could be half-human so would Zane be able to—

"*Get out.*" A grated demand, shaking with fury. Erin's head jerked toward Zane and she bared her own teeth. Wickedly sharp teeth.

A low, pain-filled cry broke from Zane's suddenly white lips, and his knees gave way beneath him. Before he could fall face-first into the floor, the witch was there, catching him, wrapping her arms around him.

Then Catalina stared at Erin with fear in her eyes.

Well, damn.

# Chapter 8

*What did he see? What did he see?*

The drumming of her heartbeat filled Erin's ears as she fought for control. The demon—the tall, dark, good-looking asshole *had* to be a demon—had slipped into her mind. She hadn't expected an attack. She'd been too focused on Jude and the demon had slipped right past her defenses.

*Broken.*

*Twisted.*

What if he knew? If he'd seen into her, he'd know her secrets. If he told Jude—

"I want you out of my bar." A woman, her long hair so blond it almost looked white, cradled the demon. Her green eyes glinted with a swirling combination of fear and fury. A combination Erin could respect. "I want you out, and I don't want to see you again—*whatever* you are."

Jude stepped in front of her. "Easy, Catalina. I think old Zane was the one to draw first blood. And he'd better explain himself, *now.*"

The fire in Erin's temples had eased, but the ache that remained sent a wave of nausea through her. A demon's touch. Her dad had warned her about demons and their tricks. Some demons could slip so easily into the minds of humans. Some were strong enough to see thoughts, to walk in dreams, and even to control their prey.

*I'm not prey.*

Zane wasn't looking quite as tan as he'd been when he first sauntered into the bar. He was braced against the woman, Catalina, and she didn't so much as buckle beneath his six-foot-plus frame.

Zane licked his lips. "Just . . . checking out the waters for you . . . hunter."

Erin swallowed. "Don't ever do that again."

Slowly, very, very slowly, he lifted his arm from Catalina's shoulders. "Don't . . . worry. Won't."

"No, you won't." Jude's fierce voice.

"Just wanted to see . . . what you were."

Her cheeks flushed. Not with fury—that would have been good. Humiliation. *What I am. No one knows, not even me.*

One person thought he knew, and that guy was a sadistic freak.

*No, I'm not like him. I won't ever be.*

She hoped, anyway. Because with her mother's genes, there really weren't any guarantees that she wouldn't go bad one day.

"Not demon." Zane's eyes were on hers now, his head up. She held that stare, refusing to look away. Erin wasn't really sure what had happened to the guy. Okay, what she'd done to him. She'd acted on instinct when she felt the probe in her mind.

There'd been a push at her, shoving at her thoughts—

So she'd shoved right back.

*Instinct.*

Her lip curled. Demon? Had he really thought she was like him? "No, I'm not." And just what the hell had Jude done? Gone running back to his hunter friends and told them about her secrets?

*Can't trust anyone.* She *knew* that.

So why did it feel like she'd just been punched?

Erin straightened her shoulders. "If this little game or test or whatever the hell it was has finished, I'll call the cops and get out of here." The sooner, the better.

"Erin." A rumble from Jude. Dark and intense.

Damn him. Her eyes narrowed. "I *told* you what I am. You didn't need to have your friend attack me."

Then, because her claws were almost out and her teeth were burning and the rage had her heart racing, Erin marched for the door. She'd call for backup once she was outside. That's what cell phones were for—screw making a call from the bar.

The demon and the witch very wisely sidled out of her way.

But Jude grabbed her arm, spinning her around, and she tumbled against his chest.

*Too close.* Her nostrils widened and she caught his heady scent. *No, no, no.*

"This wasn't my plan."

"Wasn't it?" Because she didn't believe him, not for a minute. He'd wanted to know. He'd said it himself. He'd wanted that demon to *see* her. *Thought the plan was to go to the courthouse.* Asshole. He hadn't trusted her.

Granted, she hadn't trusted him, either. But Erin decided to ignore that point, for now.

"You just told me about your mother," Jude said, his hold tight. "You never said what your father was."

She jerked away from him. Too easy, that. "He was a man, Jude. Just a man." With psychic powers, sure. But her father had been all too human. After tossing one last glare at her hunter, she shoved open the glass door and strode into the harsh sunlight.

Silence. One minute. Two.

Catalina cleared her throat and pointed to the destruction that was her bar. "Night Watch is going to be paying for that. Tell Pak I don't want a check this time. Cash only."

He nodded.

Her fingers trailed down Zane's cheek. "Never gonna learn, are you?" Then she eased away from him, shaking her head.

Jude glared at the bastard.

Zane winced and lifted a hand to his head. "Uh, some sympathy would be good here, man. I mean, your girlfriend just tried to fry my brain."

Jude's back teeth clenched. *Control.* Probably a good idea. He should stay in—

"And talk about being ungrateful. Where's my thanks? At least you know she's not a demon hybrid now. I got in her head enough to know she's human, part anyway. But she's—"

Jude grabbed the demon and lifted him a foot in the air. "You hurt her."

Zane's eyes widened even as they flashed black. "*I'm* the one with the sledgehammer banging in his head."

"Don't ever hurt her again, got me?" He didn't care how many cases they'd worked together. "A look—you told me you just wanted a *look* to see if she was using glamour." Demons could see right past the glamour that disguised others of their kind, unless you were dealing with a level ten. Nothing and no one could penetrate a level ten powerhouse's veil.

The faint lines around Zane's eyes tightened. "I was takin' a look. A real long, deep *look* into your girl."

Yeah, and judging from the way she'd looked at Jude before she'd stormed out of the bar, Erin was pissed. Because she thought he'd set her up.

*And didn't I?*

Aw, hell.

He dropped the demon. The agile asshole landed easily. "Why'd your *look* hurt her?" He'd seen Zane work humans before. They usually had no clue what was happening to them. Zane's psychic skills, his ability to ferret out secrets, were part of the reason why their cases broke so quickly.

When the two of them worked together, they were usually a pretty good team. Usually.

"Why'd it hurt her?" Jude demanded again.

Zane's shoulders lifted, then fell. "Don't know." His lips thinned. "Never happened quite like . . . that before." He exhaled. "That lady packs one hell of a psychic punch."

Physically stronger, psychically stronger. No way was she a weak hybrid.

Shifting abilities or not.

"There is something . . . something you should know—"

A groan from the floor—one that came from a slow-waking Mickey—broke across Zane's words.

Jude glanced down at the shifter, frowning.

"I didn't get deep in her mind," Zane said. "She blocked me before I could, but, hell, it was *dark* in there, man."

Jude's eyes rose to the demon once more.

"*Dark.*"

Now what the hell did that mean?

"There's power there. A lot of power. You'd better watch your step with her."

*What?* "She's the victim, Zane, not the perp. The job's to keep her safe." His goal wasn't to bring her ass down. Erin hadn't done anything wrong, no matter what Zane was rambling about with his "dark" crap.

"I don't know exactly what she is . . . yet."

Jude jabbed his finger into the guy's chest. "I do. She's the client, and our job is to keep her safe."

A rush of air as Zane sighed. "Gotta wonder . . . what would scare *her*?"

Sirens shrieked in the distance. Erin had obviously done as she'd promised and called for her backup. Being the ADA, she'd gotten that backup, fast.

Jude reached down and grabbed Mickey, jerking the other shifter to his feet. The hyena's head snapped back and his bleary eyes opened.

"What did the woman smell like to you?" he grated. Not much time. He had to know.

The bastard's lips peeled back from his pointed, yellow teeth. "*Prey.*"

No, that didn't make any sense. Sure, sometimes humans could smell like prey to a hunter, especially to one as screwed-ass up as Mickey. But Erin had shifter blood. The hyena should have recognized her true scent.

He caught sight of a patrol car outside. The car slammed to a stop. The cops jumped out, fast and ready for action.

Then they hesitated outside of the bar. They looked to the left, to the right, and Jude saw them begin to step away from the bar.

Erin grabbed the arm of the taller guy and yanked him toward the entrance. She shoved open the door. "In there!" he heard her say.

The cop blinked and gave a small shake of his head.

*Humans.*

The spell had 'em confused. Jude sighed and pushed the shifter toward the door. "My collar." So he'd be the one to take him out. He'd be earning a couple grand from Mickey's case. But, unfortunately, he hadn't learned what he'd wanted from the shifter.

The humid air hit him the minute he stepped outside Delaney's. The color had come back to Erin's cheeks, giving her skin a warm glow. Her eyes were warm, *scorching* as she eyed him with her hands fisted at her sides.

He helped load the prisoner. Jude fought the urge to give the guy an ass-kicking, and in moments, the cops pulled away with their prisoner.

Jude turned to her, his hands on his hips. Zane hadn't followed him outside. Had to give the demon credit on that one. Staying inside was definitely the best plan for him.

He stalked to her slowly. The woman didn't back up even a single step. Jude raised a brow and asked the question that was driving him crazy. "Why didn't Mickey sense you?"

She blinked.

"The hyena shifter—you recognized him, why the hell didn't he recognize you?" Her scent had been off that first day. A mix that had tempted and teased, but he'd known right away that she wasn't human. Not completely, anyway. But, Mickey had only thought of her as prey. Didn't make a bit of sense. *Like to like*. The other shifter should have been able to recognize her, too.

"You just can't keep a low profile, can you?" she grated, craning her neck to the left then the right as she searched the street. "How in the world you've kept your tiger hidden—"

"No one's around." Thanks to Catalina. He pinned her with his gaze. "Why didn't he know, sweetheart?" The words were easy, but the demand underlying them was steel hard.

Her delicate nostrils widened. "Most don't." A shrug. "Your senses must be stronger than the average shifter's—or you wouldn't have known about me at first, either."

Yeah, they were stronger. Came from being a white tiger. Rare breed, stronger shifter talents.

But if her scent couldn't be detected by the others . . .

shit. The woman had some serious camouflage going on. "So you've been just slipping right by your kind haven't you? Walking right past the shifters your whole life."

"*Not* my kind," she interrupted, voice rising.

His turn to blink. "Yeah, we are." A slow anger began to burn in his gut.

She swallowed. "I-I'm not going to do this with you, not now. You don't understand."

*Because she hasn't told me a damn thing.* The lady kept telling him, "not now." Well, when? He stared her down. "Try me."

"Shifters . . ." Her shoulders straightened. "That's not my world. When I didn't change at puberty, the *shifter* world kicked my ass out and left me in the cold."

*Her mom abandoned her, dropped her off on her father's doorstep when she was fifteen.*

"I've lived as a human since then. I don't transform. For all intents, I *am* human, and that's the only world I know."

No, last night, she'd found another world, with him. He'd felt her beast, raging just below the smooth, controlled surface she presented.

Erin turned away and began walking toward her waiting car.

*Stop her.* "Shifters don't play by the same rules as humans." She knew that. He shouldn't have to shout it at her. *Shouting.* He winced. Good thing that spell of Catalina's was keeping the humans away. "Sometimes we have to play rough." Like when he'd dug his claws into Mickey the asshole.

Erin glanced back at him, black hair sliding over her shoulders. "I know how shifters play." Anger. Fear?

"I'm trying to find the bastard after you, and believe me, I'll play by any rules that I have to. I'll *break* any rules I have to, in order to find that bastard." Find him, stop him, put him in a shallow grave.

*He'd marked her.*

The killer wasn't gonna play nice and easy. And Jude had never been that dumb nice-and-stupidly-easy type.

Their eyes held. When Erin spoke, her voice was soft but it carried easily to him as she said, "My job is about protecting the rules of the *human* world. Following the law."

Sometimes, you had to bend that law.

And maybe even break it in order to stop the bad-asses. "Human laws and human jails don't do much for *our* kind." Oh, yeah, maybe he'd put too much emphasis on the our, but screw it. She was just like him beneath the skin.

Animal to animal.

Night Watch brought down criminals and sometimes, bringing down the supernatural scum meant putting a power-mad demon, a blood-sucking vamp, or even a rabid shifter out of his misery.

No, human jails couldn't hold a strong supernatural for long. Hell, a level ten demon could blow the walls out of a jail with barely a thought. And if a guard got too close to a vamp . . .

Some monsters couldn't be stopped by the normal means.

That was the reason Night Watch had been formed.

Night Watch's mission was to bring down the supernatural criminals—one way or another.

When Mickey got to the jail, his ass would be tossed in a cage. Just where he belonged. And he'd stay in the pen, doing his time, kicking the crap out of any human foolish enough to cross him.

But someone stronger than low-life Mickey . . . hell, no, a prison would never work.

"Accept it," Jude said. "Your laws just don't work for everyone."

Her eyes narrowed.

"Like that bastard after you. Do you really think a cage will hold him?"

She swallowed and he saw the hard movement of her throat. His hands clenched when she said, "I know it won't. Why do you think I've been running?"

"Erin—"

The door to Catalina's swung open with a soft *swoosh*. Zane's head appeared and his brows lifted. "Jude, you ready to—"

Footsteps. The slam of a car door.

Jude swore when he saw his ADA drive away. *Running away*. "Not finished, Erin."

Not by one hell of a long shot.

By the time she got back to her office, her hands had stopped shaking and the ball in the pit of her throat, that weird tangle of fear and fury, had finally dislodged.

Erin managed to make it through the rest of the day in a semi-normal fashion. No snarling at the other lawyers. No flash of claws or teeth.

But Jude's words kept echoing in her head.

And they twisted with her mother's words, spoken so long ago. "*Kill or be killed, that's the only way we know.*"

Her mother had been very, very good at killing.

She hadn't wanted to be like her mother. But the freak on her trail was giving her no choice.

Hell, yes, she knew the prisons couldn't hold some paranormals. She *knew* that. But the only other option—

Death.

She'd never taken a life before.

The bastard was wrenching her choices away. Because she knew—she *knew* he wanted her to kill.

So she'd be just like him.

Dammit, no.

Erin went to court at the end of the day. A last-minute trip. The demon had been right. She hadn't been scheduled for a court appearance, but the cops needed her help, so she had to go. Erin needed a warrant to search a suspected drug dealer's house on Grant Avenue, and the cops waiting in the wings didn't have any more time to waste. They needed to get in that house before midnight.

At 6:09 p.m., the warrant was signed, the cops were ready, and Erin was so damned ready to get back to her house that she was all but growling. She headed across the middle of the big atrium of the courthouse, eager to—

A rich, musky scent teased her nostrils.

Erin froze.

*Pine trees. Sweat. Animal.*

Oh, hell.

Her heart slammed into her chest just as some guy with a too-large briefcase crashed into her back. He grunted an apology and stumbled away, but she didn't even spare him a glance.

She closed her eyes for a moment and drank in that scent. *He was there.* Close enough to smell.

The whiff of his scent was deliberate. She knew it. She'd learned that lesson the hard way. He could control his scent, disguise it. The bastard had told her about his little secret technique that fateful night. He'd bragged about it.

But now, he was baiting her with his smell. Letting her know that he was close. Watching.

Her hands curled and her claws dug into her palms. Her eyes opened and her head turned to the left. *There.* The door marked exit in bright red letters. The stairwell.

Erin was at the door before she had time to fully realize

what the hell she was doing. She shoved it open, sucking in a hard breath, then she climbed down the steps. The jarring metal echoed with every move she made, and she followed that scent with her palms sweating and the hair on her nape rising.

*Tired of running. Tired of the blood.*

The killings had to stop.

The stairs ended at another door. Big and thick. Erin knew the parking garage was on the other side of that door. She'd mapped out the building before her first court date. Since she'd attracted the freak, learning all the exits in the buildings she frequented had become a priority for her.

Erin licked her lips. The guy's scent hung in the stairwell. He'd been there, recently, and he could be waiting for her now, just on the other side of that door.

Her fingers lifted. Touched the cold metal.

Was she strong enough to take him?

Not if he shifted. No way she could handle him then, but if he was in human form, well, his ass was hers. Nice little side benefit from her mother's side of the family.

*Not that dear Mom had ever cared about how strong I was.*

Erin exhaled. Run or fight? Her choice was simple, and she really was tired of running.

Her cell phone vibrated in her purse, the shaking followed immediately by a loud chime.

*Dammit!*

Erin grabbed the phone, yanking it out. *Jude.* She recognized his number now. She pressed the receive button on the screen and lifted the phone to her ear. "He's here." A whisper.

Static crackled in her ear. Stairwells were bad for cell phones, she knew that but— "Jude, the asshole is *here.*" Waiting for her on the other side of that door.

"What?" A bark. "Where are you?"

"Courthouse." She shouldn't have been there. Another lawyer had been assigned to this case but he'd wanted to wait until morning for the court order and the cops had needed someone to move *now.* "Parking garage." A quick breath. "I can smell him." Almost feel him.

"Get the hell out of there! Don't give him a chance to get close to you!"

"This time, I'm going to get close to him." No more running. No more dead bodies or blood in her home.

"No! No, I'm coming. Shit, I'm on my way."

"Then hurry," she whispered, and ended the call. *Hurry because I'm not going to run again.*

He was too close. She couldn't just stand there and let him get away. She couldn't let him escape and attack someone else, for her.

Lee's bloody face flashed before her eyes. The guy was in ICU, hooked to a dozen tubes and needles. Because of her stalker?

*No one else could get hurt.* She couldn't stand by and let another person face the shifter's fury.

The sick bastard needed to be stopped, and she'd do her damnedest to fight him.

*Hurry, Jude.*

And then the scent changed.

Fuck, fuck, fuck!

When Jude's pickup screeched to a stop in the dim garage, his claws were out, his fangs barred, and he was ready to kick ass.

And he was scared—dammit, *scared.* When the hell was the last time he'd been scared of anything?

*She'd better be all right. Better be completely safe. Com-*

*pletely unharmed. 'Cause if she had so much as a scratch on her, the freak would beg for death.*

Beg.

He shoved open his door, jumped out, and ran across the parking area. His nostrils twitched as he caught the other shifter's scent. *He'd stalked her, tracked Erin here.*

"He's gone." Erin's voice. Quiet. Steady.

Jude whirled around and found her standing in front of an open door, a stairwell.

She was alone. Hell. "You should have gone for help." The words blasted out of him, deeper than normal, because the beast was too close to the surface. She'd stayed there, come looking for the freak. Was the woman crazy?

Her shoulders straightened. "I'm sick of running, Jude. I tried that. It didn't work." She shook her head. "That's not how I'm going to play this game anymore."

He closed the distance between them in two seconds flat. Jude grabbed her arms and pulled her toward him. "This isn't a game. He's a killer. A cold, seriously fucked-up"—he could still see the blood on her walls and the grin that he had sliced across Bobby's face—"*killer*." A game. His hold tightened on her. "If he gets hold of you, he'll—"

"I know exactly what he'll do." Erin jerked away from him. Just broke from his grasp as if he weren't even holding her. *Why do I keep forgetting how strong she is?*

Her eyes were stark. "He caught me once before."

His heart seemed to stop. No, not here. He didn't want to learn this here, with that bastard's stench in the air around him. Jude swung away from her, his gaze searching the shadows of the garage. "How the hell do you know he's gone?"

Silence.

Jude glanced back at her. "Erin?"

Her hand lifted, pointed to the right. "He left me a present."

He stalked forward and saw the roses propped up against the cement wall.

Fresh. Bloodred. Not a bloodstained message this time. Flowers.

Oh, yeah, a real perfect Romeo.

"That's Lee's parking space." No emotion in her voice.

Jude's eyes lifted and he saw the reserved spot with the lawyer's first initial and last name.

Dammit.

"There's a card, but I-I haven't read it yet."

He would. Jude grabbed the flowers, jerked out the card and tossed the roses onto the pavement. The scent of the flowers was sickeningly sweet, combining with the stench of the shifter, a stench that seemed lighter now, weaker.

*'Cause the bastard was gone.*

For now.

With steady fingers, Jude pulled out the card. Maybe he should have taken it to Tony. He should have used gloves, he should have—

***Did you like my present?***

What in the hell? His gaze flew to Erin, and he found her staring at him, her body still.

"What does it say?" she whispered.

Jude shoved the note back into the envelope. "Let's get out of here." A car horn sounded in the distance. The place was all but deserted. He knew most of the lawyers and assistants would have checked out around five. Being there, standing in that empty garage felt too much like a trap.

One Jude wasn't about to get caught in. "Where's your car?" he demanded.

But she shook her head. "The note, Jude. What did it say?"

His jaw clenched. "Screw your car, you're coming with me." He shoved the note in his pocket. If the jerkoff had been dumb enough to leave any prints, and Jude figured the guy hadn't, they were probably long gone by now. A guy smart enough to sneak into a police station and kill a man while the cops were less than twenty feet away really wasn't gonna be the type to leave fingerprints on his little delivery.

Crossing to her side, Jude reached for Erin's arm. She didn't fight him, and he knew the lady could have used her strength. She climbed in the passenger side of his pickup. He slammed the door shut behind her, raced back around, and jumped inside.

He cranked the truck and the engine snarled to life. His fingers curled around the gear shift.

"What did it say?" Her hand brushed over his. Soft. Delicate.

With an effort, he managed to unclench his jaw enough to growl, "'Did you like my present?'"

A sharp inhalation of air. Her hand fell away and she sagged back in the seat.

He twisted the wheel, slammed on the gas pedal, and got the hell out of there.

The green pickup raced down the street, the motor rumbling as the tiger drove away, *too fast.*

Running scared. He watched that truck, and he smiled.

Erin had found his note. She knew what he'd done for her. Proving his love wasn't hard. He enjoyed giving presents to his mate.

The tiger would soon realize he didn't have a place in this equation. Erin would know he didn't belong.

*Just the two of us, love. Just us.*

He'd been angry when he found the shifter at her house. *In* her house.

No other male should be so close to Erin.

But he'd investigated the tiger today. Found out that he was a hunter. One Erin had foolishly hired.

As if the bastard would be a match for him.

Perhaps Erin had already realized her mistake.

He could still smell her. He'd been so close to her today. Close enough to touch and to taste.

When she'd found his roses, had she smiled? Had her lips lifted in that slow, beautiful smile he liked so much? Erin loved red roses. Always had.

That dick of a lawyer never should have gone after her like he had in court. The prick had been in her face, screaming.

No one treated Erin that way.

The traffic light turned red and he walked across the street, keeping his gaze on the shrinking taillights.

He couldn't wait to see Erin again. Couldn't wait to claim her. It had already been so long since he'd held her body beneath his and given in to the hunger.

Did she miss him as much as he missed her? Did she long for him?

*Yes.*

The answer came from the beast inside. The beast that wanted Erin just as much as the man did.

Soon it would be time for the games to end.

Time to take what was his.

If the tiger got in his way again, well, he'd just slice the bastard apart. Wouldn't be the first time he'd killed a rival.

Not the first time. Not the last.

# Chapter 9

"You just missed my exit." The first words she'd spoken since they left the parking garage. Erin thought the words came out pretty calm. Pretty steady.

*Did you like my present?*

She'd managed, barely, not to flinch when Jude told her the words of the note. But even before he'd said them, she'd known.

It was the freak's MO.

Her gaze lifted to Jude's face. His jaw was clenched, the eye she could see narrowed. "Jude?" Her hands were balled into fists. The better to not touch him.

"We're not going to your place." He didn't take his gaze off the road. "The bastard was there last night, he was inside the night before that. Sweetheart, your place is sure as shit not safe."

But it was *hers*. And right then, she needed some security, some—

"You're spending the night with me."

She blinked.

The truck slowed, then turned off on the next exit. "And before we get there, you're gonna start talking. You're gonna tell me everything I need to know about that asshole."

*He'll turn from me. Jude won't touch me again.*

He wouldn't look at her with hunger in his eyes. Wouldn't touch her with desire.

Her fingers uncurled and pressed against the tops of her thighs. *No choice.* "I-I think he attacked Burrows and Lee because he was . . . giving them to me as presents." Yeah, sounded sick and twisted as all hell—because it was.

His knuckles tightened around the wheel but he didn't speak.

"He watches me. It's what he does." *Always watching.* "If he sees someone that he thinks hurts me or disrespects me, then he attacks." And in the case of Burrows, *leaves a body* for her to find.

Because that was the kind of present every girl dreamed of. Forget diamonds. She wanted mutilated dead men.

No, no, even she wasn't that broken.

"One hell of a Prince Charming you got there." The engine revved as he shot off the exit ramp and down the long, deserted stretch of road.

*Tell me something I don't know.* "He hurt a man I dated back in Lillian. My . . . friend was shot. The bullet barely missed his heart." A human. He'd been in the hospital for weeks. When he'd gotten out, she'd stayed the hell away from him.

Stayed away—yeah, leaving the city definitely counted as staying away. The real bitch was . . . she'd cared for him, but she'd had to leave to keep him safe.

Ben wouldn't have survived much longer in her world.

"*No one else but me. You're mine, Erin. Blood, bones, beast—mine.*" She'd never forget that voice. Whispering to her in the darkness.

"The first time I ever heard from the guy," she licked her lips and said, "he sent me roses. A dozen red roses."

Jude flinched.

*Roses.* Just like the ones that had been left in Lee's parking spot. The truck flew under the streetlights. "I used to love red roses." He'd taken that from her, too. Now when she saw them, her entire body tensed up, and she could only think of blood and death. She swallowed and looked out the window at the blur of pine trees. "He sent me a note with them. Told me I was the woman he'd been looking for his whole life."

And she'd been *flattered.* Excited. Nervous. Smiling and looking around the office as she tried to figure out who her secret admirer really was.

"I got mugged a few nights after that." A rough laugh broke from her lips. "I could have taken the guy. He was a kid, couldn't have been more than fifteen, but I was with friends."

"*Humans.*"

A nod, one she didn't even know if he saw because she wasn't ready to look back at him yet. Since moving in with her father, she'd always stuck with the humans. They might fear her sometimes, when she slipped up, but at least they'd never thrown her away. "I didn't want them to see"—*how strong I am, how deadly I can be*—"so I gave the guy my purse." Not like she'd had much money in the bag. Maybe thirty bucks. No credit cards.

"Let me guess." He turned off the winding road. Took a left. "Romeo punished the mugger."

"Used his claws to slice open his throat." She glanced down at her own nails. Short now, manicured. What a joke. "Someone saw them fighting and called the cops. He didn't get to finish the kid." The boy had survived, barely. "I wouldn't have even connected the stories. I was mugged. Some kid on the news had a knife wound." *Right.* "I mean stuff like that happens every day."

He pulled into his drive. She could see his cabin. Right where the woods and the swamp seemed to meet. A stark building standing against the glittering stars and the glow of the moon.

Jude killed the ignition, but made no move to get out of the truck. Neither did she. *Get it over with. Tell him everything.*

A touch on her shoulder.

Erin whirled around and found Jude staring at her with blue eyes that shone in the dim interior of the pickup.

"How'd you find out it was your *admirer*?"

She licked her lips again. Nervous habit. Erin saw his gaze drop, then rise, slowly, back to hers. "When I-I got home from work the next night, my purse was there. Stained with blood. He left me a note. The bastard always liked his little notes." Though he'd never left a fingerprint on them. She'd checked. The guys in the lab had owed her a few favors back in Lillian.

His note had been simple. Terrifying.

***I made the bastard pay.***

After that, he'd broken into her house. *The first time*. No security system had kept him out. And, being like she was, getting a dog, a really big, mean-ass dog, hadn't been an option.

Not that a dog would have stopped him. Or even slowed him down.

Erin wanted to drop her gaze and because she wanted to,

she didn't. Lifting her chin, she stared into Jude's eyes and said, "Things escalated from there." The scar seemed to burn.

*Tell him.*

"And you ran." Flat. Jude shook his head and drummed the fingers of his left hand against the steering wheel. "No cops—"

"Lillian isn't like Baton Rouge." Too small. Not quite the atmosphere and size most paranormals craved. "The cops there wouldn't have had the first clue about how to deal with this guy."

The drumming fingers stilled. "I've got a clue."

Yeah, she knew that and Jude had given her *hope.* Maybe the nightmare would finally end. Maybe.

*Not alone now.*

She reached for him, skimming her fingers down his cheek. She loved the soft sting of the light stubble on his flesh.

Jude stilled. His gaze held hers. Then his head moved, a graceful curl into her touch, just like a cat seeking a good rub.

The truck's cab suddenly seemed very, very small.

*Tell him.*

But he was looking at her with hunger and need and such lust on his face. In his eyes.

*I want him.* Just like before. No holding back. No worrying about hurting him.

They were alone out there. Far away from prying eyes and listening ears.

Alone.

*One more time.* She wanted him again. Couldn't she be greedy? A little greed never hurt anyone.

Her tongue swiped along her lower lip and she wished that she could taste him.

*Do it.*

She leaned toward him and heard the hard rasp of his breath. Her lips hovered over his.

"Don't you know"—the words were a growl, so deep and rough they sent a shiver over her—"not to play with a tiger?"

Oh, but a tiger shifter was exactly the kind of guy she wanted to play with. "I can't hurt you." The words slipped out and after a second, she jerked back, horrified. No, she'd said—

His head tipped back and his brows lifted. "Ah . . . makes sense."

What?

He caught her hand, pulled it between them. "The humans didn't like it when you played rough, huh?" The tips of her claws had just begun to appear.

"I have a . . . hard time holding back."

"Not gonna complain over that." His hold on her hand tightened. "Not gonna complain one bit."

"You'd be the first who didn't." Could she not keep her mouth closed? Erin tried to tug her hand back.

No dice. The tiger wasn't letting go. She *could* force the issue but . . .

"Then you've been with damn idiots. A woman with power is a fucking beautiful thing to behold." His eyes held the glow of the beast. "*You're* fucking beautiful."

He'd just—oh, hell. "I got to third base for the first time when I was seventeen. The guy was the high school quarterback. I-I've always been strong and—I didn't mean to hold him so tight." But she'd almost broken both his wrists. When she'd realized what was happening and eased her hold, he'd run, much faster than he'd ever moved on the field. Come Monday, no guy at the school had so much as given her a second look.

Freak.

"In college, I'd been seeing this guy." Lyle had always been able to make her smile. "Things got hot and my claws came out."

*Erin, what the hell? You cut me! How did you . . . ?*

Her teeth snapped together. "After that," she gritted, slamming the door on that particular memory, "I learned fast that I had to always have control and be very careful in bed." Human lovers were too weak. She could break them if she wasn't careful. So she'd taken her pleasure, weak though it had been, and she'd done it by always holding herself back during sex. If she let go, her partners would have found out what she really was.

Not an option.

Jude unhooked his seat belt and leaned over her. "I like your claws and you're welcome to hold me as tight as you want." His lips pressed against hers. Took. Tasted. His tongue slipped inside.

A moan rose in her throat.

His head lifted and he told her, "You don't have to hold back with me. Last night should have proven that to you."

It had. And being with him had made her want so much more.

The past was all around her then. Reaching out with greedy hands and claws, while the only man who'd ever made her feel like a *normal* woman waited before her with bright eyes and a mouth that made her sex clench.

*One more time.* She needed him, just once more.

And she was going to have him.

Screw the voice that demanded she tell him all of her secrets. She didn't want to see pity in his eyes.

She wanted the lust that burned hot enough to singe her flesh.

Her fingers sank into his hair as she urged him close again, and she took his mouth.

No holding back. As wild as she wanted to be. *Finally.*

The fury of lust was in his kiss. She could taste the reckless need and the hunger. She loved it. Her heart pounded, drumming hard and fast in her ears, and she pressed against him, loving that thickly muscled chest. Damn, the guy was perfect.

But he had on too many clothes.

So did she.

Her tongue snaked over the raised edge of his scar, and, this time, the moan was his.

Her nipples pebbled, the points aching and hard. She knew that he'd smell her arousal in the close confines of the truck's cab. It would be impossible for a guy like him not to notice.

If only the gear shift weren't so close to her leg, she could try to straddle him and—

He jerked back. "We . . . have to talk . . . the guy after you—"

Talking wasn't what she wanted. "We're safe here, aren't we?"

A nod. "Out here"—he ran his tongue over his lips as if catching her taste—"I'd know long before anyone got close."

That's what she'd thought. Out in the wild. The perfect place for her tiger. "Good." Her right hand dropped between them and rubbed over the obvious bulge of his arousal. "I want you—*now*." Oh, hell, had she just said that? Sounding all confident, like she wasn't shaking inside? What if he could see right through her? What if—

"I know." The edge of his growing canines appeared when he gave a hard grin. "Your smell is *driving me insane*." Then *his* hand was on her thigh, shoving up her skirt. She hadn't bothered with panty hose. Living in Louisiana, a girl learned to ditch those at an early age. So his callused fingertips touched skin and sent a little shock right through her. Especially when those fingers curled around the inside of her thigh and slid up . . .

Her breath hitched. “Inside.”

His mouth lifted in a half-smile. “Hell, yeah, sweetheart. I’m going right—”

Her cheeks flamed. “I mean . . .” His fingers worked up an inch and brushed against the crotch of her panties. Those panties were getting damp, fast. “Not . . . here.” Because the fear was always there in the back of her mind.

*Watching.*

He’d be smart enough to stay back, so Jude wouldn’t hear his movement. But he could use binoculars. She knew the guy would do just about anything to keep tabs on her.

No, no, she didn’t want that asshole to see a thing. “Your house.”

One finger eased under the elastic edge of her panties and pushed up between her folds. Erin stiffened.

Not because she didn’t like his touch, but because she did. *Too much.*

That finger stroked over her, spreading her cream in a long swipe and Erin gasped. “*Inside.*” The house. She meant the house.

He pulled away. It seemed like more beast than man stared at her from his eyes. “You’d better move fast, sweetheart.”

She shoved open the door. Fought to untangle herself from the seatbelt. Then she was all but racing for the porch, ignoring the chirp of insects and the distant lap of water.

He reached the door first, by about a good two seconds. She flew in behind him, mouth dry, body throbbing, so ready.

Jude caught her, yanking her close and crushing his lips to hers. Her back rapped against the wall and her mouth opened wider.

His cock pushed against her belly. Long and thick and just what she wanted.

No, *he* was what she wanted.

She grabbed the front of his shirt, jerked, and heard the pop of buttons.

He didn't lift his head. Didn't look horrified. No, he *growled* against her, and caught her skirt in his fist.

Her hands slid over his chest. Hot flesh. Strong man.

The skirt was bunched at her hips now and she knew her panties weren't going to last long, not when he got his claws on them.

But she didn't just want to be taken. She wanted to *take.* The tiger was about to see just how wild she could get.

The fingers that had curled to caress now flattened and she pushed against him, hard enough to make him stumble back.

"Erin? What the hell?"

She caught his arms and spun them around so that *he* was the one pinned. And she smiled. "Let's see how much you can handle." Power pulsed through her. The kind she'd never really felt before because she'd had to be so careful.

Not this time.

She locked his hands against the wall. His eyes widened. But then he flashed her that grin, that wicked grin that made her sex melt and her heart kick-start too fast. "Take your best shot at me."

She would.

Erin rose up on her toes and pressed her mouth against his throat. *Right there.* Where the pulse raced, where she could taste the beat of his heart. She touched him once with her lips closed. Then her mouth opened and she tasted him with her tongue.

And let him feel the edge of her teeth.

"*Oh, fuck.*"

"Not yet," she whispered, and her mouth moved to his shoulder. He'd played with her before, an almost exact reversal of this position.

Only she wasn't playing.

For shifters—this spot, oh, yeah, it could sure be very sensitive.

She bit.

Jude shuddered against her.

Erin's hands released their hold and her fingers skated down his chest. And her mouth followed them. Lips and tongue. She touched the small, brown nipples. Then her mouth closed over one nubbin, and she sucked.

"Erin . . ." His hands clenched around her hips and he tried to yank her closer.

Not yet.

She used her grip to hold him back against the wall. "Just getting started." There was more of him that she wanted to see, to touch, and most definitely to taste.

Her eyes dropped to the buckle of his belt. Her hands skated down his body and she lightly raked his skin.

Her fingers were steady when she unhooked the belt. The button popped free, and his zipper slid down with a nearly soundless hiss.

No underwear.

His cock bobbed toward her, the thick head glistening.

She just had to touch.

Her fingers curled around his shaft and he jerked, choking out a breath. Oh, she liked that. Erin squeezed, then stroked, a root to tip pump that had Jude tensing.

Erin lowered before him, her knees hitting the hardwood floor and her skirt fluttering around her. Just a taste. A quick sample.

Her lips closed over him.

"*Erin.*" Gravelly, barely human.

She took more of his length. Licked him. Sucked.

Enjoyed the hell out of the moment.

Her hand cradled the base of his cock, controlling the depth and motion as she tasted and took and licked.

His hands clamped down on her shoulders. He didn't push her away. Didn't pull her closer.

She looked up at him. Saw that his jaw was clenched. Those burning blue eyes were locked on her. Red stained his cheeks. And his expression—

Erin swallowed.

A ragged groan broke from his lips. "*Enough.*"

One more swipe of her tongue then she rocked back on her haunches. "Not yet."

He jerked her up. "*Now.*" A table was beside them. A big, sturdy wooden table with a lamp sitting back on the far edge. He dropped her on top of the table. Pushed her legs apart. "*Now.*"

He grabbed her panties. One slice of his claws and they fell away.

Erin knocked the lamp out of her way. She heard the thud when it hit the floor. At least it hadn't bro—

Long, strong fingers pushed between her thighs. Her head fell back against the table.

"Hot and wet." His voice was pure sex. So low and deep and rumbling.

Her legs dangled over the edge of the table.

"You're driving me *crazy,*" he charged.

Yeah, like she was feeling all sane and in control right then. Erin squirmed beneath him. "Jude!"

One finger thrust inside. He lowered over her. His left hand caught her shirt, wrenched it open. Then he shoved her bra out of the way.

When his mouth closed over her nipple, she gasped because *dammit,* she'd wanted this. Erin arched toward him, riding his finger and twisting as she fought for her pleasure.

"Aw, *damn*, sweetheart."

The eyes she couldn't remember shutting flew open. "*Now.*" This time, the demand was hers.

A grim nod. Then he pulled her closer to the table's edge. Fitted himself to her opening as he positioned the head of his cock. She loved that first brush of flesh on flesh. No condom for them. Just sex to sex and—

His cock drove into her. No tentative thrust. Just a hard plunge. Balls-deep and so thick.

Her legs locked around his hips, and she slammed up to meet him. Again and again. Her body tightened.

His mouth took her breast again. Licking and sucking, scoring her lightly with his teeth while he kept thrusting. Driving as far into her as he could go. Hard and fast.

Just the way she wanted him.

His cock withdrew, then slid right back inside her, the length rubbing along her sensitive flesh. Her sex clenched as her climax approached. So close, *so close*.

He kissed her when she came, drinking in the sounds of her pleasure even as his hips pumped faster, *faster*, against her.

Her fingers dug into his back. She wanted to feel his release inside her, the hot splash of his climax.

Jude raised his head and stared down at her.

An aftershock, warm and sweet, rippled through her sex and he erupted. Her name broke from his lips as she saw the wave of pleasure sweep over his face.

She held him, with arms and legs, as tightly as she could. Held him and tried to make the pleasure last. Tried to memorize every feeling, tried to imprint the feel of his body on hers.

Because moments like this didn't last. Especially not for her.

After a time, he sagged against her, sweat slick on his body. Erin didn't loosen her hold. Not yet.

*Not yet.*

A squeak sounded beneath her. Then a weird little creak. Then—

They fell to the floor as the table gave way beneath them.

Her breath was knocked from her and the wood bit into her back and arms.

"*Dammit!*" Jude's flushed face. "Erin? Sweetheart, are you all right?" He pulled her up, cradling her in his arms as his gaze darted over her body.

They'd broken the table.

He was still lodged inside her. Spikes of pleasure still trembled through her body.

And they'd broken the table.

Erin laughed, a helpless, rusty bubble of sound that lifted her lips.

Jude shook his head. "I didn't mean—"

She kissed him. And laughed again.

A deep rumble burst from him. Small lines appeared around his eyes and his mouth curved. She'd never seen him smile so fully before.

And she couldn't remember the last time she'd laughed. Laughed, and meant it. Not the fake crap that so often slipped out. But really *laughed.*

She stared up at Jude. The man really was gorgeous. She should have noticed it from the beginning. How had she ever thought that he looked cruel or cold?

She traced his scar with a fingertip.

*Sexy.*

And—damn it all—she was very afraid that she was falling for him.

* * *

Erin hadn't come home.

He stared up at the dark house, his body taut as a slow anger pumped through him.

He'd expected her to run home. Expected her *guard* to be there, standing watch again. He'd planned for the asshole. He'd been more than ready to rip the hunter wide open.

But she wasn't there. Neither was he.

A growl built in his throat. *Not part of the plan.*

This wasn't the way things were supposed to go, dammit. Why couldn't she ever show her appreciation? Why the hell did she keep jerking him around?

And if she'd let that cat touch her . . .

His teeth snapped together.

The tiger shifter *would* be dying soon. And it would be a long, painful death.

This time, he'd let Erin watch—every moment. She'd understand then. She'd realize how much he loved her. She'd see that he would do anything for her.

When he offered her the blood, she'd smile that slow smile, and be his.

Forever.

# Chapter 10

Jude's fingers trailed over her breast, skimming the nipple gently, then sliding under the round globe. Slowly, softly, then he touched her scar.

Erin didn't flinch and she didn't even pull away—*pretty impressive*, she thought. Swallowing, she stared up at the ceiling of Jude's bedroom. He was all around her, surrounding her with his scent and his body. A dangerous shifter. A man who could rip apart his enemies.

But she'd never felt safer.

His thumb brushed over the raised flesh. "Tell me."

No more running. She'd decided that. No more running, no more hiding. *Better start now.* "He caught me once, broke into my home, reached my bedroom." She'd woken to his touch. Cold claws sliding down her face.

Jude tensed against her, but he didn't speak and his hands didn't fall away from her.

Not yet.

"I don't really know how he does it but, he can hide his

scent." Tricky bastard. "Maybe herbs or something. Hell, maybe he can just control it at will. I don't know." A light chill seemed to cover her flesh. "Today, I caught his scent because he *wanted* me to. That's the way he plays his games."

"He was luring you out, and you walked right to the bastard." Anger there, vibrating in his voice.

"I'm tired of running," she said simply. "I can't keep doing this. He's not going to stop. He'll just keep killing and hunting me, *and I can't keep running.*" The rules in this twisted game were changing. One way or another.

She wanted the warmth of Jude's flesh against her, but she couldn't just lay there anymore. She rose, pushing from the bed, pushing *away* from him, and tugged a sheet with her. Erin wrapped it around her body and stared down at him. "You know I can't shift."

A nod. He sat up, the bed covers draped over his naked groin.

She licked her lips. "I don't—I don't have all of a shifter's enhanced senses either." *Flawed.* "My sense of smell—yeah, it's strong." Actually, she'd learned it was stronger than most shifter's. "But my hearing is just like a human's, so that bastard was able to sneak right up to me, and I didn't even know he was there until it was too late."

Blue eyes held hers. "Too late?" No emotion there. Flat and cold.

Her gaze dropped to the bed and she saw that his claws were out.

Not really so cold after all.

"I never saw his face." Now she was the one without emotion. "As soon as I woke up, he shoved some kind of hood over me."

Darkness.

Razor sharp claws.

*Fear.*

How many nights had she stayed awake in her bed? Too scared to sleep because she'd been afraid he'd come back?

"What did he do?"

"Used his claws to . . . cut away my clothes." She paced away from him. The guy had been so fast. She'd been stunned, terrified. "I knew what he was going to do." Her chin rose. "But *he* didn't know how strong I could be. I fought the bastard." The stupid scar. In one way, she was like other wolves. Her wounds always left a mark on her body. Her flesh healed, but it didn't forget. Her hand dropped to hover over the rough ridge. "I got my own swipes in, but he got his, too."

Jude jumped from the bed, caught her shoulders and hauled her close. "Erin . . . did he—"

"I got away." *Run, run.* The words had been driving her for so long. "Ran naked and bloody down the street. I was afraid he'd chase after me, but"—her lip curved in a smile she knew wasn't pretty—"he had his own wounds."

She'd snagged a pair of sweats and a T-shirt off a clothesline down the street. Sweet Mrs. Sara Copeland—still doing her laundry the old fashioned way.

"I had already planned to leave Lillian before that night. After the attack, I never went back to my house." A different hotel every night. Always looking over her shoulder. "The cops there couldn't help me. What were they going to do against a shifter?"

"*I* can help you," he told her, his fingers tight around her.

"I know." She didn't doubt his strength. "Night Watch was made for hunting guys like him."

"Made for putting 'em down."

Oh, but his eyes were bright and he was still holding her, staring at her with need and worry in that gaze.

*Tell it all.* "He's after me because he thinks I'm his mate."

Shifters and their mates. For some of their kind, a primal, instinctual thing.

"He's fucking wrong."

Was he? "He's like me, Jude. A hybrid."

"*We're the same. Not weaker, stronger. They don't have a fucking clue.*" The voice from her nightmares.

"So? There are *thousands* of hybrids in the world. He can go pick one of them for his mate."

"*Knew we were meant for each other, from the first moment I saw you.*" His weight had shoved her into the mattress.

A light shake from Jude. "Erin."

It was hard to swallow over the fist in her throat. "He's a hybrid, but-but he can still shift. I know, because I saw him change once." Deliberate. Everything with that asshole was deliberate.

"Yeah?" He shook his head. "So what'd the freak turn into? A bear? Coyote? A—"

"He's a wolf."

She caught the slight widening of his eyes.

A wolf shifter. One of the strongest and the most dangerous of the shifters. And, unfortunately, one known to sometimes cross the line that led into the realm of the *psychotic.*

But Jude shook his head. "Doesn't change a thing for me. You really think I'm afraid of some mangy wolf?"

No. She didn't think he feared much. Perhaps he should. "You know what they say about wolf shifters. They can recognize their mates—"

"Not at first sight, it can take time to—"

"He said I was his mate." Her hand rose between them. Flattened over his heart. "A wolf shifter only gets one true mate."

*Broken.*

"And for him, seems like I'm . . . it."

"The hell you are." He lifted her up, bringing her to eye level and letting her toes dangle in the air.

Erin blinked. "Uh, Jude . . ."

"Get the idea out of your head, got me? Just 'cause some fucked up psycho thinks he's your mate—hell, screw that! You don't belong to him."

*Mine.*

"And the asshole sure won't be living long enough to ever claim you."

Well, that was—

He kissed her. Hard and deep and her toes curled and her heart raced and she held on to him and she *hoped.*

*Let him be right.*

Because being the perfect mate for that freak—no, even God didn't hate her that much.

Her lips parted and his tongue swept inside. He still wanted her. He didn't care about the wolf so it was okay and she could tell him—

He broke the kiss and muttered, "Wolves are insane. Everybody knows that."

Her heart thudded to a stop.

"If they're in a pack, they follow their alpha like blind dogs," Jude continued.

Not always. Some packs were family, strong and—

"And if the bastard is Lone, well, shit, that means even the pack didn't want him. And if pack doesn't want you, then you're fucking screwed," Jude said.

She shoved against him.

"Erin?"

A quick step back. "I need to shower." She grabbed the sheet, right before it started a fast slither down her body.

*Fucking screwed.*

Her cheeks iced, then burned. Her right hand clenched, holding the sheet close to her chest.

"Erin—what is it? What did—"

But she shook her head and skirted around him. About six more steps and then she'd be in the bathroom. Just six more. "It's been a hell of a night. I just need to take a hot shower." To wash away the memories.

She pushed open the bathroom door.

"Let me come in with you."

*No. Not now. Too close to breaking.* Erin cleared her throat. "Maybe next time, tiger." Then she was inside, kicking the door shut behind her.

And turning the lock. Not that the flimsy lock would do much good if Jude wanted inside.

The soft creak of the floorboards reached her ears. *Coming this way.*

The sheet fell to the floor and she put both hands on either side of the sink, holding tight.

"Erin . . ." He sounded hesitant. Maybe even worried. "What happened, it doesn't change you."

No, it didn't. Nothing would change her.

"You don't have to hide from me."

She stared at her reflection, seeing the eyes that held their own golden glow. The cheeks that had hollowed, the teeth that had lengthened.

Her claws dug into the undersides of the sink. "I'll be out soon, okay?"

More hesitation. She could *feel* it.

Then that soft creak again. He was moving away now.

Her breath flooded out.

*If the pack doesn't want you, then you're fucking screwed.*

Yeah, she was.

Because she was a Lone wolf, one fighting to survive. She had a psychotic mate on her trail, and a lover who apparently hated her kind.

* * *

Jude stared at the closed bathroom door, his fists clenched. He could hear the roar of the shower, so trying to speak to Erin then was not really an option.

She'd locked him out. No mistaking the soft *snick* of the lock.

He could get inside, no problem. A quick shove against the door and he'd be in that small room with her, the steam from the shower around them. He could join her in the shower stall. Take her into his arms and let the spray pour over their bodies.

If she thought her story about that asshole had changed the desire that he felt for her, well, she was dead wrong.

Her story had just shown how tough she was, how determined to survive. A woman with that much strength was damn sexy.

Nothing would make him stop wanting her.

Nothing.

But he turned away from the door. If Erin wanted space, he'd give it to her. At this rate, hell, he'd pretty much give her anything she wanted.

The bastard out there would pay. He'd see to it. *A wolf.* There had been whispers and rumors about the wolves for years. Centuries.

They kept to themselves, always locking tight in their packs. Very, very rarely did they mate with non-wolf shifters. The wolves fought dirty, they fought hard, and they generally fought to the death. It was their way.

He hadn't been kidding when he'd talked about the Lones. The wolves out there who either turned their back on the pack or who had the pack turn on them were the badasses the *Other* kept away from, if they were smart. Because some of the wolves had been known to become absolutely freaking insane.

When you were crazy, *with* the full strength of a wolf shifter, folks were smart if they avoided you.

Jude liked to think he was a smart guy. Not genius, nah, but smart enough. But he wasn't gonna be avoiding that wolf. He was going after him, and he would take the bastard down.

The dog had better get ready to do some running of his own.

The hunt was on.

"Hey, Jude!" Dee's yell caught him the minute he stepped inside the Night Watch office. "I was wondering when you'd be dragging your sorry butt in here." She flashed him a grin, then bent low over her desk as she dove into a pile of paperwork. "I've been digging up your girl's past, and man, she had quite a reputation."

Jude cleared his throat.

Dee's head popped up, a furrow between her golden brows. "What? You got—"

He stepped to the side.

He saw Erin flash one hell of a *sharp*, toothy grin at the other woman.

"—something caught in your throat?" Dee finished. "Ah." Now it was her turn to make a weird-ass gurgle in her throat. "Um, I'm guessing you're the new ADA, huh?" Dee didn't flush. Come to think of it, he'd never seen her cheeks redden. But her eyes did narrow as she fired an assessing glance over Erin.

"Guess you're right," Erin murmured, her fingers tightening around her purse strap. "The woman with the reputation."

Dee blinked and pasted what Jude knew to be a false smile on her face as she pointed to the left. "There's a waiting room for clients down that way. You can just go take a seat while I brief Jude on—"

"My life?" Erin shook her head and took a step forward. "Thanks, but I think I'd rather hear this."

Dee glanced at him. Jude shrugged. He didn't know what to expect from Dee's reports. She'd been on the computer, with her hacker buddy Jasper, for the last twenty-four hours. If there'd been secrets to uncover, she would have found them all.

So what kind of reputation did his little hybrid have?

He stepped toward Dee's desk. There was no sign of Zane, for now, and he figured that was probably a good thing. His associates sure seemed to be making friends right and left with Erin.

"Asshole," Dee whispered when he got close to her. Her skin looked even paler today. The lady must be getting too much night hunting. If she didn't watch it, she'd start to look like the vamps she tracked. "You *knew* I didn't realize she was there. Hell, I'm not you, I can't smell a person from thirty feet away."

"So you were digging in my past." Erin's smooth voice cut across Dee's furious snap. She paused next to the smaller woman. Dee's skin seemed too white next to Erin's burnished gold. "What did you find?"

Dee's eyes narrowed on him. A look that promised she'd get her payback. Then she grabbed the leaning pile of paperwork. "I found out that you can be a pretty tough bitch."

Erin's expression didn't alter.

"So can I," Dee said, flashing a real smile. "So I tend to respect that."

The mask cracked on Erin's face for a moment as confusion flashed through.

"There were some stories about you getting a bit rough with some guys back in high school and college."

Her golden gaze shot to Jude's.

"Nothing too bad. One guy had a sprained wrist, the other mild lacerations."

Erin winced at that. "I can explain those."

Dee waved her hand in the air. "You're *Other.* You like to play rough." Her hand stopped the wave and her index finger pointed at Erin's chest. "You stopped playing with the humans, though, when you realized you could hurt them."

"Did I?" Erin asked quietly.

No, she hadn't. Jude knew she'd just learned to play better. *Holding the beast back.* Not a lot of fun in that for their kind. Especially not during sex.

Shifters were wild for a reason.

Dee's head cocked to the right. "I don't know. Maybe you just learned how to play better. But either way, there weren't any more stories about the down and dirty Erin after you hit twenty-one."

*The down and dirty Erin?* Jude tensed.

"You graduated from Tulane—both for your undergrad work and your JD—with honors. I figure you must have hooked up with some of the paranormals while you were in New Orleans. Always happens in the bigger cities. Guessing they didn't care about you being a bit out of control in the bedroom, or they showed you how *to* control yourself."

Erin gave a nod at that and Jude had to wonder—which option was she agreeing to? And why the hell did the idea of Erin with other men make his jaw clench, his heart race and—

"Dude, get your claws out of my desk." Dee's pissed voice. "This desk is new! I don't want you marking it the way you idiots always mark everything you want."

He jerked his claws from the wood. "Sorry." Hell, he'd have to repair her desk. He hadn't meant—

"Shifters do have a habit of marking things that don't belong to them." Erin seemed way too calm when she said that. "A flaw in genetics, I think."

"*I'm not like him, sweetheart.*" The words rasped out before he could stop them. Not that he would have stopped them. She'd put an icy wall between them since last night. He was tired of the distance and more than ready to knock that wall apart.

He wasn't like that asshole. Erin should know that by now.

Her eyes held his. *So beautiful.* "No, you're not."

Was that a thaw? Was she going to open back up to him? Last night had been heavy for her, he knew it, but he sure didn't want her turning from him now.

No, now, she was supposed to turn *to* him.

"Uh, yeah, great. Whatever this is"—Dee's hands fluttered between them—"keep it in the bedroom, okay? I haven't been laid in two months and all this weird-ass tension in the air is making me jealous."

Now Erin did smile, a slow stretch of her lips.

Jude's heart kicked into his ribs.

"Ease up, Romeo." Dee's elbow rammed into his chest. "Back to business."

Right.

"After law school, you did some work in different parishes. A few years later, you settled in Lillian. Started working for the DA's office and got the reputation for being the bitch who went after the monsters." A fast glance at Jude. "Not your kind. Rapists, domestic abusers. Those pigs that make me want to deliver a bit of my own abuse."

"Dee, we've talked about your eye-for-eye punishments before," he murmured.

"Yeah, we talked about how *they work.*"

Phones rang in the background. Jude caught Zane's voice, the guy was talking to Pak. "Cut through the crap. Did you find anything we can use on this guy?"

Dee's mouth tightened, just a bit, and her focus shifted back to Erin. "I found out you were working the biggest case of your career and all of a sudden, you seemed to lose your nerve."

"*What?* I sure as hell didn't. I've never lost—"

"Two missed court appearances. Five late arrivals. You didn't have your witnesses ready, and when it came time to step up to the plate in the Trent case, you struck out."

Dee could be a vicious fighter, one who went right for the jugular when a person least expected it.

Jude lifted his hand toward Erin because the lady looked—

"You don't know me," she snapped at Dee. "You get on your computer and you sneak around and you think you're looking into someone's life and you're learning about them. Well, *you're wrong.* I worked my ass off on that case. I did everything I could, but Trent had an in with Judge Harper. Court times kept changing, with *no* notice to me. Witnesses vanished, and even though I did my damned job, that bastard walked."

Dee didn't back down. He'd never seen the woman back down. "And when you were in the middle of this case, fighting to get that abuser locked up, that freak out there made first contact, didn't he?"

"What?" Erin shook her head.

"I saw his pattern. The attacks on the people around you. When someone hurt you, pissed you off, or just got in your face, he attacked. This case was the deal breaker. You were fighting on your own, getting knocked around by the judge *and* the defense attorney—and that guy out there made his move . . . on you."

Jude wrapped his fingers around Erin's shoulder. "Is this when he made first contact?" Dee was the best research agent he'd ever met, and the best attacker he'd ever seen in a bar fight.

A nod. "Yeah, yeah. I-I was working three other cases at the same time, but the Trent case was the one eating me alive." Echoes of frustration. Anger.

Dee tapped her chin. "He found you on that case." Her gaze drifted to Jude as she eased into her chair and leaned back. Like the lady didn't have a care. "Jude, I'd lay odds that if you went to that city, used your usual *finesse*, you'd be able find him through that case."

The beast inside jerked on his leash. *Hunt.* "Oh, I'm sure I can finesse my way in Lillian." Finesse had to be slang for biting and clawing his way to some answers. His shoulders rolled. "Looks like I'll be taking a road trip."

"You mean *we* will." Erin's determined voice.

Dee's eyes widened. "Uh, civilians don't normally go on hunts."

Erin flashed her perfect smile, then punched down at Dee's desk. Her claws plunged into the wood. "Not your normal civilian."

"*Dammit!*" The human glared at them, hands fisted on her hips. "New desk, Donovan, got that? I expect a new freaking desk! I will go to Pak with this, don't think I won't!"

Erin's dainty hand lifted. The claws were gone. Nice control. "I'm going with you," she told him.

Despite the little show she'd just given, he shook his head. Claws really weren't going to do the trick on this one. "No."

"I'm paying you. I go."

He braced his legs apart and stared her down. "Twice before, I've had clients bitch to ride shotgun with me. The first guy wound up with two broken arms and a concussion."

" 'Cause hunts aren't for civilians," Dee chimed in.

Erin's gaze didn't waver.

"The second guy," Jude continued, "died on me."

Her lips parted.

"Lucky for him, I managed to bring the asshole back." But for that five minutes when the guy had lain lifeless, Jude had been nervous as all hell. A dead client didn't pay.

" 'Cause hunts aren't for civilians," the too-helpful Dee said again.

Erin's nostrils flared. "I'm tired of standing on the sidelines and being afraid. Things are changing for me, *now.* I know that city. I've got connections that you don't. I can help you."

"You can get killed." And if she slipped away from him, well, *nervous as all hell*, really wouldn't be how he'd be describing the—

"And if I stay here, without you, what's to say the bastard won't make a try for me?"

"If he comes, I'll be by your side." Zane sauntered in, halting close to the now ravaged desk.

"Hell, no." Erin's hair whipped as she shook her head. "Not an option."

"Look, I can explain about yesterday."

"Not an option." Her hand lifted toward him, palm flat. "And it's not because of that bullshit yesterday. It's because you can't handle this guy."

"Shot down," Dee murmured and it looked like she was biting back a grin.

And Zane looked insulted. "The day I can't handle a shifter is the day you can—"

"He's a wolf."

"—throw my ass in the grave. *What? A wolf shifter?*" Not fear in his voice. More like shock.

Dee whistled. "I am so jealous. You get all the good kills, Jude."

He slanted her a quick glance. The lady needed some therapy.

"What's your power scale, demon?" Erin asked and her voice was *loud*. It seemed like the gloves were definitely off now. Jude figured it was a good thing the office was pretty much deserted. Most of the agents were out on their own hunts.

Choking out a laugh, Dee shook her head. "You can't ask a demon that. I mean, it's like asking a man the size of his di—"

"High damn enough!" Zane cut through, face reddening.

But Erin's lips curved down. "Doubt it. If the stories are true, a wolf shifter can take down a level ten demon. Are you really up for that?"

"Hell, yeah, I—"

"*I'm going with Jude.*" Her steely words sliced through the air. "So all this doesn't really matter. My life, my choice." Her eyes had begun to glow.

Jude stared down at her. Weighing. Deciding. "I can't risk your safety."

"If you leave me here, you risk my safety."

"That's not—" Zane began hotly.

Erin flashed him a feral stare. He shut up.

"You take me, you risk me." A shrug. "Guess it's one of those lose-lose situations."

Those were real bitches.

"It's *my* life," she said again. "And I am sick of running and sick of blood. It's time to go back. Escaping didn't work. Trust me, I can see that now." She licked her lips. "He won't stop until I stop him."

"Or until you're dead." A piss-poor comment from Dee.

Jude glared at her. Like fuck that would happen.

Erin's chin lifted. "If I have to, I'll just follow you to Lillian. But I *am* going."

"Uh, don't you have a job?" Zane asked. "Cases to prosecute?"

"I'm off until Monday." She waited until Jude looked back at her and asked, "So what's it gonna be, tiger? You taking me?"

*Again and again, sweetheart.* He bit back the words and sucked in a sharp breath. "You go, you follow my rules."

"Ah, hell, fool number three riding shotgun." Dee squeezed her eyes shut. "Can no one trust professionals these days?"

He ignored her. "At the first sign of trouble, you back the hell off and let me handle things."

A nod.

*Mistake. Oh, this was such a mistake, but—*

But if he left her behind, he'd worry about her every second. Because the truth was that Jude could all but feel the bastard's eyes on them.

Watching.

Waiting.

Poor fucked up Lee Givens—the guy still hadn't woken up yet. He was in the ICU, with a guard stationed at his side, courtesy of Tony's pull. Erin had called to check on him first thing that morning, but there had been no improvement.

The docs thought it was a miracle he was still breathing. Well, breathing with the help of all those beeping and buzzing machines.

The guy out there after Erin didn't play around. Vicious, twisted, and quick to kill.

Not exactly a dream date.

No, leaving Erin in Baton Rouge, even with Zane for protection, wasn't an option he liked.

So that just left . . . shotgun.

Jude gave a grudging nod. *Dammit.*

* * *

The tiger brought her back. Fucking finally. His body tensed when he saw the familiar pickup truck. Then Erin appeared, midnight hair shining, and the two of them hurried toward her house.

The shifter's hand pressed against her back right before they disappeared inside.

A familiar gesture. Too familiar.

He waited, barely glancing at the truck. He'd already marked the license down. He'd done that days before.

Less than five minutes later, the shifter was back at the door. The hunter glanced down the drive with narrowed eyes. He held a suitcase in one hand, the other hand was intertwined with Erin's.

*Too familiar.*

They hurried out. Erin climbed into the passenger seat. The shifter hesitated. Looked around. Seemed to stare right at him.

Then the tiger smiled.

He leaned back inside the truck, caught the back of Erin's head, and kissed her.

*No.*

A snarl broke from his lips and the tiger jerked up, gaze sweeping past the azaleas.

He shoved back the fury, nearly choking on the rage.

Erin's slender hand reached up and touched the shifter's chest. "Jude, what is it?"

Her voice drifted to him on the wind. So sweet and husky. Sexy.

And saying another man's name.

*You're next, bastard. You'll beg.*

The tiger's fingers closed around hers. "Thought I heard a damned dog," he said, voice loud.

Too loud. Deliberate that.

So the cat wanted to play.

The fool didn't understand who he was going up against. The tiger was big, tough, and deadly in his own right, but he didn't understand a hybrid's strength.

His mistake. One that would be fatal.

The tiger shifter tossed her suitcase in the bed of the truck, then took his time stalking around the back of the vehicle.

The urge to attack, to rip and kill and smell the sweet scent of death, had his blood heating in his veins.

But he wasn't stupid. He knew how to hunt. And *when* to hunt.

Too many witnesses. Too many neighbors out and too many cars buzzing on the street.

For this hunt, this kill, he wanted to take his time and enjoy the moment.

Because after this, there would be no more games. The chase would finally be over and Erin would be his.

He just had to kill the cat first.

Easy.

The bigger they were, the louder they screamed.

And Erin would scream too. She'd have to be taught a lesson. He'd enjoyed the games. They roused his appetite, but her playing with the cat hadn't been part of the deal.

The truck drove past him. So close.

He glanced down, surprised to see that his claws were out and embedded in his palms. Blood dripped onto the ground. The blood was dark on the dirt. Fat blobs that spread over the grainy surface.

He looked back up just as the tiger turned the corner.

*Where are you running to now, mate?*

Didn't matter. Wherever she went, he would find her.

That was the way he played the game.

# Chapter 11

"Okay." Erin turned away from the traffic and focused on the sharp lines of Jude's profile. "What was all that about back at the house?"

His fingers were at a perfect ten and two position on the wheel. He didn't glance her way, but the truck accelerated, and weaved in and out of traffic as he flew through the intersection. "Thought I heard something."

"Something," she repeated quietly, "or someone?"

She caught the curl of his lip. "What do you think, sweetheart?"

"I think baiting the asshole out there might not be our smartest move, and I think that next time, you better let me know your plans." Because being in the dark sucked, and if she was going up against the wolf, she wanted to know *everything.*

"Got it." A quick glance her way. "But, for the record, I kissed you because I wanted to do it. Because you've got the sexiest mouth I've ever seen, and because I wanted to taste you."

"Ah . . . okay." Erin reached out and fiddled with the air conditioning vent because she was suddenly feeling a little warm. "Fair enough." His mouth had sure given her plenty of fantasies. It was the scar—scars weren't sexy, she knew that. Well, they weren't supposed to be sexy, but his . . .

Damn. It was his mouth. The man sure knew how to use those lips.

And his tongue. He was very, very good at using his tongue and—

"Your breathing's changed on me, Erin." She caught the flare of his nostrils. "And your scent . . ."

*Shifters.* She couldn't quite get used to being around another shifter again. The rules were so different. The whole polite society thing was thrown right out the window. Her legs stretched. Yeah, her scent had changed, and she figured the guy probably had caught the smell of her arousal. No point playing a game with him. "I want you, Jude." There. That sounded confident and tough and like she didn't give a crap if he knew that her panties were getting a bit . . . wet.

*Just from thinking about the guy and the things he could do with his mouth.*

"Oh, baby." He accelerated as the pickup zoomed off the ramp and onto the interstate. "You know how to make me suffer, don't you?"

No, she didn't.

"Just so you know, we're getting *one* room when we get to Lillian." Gruff words, hard with a lust she couldn't miss.

Her hand reached out, trailed up his thigh and she felt the strong clench of his muscles. "So I have to wait until then, huh?" A couple of hours. Shouldn't be too bad.

Her fingers rose just a bit more and traced the swollen length of his cock. Maybe she could—

Jude caught her hand. He tangled his fingers with hers. "Unless you want me plowing into the semi in front of us, yeah, you have to wait."

Her gaze shot to the windshield and she saw the lumbering big rig.

He rubbed the back of her hand over the ridge of his cock in a rough caress. "But don't worry, I'll make it worth the wait."

*Lillian.*

She cleared her throat. "You'd better." Because going home was hard. There were too many secrets there. Too much pain. Being with Jude, touching him, taking the pleasure from his body would help her pull through.

She tugged her hand back. After a slight hesitation, he let her go. Erin settled into her seat and tried *not* to look at his crotch. Maybe she'd sleep. *If* she could stop thinking about him. Maybe she'd—

"Gonna tell me about the 'down and dirty' Erin?"

She winced. Oh, but she'd known this would come. Her eyes closed. "You've already met her. Not much to tell."

"Ummm . . ."

Her left eye opened. Then the right.

"Playing with humans, were you?" He shook his head. "You'll find those males don't always have the stamina you need."

A choked laugh broke from her. "Wasn't really a question of stamina. More like the problem of them freaking out when I got too, um—"

"Rough? Wild?"

Yes, to both.

"Don't worry. I like wild and I like rough." His index finger tapped on the wheel. "But I think you already know that."

*One room.*

This drive was going to be hell.

"Just so you know . . . I can also do slow."

She gulped. Damn dry throat.

"I can do easy. Thrusting as light as you want, kissing and stroking the whole night long."

Her clothes were too thick. Or maybe the truck's cab was too hot because she was sure starting to sweat.

"Whatever you want, I can give you."

Didn't she know it.

"But, Erin, you've got to trust me."

Easier said than done.

And Jude knew it.

She crossed her legs, fought to ignore the growing tension in her body, and stared out her window at the pine trees.

The silence in the car wasn't comfortable and it wasn't easy.

Just like her relationship with Jude.

Loose ends were a bitch.

He paced down the shining white hospital corridor, the green scrubs rustling softly as he walked.

If Lee Givens had been an accommodating bastard, he would have already been dead. But no, he was still alive. Still fighting to survive as he clung to life.

And why?

There was no reason for that piece of garbage to keep living.

A woman brushed by him, pretty, but scrawny. Her thin arms were around a kid, some little freckle-faced brat who had thick tears sliding down his cheeks.

"It's gonna be okay, Tommy," she whispered, clutching the boy. "It's gonna be—"

He rounded the corner and caught sight of the room he wanted. 409.

But a guard stood outside. *What the hell?* He stumbled to a stop. Why was a cop there?

*Loose ends were a bitch.*

He'd learned that back in Lillian when one of those loose ends had tried to confront him one night. Better to just cut them off before they could do any harm.

Givens hadn't seen his face. Well, he didn't *think* the lawyer had. The road had been dark. Too dark for a human to see, surely and—

"Something I can help you with?" The drawling voice came from behind him and was followed by a tap on his shoulder. One that was a little too hard.

He spun around, his clipboard up and ready. "Uh, what—" He let his eyes widen, then narrow as he studied the man before him.

*A Night Watch hunter.* He'd seen the guy with Donovan. Tall, dark, with eyes that seemed too sharp for a human's.

Probably because the guy wasn't.

His nostrils flared, just a bit, as he caught the hunter's scent. Not shifter.

But that still left at least a dozen *Other* possibilities.

He forced a smile. "Just making my rounds." He shifted the clipboard, a light move to draw attention to it.

"Room 409 *isn't* on your rounds, Doctor"—the green gaze dropped to his nametag—"Walters."

Smug jerk. "No." He bit back the rage and kept his voice flat. "But room 407 is." And he was standing right in front of that door then. "So if you'll excuse me—ah, sorry, *who are you?*"

"I'm one of the babysitters for room 409." A grim smile. "Since you don't know my patient, there's no need to know me."

Ripping him apart would be fun. One fast swipe with his claws. He could slash the jerk's throat. Let the blood spray and soak the too-white tiles and walls. Or he could cut down the guy's chest. Catch the bastard's heart and tear it out.

So many choices.

The hunter inclined his head and sauntered toward the waiting cop.

Two guards. Too much attention. The lawyer would have to wait.

A loose end he'd get—sooner or later.

The hunter glanced back at him, eyes narrowed.

Asshole.

With a curt nod, he hurried into room 407. The patient, an elderly man with a white mane of hair, glanced up at his approach. "Fuck. Another one of you assholes?"

Really, it was the wrong thing to say. Because his day was already pretty shitty.

"I'm tired of you pricks coming in here! I'm tired of everybody poking and prodding me. I'm eighty-seven. You can't fix me. I'm just gonna die."

*Sooner than the jerk realized.* He shoved his hand into his pocket. Felt the capped syringe he'd prepared especially for Givens. No sense in letting all that preparation go to waste. He'd known he wouldn't be able to attack with claws and teeth on this one. Though he sure did prefer to kill that way.

So he'd bribed a nurse. Gotten exactly what he needed for a fast, clean kill.

"Why don't you just take your overpaid, arrogant ass right back out of my room!"

He smiled and headed toward his patient. Some people really didn't do much for the world. He stopped at the foot of the bed and glanced at the patient's chart. "Tell me, Mr. Pope, have you had a good life?"

"What the hell kind of question is that? No, asshole, I haven't. I got my knee blasted in the war, stupid bitch of a wife sent me to jail for ten years, the cancer fucking ate me up when I got out, and now I have to look at your sorry ass!"

*No, some people really didn't do much for the world.* "Don't worry, sir, you'll be leaving the hospital soon."

"The hell I will! I heard them other assholes! I'll only be leaving in a body bag!"

True enough.

He uncapped the syringe. This wouldn't hurt. That was the only downside. He rather liked to watch pain and blood.

Hmmm . . . no blood. Another downside. But it would be fast. And the doctors and nurses would run in, so worried about this patient that they wouldn't even notice him slipping out.

And a kill would really improve his day.

Not one for Erin this time. Just for him.

It had been so long since the kills had been for him alone.

He rounded the bed. "Just relax, Mr. Pope, this will only take a few seconds of your time."

The old man gave a grim nod. "Fine, just hurry the hell up."

They reached Lillian just after lunch. Jude didn't drive to a motel first, good thing that because she probably would have jumped him. Instead, he took them straight to the police station.

Erin licked her lips as she stared up at the gleaming doors of the Lillian PD. The place was less than half the size of Baton Rouge's department. It was a fat, square building, one surrounded by police cruisers and motorcycles.

She'd spent hours there before, grilling cops, talking to suspects and perps.

Coming back was bittersweet.

Erin climbed the steps with her head up.

Jude shadowed her. "We need to find out if there were any more attacks after you left town."

"I didn't tell a lot of folks I was leaving," she said, as the doors drew closer. "I didn't want everyone to know—"

"Because you didn't *trust* them."

She didn't trust anyone. "I still don't." Her clothes were wrinkled, courtesy of the long ride and she hadn't bothered with makeup that morning—there hadn't been time—so Erin knew she probably looked like hell.

Not the perfectly pressed ADA image she'd worked so hard to maintain.

Her shoulders straightened. "Only one person knew I was up for the job in Baton Rouge. I wanted to keep it as quiet as possible. The bastard after me seemed to know too much."

"He still does." Jude reached for the door and closed his tanned fingers over the gleaming handle. "We're gonna be seeing the one who knew about your transfer after we leave the station."

Yeah, they were. Seeing the DA again was one of the reasons she'd wanted to come along. She'd worked hard to disappear. The stalker shouldn't have found her. Unless someone had told him about her plans.

"Hey, Jerome!" A bellow loud enough to shake her bones. A cop, a tall, skeletally thin black man with faint gray in his hair, jumped up from behind the check-in desk. "You finally brought your butt back home!"

She smiled at him. "Hi, Pat." Patrick Ramsey. Patrick one-more-year-til-I'm-out-give-me-a-desk Ramsey. The guy had taken four bullets in his career. Tossed hundreds of perps into the pen, and he'd once told her he couldn't wait for the day he got to kiss the badge good-bye and go lay on a Mexican beach.

He shot around the desk. Pretty fast for a guy whose knee had been blasted two years ago. He wrapped her in a hug that squeezed her bones. He'd always been so much stronger than he looked. "*What the hell?* You didn't even tell old Pat good-bye! That tightass DA had to give me the news."

She tried to breathe. Quick, shallow breaths. That was all she could manage right then.

He dropped his hold.

She sucked in a deep gulp of air. "Sorry, Pat, I-I had some personal things I had to—"

"Personal, huh?" He fired an assessing glance back at Jude. "Guess he's to blame?"

Her jaw dropped.

But Jude gave a nod. "Guess I am."

Pat sized him up. "You look like a cop."

"I'm not."

Pat's raised brows called him a liar.

"Bounty hunter." Jude pulled out his ID. Pat never glanced at it. "Erin's helping me on a case."

"You?" He stared down at her and then gave a nod. "Always said the law was too tame for you."

*Too tame.* Pat had always been good at seeing below the surface. That was one of the reasons he'd done such good undercover work back in the day. She smiled but the motion of her lips felt too fake. "I need a favor."

A shrug. "Figure I owe you a few of those."

Yeah, he did. And she was sure glad he'd been the first cop she saw. Maybe fate was trying to throw her a bone.

But, ah, now for the delicate part. "I need to check some case files. We're after a guy, a real bad asshole, and I need to see if his MO matches up with any unsolved crimes here."

Pat scratched his chin. "That's a bit dicey."

She stared up at him. "I need this. You know me, I wouldn't ask if it wasn't important."

His gaze held hers. Then he smiled and looked ten years younger. "What the hell. I'm down to days here now and it's not like the bastards are gonna fire me for letting the ex-ADA review some of her old files, right? Besides, Ben isn't here now. Gone on vacation. So it'll be all right with the other guys in the—"

*Ben isn't here.*

Erin exhaled. One less worry. Because she'd sure been dreading seeing her ex-lover.

She still wasn't sure what to say to him. How to explain . . .

"Erin?"

Her head jerked. "Uh, thanks, Pat." She pointed toward the stairwell. "This way, Jude." Vince would be on duty. He was always on the day shift. He'd run the search for her, and they'd see what turned up.

The door slammed behind Jude, echoing hollowly. "Who is Ben?"

Her right foot came down too hard on the step.

"I saw your face when the cop mentioned him." A pause. "He's . . . something to you."

She turned to face him, slowly. "You caught any other shifter scents while you've been in the station?"

His brow wrinkled.

"Didn't think so." Her arms crossed. "You won't. The city's too small. Full of humans. Humans like Detective Ben Greer. Humans who don't realize what's really happening in this world."

"Ah . . . like that, is it?" But there was still something in his eyes and in the lines bracketing his mouth. Anger.

"The bastard after me—he shot Ben." Her left foot was tapping. With an effort, she managed to still its fast beat. "Cops on the scene thought it was a robbery gone wrong, but I *knew* it wasn't. The bastard left me one of his notes."

Always the damn notes.

"This Ben—you were seeing him, weren't you?"

Seeing him. Hoping to live a normal life with him. Even

thinking about the brick house and the stupid picket fence with him. "I was, until I realized that being with me wasn't safe for him." Not safe for many guys. But it had been easier with Ben. He'd been a good lover. She'd held tight to her control with him. So tight. He'd always been patient, and if he sensed she'd held back, he hadn't said anything.

Jude caged her with his body. The stairs put them at eye level. "I'm not real worried about being *safe*." His gaze searched hers.

Her stomach knotted. "Maybe you should be. You know this guy could set his sights on you, too."

The tiger's smile. "That's what I'm counting on, sweetheart. That's what I'm counting on."

And why he had kissed her so hard and deep back at her house. *Thought I heard something.* "You're playing a dangerous game."

He shrugged. "I know the rules and the risks—and I've always liked to play."

Yeah, she just bet he did.

His hand lifted and cupped her cheek. "Something I need to know, though."

His touch jolted her. Callused fingers should never have been so gentle. And his claws, just waiting below the surface. *I can do soft and easy.* "Wh-what's that?"

"You carrying a torch for the cop?"

The grated question had her mind going blank.

His eyes narrowed. "I won't be a stand-in, not for any damn one."

As if he could ever be. No, Jude was too strong, too *dominant*, for something like that. "I wanted to be with Ben." Wanted to fit in. To be loved. "But—"

"But what?" His thumb brushed over her mouth. Her eyes closed at that touch and heat streaked through her.

"But I knew, even before the attack, that we weren't going

to make it." She'd broken it off with him just days before the attack, but the bastard out there had still gone after him. Her eyes opened and she found Jude watching her with a predatory stare. "Ben had no clue about me." She swallowed. "Our relationship wasn't fair to him or to me. So I ended it." He'd wanted her to be someone that she wasn't. Someone that she could never be.

Someone normal.

"You got regrets about him?"

"Some." She'd be honest about that. "But what we had is over."

He flashed his fangs. "Good."

His mouth crashed onto hers.

Her hands flattened against his chest. Not normal—she wasn't, he wasn't.

But she was still pretending, dammit.

Jude would have to learn the truth about her sooner or later.

Maybe later . . . much later.

His breath panted when he raised his head. "Now let's go see what we can find out about the bastard."

Jude realized right away that the cops liked her. Respected her. It was in their eyes. On their faces. They opened their offices to her. Broke rules that they shouldn't have and they did it for her.

Jude and Erin poured over files. Searched databases. They looked for clues in the crimes that might have been overlooked. Links that weren't noticed.

They found jackshit.

At six o'clock that night, Jude leaned back in his chair, rubbing his eyes and stretching his back. As far as they could tell, the attacks by Erin's stalker had ended as soon as she left town.

The precinct had been a dead end for them.

Time to try *his* way.

"Here you go." A slim female cop with a long braid of red hair tossed a file onto the already overflowing desk. "Last info on the Trent case. Shame about the wife . . ."

"What?" Erin's brows snapped together. "What are you talking about, Wendy? What happened to the wife?"

"Ah . . ." Wendy shifted from her right foot to the left. "Thought you'd heard. Sylvia was the vic in a hit and run. The kids were with the grandmother at the time. Sylvia had just gone out for some groceries. She was walking across the street, headed back to her car when she got hit. Such a shame."

Erin grabbed the file and began flipping through the notes. "Yeah, it sure as hell is."

Jude waited until the cop shut the door, then asked, "Did you know her well?" She'd paled at the news of the woman's death. Her breath had caught.

She glanced up at him. "Donald Trent spent five years beating his wife whenever he wanted. *I* wanted to put the bastard away, but Sylvia recanted on the stand." A hard exhalation of air. "She had twins, two little boys, real cute kids." She licked her lips. "But the boys would jump anytime a door slammed or a voice was raised."

His hands clenched. Through Night Watch, he'd seen kids, human and *Other*, with shadows in their eyes—and it always pissed him off to know where those shadows came from. Whenever he could, he tried to make that fear go away.

Permanently.

"She didn't want him back." Erin was definite on that. "She had a new life going. She'd moved in with her mother. Filed for divorce. But he got to her. I know he did. Threatened her or the kids, and she changed her story so that he could walk." Her gaze fell to the folder. "Now she's dead."

And the kids would grow up without a mother and with a piss-poor excuse for a father.

"She's dead and"—her brow furrowed—"and the kids are living with her mother because"—she glanced back up at him—"because Donald Trent has been missing for the last two months."

Well, well. The trip to the PD might be paying off, after all. They'd already figured the stalking began with the Trent case.

Maybe because the stalking had come from the asshole Trent? "You ever get a sense this guy was more than human?"

"I got a sense the jerk was *less* than human."

He reached for the file. Scanned the details available about Donald Trent. Age: forty-five. Height: Six-foot-three. Weight: one ninety. An ex-football player who'd busted his knee the first year in college. He'd bounced around after that, gotten into bar fights, racked up a few restraining orders from former girlfriends.

The guy liked to play rough. And he liked to hurt his ladies.

"You ever see any sign of this guy in Baton Rouge?"

A shake of her head. "You think Trent could be the one after me?"

Maybe. One way to find out. "Let's go see the grandmother."

"What? Why?"

"Because old Trent might have been able to hide his shifter scent, but he left his kids behind. They won't be so skilled at cloaking without dad around."

"I've been around the boys, I never noticed—"

"You said he might have been taking herbs to hide his scent." He'd heard of that before. Even used some herbs himself once on a case. "Could be he was feeding the kids the same herbs he was taking." He wouldn't overlook any possibility. "But with him gone . . ."

Their systems would be clean.

Erin grabbed her bag. "Let's go."

With him gone, no one would have been around to pump the kids up, and if they were hybrids, he'd know it on sight.

Or rather, on scent.

"They don't talk about their father. They never ask about him." Katherine LaShaun brushed away a stray lock of gray hair that had escaped from the bun at her neck. "It's Sylvia they talk about. They keep asking when she's coming home."

Erin glanced into the kitchen where the two boys were sitting at the table, pushing bright race cars back and forth. Jude stood over them, talking and smiling.

One of the boys—she'd never been able to tell Jake and Joseph apart—gave a loud laugh and revved his car.

"I'm glad the bastard is gone, and I hope he never comes back. These boys, *they're mine*. I know what he did to my Sylvia. He's not gonna get the chance to hurt my boys, too."

No, he wouldn't. "You're going to call that lawyer, right?" Erin had written down the name and number of the best child custody lawyer she knew. She'd given the slip of paper to Katherine. Just in case, *just in case*, Trent showed up again, she wanted to make sure Katherine and the boys were protected. Permanently.

Katherine gave a grim nod. "I just—I don't have much money."

"Don't worry about it. Larry does a lot of pro bono work." Larry Myers. He didn't handle many cases anymore, but she'd call him and tell him this one was important. His semi-retirement was built for cases like this.

"You sure I can trust him?"

"Yes." Larry had been the lawyer her father used all those years ago, when she'd first appeared on his doorstep.

*Is she coming back?* The question had been hers, as she watched her mother's taillights disappear into the darkness.

Her father—a stranger—had pulled her close. "I hope to God not."

Erin glanced back at the boys. She'd looked for her mother for so many days after that. Years. But her mother never came back.

Erin blinked, clearing vision gone foggy. Kids always got to her. They were so vulnerable. Too easily hurt.

"You okay?" Jude stood in front of her, eyes seeing too much.

Great. Just what she wanted. Him to see her as some kind of emotional wreck. "Fine. We should go. The boys need to eat their supper."

"Right." He offered his hand to Katherine. "Pleasure, ma'am."

She gave him a weak smile, and her gaze drifted back to her grandchildren.

Moments later, they were out of the house. Back in the heat and the darkness.

Erin waited until they were in Jude's truck, then asked, "Well?"

He shook his head. "Didn't catch a trace of shifter on 'em. You?"

"No." So much for that theory. But if Donald Trent wasn't the shifter after her—

"Trent pissed you off. Beat his wife. Was a general ass-hole who made the world a hell of a lot worse by living in it." He drummed his fingers on the steering wheel and glanced her way. "You went toe-to-toe with this guy in a courtroom."

Yes, she had. He'd threatened her. Screamed at her. Even had to be restrained by his lawyer once.

"Can't help but think . . . the last guy who went after you in court wound up left for dead."

She knew where this was going, dammit.

"Sure does make me wonder—if Trent isn't the perp, maybe he's the victim."

And in that case, Donald Trent wouldn't be making an appearance in that town again.

Another present? Hell.

And what about Sylvia? Had she been some twisted gift, too? She and Sylvia had fought that last day in court. In the hallway, where she'd thought they were away from prying eyes.

*"Why, Sylvia? Why the hell are you doing this? He'll walk, and he'll come after you."*

*"I don't have a choice!" Sylvia had screamed at her. "My life, not yours! You don't understand, you don't know—"*

Her forehead fell against the glass of the window.

An image of the two boys flashed before her eyes.

*Damn you, bastard—stop!*

# Chapter 12

The motel room was small. The bed was big. And Erin was close.

He'd never been good at resisting temptation, but, this time, he was gonna have to fucking try.

Jude clenched his back teeth and tried not to notice the way her breasts stretched the front of her blouse, urging the buttons to pop loose.

He'd been trying not to notice and so had all those cops at the precinct.

Seeing the other men eyeing his lady . . . well, his beast had been ready to attack.

"What's the next move?" she asked, kicking off her pumps and making her way to the bed.

The next move? Stripping her, spreading her out over that bed, driving deep and hard inside her sex.

Jude cleared his throat and glanced up at the ceiling. *A job.* The job came first.

Hell, she *was* the job. And as much as his dick would like to lead him around on this case, he had to focus.

And keep her safe.

"You're going to sleep, and I'm going to find out just what kind of paranormals rule this town."

The mattress squeaked when she sat down. "What? Jude, I told you, there aren't any supernaturals—"

"Ah, sweetheart, you're not the only *Other* here." Sure, the paranormals loved the big cities, but there were just *too many* of their kind. If you looked, you could find paranormals just about everywhere, and he *knew* there had to be more *Other* in this city—more vampires, shifters, demons.

To find them, you just needed to know exactly where to look.

"You were at the station with me, you saw the cops—"

"Yeah, none of 'em were shifters." Wouldn't have been vamps either. He'd never met a vamp cop. Vamps couldn't usually hold day jobs. They just weren't cut out for it. They were stronger at night, so most of them just stayed shut in when the sun was up.

There could have been some demons on the force, though. Maybe one or two, but without Zane there to spot his own kind, Jude wouldn't see them.

"I worked with those cops for years." She shook her head. Her dark hair gleamed. "I never saw *anything* that made me think they weren't humans."

He shrugged. "Maybe they were all human, but, see, the problem is, you're looking at this situation all wrong."

She blinked and a furrow appeared between her brows. "Uh, I am?"

"Yeah." That top button would be popping soon. Hell, he could use one claw and have it off in less than a second.

Then he could see those perfect breasts, with the pink nipples that were so sweet.

*Focus.*

He looked back up at her eyes. "You were looking for a supernatural to help you. In a town this size, you've got to realize, not all paranormals will be the good guys."

"So I found out."

Right. "I'm not gonna look for the good guys tonight." Hunting the bastards was always easier. "I'm gonna go out, rattle some cages, break open some coffins, and see what the hell shakes loose."

"You—you really think you can come into this town, knowing *nothing* about the place, and find *Other?*"

He flashed her a smile. "One of my talents, sweetheart." It was all in knowing where to look. He hadn't worked his way up the food chain at Night Watch by not knowing his cesspools.

Walking on the dark side was old hat to him. He knew, better than most, just how deadly the beast inside could be.

White tigers . . . rare. So very rare. Because they had an unfortunate reputation and an appetite for death. Other people's.

Erin didn't know that about the tigers. If she did, she would be running away from him as fast as she could.

And she thought a wolf was bad.

"Stay here," he ordered, turning away. "I'll be back before dawn." Not much use hunting in the daylight. The creatures he wanted lived by darkness.

So did he, most of the time.

"I want to come with you."

He froze, hand poised above the door knob. Hell. Hadn't she seen enough at Delaney's? Much more and—

She wouldn't want him near her. Wouldn't want him touching her. Kissing her. Taking her.

Wouldn't want him in the same room, much less the same bed.

Not when she saw just what he could become.

Had become, so long ago.

*No, no, I won't lose control again.*

There was more to this world than blood and screams and claws and death.

There was—

"Jude?"

*Her.*

"You don't need to see"—*what I do*—"the bastards out there. Where I'm going would be hell to most humans." He always knew just how to get to hell.

*Like to like.*

"I'm not human."

He glanced back at her. She'd risen from the bed and put her shoes on again. Her lips were pale and plump.

"I can handle a few interrogations." Her smile was twisted. "I've seen my share, you know."

No, she hadn't. Not his way.

But he didn't want to leave her in the hotel. Didn't want her to be alone, not with that freak out there.

*Freak—and what am I?*

So fucking be it. "When the blood starts pouring, just stand back, got me? Don't interfere and don't try to stop me."

Her eyes widened. "What are you—"

"I'll do what has to be done." Always did. "No innocents will be hurt." His one rule. "Just . . . stand back, okay?" *Don't try to stop me.*

*And, hell . . . don't fear me.*

He wouldn't cross the line. Hadn't, in years.

Because the one time he had lost control, the beast had run wild.

* * *

The guy was looking for a hooker.

Erin sat beside Jude, her lips pressed together, as he cruised down the strip she'd never visited.

Oh, she knew this particular strip was there. It just hadn't been on her list of places to visit in Lillian.

"Uh . . . can we go over this plan again?" Because the fist in her stomach told her this was a bad idea. Very bad.

Searching for a hooker with her lover. Um, not really her thing.

But Jude didn't even seem to be listening to her. His gaze was on a blonde. A woman with long hair, the shortest skirt Erin had ever seen, and legs clad in fishnet stockings.

*Fishnets? Seriously?* She'd thought that was just some kind of really lame-ass stereotype, but no, the lady was strutting in her fishnets.

The blonde led the guy with the thinning hair—the guy who'd just hurried out of his car and run to her—into the mouth of the nearby alley.

Jude shoved open his door.

"What are you doing? Jude—"

"She's feeding. Come on!"

*Feeding?* Was that really the right word for it? Erin unhooked her seatbelt and bolted after him. Her stupid shoes didn't make for the easiest of runs, but she kept up with him, snaking across the street and into the alley that reeked with the stench of garbage and sewage and hell knew what else and—

And the john was on the ground, head twisted to the side. The blonde was over him, her mouth working on his neck even as her fingers shoved into the front of his jeans.

Erin's head jerked to the right. She *really* didn't need to see this scene. Watching others screw wasn't her idea of a good time.

"So what, drinking from the idiot isn't enough? You're robbing him, too?"

Now *that* had her gaze flying back toward the couple on the ground.

The blonde's head snapped up and she glared at them with—was that blood dripping down her chin?

The guy on the ground gave a weak moan and whispered. "Don't . . . stop . . . don't—"

"Get out of here!" the woman screamed, her barely covered breasts heaving. Erin noticed that the hooker had the guy's wallet in her right hand. Ah. So *that* was what she'd been looking for in his pants.

Jude took a step forward and a rat raced across the alley.

*Not my kind of place.* Erin braced her legs apart and tried to look like she wasn't in the middle of hell.

The woman swiped her hand over the back of her mouth, leaving a red swatch on her chin. "Unless you're a cop, you ain't got no business—"

Jude growled. A low, menacing rumble that wasn't human. Not even close.

The woman rocked back, eyes widening. "Wh-wh—"

*"Don't stop!"* A fierce cry from the man. His eyes were open, but he didn't seem to be staring at anything. Erin wasn't even sure he'd noticed them.

The woman's lips peeled back, and Erin caught sight of her teeth.

Fangs.

Vampire?

The hooker shifted, moving like a snake on the ground as she sized them up and put her prey between them.

Her eyes—why hadn't Erin noticed the woman's eyes before? They were black. A vamp in hunting mode.

Erin's breath jerked out. She'd only ever seen two vampires—*okay, three now*—in her life. The assholes she'd seen before had done nothing to make her like the bloodsuckers, or even to have vague semi-warm feelings for them.

The first guy had jumped her in a park when she'd been in New Orleans. Her first week in the city. She'd broken his nose, possibly given him a concussion, then she'd run like hell.

And she'd run right into another vamp. The two had been some kind of sick team. Caging in their prey.

They'd picked the wrong prey.

That guy had gotten tossed ten feet. By the time he'd gotten up, she'd been gone.

But Erin had never forgotten their eyes or the stench of death that clung to them like a second skin.

"Come closer, and I'll kill him," the blonde grated, lifting her claws over the man's throat.

Erin believed her. One swipe would be all that was needed to cut open his jugular and—

Jude lunged forward. He grabbed the man's arm and jerked him away from the vamp in a lightning fast move. The vamp's claws raked across the john's neck and shoulders, drawing blood and eliciting screams from him.

Jude snapped, "Shut the hell up!" Then he shoved the guy away from him and away from the rising vampire.

The man's eyes were finally open and *aware*. He raised a trembling hand to his throat and touched the trickling blood. His saucer-sized eyes stared first at Jude, then the vamp. After a few stunned seconds, he turned and ran.

"Now what are you gonna do?" Jude put his hands on his hips and sized up the vampire. " 'Cause I doubt you're gonna be able to take me." Erin saw that his claws were out. "But, just for fun, why don't you come and try?"

Well, damn.

So much for using the victim.

The vamp's chin lifted and her eyes narrowed. "You know how hard it is to find a donor in this city? One who *likes* the bite?"

A donor. Nice way of putting it.

"Do I look like I give a shit?" Jude demanded. "Besides, I get the feeling you don't care if your donors are willing or not."

A smile from the vamp. One that probably would have been pretty, if the woman hadn't been flashing bloodstained fangs. "No, I don't." Then her gaze shot to Erin.

Hell.

That toothy grin widened. "Hello, there."

Jude's hands flew up, and those claws were wicked sharp. "I don't have much use for vamps, so let's make this short."

"Umm . . . and I don't have much use for shifters." Her gaze was still on Erin. "Even those who bring me pretty presents."

Pretty what? *Presents*? And why had the blood ho been looking at her when she said that?

"She's not for you." Jude moved a bit to the right, putting himself between Erin and the vamp.

"Oh?" The woman's voice was low, taunting. "And I'm to think she's for you? Humans don't go for shifters. Everyone knows that. They hate the beasts in you."

Jude just shook his head. "I don't have time for this shit." He flew toward her. Seriously seemed to fly although Erin knew he had to have jumped or—or something. His hand locked around the vampire's throat, and he lifted her up into the air. Her feet kicked out at him, her claws ripped at the flesh on his arms, but he didn't even flinch. "I need information."

She stilled, her claws buried in his arms. "And I need you"—she spat at him—"to get the fuck off my street!"

His fingers tightened.

She laughed. "Can't . . . kill me . . . this way." Her voice was hushed, broken, but her lips were still twisted in a smile.

Erin stepped forward. No, this wasn't what she wanted, there had to be—

Jude lifted the vamp higher, then threw her back.

*"Jude!"*

The vamp twisted in midair, and landed easily, too easily on her feet. Then she charged, running fast for her prey.

Not Jude.

*Me.*

Jude snarled and reached for the vamp, but she struck out, swiping her claws over his chest and arms and sliding right through his grasp. She came toward Erin, laughing, mouth wide, fangs bared, eyes too dark and—

Erin punched her as hard as she could, right in the face, aiming for that wide, gaping mouth and those freakishly long fangs. There was a crunch, then a crack, and something flew to the ground.

Then the vampire fell backward, hard.

Before she could rise, Jude was there, crouched over her, his claws at her throat. "Never said she was human," he murmured.

The vamp stared at Erin in horror. There was more blood on the vamp's mouth now. No, more blood *coming* from her mouth.

Erin glanced down at the broken cement. What was that? Was it a—

*"My tooth!"* At least, that's what Erin thought the vampire said. It was a bit hard to understand her.

"It's not like it won't grow back." Jude's voice was mild.

The vamp heaved against him, but his hold was unbreakable. Erin glanced around the alley, then back at them, worried someone else would come by.

"But your head, now that's a different matter." His smile sent a shiver through Erin. "That won't be growing back once it's cut off. And if you don't answer my questions, fast, well, I'll just have to start using my claws."

Erin tensed. He could do it. The surefire way to kill a vamp was to take off the head. A tiger's claws could cut through bone and muscle so easily.

*No.* They hadn't come to kill. Just to get information.

*I don't hurt innocents.* His words drifted through her mind. No way could the vamp count as innocent.

How long had she been in the city? Taking her donors—willing and not? How long?

*And I never knew.*

No, she hadn't wanted to know. She'd been working her cases, taking down the humans who broke the law, thinking she was safe in her little town. Far away from the *Other*.

She'd been so wrong. Dead wrong.

"I'm looking for a wolf shifter."

The vamp froze beneath him.

Her eyes gave her away instantly.

"You know where the wolf is, don't you?" His claws broke the skin of her neck, just a bit. Blood welled.

"You . . . don't want to . . . find the wolf." The vamp pulled her head back, trying to ease away from those claws. "Kill . . . you."

"Yeah, well, don't worry about me. I think I'll be just fine." He leaned in a bit closer. "While you—you're gonna find it real hard to keep bloodsucking without a head."

That would be a challenge. Erin cleared her throat. "Jude . . ." She wasn't going to let him do this. Couldn't let him.

"*My* rules, Erin, remember?" He didn't glance her way. The air in the alley was thick and hot and sweat trickled down her back.

"Mort's Bar! S-seen the wolf . . . last Saturday."

Mort's Bar. Erin's breath rushed out. She knew the place. The owner, Jacques, was old-school Cajun. And *Mort* . . . that meant death.

"Guess you get to keep your head." Jude rose slowly, keeping his eyes trained on the woman.

"*Asshole!*" She scrambled to her feet. Her hand rose to her mouth and she touched the hole that had been her right fang. "*Bitch!*"

Erin stared back at her. The blood ho had been trying to attack her. Defending herself had been the only option.

"I hope the wolf . . . rips you apart!" Screamed at them. Then she was gone, bounding toward the back of the alley. Disappearing into the shadows.

Erin finally took a deep breath and tasted shit.

She choked back her gag.

"Come on," Jude ordered. "Let's get out of here."

Yes, that sounded like a great plan to her.

Jude slammed the door to the motel room. He threw the lock and waited for Erin to pounce.

But she didn't pounce. Didn't glance his way. Didn't speak.

Same routine she'd had in the car.

*Hell, I let the vamp live. Shouldn't that count for something?*

"Erin."

She jumped. *Jumped.* She'd been the one to knock the vamp's tooth out, and, he was pretty sure she'd broken the blonde's jaw.

The lady had a killer right hook.

He'd remember that.

"I—it's late." Said without looking at him. But, yeah, it was late.

Hitting close to three a.m. late. It had taken him forever to find a working girl he *thought* might be a vamp.

Same rules, different city. Vamps liked to get their prey in the easiest possible way.

Sex worked. Always had. Always would.

While the men were getting ready, so busy fantasizing and stroking their dicks, the vamps locked those teeth on 'em and took.

Some humans liked the pain of the bite.

Some were scared shitless.

Some fought. Some died.

Vamps didn't usually care, no matter what the victim did.

Erin's fingers rose to the front of her shirt and fumbled with the buttons.

Jude swallowed. Okay. She was stripping. Right in front of him. He could see the edge of her bra, dark blue. So if she was stripping here instead of heading to the bathroom, she *wanted* him to look and that meant—

Her fingers paused and she glanced up at him. The woman totally froze him with her stare.

*It meant jackshit.*

"You're a hard man, Jude Donovan. Dark—darker inside than I realized."

A slow rage began to simmer in his veins. He took a step toward her, then another. His hands fisted. "I'm not a man, sweetheart. You can't make that mistake with me."

Her lips parted. Pale and moist and he could see the tip of her tongue.

The beast inside lunged against his leash.

Maybe he'd let the tiger go. Show her how *dark* he really was.

"You've killed, haven't you, Jude?" The top two buttons on her shirt were undone, but the striptease seemed to be over.

And the interrogation had begun.

He hadn't lied to her yet. Wouldn't start now. So he kept his eyes on hers, didn't look at those sweet breasts, and left the leash in place, for now.

"Hell, yeah, I have." And to protect himself, or her, he'd do it again. In a heartbeat. "Want to know how old I was the first time? Want to know how I did it? Want to know who I—"

She turned away from him, and he clenched his jaw, biting back the words. *What the fuck did she want?* She *knew* what he was. She'd seen everything. Every fucking thing.

Man to beast.

She hadn't run. She'd turned to him. Taken him after the brutal shift. But now, because he'd gotten rough with the undead scum *in order to help her*, Erin was acting like he wasn't good enough for her.

*Because maybe I'm not.*

He hadn't told her about his folks. Not yet. With that asshole after her, he just hadn't wanted to—

*Make her run.*

*Make her fear me.*

"I want to be normal." A whisper that he could hear all too easily. "I want a normal life, normal—"

He lunged across the room. Grabbed her elbow and spun her back around. He was afraid, very afraid, that her next word would be—

Lover.

*I want a normal lover.*

He sure didn't fit that bill. "You're not normal. You're damn better than normal. Normal isn't for us. Fire, lust, the power of the beast—*that's* for us. Ball games and barbecues aren't our cup of tea."

She didn't blink. Just stared up at him, her gaze stark.

He fought to pull back the fury. Because she was slipping away.

Standing right in front of him, but slipping away.

*No.*

"I've killed, and if it comes to it, I'll kill again. My job's not easy." Hunting freaks like Burrows sure wasn't easy, and he had the scars to prove it. But someone had to do the dirty, bloody work. He'd been born stronger than others so hunting, yeah, he could do it. Sometimes, he needed to do it. "And yes, there's *darkness* in me, but, sweetheart, that same darkness is in you."

He'd seen it from the beginning.

Her lashes lowered.

Then, softly, she said, "I know." She looked up at him again. "That's what scares me."

What?

Her hands lifted to his chest and he felt the sting of her claws press into his flesh.

"Erin, what are you—"

She rose on her toes and kissed him. Not an easy kiss. Hard and fierce, bruising in its strength.

The tiger jerked free of his leash.

They fell onto the bed. Hands ripping, fighting the clothing. Mouths taking. Hearts pounding.

He tossed her bra across the room, then caught her breasts in his hands. The nipples were tight and hard and when his fingers plucked them, she moaned into his mouth.

*Fuck.*

He pushed her onto her back and took her breast in his

mouth. Jude sucked and licked and bit and had her arching off the bed toward him. The scent of her rich cream flooded his nostrils and the drumming beat of his heart just grew louder in his ears.

Her claws raked down his back.

His shirt was gone—hell knew where.

He caught the waistband of her skirt and yanked it down, jerking her panties away at the same time.

*My turn.*

Jude shoved her thighs apart. He eyed the ripe flesh just waiting for him. Dark pink, plump, glistening and—

He put his mouth on her. Jude swiped his tongue over the button of her need, got that taste of sweet and tangy cream and wanted more.

So he took more.

Her hips slammed up toward him as he drove his tongue inside of her. She came against his mouth, shuddering, legs trembling around him, but he didn't stop.

No, he wasn't even close to stopping.

*More. More.*

Lips and tongue took. Learned every curve. Every secret. Drank up her taste and had her twisting against him.

"Jude! *Jude!*"

His head lifted and his tongue snaked over his lips. Damn but she was beautiful.

Spread and open, ready for him.

She might not be his forever, but he'd take her for as long as she'd let him.

"Roll over." Guttural.

He heard the rasp of her breath. The hitch that could have been fear or hesitation, but he also caught the surge of her arousal. The thickening of that rich scent in the air.

One thigh lifted over him and she rolled onto her stomach.

"No, like this." He caught her waist, lifted her up onto her knees. That perfect heart-shaped ass stared him right in the face.

*Damn.*

Her palms pressed into the mattress and she rose up, glancing back over her shoulder. "*Now.*"

Yeah, oh, yeah, now.

He gripped his cock in one hand. Pushed the head toward the gleaming entrance of her sex. Sank deep.

This time, he was the one to moan.

She gripped him, squeezing so tight he thought he'd go *insane* and he withdrew, only to thrust deep again.

Even as she slammed back against him.

The rhythm was wild, unsteady. Deep and hard. Sweat slickened his body and the bed sagged beneath them.

*Thrust.* Her ass was so soft and round.

*Thrust.* She gripped him so tight. *Fuck!*

*Thrust.* His. She was his.

The release barreled through him, a white-hot burst of pleasure that rocked every cell in his body.

He moved by instinct. Jude clamped his mouth over her right shoulder. That sweet, sweet curve near her neck. Pleasure spot.

And he bit.

Her sex contracted around him as she came.

The power of his release seemed to double. Emotions flooded through him. Needs. Whispers of longings he'd buried years ago.

*Erin.*

He held her tight, held her wrapped in his arms and rode out the fury of the climax.

She sagged against him, and he kissed her flesh.

*Mate.*

The word trembled through his mind. No, no, that wasn't possible. The sex was great, but there was no way she could be a mate for him.

She turned her head, looking back over her shoulder at him, and her eyes were sleepy and satiated.

Mate.

Hell.

Talk about a case of seriously screwed up bad timing.

*Fate, you bitch.*

# Chapter 13

"Why did you join Night Watch?" Her quiet voice pierced the silence that had hung so thickly in the room. Her hand was on his chest, right above his heart. The sheet curved around her, hiding her hips and breasts, revealing a hint of the flesh along her side.

At her words, he tensed. He'd known he'd have to tell her. Sooner or later.

He'd just wanted the later part.

"Jude?"

He brought her hand to his lips. Kissed the palm. "Dawn's coming. We need to catch a few hours of sleep before going back to the station." There'd be more files to search. Witnesses to question.

Then, when the darkness fell, they'd get the wolf.

"I want to know about you."

He turned his head, just a bit, and met her stare. He could see her so well, even in the darkness.

"There's more to you than you let the world see."

More than being a hunter.

A killer.

"Hate to tell you, sweetheart, but there's not." The words were cold and distant, but he couldn't make himself let go of her hand.

Her eyes narrowed, but she repeated, "Why'd you join?"

*Mate.*

Okay, so the beast inside had recognized her. It was the way with his kind. The animals could recognize potential mates. It was a physical thing. Genetics.

Mates could produce children. Shifters couldn't reproduce with just anyone. Their genetics were too complicated for that.

But the animals knew . . . they always knew.

It was survival of the fittest kicking in. The beasts inside were sure all about surviving. Propagating the species.

But just because someone was your mate didn't mean you loved them. Or that they loved you.

His parents were proof of that.

And proof of just how screwed up and twisted the world could be.

*When I tell her, she won't let me touch her again. She'll fear me, just like she fears that bastard out there.*

Her stare was so steady. Her body so soft and warm against his.

*Lie.* The whisper came from deep inside. He could invent some sob story for her. Get her to keep trusting him. Get her to keep giving him that beautiful body.

Her fingers moved in the smallest of caresses against his heart.

*Can't lie to her.* Not her.

"I joined Night Watch because the tiger needed prey." Staying in control—when he wanted to hunt and fight every day, when the tiger wanted to roar and bite and claw—had been pushing him to the very edge of his sanity.

Night Watch had been, *was* his release. "I know just how dangerous the *Other* are in this world. I know that humans can't handle them. They don't have a clue. And the bastards that cross the line, the ones that torture humans and kill 'em . . . they have to be stopped." He knew too well the nature of the beasts hidden inside the façade of men. Too well.

"The men I've hunted"—mostly paranormals, though he'd been sent after a human or two in his time—"you don't want to know what they've done." Even he'd had nightmares. "I stopped them. I made a difference." When he hadn't been able to before. "You might not like my methods, but I get the job done." Period.

"Making a difference . . . that's important to you?"

*You can't change the past, boy. You got to look to the future.* His grandfather's words. Hard with grief. He'd been twelve that day. And he hadn't really understood what his grandfather meant.

But he did now. "Yeah, it's important to me." He inhaled, catching her scent and the lingering fragrance of sex in the air. Not the best time to tell her, but, hell, when was there ever a good time to say something like this? "Erin, my parents . . . there's something you need to know about them."

A frown pulled her brows low, and she eased to a sitting position beside him, dragging that damn sheet up with her. "What is it?"

Trust. He'd give her all of his. For the first time in his whole damn life.

*Can't look into those eyes and keep the truth back.* "They were mates."

A faint smile curled her lips. "Well, they would have had to be or you wouldn't be here."

True. But . . . "My mom didn't love my father." He'd

known. Always felt the coldness there. But he'd seen the heat in his father's stare every time he looked at her. "He was crazy about my mother though." Crazy. Good word.

Hell. It was hard to tell this story with her watching him with those big, golden eyes. Hard to speak when he was scared spitless that his words would send her running away.

*Not just one screwed-up asshole in her life—two.*

"This story doesn't have a happy ending, does it?" Quiet, tense. Her knuckles had whitened around the sheet.

He gave a hard shake of his head. If only . . . "Most of the talk in the *Other* world about the shifters who go fucking psycho, well, it's about the wolves."

She tensed a bit. "Did a . . . wolf do something to your family?" Her voice seemed stilted.

"No." The wolves had hurt plenty of others, but not him. "The Lones are the wolves you know to avoid. For tigers, we have our own twisted assholes who love to kill."

"Ferals." A whisper.

They were rare, luckily, but every now and then, a tiger shifter gave into the bloodlust of the beast. When he did—and it was always a male, no one knew quite why—the hunger took him over. The only way to stop a Feral was to put him down.

"My mom didn't love my dad. Never did." Matings couldn't force feelings. Nature didn't work that way. "One day, she told him she was leaving him. She fell for a human. She wanted to start a life with him, and she wanted to take me with her." His mother had loved him. He knew that. Never doubted it for even a single moment.

His grandfather wouldn't let him doubt it.

"I could see the pain in my dad's eyes, but what could he do? Not like you can make a tiger stay." Not when the tiger wanted to be free, and his dad had loved his mother enough to let her go. "She went to the human. She was going to send for me as soon as she was settled but—"

But she'd never gotten settled, and he'd never seen her again.

He glanced away from Erin's eyes. Had to. "A Feral attacked her human. She jumped in to try and save him—and the Feral killed them both."

Jude heard the swift inhalation of her breath. He didn't look back at her. Not yet. This screwed-up story, on top of the hell that bastard was putting her through—

*Oh, yeah, she'll be running. Moving that sweet ass as fast as she can, dammit.*

But she deserved the truth from him. Especially if the beast inside was right.

"When my dad found out, he broke." No other word for it. His father had shattered before him. "Blamed himself. He thought if he'd just been able to make my mother love him, she would have lived."

"You can't make someone love you."

No, you couldn't. His father had even told him those same words the night his mother left to join the human, but the grief had wrecked his mind.

His father loved his mother so much that when she slipped from the world, he'd seemed to slip away, too. "He went after the Feral."

Her hands reached for his. She unfurled the fingers he'd clenched. Lightly traced the marks made by his growing claws.

Jude took a breath and caught her scent. He closed his eyes. "He never made it back from the hunt."

His grief had made him weak, and the Feral had been too strong.

Silence.

Too heavy. Too thick.

His father had been too consumed with rage and grief.

And his old man had left him alone. With the same rage and grief gnawing at his soul.

An image of those twin boys flashed before him. When he'd seen those boys tonight, he'd seen himself.

"*When's Mom coming back?*" Stupid. He'd been twelve. He knew about death. Fucking knew. But he'd asked and asked Grandpa Joe. "*Where's Dad?*"

Asked and asked.

And broken when his parents never came home and he saw those coffins days later. His mother's wooden coffin had been covered with red roses.

Because she'd loved red roses, too. Just like Erin.

*Just like Erin.*

"How old were you?"

He flinched at her voice. "Twelve."

"Where did you go?"

Not the questions he'd anticipated. "My grandpa Joe—my mom's dad—took me in." Grandpa Joe had been his anchor, and when he'd finally let loose his own grief and rage, his grandpa had been there.

"What—what happened to the Feral?"

This was the part Jude dreaded. His eyes were on her hands. So delicate next to his. "When I turned twenty-one, Grandpa Joe died." There'd been no one to hold him back then. No one to grieve, in case he failed. "The next day, I started hunting."

And he hadn't stopped until he'd found his prey. "I hunted the bastard down and I ripped out his throat." The blood had been hot on his tongue. The tiger had been so very thirsty. "I found out I was good at hunting." At killing. Too good.

"That's why you ended up with Night Watch."

His gaze lifted to her face. "Yeah. Pak heard about me. I'd shoved my way deep into the *Other* world." It had taken months, but he'd tracked the bastard. "Pak offered me a job." An outlet for the rage the guy had still seen brewing beneath his surface.

"Why'd you take the job?"

Huh. Again, not the question he'd thought she'd have. "Because the tiger's always been fighting his leash and hunting satisfies him." *Me.*

She didn't speak. Was she afraid now? Did she think he was a twisted freak like that asshole after her?

A revenge kill. Yeah, not something nice and orderly. Not something the good guy was supposed to do.

But he'd never told her he was good. There were dark places in him. So damn dark.

That's why he was so good at his job. It was easy to hunt the sick freaks when you could think like them.

"Don't be afraid of me." The words were ripped from him. They came out as a demand, instead of the plea they should have been. "I swear, Erin, I'm not like the asshole out there. I would never, *never* hurt you."

More silence.

He turned away. Jumped from the bed. "I-I'll—" What? What was he going to do? He couldn't leave her, not with that prick out there. He couldn't—

"Why did you tell me this?"

His head jerked back toward her. She'd risen from the bed and was walking toward him. "Because I wanted only truth between us. You deserved to know." She'd taken him into her body so sweetly. Given him so much.

Trust—he'd given it to her.

She knew his darkest secret now. His darkest shame.

The next move was hers.

She stopped in front of him. Her hand lifted and stroked his cheek. Then her arms wrapped around him, and she held him close.

And he held her tighter than he'd ever held anything in his life.

The bastard was in the motel with her. Touching her. Kissing her. Taking her.

Did Erin really think that cat would keep her safe?

Or was this to punish him? Was she angry with him? Hadn't he shown her how much he cared for her?

That he'd do anything for her?

*Anything.*

She'd gone to the Trent house. He knew it. She'd seen those kids.

Did she know what he'd done? *For her.* Always.

Maybe she'd wanted that kill for herself. Maybe that's why she was with the hunter. She was angry—

No, no, he couldn't have that.

She had to understand that the kill had been for *her*.

He yanked out his cell phone. Punched in the numbers for 911. Yes, yes, this was the easiest route. They'd report his call, but they wouldn't be able to trace him. Not with a disposable cell like the one he'd picked up hours before.

The call was answered on the second ring.

"911. What is the nature of your emergency?"

"Tell Detective Benjamin Greer that he can find Donald Trent's body buried in the woods behind Trent's mother-in-law's place."

"*What?* Wh—who is this*?"*

He pressed the small button on the cell, ending the call.

When Erin found out exactly what he'd done, she'd appreciate him again. After all, he'd returned Donald to his boys. To his family.

"For you," he whispered, and turned away from the hotel window.

The next day, Jude worked beside Erin, digging into case files she'd snagged from her old office. *Good thing the DA was slow as hell about reassigning cases and cleaning up paperwork.*

They were in the old Lillian government building, home of the District Attorney's office, and the files were spread around them. Jude still thought there was a link to the crimes somewhere but she—

She didn't know what was happening.

Erin snuck a glance at him. Last night, he'd pulled away after his confession. She'd tried to reach out to him, but, she'd hesitated.

Because his story had scared her. To know that he could kill so easily. *Had* killed so easily.

Two men in her life. One who swore she was his mate—and he was killing for her.

The other man—*her lover*—with a past bloodier than her own.

But at least Jude wasn't claiming to be her mate.

What should she say? She knew he wouldn't hurt her. Maybe she should just start with that. As for the darkness inside him—

*Like to like.*

Who the hell was she to judge?

"*Erin Jerome*?"

The deep voice, rich with surprise, had her tensing.

Jude shot to his feet and turned to face the door.

A man stood there, tall, with broad shoulders, his black hair graying just a hint at the temples. He wore a gray suit, not his usual long, black enveloping judge's robe.

*Because they weren't in court. Because it was a Saturday and they were in the bowels of the pit and I sure didn't expect to see—* "Judge Harper?"

He smiled at her, but then flashed a worried glance Jude's way. "Ah, I . . . didn't realize you were back with us."

She stepped forward. "I'm not. Just finishing up some old business." True enough.

Judge Lance Harper. The judge with a reputation for playing with the ladies. The judge with three ex-wives. The judge with the giant house on Blakely Road.

The judge who'd let Donald Trent walk.

He was the judge she and a half dozen cops suspected was on the take. Because Harper let too many criminals walk from his court.

Too many bastards like Trent.

His handsome face turned solemn. "If you're reviewing your files, then you know about . . . Sylvia."

Her eyes narrowed. What was that? Regret? Did the guy feel *guilty* about what had happened?

She sure did. "Yes, I know."

"Pity." He sounded like he meant it. Where had his pity been when he'd let Trent walk? "I remember she had those two boys . . ."

Jude straightened his shoulders. He had at least three inches on the judge and a good forty pounds. "The boys are being taken care of."

Harper blinked. "I'm sorry. Are you the new ADA?"

"No." A growl. His gaze raked the older man. Harper was in his early fifties but the guy could have passed for forty. All those gym memberships she'd heard about.

Brown eyes narrowed. "Then who are you?"

Erin grabbed Jude's hand. "He's with me." That was really all the judge needed to know.

Arrogant ass. She'd always hated going into his court. She'd made a point of wearing her longest skirts and her most concealing blouses.

*Hot Harper* might have been a favorite with some of the other female lawyers, but no way had she ever wanted to be considered for wife position number four.

"Ah . . . I see." Harper blinked. "Does Cartwright know you're down here?"

District Attorney Kent Cartwright. "Yes. He knows." Kent had been the one to help her get the job in Baton Rouge. He'd also been the guy Jude grilled for half an hour that morning. Kent swore he hadn't told anyone where she went, and Erin was inclined to believe him. His responses had been too genuine.

"And why are you down here, Judge?" The demand came from Jude, but it was a question also on the tip of Erin's tongue. Being in the basement was on par with slumming for Harper.

And on a Saturday?

His lips thinned. "I was . . . planning to meet an associate here. To discuss a private matter."

Oh, yes. Right. Ten to one odds said the associate was a female.

A most likely *married* female if they were meeting in the basement, far away from prying eyes.

"Erin!" Cartwright's sharp voice. He shouldered into the room, casting a quick, somewhat bemused stare at Harper. "Erin, I just got a call from the PD, thought you'd want to know . . ."

*Not good. Couldn't be good.*

"A tip came in last night." The tiny room was too crowded. "The caller said he knew where Donald Trent's body was buried."

The air seemed to leave her body in a hard rush.

Her eyes locked on Cartwright. The DA was just a few years older than she was. He had a politician's open face. Light brown hair. Worried blue eyes.

Good old Kent. *He hadn't given her secrets away.* No, not him.

"Where?" The question was soft.

His lips thinned. "According to the tapes from 911 . . . the body is in the woods behind Katherine LaShaun's place."

*Sonofabitch.*

She slammed the files closed. Jude was already moving, shoving past the other two men. Clearing her way.

He was real good at clearing the way.

Erin hurried into the hall. Rounded a sharp corner behind Jude and—

Smacked right into Lacy Davis. A clerk in the DA's office. Friendly, flirty, *married* Lacy.

The woman grunted and stumbled. "Erin?" Her eyes, dark green, widened. "When did you get back in town?" Her gaze drifted over Erin's shoulders and a red flush stained her cheeks. "J-Judge H-Harper, what are you doing here? I thought you'd—"

She did not have time for this. Jude stood next to the elevator, holding the doors open and waiting for her. Great. "Got to go, Lacy, we'll catch up"—not really, they'd never been close—"later."

She hurried forward, heart racing. Donald Trent's body? Oh, hell.

"Not so fast, Jerome."

Kent's voice. The hard and sharp tone that he usually just delivered in court.

She glanced back at him. She saw the judge reach for Lacy's hand. He leaned in close and murmured something to her. Erin's jaw locked and she gritted, "Kent, if they found his body—"

He slanted a quick glance over at the judge, then stalked to her side. "You don't work for me anymore," he said, softer now. Probably so the judge wouldn't overhear. Like that guy was paying them any attention now. "You can't go storming onto a crime scene."

"But it was *my* case." Still was, if he only knew what was really happening.

"*Was*," he threw back at her. "It's just mine now." His shoulders straightened. "I always liked you, Erin." A gentleness in his eyes. Flashed there so briefly. "You're tough, smart, but my favors for you end here. You don't work for me anymore," he said again. "And I can't let you interfere with an investigation."

Hell. The damn thing was—he was right. No way should she be at a crime scene. But she *needed* to be at this one.

"Who is the detective on this?" Jude asked.

"Ben Greer. He's coming in early to handle things." Kent's stare bored into her. "You know he'll do this right."

Yes, and she also knew he wouldn't let her anywhere near the case, either. Erin gave a grudging nod.

Then the DA brushed by her. He caught the elevator Jude had kept for her and vanished behind the heavy metal doors.

Erin looked over her shoulder. The judge and Lacy were gone. They'd probably ducked into one of the rooms for a "meeting."

"They won't have anything for hours anyway," Jude said. "The cops will have to search the woods with dogs."

He was right.

"Then it'll take 'em time to dig up the body."

Her eyes closed. "What will it do to the boys?" They'd already been through enough.

A brief hesitation, then, "Call Katherine. Tell her to get the boys out of there—and to keep 'em out until this mess is over."

Erin's lashes lifted. "But that's against protocol—" She stopped. She didn't work for the Lillian DA any more. He'd just said so himself.

"Call her," Jude repeated, eyes intense. "Tell her to get the boys the hell out of there."

The cops would be on their way over to her place now. There wouldn't be much time.

"They don't need to see their old man's body dug up."

No, and they didn't need their only safe haven turned into hell right in front of their eyes.

Screw protocol. Not her case? Fuck it. Those boys were hers. She snatched out her cell phone. Dialed the number she'd memorized yesterday. When a woman's soft voice answered, she said, "Katherine, it's Erin Jerome. We don't have much time, and I need you to listen carefully . . ."

A line of motorcycles blocked the entrance to Mort's Bar. Pickups snaked and twisted, filling up the parking lot, and the blare of country music trembled in the air.

Erin slammed the door of Jude's truck and stared at the bar. Night had fallen, bathing the city in darkness. The thick darkness hid the sagging sides and the dipping roof of Mort's.

She'd been in this bar once before. A blind date that had gone to hell very fast.

Not her kind of place. Too loud. Too drunk. Too many men with free hands.

Gravel crunched beneath Jude's shoes. She glanced at

him when he rounded the front of the vehicle. "You think the vamp was telling the truth?" The guys in this place tended to run more toward the "good old boys" and not the paranormal predators.

Though she sure knew those good old boys could be predators, too.

"She was." He sounded absolutely certain.

Erin raised a brow.

"She knows if she lied, I'll just come back for her." A barring of his fangs. Damn, he already had his fangs out. This wasn't going to be a good night. "And if I do that, I won't be so nice."

Right. Because he'd been all goodness and light during that first showdown.

Her eyes darted back to the entrance. Smoke drifted lazily from the front door. Not a fire, just a shitload of folks with cigarettes, cigars, and who knew what else inside. Her hands balled into fists. "No sense standing around here all night. Let's go."

They started forward together. A loud wolf whistle split the air, and Jude froze. His gaze immediately tracked to the left, to the two men sitting on the back of a gray pickup truck. His growl vibrated in the air. "Don't make me come over there and kick the shit out of you."

The men jumped up and hurriedly ran into the shadows. Erin figured they weren't in the mood to lose their shit.

Jude spared her a glance. "I don't have time for assholes."

"Neither do I." But she smiled. Because Jude made her feel . . . aw, hell, he just made her *feel.*

A burly bouncer blocked the bar's door. "Twenty bucks." He didn't look up from his comic book.

Jude tossed him the cash and sauntered inside.

As soon as she crossed the threshold, the smoke got five times thicker. It flooded her nostrils, seeming to burn her nasal passages. What *was* that? Not cigarettes. This was stronger. Almost like incense but—

"Got us someone smart in here," Jude whispered, reaching for her hand and pulling her close as he surveyed the crowd. "Bastard's blocking all the scents with the kymine."

"What? Ky-kymine? What's—"

"A scent that fucks up a shifter's nose, that's what." His eyes swept the crowd again. "Vamps in the west came up with it a few years back. They use it to even up the hunting field."

Erin felt like she had to sneeze. She rubbed her nose, trying to stop the itch.

"Won't do you any good." He glanced up at the air vents. "Bet they're pumping it in from there."

Great. "So . . . they knew we were coming?" Not a good thought. Hell, she didn't even know who "they" were. The good old boys? The not so good old boys?

She inched a bit closer to Jude and felt the sting of her claws as they began to stretch beneath her skin. If they were in for a fight, she wanted to be ready. "You think the vamp sold us out?"

"Could be." He didn't sound particularly concerned. "Or maybe this isn't for us."

*The wolf.*

"If the bastard has been hunting here, the kymine could be for him." A man in an oversized cowboy hat and his giggling girlfriend staggered past them. "It'd explain how the vamp knew he was here."

Yes, it would. Erin breathed slowly through her mouth. If she didn't use her nose, didn't move it at all, she'd be fine.

Maybe.

"So what do we do next?"

"Well . . ." He steered her away from the door. *So much*

*for not moving.* Jude didn't stop advancing until his back was against the wall and he had a good view of the crowd. "We can march up to the bar and announce that we're here for the wolf."

She eyed the bar. It was surrounded by men with thick stomachs and big arms, and the women with them—short skirts and give-em-hell grins.

How would that conversation go? *Hi. We're looking for a werewolf.* Um, no. "What else can we do?"

He turned to her. Winked. "Got a little voyeur in you?"

"*What?*"

"I can't hunt in here, and neither can he. But outside . . . that's fair game." He pointed to an exit in the back. A rounded ceiling led the way to darkness. A couple, kissing, groping, headed for the thick door.

*Voyeur.* "Watching's not so much my thing." But she had a feeling choice wasn't going to be a big option right then. "I'm more for doing."

His teeth were a brilliant white flash. "I'll remember that."

Then he stalked toward the back exit.

Dammit.

And she followed him.

No choice.

The kymine was driving him crazy. Jude shoved open the back door and sucked in a sharp breath of clean air.

*Vampires.* One day, he'd pay them back for the kymine. That crap was being sent all over the U.S., funneled by the undead freaks.

Sometimes, he really hated vamps.

"Jude? You okay?" Erin's voice. He glanced back at her.

She hadn't been hit as hard. He'd noticed that right off. So he hadn't told her that the kymine was blistering the inside of his nostrils. Hadn't told her that if they hadn't gotten the hell out of that stinking bar, blood would have started pouring from his nose in another two minutes.

But now that they were out, he'd start healing. Unfortunately, even for the strong shifters, it took some time to get kymine out of the system.

Admitting weakness with so many others around hadn't been an option. Better to just suck up the pain and move on.

Story of his life.

Whispers floated to his ears.

"Jude?" A thread of worry thickened her voice. "Are you sure you're—" "

"I'm fine," he muttered.

But her brows were drawn low and she crept closer to him. "You don't look so good."

The door swung shut behind her.

Moans teased his ears. Pants. The couple he'd followed outside were already busy. Judging by the man's groans, they sure seemed to be having one great time in the dark.

"I'm *fine,*" he said again and turned away to scan the thicket of woods around the bar. The perfect place for sex. Groping in the dark. Fucking in the wild.

The man and woman were completely oblivious to everything but their need. Great prey for a wolf, one who wouldn't have to bother going inside the bar—*damn hole in the wall*—and dealing with the kymine.

The vamp hadn't told him about the kymine. Probably because she'd been the one to sell it to the bar owner. No wonder she'd known about the wolf.

This really was the perfect place to hunt. Pity he wouldn't be able to smell the beast coming. It would take at least an hour for the kymine's side effects to clear up, but if the wolf came hunting, he'd be able to hear the bastard.

The door squeaked behind him. He reached for Erin, pulling her into his arms and dipping his head toward her mouth. They'd pass for a lust-driven couple. Hell, he *was* lust driven around her and—

*Click-click.* Fuck. He *knew* that sound.

The unmistakable cock of a shotgun.

Jude froze. His lips hovered over Erin's, close enough to taste the sweetness of her breath and the sudden fear on her tongue.

"Move away from her! Do it, *freak*!"

His fangs burned as they lengthened even more in his mouth. His claws ripped through his skin.

"I'm fuckin' tired of yer kind comin' here, screwin' with my bar!"

Slowly, Jude dropped his hands and moved his body a few precious inches from Erin's. He kept himself between her and the asshole with the shotgun.

He turned his head and found himself staring down the double-barrel.

A short, gnarled old man with tufts of greasy gray hair had a white-knuckled grip on the gun. His finger looked all too ready to pull that trigger.

"Get away from him, girl!"

Jude tried to figure out his next move. He was fast, but that shotgun was *close.*

"No."

He blinked. Erin's voice had been too calm. Didn't the woman see the gun?

The old guy's face scrunched. "Girl, I'm savin' yer life! Knew what he was soon as I saw his face. Bastard couldn't take that gas."

Ah, so he had this gun-toting jerk to thank for the kymine.

The jerk spat a wad of tobacco on the ground. "Get away from him. He'll rip ya apart!"

"The hell I will," Jude snapped and got ready to rip that little gnome apart.

"I'm not a girl." Her fingers curled around Jude's shoulder. He looked down, saw her claws and knew when the gnome whispered, "Shit" that he had, too.

But the hold on the gun never wavered. The gnome just shrugged and said, "Then I'll blow both yer asses away. No fuckin' werewolves are comin' in my bar and wreckin'—"

"We're not werewolves," Jude said quickly. He could take the gun, but what if the gnome got off a shot and it hit Erin? He didn't know how fast she could heal.

Or *if* she could heal like a shifter.

No. No way could he risk her.

"The fuck ye say. I see them claws!"

Yeah, and the guy didn't look like he was real interested in learning about all the differences between shifters. No, the fellow looked like he was only interested in firing that big-ass gun.

"Sorry, sweetheart," Jude said to Erin and meant it. Odds were good this would hurt her.

But not hurt as bad as a shotgun blast.

"What? Jude—"

The gnome's finger tightened around the trigger.

Jude shoved Erin away—shoved *hard*. Her body flew into the air.

He grabbed for the gun just as the deafening blast blew the hell out of his ears.

Fire scorched his right side. *Sonofabitch.*

He caught the smoking barrels and wrenched the gun from the old man's hands.

The guy whimpered.

Jude glared at him, all too aware of the blood trickling down his side. He didn't even want to *look* at that wound. "Now you've pissed me off," he snarled, the words sounding distorted to him, thanks to the ringing in both ears. "You have no idea who you're messing with."

The man's eyes widened. Fear had his face going slack.

"Yeah, yeah, now you're getting the picture." He threw the gun aside. The day he'd ever choose a gun over claws, well, that was a day that hadn't ever come for him.

The gnome scrambled back, his fingers clawing at the door.

Ignoring the pain, Jude lurched forward. He caught the little bastard around the neck and lifted him high into the air. "You're not going anywhere." His side *hurt.* "Erin?"

A muffled groan. He jerked around and saw her pushing up onto her knees. She tossed back her hair, glaring at him. "You could have just said 'duck.'"

Duck or fuck? He couldn't tell for sure because his hearing was still screwy, but since they had an audience he'd go for duck.

Jude shook his head. Ducking hadn't been good enough. He'd needed her clear and safe.

"Oh, hell, Jude!" He saw her lips form the horrified words. Erin jumped to her feet. Raced to him. "You're bleeding!"

Like a stuck pig.

She reached for his shirt, but it was already wet with blood and plastered to his skin. Or what was left of his skin.

His fingers tightened around the old man's throat. A wheeze slipped from the guy's mouth.

"I've got to shift," he muttered. No choice. The tiger was stronger than the man. He'd heal faster with the beast's power.

No choice.

Erin gave a grim nod.

And the gnome suddenly started fighting in his hold. Clawing at him with stubby nails and kicking out. "No, no, *no!*"

This was the last thing he needed. Jude could hardly hear, and he still couldn't smell a damn thing.

Some hunter he was right then.

With a growl, he slammed the gnome's head into the back of the building. A nice thud sounded and the guy's eyes fell closed. Jude dropped him to the ground.

Then fell down beside him.

Erin dropped to her knees. "Jude, what can I—"

Fire heated his veins. The tiger roared, and Jude arched his back, more than ready for the burn of the shift. The tiger fought his way to the surface as the man sank back into the pain and let the beast have his way.

Bones popped. He saw the fur spring up on his hands and arms. This was it, this was what he needed—

"*Behind you!*" Erin's scream.

He realized that her arms were pulling at him, trying to yank him closer to her. He hadn't even felt her touch because the shift was too intense.

Jude forced himself to glance back. Caught between man and beast, he struggled to hold on, just for a moment more.

Glowing yellow eyes stared at him. Shining from the darkness of the woods.

*Oh, shit.* The old man hadn't been afraid of him in those last few moments. No, not of him.

The wolf raced out of the trees, body thick with muscles and black fur. Its mouth was open, the razor sharp teeth glinting with saliva.

The bastard was heading straight for them.

Jude opened his mouth to cry, but he couldn't speak anymore. The hellfire of the shift blasted through him. Sweet, sweet pain.

No, the man couldn't speak, but the tiger roared his challenge into the darkness—and to the wolf.

# Chapter 14

A shifter's weakest moments came during the time of change from man to beast. The shift wasn't instant. It was fast, yes, but the bones had to snap and reshape and the flesh had to change and the—

*It was brutal. Hard.*

And dangerous.

Erin had seen her share of shifts before. She knew the game. And she knew that Jude couldn't take the wolf right then.

So she did the only thing she could.

Erin ran in front of him. The tiger snarled in fury behind her, but he couldn't attack yet. He was trapped between man and beast.

She stared at the wolf. She hadn't smelled him. Because of the kymine or because he'd cloaked his scent? The bastard had been able to sneak right up on them.

All the better to kill.

"You stay the hell back!" She lifted her claws, ready to do as much damage as she could.

The wolf was big, with a long, muscled body. A thick muzzle, pointed ears, and those glowing eyes—

Her heart slammed into her chest.

*Those eyes.*

The wolf froze, staring up at her. A rumble rose in the beast's throat.

Oh, God, no.

She'd seen those eyes before.

Something bumped against her thigh, a hard jolt that had her stumbling. Erin looked down, eyes wide, scared, stunned.

Jude had finished his shift. The tiger stood near her, using his weight to force her to the side.

So *he* could stand before her.

Red stained his fur, darkening that thick, white and black pelt. But the tiger easily outweighed the wolf. Hell, he had to be twice the other animal's size. His teeth were bigger, sharper. His claws far longer and stronger.

"*No!*" The cry was ripped from her. She couldn't let this happen.

The wolf's head swung toward her and the beast howled. A long, mournful sound.

A sound she knew too well.

"No," a whisper this time.

The tiger's muscles bunched as he prepared to attack.

She couldn't let him do it. Erin threw herself against him, holding on tight as she sank her fingers into that fur and clung with all her strength. "Jude, let the wolf go!"

He trembled against her, and his head turned toward her as he opened his mouth with a cry loud enough to rattle her bones.

The wolf lunged forward, ready to attack.

"*Leave him alone!*" Erin screamed and held on even tighter. *This couldn't be happening.*

But the wolf was there. Watching with eyes that never blinked.

"Get out of here." Erin stared into those eyes. The tiger's body was too tense against her, and she knew Jude was using all of his control in an effort to hold back his attack.

The wolf's black muzzle lowered toward the ground.

Jude's left claw lifted as he got ready for a deadly swipe.

"*Run, now!*" Erin pressed all of her weight against the tiger. *Dammit, go!*

The wolf turned and fled into the darkness.

Her breath choked out. She turned her head and buried it in the tiger's soft fur. Oh, hell.

Jude leapt away from her. Erin slipped and almost fell flat on her face. *For the second time that night.*

Jude shot toward the twisting trees.

"No! Jude, stop!" She knew the man inside the tiger understood her perfectly.

She just wasn't sure if he'd *listen* to her.

When he didn't slow down, she shouted, "That's not the asshole after me!"

Still didn't slow.

Another few seconds and he'd be gone.

"Jude, that—that's my mother!"

The big cat's claws dug into the ground as he came to a shuddering halt. He glanced back at her, blue eyes too bright in the darkness.

*Now he knew.* The last secret.

She pushed to her feet. Wished that her knees didn't feel so weak. "Remember those crazy, psychotic wolves you told me about? Guess it's time I told you, I'm one of them."

In the distance, a wolf howled and the sound ripped right into her heart.

"Jude! Jude, dammit, wait! You're still bleeding!"

He shoved open the motel room door, heard the crash as it banged back and hit the wall. Keeping his head low, he stormed across the threshold, fighting to keep his rage in check while—

Erin grabbed his arm. "Stop! *Listen* to me!"

Teeth clenched, he spun to face her. He'd managed to jerk on the spare jeans he kept in the truck, for shifting emergencies, but with his side still burning like hell, a shirt hadn't been an option.

Erin stared up at him, face stark, lips quivering. So beautiful.

*A wolf?*

Hell.

"I-I should have told you before."

Uh, yeah. She should have.

Her fingers curled around his arm. "You made it clear how you felt about wolves—"

"Sweetheart, that's the way *everyone* feels." All the *Other* anyway. They all knew the rule: If you were smart, you stayed away from the wolves.

Smart. He grimaced. Not him because he sure hadn't stayed away. He'd run straight to her and gotten his ass addicted to her sweet flesh.

Sweet wolf flesh.

A tiger tangled up with a wolf. His grandfather had to be someplace, laughing his striped ass off.

Her hand fell away. "How many wolves have you actually met, other than me?"

His brows flew up, and he ignored what was turning into a dull throb in his side. At least he was healing. "Um, you mean other than the asshole stalking you?"

She kicked the door shut with her heel even as her eyes slit. "No one's perfect, Jude. Not wolves. Not tigers. You should know that."

Oh, hell, no, she hadn't just thrown his past into his face. He grabbed her shoulders and pushed her back against the mud-brown wall. "Don't go there, sweetheart." He'd trusted her. Bared his soul. While—what? All the time she'd been keeping her secrets from him? He'd been trying to *help* her.

But the woman was working her own agenda.

*Wolf.*

"I-I didn't mean—" She broke off, shaking her head and sending those silky locks flying. His nose was working again—he'd felt lost for a time without the onslaught of scents teasing him—and the heady fragrance that was Erin filled his nostrils.

"What did you *mean* then?" Her mouth was close. Tempting and close and he would not kiss her. Not now. Because, dammit, he couldn't help but wonder . . . what other secrets was she keeping?

She wet her lips.

*Damn her.* That swiping pink tongue had his cock jerking.

"Do you—do you remember what you told me about Lones?"

No, he had no idea.

His expression must have said as much because she glared at him. "How screwed up do you have to be," she quoted, "to get kicked out by the pack?"

Okay, he remembered. Jude tried real hard not to wince. So he'd been a hardass on the Lones, but after that Feral butcher who'd killed his family—

"I got kicked out." Said with dignity. Said with a stare that was straight and unflinching. "They thought I was weak. Unworthy." A pause. "Not fit for the pack. When I couldn't shift, they threw me away."

His hands clenched into fists. It was either ball 'em up or grab her again and hold tight. And he couldn't hold her, not yet. She'd kept this secret from him after he'd bared his soul to her.

He should have seen this coming.

*He says I'm his mate.*

Because the bastard after her was a wolf. Just like she was. Like to like.

So why the hell was the beast inside him screaming that she was *his* mate?

No way could a woman be a mate to two shifters.

"My mother took me to my father's house. Dropped me on the doorstep without a word, and left." Memories trembled in her voice. "She'd kept me from him for fifteen years, because while they were *mates*"—Erin said the word like it was a curse. Maybe to her, it was—"she didn't love him, because he wasn't pack."

He tried to think. Hard to do, when she was so close and his fury still rode him. "You could have just been delayed. Shifters don't change until puberty. If you were just fifteen—"

A slow motion of her head, back and forth. "I don't change, Jude. The claws and the teeth are all I have. All I'll ever have. There's no running in the woods for me. No beast who can break through the surface. There's just"—her hands lifted, fell—"what you see. And that wasn't enough for the pack or for my mother."

The mother who'd appeared tonight, more than ready to attack him. "Why is she here?" He didn't believe in coincidences.

"I don't know."

He snorted.

"*I don't.*" Erin exhaled on a hard breath. "I haven't seen her since then—until tonight, anyway. I-I remembered those eyes." She straightened her shoulders. Stiffened her spine. "My father was scared of me because he was scared of *her*. He loved me, I know he did, but I think he was always worried the wolf would come out."

"Your dad—you said he was human?"

"He was a shaman for his tribe. He was used to helping people. When he first met my mother, she was hurt. He told me she'd been attacked by vampires. He wanted to help her, but in the end, she didn't want to be helped. She wanted the blood and the violence and *pack*."

And she'd taken Erin into that world.

Then tossed her out.

Bitch.

"My father was psychic. He could see things, change lives." She blinked quickly. "He was a good man."

Erin had loved him. No denying the emotion in her voice. "What happened to him?" he asked, because there was so much pain there.

"He was killed. One of those horrible wrong place, wrong time things. He was mugged. Caught one night coming home. The guy stabbed him and my father bled out on the street. On the filthy street, with his eyes wide open." Her lips twisted. No smile this time. "I saw it happen. My damn dreams. But by the time I got there, it was too late. He'd left me, too."

He jerked her into his arms. "I'm pissed as hell at you," he growled, but held her all the tighter. What was she doing to him? *What?*

"I couldn't let you kill her," she said, words muffled against him.

His side stung, but no way was he gonna let her go.

"Yeah, well, sweetheart, looked to me like she was the one wanting to do the killing."

No response.

"And if that gnome with the gun was anything to go by, she's made a habit of hunting folks at that bar." A wolf who hunted humans was a wolf that had crossed the line.

Rogue.

Her pack wouldn't take her ass back if she'd gone Rogue.

Erin's head lifted. Her long lashes were spiky, wet. "I don't know what's going on anymore. I just want things to go back to normal."

Ah, normal. That word again. The one she liked so much. "Not gonna happen." His nose twitched. So many scents assaulting him now that his enhanced smell was back. But, what was—

*Hell.*

He pushed Erin behind him and glared at the door.

"Jude!" Erin's nails scraped down his arm. "It's her!" Looked like Erin's sense of smell was working, too.

This time, he could catch the lighter, feminine scent of the wolf shifter. Yet knowing that it was Erin's mother on the other side of that door didn't make him relax his guard for a second. No, it only made him tense more. "Stay back."

He grabbed the doorknob. Wrenched it open—

And came face-to-face with Erin. No, not his Erin. An older version, one with faint lines around her eyes. One whose face was more haggard, whose hair was a bit shorter.

And whose eyes were more yellow than gold.

Sonofabitch.

She stared at him, measuring him. Then one black brow shot up and she said in a voice *too much like Erin's*, "You gonna stand there staring all night, cat, or are you gonna let me see my daughter?"

* * *

Detective Ben Greer eased under the bright yellow line of police tape, his gun holster pressing into his side. He'd had exactly two days of vacation—two days of sitting on his ass and going insane at the cabin—and then he'd gotten the call about Donald Trent.

*Trent.* Like he'd ever forget that bastard. He'd put down ten to one odds that the guy had offed his wife a few months back. Not that Ben had enough evidence to prove it, though.

But after being on the job for ten years, some things were just pure instinct.

Trent was a killer. A psychopath who got off on hurting women. If Trent's body really was buried in those woods, then the women in Lillian would be one hell of a lot safer, and their sleep would be easier.

"Detective!"

A female uniform waved him over. Kristen Langley was still pretty fresh to the force, but she was a fast learner, and she knew how to keep a scene safe.

"What have we got?" he asked as his gaze swept the area. That house. He'd been there before. Been to tell Katherine LaShaun the news about her daughter. He'd seen the boys, peeking from behind the stairs.

Sometimes, the job really sucked.

"The dogs found something . . ." Excitement had her voice cracking. "Come on, we're pretty sure it's—"

Ben ran past her. He could hear voices rising in the distance. The rest of the team. He caught the thud of a shovel. Dammit, they'd better be careful with his scene.

He twisted, avoiding the thick brush as best he could, then he broke into the area with his group. Stumbling to a halt, he eyed the large hole his men had sectioned off. Not too deep. Not deep at all, really. The spotlights lit up the area, and in the black dirt, he saw the faded blue fabric.

A shirt. Ragged.

More of the thick dirt was carefully brushed aside and he glimpsed—

Bones.

"Think it's Trent?" Kristen asked, that excitement still in her voice.

He glanced at her, mouth grim. "It's him." Tests would have to be done. Dental records checked. But he could see a long, thin necklace, one with intertwined snake heads, laying across the bones.

Trent had worn that piece of crap around his neck every time Ben had seen him.

"Careful, people!" Ben yelled. "I want every piece of evidence here! Tag it, bag it, and don't miss anything!" This case was going to have a shitload of media scrutiny. There would be no room for mistakes on this one.

Buried behind his kids' house. How freaking twisted.

And who'd done the bastard? Who'd finally managed to kill Trent?

Even he'd been tempted. Especially after he'd seen Sylvia's broken body.

Ben rubbed his hand over his face. His eyes were gritty. "I want to talk to the family." Had to be done. Better to just get it over with now.

Kristen nodded, her short red hair bobbing around her face. She looked barely eighteen, but Ben knew that image was deceptive—and one that Kristen used to her advantage on the streets. When you were expecting fluff, it was easy to get taken down by a bulldog.

Crickets chirped around them. The cadaver dogs barked as their handlers held them back.

When they approached the house, he saw Katherine walk onto her back porch. A worn robe covered her thin shoulders and she hugged herself. "You found him, didn't you?"

He didn't want to suspect her, but the questions in his mind wouldn't stop. *Had she known about the kill? Been in on it?*

Katherine LaShaun. A strong woman. One who would do anything for her family.

*Buried behind the house. In the woods that the boys probably played in every day.*

Sick.

He walked onto the porch. He hesitated under the bright light. "We've found a body. Too early for identification yet."

Kristen crept to his side, almost soundlessly. The lady knew how to move and she knew how to track killers. One day soon, she'd make a good detective.

Katherine nodded. "It's him, then." Certainty. A jagged breath. "My boys won't have to worry anymore."

Ben glanced around. The house seemed too quiet. Sure, the boys should have been sleeping—but no, they would have woken up with all the cops and dogs there. It was too loud for the kids to still be sleeping. "Katherine, where are the boys?"

Her gaze left the woods and came to rest on him. "At a friend's house. They're safe. They don't know . . . won't know . . . about this." Her lips shook. "They play there—*they won't know*."

She'd moved the boys before the cops arrived. How the hell had she known to do that?

"You knew we were coming, didn't you, Mrs. LaShaun?" Kristen asked.

Katherine glanced her way. Slowly. "Don't believe I know you, honey."

Kristen slapped a smile on her face. The non-threatening one she wore so well. "Kristen Langley." She offered a hand. One that wasn't taken.

Katherine rocked back on her heels. "All this time, I was

afraid, and he was right here." Her gaze skittered back to Ben's. "Do you know who killed him?"

Not yet. But, God willing, he would soon. "Who told you we were coming, Katherine?" The person who'd given her the tip could well be the killer.

Only the officers on his team knew about this body. The cops—and the killer.

Her lips, already thin, flattened even more. "I need you cops to be done by tomorrow afternoon. My boys will be comin' back then."

Kristen opened her mouth—

"You got a phone call, didn't you?" he pressed, not about to be led off track. He wasn't new to this game.

Kristen's mouth snapped closed.

"We can subpoena phone records, you know. We're going to find out, one way or another."

She stumbled back. "You didn't do a damn thing to help my girl! Not one damn thing! You let that bastard out and he killed her—he *killed* her!"

"We don't know that, Mrs. LaShaun." *Yeah, right.*

"Bullshit!"

Katherine had never been one to mince words. One of the things he liked about the woman. "I'm sorry about your daughter, Katherine. I *did* try to help her. Erin—" *Don't think about her now* "and I did everything we could." It just hadn't been enough.

Her gaze fell. "Erin Jerome fought for my daughter even when Sylvia wouldn't fight for herself." Soft. Sadness passed over her face. She sucked in a sharp breath and her shoulders shoved back even as her chin came up with new determination. "Get your subpoena if you have to! Do it! But I'm not tellin' you another thing!" Then she turned and stormed into the house, slamming the back door behind her.

Well, well. Katherine was hell-bent on protecting someone. From the look on her face, she thought that *someone* might have been involved in the killing.

*Who*? Who would Katherine protect? Only her boys. Just the boys.

His eyes narrowed as he stared at the back door. "Kristen, get the DA. Let him know we need that subpoena yesterday."

Ben kissed the rest of his vacation good-bye and got ready for his business of murder. Murder—just what he did best and—

Voices. Shouting, the snarls of fury drifting on the wind.

His stare snapped to Kristen's. *What the fuck?*

He vaulted off the back porch. She was with him, her smaller body hurtling behind his.

They rounded the house. Good, more police tape was up. That should keep the gawkers back, for a while anyway.

"*Get out of my way! Don't you know who I am*?" An asshole was all but screaming at one of the uniforms, shoving a long, thick finger at the young guy's chest. "I'm—"

"Judge Lance Harper." Bastard extraordinaire. Ben braked to a halt and glared at the idiot who would no doubt be headlining the local news for the next three days.

The judge's head jerked toward him and his muddy brown eyes slit. "*Greer.*" Sounded more like a curse than a name because, yeah, there wasn't exactly a whole lot of love lost between him and the judge, arrogant SOB that the guy was.

Ben braced his hands on his waist, knowing the move would show his holster. Shooting the judge probably wasn't an option, but a man could dream.

Oh, yes, he could dream.

"I've got this one," Ben said to the uniform. "Langley"—Kristen's gaze was on the judge—"go make that phone call."

From the corner of his eye, he saw her head bob and then she backed away.

The judge's hands fisted. "I demand that you tell me what is going on here."

"Ah, you demand, huh? Since when do you have the right to demand *anything* at my crime scene?" What was the guy even doing there? No way was this the man's business anymore.

A muscle flexed along Harper's jaw. "Cartwright told me about the body on the property."

Did no one in this city believe in keeping things under wraps? This was a murder for shit's sake! "His mistake," Ben managed, the words grating in his throat.

"It was *my* case, detective. The man was in my courtroom, he was—"

"You let him walk." A mistake. Not Harper's first, not his last, and the judge's insanity on the bench was only part of the reason why Ben couldn't stand the guy.

The other reason? Ben had once had a lover leave him . . . for the judge. The guy might be old, but the bastard was hell with the ladies.

Very slowly, Harper's fists unknotted. "You think you know me, don't you, detective?"

No, he didn't know him particularly well. Didn't want to, either. "I'm working a murder, Harper. I don't have time for your games."

Harper's chin rose. "I didn't want to let that bastard walk, but I had no choice." He shook his head. "When the wife changed her story, what was I supposed to do? There wasn't enough evidence to hold him."

"You know he probably killed Sylvia, don't you?" Ben fired right across his words. "He walked and he killed her." That knowledge had burned in Ben's gut more nights than he could count.

Harper's Adam's Apple bobbed. "I-I know." A rasp. Remorse? *What?* From Harper? Their eyes locked. "What I do in this world isn't easy," Harper said. "Justice never is."

Ben thought of those dirty bones. Of the boys who'd grow up without their mother or their worthless excuse for a father. "Go home. There's nothing left for you here. This isn't your case anymore."

Harper's gaze drifted to the house. "No—no, I don't guess it is." His shoulders slumped and he turned away.

For an instant, Ben could almost feel a stir of sympathy for the fellow. Almost.

Then the instant passed. He wheeled around. Back to business. "All right, people, I want this scene combed for every bit of evidence you can find. We've got a body, and we're damn well gonna find his killer." Because Ben didn't believe in letting monsters walk. Not in his town.

Even if the vic had been a cold-blooded asshole, he'd find Trent's killer. That was his job.

He was good at his job.

"What are you doing here?" Erin stared at her mother—oh, damn, *her mother*—and kept every muscle in her body locked tight.

*Not going to her.*

*Not going to hold her.*

*Not going to hit her. Not!*

"I came to see you." Flat. No emotion there. Never had been. That one eyebrow rose again. "Can I come in or do I have to stand out here all night?"

*Leave.*

"Come in," Jude growled. "But at the first sign of a shift, your ass is gone."

She sniffed and crossed the threshold. "I can't talk to my daughter in wolf form. She doesn't change—"

"Yeah, I fucking know. Big damn deal." Jude shut the door behind her. Too quietly. He crossed his arms over his chest and glared.

Her mother—Theresa—blinked and glanced over at Erin. "You told him? And he's still with you?"

Oh, yes, her mother was full of love and maternal instincts.

Erin felt her blood heat. "He's still here."

"Standing here, big as day," Jude murmured. "Not planning to go anyplace."

In a flash, her mother attacked, jumping back, and thrusting her claws right up to Jude's throat. "Don't even *think* about hurting her. Just 'cause she's weak, you can't—"

"Get away from him." Not screamed. Not shouted. Erin gave the demand coldly, despite the fire in her gut, and she felt the rip of her claws tearing through her flesh.

Her mother's head swung toward her. "Erin? What are you—"

Jude threw her back. A hard toss with his hand that had Theresa flying through the air and slamming into the floor. She scrambled up, fast, crouching, snarling, and spitting.

Erin hurriedly stepped in front of Jude. "Don't come at him again."

Her mother's face went slack with surprise.

Looking at her *hurt.* Erin sucked in a breath. "I don't know why you're here, and I really don't care." Lie, lie. "But you are *not* going to attack Jude. He's done nothing but help me, and he doesn't deserve that shit."

Yellow eyes slit. "You care for him?"

The silence behind her was thick. Good thing Jude couldn't see her face right them. "What I feel for him is *not* your business."

But her mother saw too much. Always had.

After a moment, Theresa rose to her feet. Tossing back her hair, she said, "You've grown up hard."

Yeah, because being abandoned by her mother should have made her grow up *easy.* A growl built in Erin's throat.

Jude's hands came down on her shoulders. Squeezed.

She stiffened. He shouldn't touch her. *No. Don't do that. Don't show her any weakness.*

Too late. Her mother's gaze had already noted the telling move.

"Attached to her, are you, tiger?" She smiled and seemed satisfied. "I hope you're a fighter."

"I am." Close to a snarl.

"Good."

Her eyes raked Erin. "Long time, baby girl."

Baby girl, her ass. This wasn't some movie-of-the week reunion. "What do you want?"

A shrug.

Red lights danced before Erin's eyes. "Then *get out.*"

Jude pulled her back against his chest. "Easy." Breathed in her ear.

But she didn't want to be easy. She wanted to scream. To rage. Like she'd done years ago.

The yellow eyes dropped. "Been looking for you," Theresa said, lifting her hand to rub the back of her neck. "You disappeared on me. I got . . . worried."

*What?* "*You* left me years ago. You knew where I was." She hadn't moved until her dad died. "Not like I was real hard to find." Theresa had never come looking for her. Not once.

Still gazing at the floor, her mother said, "Not then. I . . . watched you then. Had to stay far back. You would have caught my scent."

It wouldn't have hurt more if someone had carved her heart out with claws right then.

"Lost you . . . a few months back."

What? All that time? All that damn time, her mother had been close by—and she'd never contacted her. *Why?*

Theresa glanced up. Her mother had to see the question burning Erin alive because she said, "You didn't fit in my world."

Like Erin didn't know that.

"I didn't fit in yours." Another shrug of Theresa's shoulders. But this time, the move seemed . . . tired. Sad. "But I still . . . wanted to make sure you were okay. I-I needed to see you."

Erin shook her head. Jude felt solid behind her. Strong and steady—just what she needed then. "You threw me away." A whisper, one she hadn't meant to voice.

That stare bored into her. "Had to. You couldn't shift—"

She flinched.

"—and the pack would have torn you apart. No way were you strong enough to handle what they would have thrown at you." Theresa's shoulders set. "I did what I had to do in order to protect you."

Erin stared at her mother. At the tense expression on her face. The steady hands. And she said, simply, "Bullshit."

Theresa's jaw dropped.

"You didn't leave me on that doorstep because you wanted to *protect* me." Not buying that. Not for a minute. Jude's hold on her tightened. "You did it because you were ashamed of me."

She saw the hit in the slight widening of her mother's eyes.

"You think I didn't know?" Erin asked, stomach knotted. "You think I didn't see the way you looked at me?" Not a proud mama. Never that. Always pushing her into the shadows. Away from the others who might see her.

"*You were supposed to be like me!*" A scream of fury and pain that broke fast and hard from her mother's lips. "Supposed to shift and fight—*just like me!*"

"But I wasn't just like you." Sadness there. "I was like my dad."

Theresa's head jerked. "I should have been mated to the alpha! He *loved* me! We were supposed to be together, but then I screwed everything up and—"

"And had me."

Her mother's mouth snapped closed but she gave a grim nod.

Honesty, at least.

"You had me," Erin continued, "and you didn't think I was good enough for the pack—or for you." This *hurt*.

"I wanted to be with him," a stark whisper. "I loved him."

Erin knew the *him* hadn't been her father.

"He saw me," Theresa said, voice soft. "Such dark, dark eyes that saw into me so well." Her shoulders sagged. "He didn't look at me the same way after he learned about your father."

And what? That was Erin's fault? Her father's? Erin bit back the snarl that rose within her.

"When I got pregnant," her mother said, "he knew I wasn't his mate. Knew that somewhere out there, another woman waited . . . only a matter of time." A tear trickled down her cheek. "I lost you."

Not real hard to lose something when you threw it away.

"But first, I lost him." She swiped away the tear with the back of her hand. "He left the pack before you were born. I-I kept thinking he'd come back, but he . . . turned his back on everyone. On me."

Just like Erin's mother had turned away from her. The woman wasn't going to be getting any sympathy from her.

"Why did you come here tonight?" Jude's gravelly voice.

Her mother blinked. "To . . . see Erin. I caught her scent at Mort's. I wanted to . . . talk to her."

"And what? Make up for lost time?" he demanded. "Or just jerk her around some more?"

Theresa's hands fisted. "I wanted to make certain she was happy and *safe*. I didn't know what you were to her, I was afraid—" She exhaled. "Shifters go after the weak."

*Weak.* Was that how her mother truly saw her? Erin glanced down at her hands. Her claws were gone.

But they could come back in a second's time.

"Other hybrids were in the pack," her mother said, swallowing, "but you were the only one who couldn't change. You were in danger, you were—"

"When I was fourteen," Erin said softly, cutting through her words, "the girls in the pack jumped me."

"What?"

"They thought I was weak, too." They'd taunted. Teased. Then attacked her with claws and teeth.

But, luckily, they'd been in human form.

So she'd wiped the floor with their asses.

Erin met her mother's shocked stare. "They were wrong about me, too." She'd bet some of them still had the scars to prove just how wrong they'd been.

"Y-you never said—and they didn't—"

"I didn't tell you because I didn't want you to worry." She'd always tried to protect her mother. Stupid really. Theresa was the last person on earth who needed protection. "They didn't tell—well, I guess because they didn't want everyone knowing the little freak had kicked their furry butts."

They'd left her alone after that. No more teasing. No more taunts. She'd thought she was fitting in—

Until she'd been forced out.

Her spine straightened. "So don't talk to me about being weak, okay? I know why you left me, but what I don't know is why the hell you've come back now." Or why she'd been coming back. Spying, all these years.

She'd never known. *It hurt.*

"I . . . missed you."

She wouldn't weaken.

"I wanted to see how you turned out."

"And when Dad died? When I stood by his grave, crying, *alone*, where were you?"

No answer. She hadn't expected one. *Enough.* "The reunion's over, mother. Time for you to go." Hopefully, before her mother decided to go after Jude—or her—with claws and teeth.

Theresa held her gaze, then gave a grim nod.

Erin and Jude stepped away from the door.

Her mother hesitated. "Things are . . . good for you. I know you used to be a lawyer—"

"Still am."

"—but now you've got a mate." A smile. Wistful, dammit. *Her mother had been given a wonderful mate*. "A strong shifter, someone who can—"

"My *mate* is a fucked-up wolf shifter, a hybrid like me who kills and tortures people because it gets him off."

The smile vanished. Horror took its place on her mother's face. "A-a hybrid . . . wolf?"

"Erin." Jude's tense voice. "Don't. There's something that I need—"

But she just rolled right over him, the rage too much to hold back. "So don't think I've walked off into some sort of happily-ever-after la-la land for wanna-be shifters. I've got a mate, all right, mother. A mate who thinks he's my perfect match in every single, sick way."

# Chapter 15

"She doesn't know, does she?"

Jude led Erin's mother outside and closed the door behind him. A thud shook the motel room wall. *Huh. Wonder what Erin threw.* "Ah . . . Doesn't know what?"

"That she's yours."

His brows rose. Oh, but he hoped the door and walls were thicker than he'd thought.

He grabbed the woman's arm and hauled her away from the room. "You don't know what you're talking about."

"Don't I?"

His jaw locked.

"I smell her on you. Smell you on her. That's the way with mates. Like she's under your skin and you're under hers."

He wouldn't deny it, because Erin was under his skin. In his very blood. "Then you tell me . . . how is it possible for a woman to be a mate to two shifters? One a wolf and one a tiger?" Because it wasn't possible. No way.

"Erin's not your usual shifter. Maybe the rules don't apply

to her." Her fangs flashed as she said, "Or maybe that asshole who's claiming her is dead wrong."

Good emphasis on dead.

"I want to be with her again," she told him. "I know I've screwed up, but *I miss her*. I've missed her for years and I want back in her life."

"That why you're in Lillian? Hunting the locals? 'Cause you're looking for her?" This setup wasn't making sense to him.

"Yes." A hiss.

He just stared at her.

"Hunting the local idiots was just bonus." Her hands went to her hips. "I didn't *hurt* anyone. Just had some fun."

Right. The kind of fun that had led the gnome to his shotgun. Jude figured he owed the wolf before him for that. Another damn scar on his body.

But, curious now, he asked, "If I'd been after Erin at Mort's, if I'd been going to have some . . . fun with her, what would you have done?"

"Ripped your throat out." Said immediately.

Good to know.

"I know I'm messed up," she told him with a straight stare. "And I know I'm not the mother she needs." The woman wet her lips. "But I need her." Her hand dove into her back pocket. When her hand came back up, she shoved a bent business card at him. "When . . . *if* she ever wants to talk to me, give her that number, okay?"

Not waiting for his answer, she spun away from him and marched toward the line of cars waiting in the parking lot.

After five feet, she stopped. "You gonna get that bastard claiming to be her mate?"

"Count on it."

She tossed a quick glance over her shoulder and the smile

on her face was pure Erin. "Good. Do me a favor—rip his throat out for me."

Then she jumped into one of the cars and spun out of the lot.

"Will do," he whispered, watching her go. Ripping the bastard's throat out was the plan, after all.

The early morning sunlight burned her eyes. Thanks to her mother and the not-so-small matter of a murder, last night had been a real bitch. Erin marched away from the motel room, her bag clutched tightly in her hand. Coming back home had been exactly as hard as she'd thought it would be.

And just when she'd thought her life couldn't get any more screwed up . . .

"*Erin.*" Jude grabbed her arm, jerking her to a stop. She blinked, trying to shove her way out of the pity party and focus on him.

"Company," a breath of a whisper from Jude.

She followed his gaze and saw the gleaming curves of a BMW sweep into the old lot. Erin caught a glimpse of the driver's face.

Judge Harper. "He must have another meeting," she muttered. A meeting at the motel. No big surprise for the judge. "Come on, let's get out of here." She was more than ready to hit the road.

The BMW jerked to a halt, and Harper shoved open his door. He sprang from his car and his gaze instantly zeroed in on her. "Jerome! Erin Jerome! Wait!"

Great. Erin took a deep breath, aware of Jude stiffening behind her. Pasting a fake smile on her face, she asked, "Something I can do for you, judge?"

He stalked toward her. As usual, he looked all determined and cocky and confident—then he stumbled. The judge jerked to a halt and stared down at her.

She lifted a brow and stared right back.

"I-I had to find you. Cartwright told me you were leaving." A heavy pause. "I went to Katherine LaShaun's house."

Erin blinked. "*What?*" The last thing she'd expected.

"I had to go! When I heard about the body"—his nostrils flared—"I needed to see for myself what was happening out there."

Yeah, she'd wanted to see the scene, too. But she hadn't been allowed on sight.

Harper's eyes darted to Jude, then back to her. "Erin, can we talk, privately?"

"No." The instant answer came from Jude *and* from Erin.

Harper's lips thinned and he dragged a shaking hand through his already tousled hair. "You and Greer have to understand. Trent's death wasn't my fault."

Oh, what? Was it hers?

"The wife recanted, she—"

"Even without her testimony, there was more than enough evidence to convict." Flat, cold. "We both know that Trent was abusing her. The guy was guilty as the devil, and we had the chance to stop him." But he'd walked.

Then, well, died.

"We did." The judge rocked back on his heels, and for a moment, he didn't look as strong or as fit as he'd appeared in the past. He looked . . . tired. "I guess he's stopped now, though, isn't he?"

"I guess he is," Jude said, voice like a cool breeze.

Death had a nice way of stopping folks.

Harper flinched. "I didn't know this would happen. I just—I just made the only judgment I could."

Erin didn't know what to say to the judge. After a moment, he turned away from her and shuffled back to his car.

Erin watched him, aware of Jude's strong presence at her back. Harper felt guilty. She could see it, feel it. Guilty enough to seek her out.

And he'd come—to what? Neither one of them could go back and change the past. Too many *ifs* in the world. If he'd convicted Trent . . . if she'd worked harder to prove the bastard's guilt . . . if Sylvia hadn't faltered . . .

*You couldn't go back.*

The judge knew that and so did she.

Harper stopped at his car. He glanced back at her. "I know what they say about me."

*On the take.* So many criminals walked right out of his courtroom with barely a slap on his wrist. "Do you?" She murmured, but Erin knew he heard her.

"I want those bastards who break the law to pay," he told her. "Just like you do."

Then why didn't they? Why did so many ease past him?

He pulled open the driver's side door. "I do the best I can, Jerome. Guess it's not always good enough." His eyes narrowed. "Don't you ever have regrets?"

Too many. Erin gave a grudging nod.

"Is the bastard ever gonna leave?" Jude murmured in her ear and wrapped his arm around her shoulders.

A ghost of a smile curved Harper's lips. "I thought you might." Then he climbed into his car.

Erin leaned against Jude. Damn but the man felt solid.

Harper drove away with a soft purr of his engine.

"You ready to get the hell out of this town?" Jude asked after a moment of silence. The thick, uncomfortable kind of silence that made her want to squirm.

"More than ready." Before she had any more unwanted

visitors from her past. Like a certain detective she'd prefer to avoid. *Talk about regrets.* Erin swallowed and tried to shove the past away. "We didn't get any closer to finding the bastard, did we?"

He turned her toward him. "We're gonna catch him, sweetheart." Absolute certainty there.

But when? Before or after he killed someone else?

"We *will* catch him," Jude repeated.

And, once again, Erin forced herself to nod.

Once they were in Baton Rouge, Erin tried to get back into her routine as fast as possible. But, her routine had an unexpected addition.

She'd been given a babysitter. Okay, not a babysitter so much as a six-foot-two, two hundred pound, pissy demon who tailed her every move.

Erin looked up from her files and stared at said pissy demon.

Zane raised his brows and stared right back at her.

He was five feet away. Slouched in her ratty spare chair.

And the man wasn't going anywhere.

When she and Jude had returned to Baton Rouge, Jude had dropped his little protection bombshell on her.

Until the wolf was caught, she'd have twenty-four seven protection. One of the Night Watch hunters during the day—while Jude was out digging up leads. And at night, Jude would be with her.

Now, she was all about the Jude at night part. Yeah, that worked for her. More than worked.

But Zane, and the irritating humming the guy kept doing under his breath, well, he wasn't so much her thing.

Jude even had the human woman scheduled to take a shift with her. A human.

For protection?

That was just insulting.

One of the assistants came bustling in. "Erin, here's the transcript from the Parsons trial—"

A long, loud whistle.

Amy jumped and dropped the folder. Her hand flew to her chest as her head jerked to the right and Erin saw her spy the lurking demon.

He smiled at her. "Hi there."

Erin growled.

He kept smiling at the assistant.

*Don't need this. Don't. Need. This.*

"Thanks, Amy, I'll review it later today." A dismissal. Probably too curt, but damn if Amy wasn't starting to smile right back at the demon now. Great.

Erin cleared her throat. Twice. Amy finally darted out of the office, but not before she gave one long, last look at Zane.

"You're an ass." Erin told him, meaning it.

He blinked. "Ah, you're just mad 'cause I'm not flirting with you." He shook his head. "But I don't flirt with women who can fry my brain."

Well, at least she was in his safe zone. Erin bared her teeth. She really didn't like the reminder of that vicious encounter. "Didn't we already go over this? Demon versus wolf? Why did Jude send *you* to watch me?"

A lazy shrug. " 'Cause he trusts me." A pause. "And he knows I'd fight like hell to protect you."

Her eyes widened. That was new. The guy sounded like he meant those words, too. "You don't even like me."

"Sure I do." A slow stretch. "Would even want to fuck you, if Jude hadn't already claimed you."

Heat burned her cheeks. No, no, he hadn't just said—

A soft chuckle escaped his lips. "Relax. I said I *would*

want to. Didn't say I was going to." His right foot swung in a small circle. "I like women with a wild side."

Oh, then he'd probably love her.

But—

But she wasn't interested. Not at all.

He wasn't Jude.

*Jude.*

Erin rubbed her right temple. A vague ache was starting to build there. Not enough sleep, probably. After seeing dear old Mom, she sure hadn't been able to sleep well.

And knowing that the wolf was still out there—

Not exactly a situation conducive to rest and relaxation.

"Where is Jude?" she asked him, sinking deeper into her chair.

"Hunting."

She *knew* that. "He's got backup, right? I mean, he's not out there alone?"

"Jude really isn't the backup type."

The ache turned into a throb. "Everyone needs backup."

Another rap at her door. Sighing, Erin called out, "Come on in, Amy, it's fine for you to—"

The door swung open. Not Amy this time. Jude.

Her lips wanted to curve at the sight of him. She could almost forget about the ache in her temple because she was just so glad to see him.

*Jude.* Tall and strong, with that thick mane of blond hair. Blue eyes shining so bright.

His stare heated when it landed on her. Erin rose, bracing her hands behind the desk. "Ah, Jude, I was . . . ah . . . wondering where you—"

"Wanted to check on you," he said, breaking into her stumbling and so not suave words. He jerked his thumb toward the door. "Zane, give us a minute, okay?"

"A minute? Damn, man, no woman likes it *that* fast."

Her eyes widened. No, that jerk just hadn't said—

Jude's snarl had the demon jumping from his chair and heading for the door.

When the door shut behind Zane, Jude stared at her in silence.

Then he locked the door.

Erin swallowed, realizing her throat was way too dry.

"We need to talk."

She flinched because, those words, oh, they were *never* good.

*Knew this would happen.* Jude knew all her secrets now. Everything about her mother and the wolf within.

*How screwed up do you have to be to get abandoned by the pack?*

"Erin?" A deep rumble as he took a gliding step closer to her.

Right then, she was very grateful that the desk was between them. "Ah . . . okay. Wh-what do you want to talk about? Have you—have you found out anything about the stalker?"

His lips thinned. "I got some places to check out today. I might have some news after that."

"Good." Her fingers knotted together. What was she supposed to say? *Sorry my mother tried to attack you and sorry I've been lying-slash-keeping-the-truth-about-myself-from-you, but, hey, the sex between us is great and when I'm with you . . . I feel good.*

Better than good.

Almost happy.

No, not almost.

Even with that bastard on her trail, when she was with Jude, she felt safe. Like she belonged.

And, yes, dammit, *happy.*

"I need to know . . ." Jude's jaw set as he walked around the desk.

*So much for that safety.*

He caught her upper arms and held her with fingers too tight.

Both temples throbbed now in a hard, fast beat.

"Are things different between us?" Jude asked. "Because of what I told you? Do you . . . ? Ah, hell!" He kissed her. A deep, toes-curling-*yes* kiss that had her heart racing and her sex clenching.

His tongue slipped past her lips. Tangled with hers. Tasted.

And she sure tasted him.

Her nipples hardened against the lacy edge of her bra. The points ached and she rubbed them against his chest, seeking relief. No, pleasure.

Because Jude knew just how to offer pleasure.

His lips broke from hers. "Erin, the way you smell"—his nostrils flared—"sweet cream and candy—my own treat."

She gulped and knew that her smell—*sweet cream and candy*—had to be flowing stronger right then.

His forehead pressed against hers. He sucked in a sharp breath and shuddered.

Or maybe she did.

"Tell me it didn't change anything," he growled. "Tell me you know I'm not like that psycho after you."

Understanding broke through the sensual need. Jude was worried she'd turn from him? Because of his past?

And here she'd been afraid that her wolf heritage would send the guy running.

"I'd *never* hurt you, Erin. I swear."

Her lips brushed over his. Soft, so soft. When there had never been much softness between them. "I know." And she did. His past might not be pretty. Neither was hers. But the truth was that she trusted him.

Dangerous, she knew. Trusting anyone, especially a shifter, was a big risk. Born with two faces, meant to lie—that's what some said about the shifters. But Jude was different.

He was fighting to protect her. Not trying to hurt her or control her.

Yes, he'd killed. There was darkness in him. She'd felt it, seen it. Yet Erin didn't think Jude would ever turn that darkness on her or on anyone else that didn't deserve the fury of his hunt.

*No innocents will be hurt.*

She pulled back a bit and tried a smile, hoping to lighten the thick mood and ease a grin back to his lips. That sexy scar—she loved to see it rise up. "Besides, since we're not mated, I know you'd never go territorial on me."

He stiffened.

No smile and his face, if anything, seemed harsher.

"Jude?"

His hands dropped. "Mated or not, I already am territorial when it comes to you."

Her mouth dried. What did he mean? Was it more than sex for him? It was so much more for her, but she hadn't wanted to hope—

"I'm not an easy man, Erin. Never will be." His shoulders were so straight. His hands had fisted. "I'd sooner fucking cut off my own hand than ever lift it against you."

His voice shook.

So did her knees.

"But, hell, yeah, I'm *territorial* about you. You're in my head every minute. I close my eyes, and I see you and I want you so much I can hardly breathe."

Oh, that was—

"The timing for us is shit."

True. Her timing was generally always like that.

"And I know with that asshole out there, the last thing you need is a man trying to get too close."

Jude already was too close because the things he'd said . . . *You're in my head every minute. I close my eyes, and I see you and I want you so much I can hardly breathe.*

She could have said the same things about him.

All true.

"So I'm gonna take him down," Jude growled, "and I'm gonna take the fear out of your eyes and I'm gonna prove that you can trust me, that I'm not some sick freak like him."

"No, Jude, I know—"

"You'll see who I am." He stared down at her. "And we'll see if we can't fix this damn timing." She saw him take a hard gulp of his own. "And as for the mating . . ."

Her chin lifted. "I can't control the mating. If that—that wolf is right, then—"

"Then nothing! You . . . you're different from every other shifter out there, sweetheart."

Yeah, different. Nice, easy word for her situation.

Because she'd always been *different*.

"You're different . . . human and shifter. So what makes you so sure that you'd mate like the others? What makes you so sure you'd only have one mate?"

Her lips parted in surprise. "Jude." What was he telling himself? No, no, he had to see—shifters only had one mate. One chance for children. Fate didn't care if a shifter's mate was a killer or a savior. The mating was forever.

The beast inside her had recognized the wolf. That part was the most humiliating for her. So humiliating, she hadn't told Jude. Her body had known the wolf shifter at the first touch. No, not her body, but the dormant beast inside. Erin had been horrified, afraid, but, dammit, *aware* of him. An instinctual response she couldn't control. One that made her sick.

"I know." Simple words, gruff.

Her gaze met his and she saw the understanding in his eyes. Understanding and a banked rage. Erin licked her lips.

"I know," he continued, "but I also *know* how your body responds to me, and I *know* the beast. It's awake when I'm near, and it's hungry for me."

He was right.

Erin rocked back on her heels, banging her hip into the desk. She'd thought the sex was just great because she wasn't having to hold back and because, well, Jude was freaking fantastic, but what if there was something more there?

What if . . .

*No. No one got two mates, and sure as hell not someone who couldn't even manage one shift.*

"Forget the mating," Jude told her and his eyes burned with intensity. "The mating isn't what matters anyway."

He'd know. He'd seen firsthand just how wrong those fated matings could be.

So had she.

"I'm not looking for a mate for the beast."

But with full-blood shifters, the beast was never separate from the man. Not really.

His fist thudded against his chest. "I'm looking for someone who—"

"*Get the fuck out of my way!*"

Erin jerked at the raised voice. Her gaze locked on her closed door. That voice . . . she hadn't heard that deep baritone in months.

"Back up, Boy Scout, or I'm gonna have to hurt you." Zane. Loud, confident, pissed.

"What the hell?" Jude strode toward the door.

Erin, moving much slower, did the same. *Shit for timing. Always.*

"Try it, asswipe. I'm a cop. Lay the first finger on me and—"

Jude yanked open the door, a snarl on his lips.

Erin scrambled after him.

She caught sight of the two men in the outer office. Tall and strong, almost nose to nose.

And she knew that her day was about to get even worse.

The throbbing in her temples flared again. Harder. *Aspirin. Need aspirin.*

"Zane!" Jude's voice snapped. "Who the hell is this guy?" His nostrils flared and Erin knew he was trying to catch a scent.

But he'd only smell a human because Lillian Detective Ben Greer was human through and through.

Ben shoved Zane out of his way and locked his warm chocolate eyes on her. "Erin." Softness there, and anger.

She eased to Jude's side, far too conscious of all the curious stares. Way too many people were around. Amy. Another assistant, Donna. And Karrie, the ADA next door was also peering in, though it looked like she was trying real hard not to be obvious. "Ah, Ben, it's been a while."

"A while since you left me bleeding out in a hospital bed, you mean?"

Okay, no softness that time, only anger. She stiffened and took the hit because the way she figured it, she deserved his rage. He'd been hurt because of her.

"Aw, Jude, come on! Let me take this prick outside and teach him some manners," Zane wheedled.

Ben jerked out his badge. "*I'm a cop*. I'd like to see you *try* to teach me some—"

Zane grinned and stepped eagerly forward. The fact that Ben was a cop didn't seem to matter much to him.

"I take it you're Ben Greer?" Jude asked quietly. His legs were braced apart. Hands loose at his sides.

Ben's gaze raked him. "And I take it you're the asshole who's sleeping with Erin now?"

Amy sucked in a sharp breath.

Jude just smiled. "Yeah, I am."

"Then you're also the prick who was screwing around with my case files."

Jude just shrugged.

Erin knew it was time to take charge. She stepped forward, putting herself between Jude and Ben.

*Ben.* He looked the same. Handsome face. Thick, slightly curling brown hair. A dimple in his chin.

A solid guy. A good cop.

Human.

*Not for me.*

He didn't understand her. Never would.

*Not like Jude.*

"Ben, perhaps we should go into my office and talk." Away from all the watching eyes and straining ears.

He pulled in a deep breath. His fingers whitened around his badge. "Yeah, yeah, let's do that." His head cocked to the right. A move she'd seen a hundred times. A move he always made just before he threw out a challenge to a suspect.

Her heart thudded too hard in her chest. *He'd come to Baton Rouge. Why? Not for me, but for . . .*

"Let's go *talk,* Erin, and you can tell me just why you interfered in a murder investigation this weekend and why the hell I found your picture clutched in the hands of a dead man."

Ah, that would be why.

# Chapter 16

His claws wanted to spring free. Jude could feel the burn beneath his fingertips, but he held onto his control.

*The cop.* The one he *knew* Erin had cared for back in Lillian. They were in Erin's office now. The guy stood less than five feet away—and he was watching Erin with far too much knowledge in his eyes.

"Jude, do you mind if I speak with Ben alone?"

Yeah, he did. He crossed his arms over his chest and glowered down at her.

She stared right back up at him. "I *need* to speak with him alone."

Dammit. He was not happy with this crap. "I'll be right outside." He glanced at the cop. The guy had moved back and leaned against Erin's desk.

Human.

Her fingers skimmed over his arm. "Thank you."

*Territorial.* The word echoed in his head. The lady had no

idea just how *territorial* he was feeling right then or how badly he wanted to rip into the cop.

Her lover. He knew it. He could see it in the man's eyes. The detective had been with Erin. Hell, maybe he'd even loved her. Jude had heard the way the asshole first said her name.

And Erin—how did she feel? She'd told him things were over with the cop because she couldn't fit into his "normal" world, but—

But Jude knew just how badly Erin longed for "normal."

*Rip him apart. Easy prey. Fight. Claim.*

*Mate.*

The beast raged inside.

But he was more than the beast, and he was trying to prove that to Erin. Besides, she had her own choices to make.

He clenched his teeth and stepped back. "If you need me, I'm right outside." Course, she'd be able to take down a human no problem, so the message wasn't so much for her.

*For the cop.* His gaze held the other man's. *Right outside.*

When he left the room, Erin swung the door shut behind him.

"Man, are you freaking insane?" Zane demanded instantly. "You're gonna let that cop stay in there alone with your woman? Did you *see* the way he was eyeballing her, like a good fu—"

Jude turned his stare on the demon, and Zane wisely shut the hell up.

Then Jude crossed his arms over his chest and got ready to wait.

He'd agreed to stay outside, but it wasn't like the thin walls would give Erin much privacy. Not to someone like him, anyway.

If that asshole cop yelled at her again, Jude was going inside, and the claws would be coming out.

"How did you find me?" Erin asked, keeping her voice cool and easing into her desk chair.

A shrug. One that tried to make him appear careless, but the lines bracketing his mouth belied the move. "When I linked the call at Katherine LaShaun's place to your cell, the DA had to cough up the info."

Ah, the cell call. She'd figured that would be traced back to her sooner or later. She just had been hoping more for later.

She'd forgotten just how good Ben's contacts were. "I had to call her. I couldn't let those boys see their father's body. They never would have felt safe at that house, they never—"

"Still trying to save the world?" he asked softly.

Her lips pressed together.

Jude had understood. She'd seen the way he looked at the boys.

*Had he seen himself in them?* Yeah, she'd bet that he had. Just like she'd seen herself.

Her hands flattened on the desktop. "I didn't break any laws by calling Katherine."

"You tipped off a suspect."

She jumped to her feet. *So much for playing it cool.* "Please! You and I both know there's no way Katherine killed Trent! That's not the kind of woman she is!"

"She thinks he killed her daughter. She'd do *anything* for her girl, you know that."

She did, but . . . "Katherine didn't kill Trent."

"You seem awfully sure of that." He walked around the desk, moving until he stood less than a foot away from her.

"Why is that, Erin? And why is it that Trent had your picture in what was left of his hands?"

*Because he was another freaking present.* She didn't flinch. "There are things going on here that you wouldn't understand."

"Oh?" His lips twisted into a cruel smile. The smile didn't suit him. Not at all. "Like I didn't understand about you back in Lillian? Every time I tried to get close, you just shoved me back. When I was in the hospital, you didn't even come to see me."

"Because I was trying to protect you!" The words burst out. Oh, no, she hadn't meant to tell him that. Now she was—

"And I find out now that you're cozying up with some low-rent bounty hunter!" His face reddened as his voice rose. "I saw the way he looked at you, the two of you are—wait, what the hell did you say?"

"Uh . . ."

The door flew open. "Asshole, don't *raise* your voice to her again." Jude stood in the doorway, his claws out and his eyes glowing.

Ben looked at him and his jaw dropped. *"What. The. Hell!"*

Jude kicked the door closed with his heel but never took that deadly gaze off the cop.

"I told you there were things you wouldn't understand," Erin said. Then, "Jude, back off, okay? I've got this."

"Bullshit. I could hear the prick yelling at you."

Yeah, well, with his shifter hearing, he probably would have been able to hear a whisper. "This isn't the way to handle the situation, okay?"

"He's got claws!" Ben shook his head, hard.

"All the better to rip into prey." Jude took a step forward.

"What's up with his eyes? Why are they—"

"All the better to see the asshole who doesn't need to be attacking my lady."

"Jude!" Her snarl had him faltering and glancing over at her. "I can fight this one on my own." *Not helping.* No, his big show and tell was making everything a thousand times worse.

"Sweetheart, it's time your cop learned the truth." In that devil-may-care grin, she caught the edge of his teeth, those too sharp canines. Erin swallowed and really hoped that Ben hadn't seen them, too, because if he said something about the fangs, she could already hear Jude's smart-ass response.

*All the better to bite.*

As much as she enjoyed his bites, Ben wouldn't appreciate the sentiment.

And he might run screaming.

It looked like that response could be a near thing right then.

*Thanks, Jude.* "Ben, relax, okay? Everything is all right."

"*All right?*" he thundered, still shaking his head. Then he shoved her behind him. "Do you see that guy? He's got *claws!*"

She peered around Ben in time to see Jude shrug. "So does she."

"*What?*"

"There are some things I never told you about myself," she said to Ben, using a tone she hoped was calm and easy.

He twisted around and eyed her with too-wide eyes. "What things?"

"Like the fact that I'm not . . . completely human."

A shocked laugh. "Right."

She held up her hand. Let him see her claws.

He jerked back from her and rammed into the desk. Horror was etched on his face. Disbelief filled his gaze.

The reaction she'd always feared.

"You've stumbled into a hell you can't fully imagine," Jude said.

Ben just looked between them, shaking his head. "No, Erin, I cared about you, I—"

"You cared about the woman you thought I was." And she'd just wanted someone to love her, as she *really* was.

Claws and all.

"This isn't real," he muttered, running a trembling hand through his hair. "Can't be, it's—"

"The guy outside the door,"—Jude jerked his thumb over his shoulder—"is a demon. I'm a white tiger shifter."

"*Not real.*"

"And the killer you're after—the one who left Erin's picture in the hands of a dead man—is a wolf shifter."

Ben's brows bunched. "Were . . . wolf?"

"Close enough." Jude nodded.

"No, that's not even possible, there's no way—"

Jude held up his claws and this time, he bared his teeth.

The gulp that clicked in Ben's throat seemed way too loud right then.

Erin reached out her hand to him, claws gone, but he flinched back. *Knew it would happen.*

Jude had never flinched away from her. She glanced at her shifter. No, he'd never flinched away, not even when he'd found out she was part wolf.

He'd wanted her from the beginning. No holdups. No hedging.

Taking her, as she was.

Jude's bright blue gaze held hers.

"Erin saved your ass by getting the hell out of Lillian," Jude told the cop. "The *werewolf* who killed Trent is after her and, if she hadn't left you behind, odds are high he would have killed you."

*"What?"*

She managed to look away from Jude and turn her attention back to Ben. "Seems that I acquired an . . . admirer, of sorts." Her lips pulled down into a frown and she rubbed her temple. "He does things, hurts others, even kills, and he thinks he's doing it for me."

Jude eased closer. "He killed a perp here in Baton Rouge and smeared the bastard's blood all over the walls in her house. Another guy, a lawyer, made the mistake of arguing too much with Erin in court. The freak put him in the hospital. ICU."

Erin flinched at that. She'd gone to the hospital that morning, before work, hoping to hear better news about Lee. His son had been sitting in his room, holding his hand. She'd stepped away, ducking into the empty room beside Lee's as she fought to control her tears.

Seeing that boy, praying for his father to wake up . . .

*He has to be stopped.*

Clearing her throat, she tried to push the memory of that kid aside. Lee would wake up. Oh, but she hoped he would anyway. "I have very good reason to believe that this guy is also the one who attacked you."

"Erin, there's no way to know that!"

"I've got good reason to believe it, because he told me he did," she broke across his words and dropped her hand. *I took care of your lover. Fool wasn't worthy.* He'd been so proud of nearly killing Ben. He'd whispered his words to her that terrible night. "He's been making my life hell for too long now. I tried running from him, hiding, but he just found me, and he started killing again."

Ben's mouth hung open. After a moment, he snapped his lips closed.

"It's the truth," she said. Might seem crazy, but crazy was her world.

"Wh-why didn't you tell me? I thought you left because you didn't care."

"He's a paranormal." Simple. "You couldn't have handled him. The other cops in Lillian are human, too. They wouldn't have known how to stop him. He would have sliced right through them and—"

The cop's head craned toward a watchful Jude. "This guy—let me guess, he can *handle* him, right?"

Jude shrugged.

"Yes." Erin was definite. "When he's in his tiger form, he's the closest physical match the bastard has." More than a match. Jude would be able to take the bastard down, she knew it.

"*Werewolves?*" Ben asked again and rocked back on his feet. "Come on, babe, I've dealt with some screwed-up killers in my time, but I haven't—"

"Shifters have been around for as long as humans have walked this earth." Jude crossed his arms over his chest. "Deny it if you want. If it makes you sleep better, do whatever the hell you have to do. But, the fact here is . . . you've got a paranormal killer out there. One who is obsessed with Erin, and you—well, you're playing out of your league, human."

There wasn't room for Ben in this fight. "If you try to get involved in this, you'll just get hurt." The freak out there would like his pain too much. "Go back to Lillian. We're going to stop him, and when we do—"

"What?" Ben's voice snapped out, high and sharp. "When you stop him, I book a werewolf for murder? How's that going to fly with the mayor and DA, huh? And what kind of cage am I going to toss him into?"

"This one won't stay in a cage." Jude's voice was soft, deep. A calm opposite to Ben.

Erin knew he was right. The killer they were looking for

was too strong for a human prison. "A cage won't ever hold him," she said, her stomach knotting. She'd known it would come to this.

"What are you saying?" Ben reached out a hand, as if he were going to touch her, but stopped, the fingers freezing in midair.

*Can't touch the shifter. Not normal.* Her chin lifted. "I'm saying we'll let you know when this threat is gone." That was all she was going to say. She couldn't really tell a cop that murder was the only option. Not really murder, though. Self-defense. "Now, I'm sorry, but I have work to do."

"If you've got more questions, *human,* I'll answer them," Jude said.

Ben's gaze drifted over her face. "This is the last damn thing I expected."

"I know."

"Erin . . ."

But there was nothing more to say. Like she'd told Jude, they'd ended in Lillian.

His hand fisted and he turned away from her. "I want to know everything you've got on this bastard."

Jude's claws were gone. For now. "Then I guess you'd better get ready for a little visit to Night Watch."

Jude took the human to the agency. Introduced him to a few of the hunters. Left him with Dee for a while so that she could brief him, one human to another.

And the fury inside him built.

*Erin had been hurt.* The human asshole had hurt her. He'd looked at her like she was . . . like she was some kind of freak.

*Erin.*

Jude growled.

*That* was the prick Erin had been dating? An ass who didn't recognize how great she was?

Idiot.

The cop's hands were shaking when he finished his briefing with Dee. Yeah, she usually had that effect on men.

"Heard enough?" Jude asked from his slouch against the wall.

A jerky nod.

"Good, then it's time to get your ass back on the road and head home to old Lillian." He straightened, then remembered the way the guy hadn't even been able to *touch* Erin after he'd learned the truth. "But first"—his fingers clenched around the prick's shirtfront, and he yanked him inside the nearest office.

"Jude! What the hell?"

"Beat it, Gomez." Gomez Montiago, charmer extraordinaire.

"This is *my* office, I'm not just gonna—"

Jude slanted him a hard look.

The charmer jumped up from his chair. "I had to go talk with Pak anyway."

The door slammed behind him.

Jude turned his focus back to the cop. "I ought to kick your ass."

The human got some spunk then, because his jaw clenched and he gritted, "You can try, but I'm not as weak as you may think."

"No?" Yeah, he was. "Are you as stupid as I think you are?"

Ben blinked and a furrow appeared between his eyes. "*What?*"

"She's not less because she's a shifter. She's not some kind of freak or abomination or *monster.*" The tiger roared inside. "She's still the same woman you knew. Still smart, still sexy, still *Erin.*" He shook his head now, the rage burning his tongue and leaving an acrid taste in his mouth. "But after you knew the truth, you couldn't even look at her the same way anymore."

*Humans.* They could piss him off so easily.

Dee and Tony were the only ones who'd ever been different. Dee because well, she'd been introduced to the paranormal world at a very early age.

And Tony . . . he'd come across Jude mid-shift once. The guy hadn't run or screamed. He'd just stayed and watched, gun drawn because he wasn't totally stupid. When the shift was done, that gun hadn't wavered. *"That you, man? You still fucking understand me?"*

Jude had managed a nod.

The gun hadn't disappeared, not right away, but he'd helped Jude ambush two killers who'd been hiding in a slum.

When a guy had seen you at your worst and he didn't flinch, but instead stepped up to the plate and helped get the job done—yeah, you could respect a guy like that.

"I didn't know what she was."

It would be so easy to rip his head off. "What she *is*. She's a woman. Strong and beautiful. The same as she's always been."

"It's a lot to deal with, all right? My head is spinning, I've got a body to deal with—"

"And you didn't have to treat Erin like she's something *less.*" Would Erin get too pissed if he clawed the guy a bit? What she didn't know . . .

"I-I *care* about her," the cop mumbled and his eyes fell.

What? *Care*, not cared. A snarl from the tiger that was echoed by the man as he said, "You didn't act like you do."

"Because I saw the way she looked at you!" Ben's fists rose up between them and he shoved against Jude's chest.

Jude didn't move. "Run that by me again." Maybe he wouldn't use his claws on the guy. Not yet.

"I always knew Erin had secrets." Another shove with those fists. Hmmm . . . the guy *was* stronger than he looked.

Jude still didn't move.

"I tried as hard as I could to get close to her, but she always kept me locked out." His eyes narrowed. "She doesn't keep you out, does she?"

A smile curved his lips. "The woman tried." *A wolf.* Who would have thought—

"But *you* got close to her. I saw it, when she looked at you, I *saw it.*" Another shove. Okay, more of a two-fisted punch this time.

Jude went with it and let his body slide back.

"You're sleeping with her." Bitten off. "Don't bother lying, I could *see* that, too. When you looked at her, it was all over your face."

"And Erin thinks I'm not territorial," he murmured.

The cop's eyes were slits. "She cared enough to protect me, but not to confide in me, not like she's done with you." Bitterness there.

Jude realized if the situation were reversed—damn lucky it wasn't—he'd be bitter, too.

A hell of a lot more than bitter.

A muscle flexed along Ben's jaw. "She left me behind. Do you think she'll do the same to you?"

Not if he had anything to say about the matter. He was playing for keeps.

"You gonna be able to handle things if she walks on you?"

Jude stared at him.

"Guess we'll see," the cop said and Jude thought about

punching him. Ben straightened his shirtfront. "I'm not leaving the area just yet. I'll be around if Erin should need me."

"Out of your league," Jude told him again, meaning the words as a warning. He'd hate for the cop to get killed. Explaining his death to Erin would be a bitch.

"Yeah, well, maybe it's time I got into a new league." He shouldered past him and headed for the door.

Jude watched him, brows low. Easy prey, but . . .

Ben glanced back. "If you let that bastard hurt her, I'll come after you, tiger." A pause. "She's not mine anymore, but—"

He broke off and shook his head, but Jude understood.

*But she's still Erin.*

"Now you're getting it," he said softly.

The human let out a growl of his own and jerked open the door.

Gomez stood in the doorway, his hand raised. "Ah . . . Jude." The hand dropped. "C-call for you. Some guy named Mickey."

He'd known the guy was there, of course, but—wait, *Mickey?* Hyena-asshole Mickey?

Ben moved around Gomez and marched away.

"The guy says he's got a tip, but only for you."

Now wasn't that some new shit. Mickey, offering him help on a case?

Jude went back to her, almost helplessly.

A jerk of his thumb had Zane heading out of the office, and Jude shut the door behind the demon.

Then turned the lock.

Erin glanced up at the soft click.

"Got rid of the boyfriend," he told her and stalked slowly forward. He eyed the room. Too much paperwork on her desk and the thing didn't look sturdy enough. He could always stand but—

Ah, that chair to the left, the one made of old leather would work fine.

"Ben's gone back to Lillian?"

Jude didn't want to lie. "He's not in the game." He'd better not be. The last thing he wanted to do was stumble on to the human while he was hunting.

And he'd be hunting again, very, very soon.

But first . . .

Erin rose and hurried toward him. "Jude, what is it? Why—"

He caught her hand, brought her fingers to his lips, and pressed a kiss to her palm.

Her nostrils flared, and he saw the dilation of her pupils.

"Don't have much time," he managed, his cock digging hard into his zipper. "I had to come and see you." Jude swallowed. Hell, he sucked at this relationship shit.

A frown pulled her brows low. "I don't understand."

He tugged her over to the chair, fell back, then pulled her down on top of him.

She straddled him when she came down, the skirt of her dress fluttering over his thighs.

Convenient.

A startled laugh burst from her lips. "Okay, hard to misunderstand *that.*" She rubbed against his straining erection, pursing her lips. "But, seriously, I've got to be in court in half an hour. I can't—"

"I don't want you to walk away from me." The words fell out, hard and flat. "Not like you did with Ben, with no looking back."

Her hands rose to push against his chest. The laughter was gone now. "Who says I never looked back?"

His fingers dug into her hips. He hadn't expected that. "I thought you said that you and the human were finished."

"We are." Her chin titled up and her hair brushed over her shoulders. "But I can still have regrets."

Not what he wanted to hear. "A human wouldn't be strong enough for you. He wouldn't be able to handle things when they got . . . wild." Not just talking about the shifter bastard out there.

"Doesn't always have to be wild," she told him softly, and her right index finger smoothed down the front of his shirt. "I'm wolf, but I'm human, too. Sometimes—sometimes a woman likes to go slow."

*Slow.* Not really his thing.

"Can you handle that, Jude?" she asked him and he really, *really* didn't like the look in her eyes. "Could you handle slow with me . . . and soft?" She tossed a look toward the shut door. A wooden door, but too thin. He could catch whispers and phone calls and about a hundred other sounds too easily.

He stared at Erin, at the elegant lines of her face. "I can handle anything you've got, sweetheart." That was why he'd come to her. To tell her that he wasn't the kind she could throw away when the danger was over.

He wasn't just dicking around with her. With Erin, he wanted everything.

*You gonna be able to handle things if she walks on you?*

"Let's just see." Erin's fingers fumbled with his belt. Eased open his zipper.

With a shifter, generally, the fewer clothes, the better, so he never bothered with underwear.

His cock sprang into her hands and he had to watch her. Had to watch the sight of those delicate hands pumping him, clenching and stroking.

*Oh, but that felt good.*

"You're ready." Her pink tongue swiped out.

Sweat trickled down his brow. *Hadn't counted on this.*

"So am I." With her left hand, she reached under the folds of her skirt. She twisted a bit, the movements clumsy but still sexy, then she had a scrap of lace dangling from her fingers.

*Fuck.*

"No sounds, Jude. Not fast. Not hard. Not this time." Another swipe of that tongue.

His head jerked forward and he locked his mouth on hers.

She nipped his lower lip and his cock jerked. *Oh, come on, that was just too—*

"I said soft," she whispered before her lips took his. She was soft. Her lips brushed across his mouth. Feathered over him, then broke away.

*Not enough.*

Her hips rose. Jude glanced down, desperate for a sight of that pink flesh, but her skirt covered her and he couldn't see a damn thing.

But he could *feel* her as she slid down onto his throbbing erection. Warm, wet flesh. A straining entrance that took in the tip of his cock, squeezed.

He wrenched his hands away from her and locked them onto the arms of the chair. *Can't hurt her.*

Leather tore as his claws dug deep.

She lifted herself higher, bracing against him, then pushed down, taking all of him in one long, slow glide.

His breath shuddered out. "Is . . . this . . . some kind of . . . fucking test?"

She rose, sank down, rose again. "Maybe . . . for both of us."

*Too slow.* He wanted her creamy flesh. Wanted her breasts in his hands, her tongue in his mouth.

Her inner muscles clamped around him, her sex squeezing so tightly that he lost his breath.

Then she smiled that sexy smile. "So far, so good."

Better than good.

"Let's see how long we can last," she murmured and lowered her face to his neck. She swiped her tongue over him, and Jude's head tipped back against the chair.

The tiger jerked against his chains, desperate for more, faster, harder.

Jude's hips arched against her when she tried to rise.

He couldn't help it.

Her gasp said she liked it.

So did the sting of her claws.

Her cream coated the length of his arousal, and when she pushed up onto her knees and then drove down, he met her with a deep thrust.

*So fucking good.*

Another thrust. Deeper.

His cock slipped over her clit and Erin bit her lip, smothering a groan.

Slow and deep.

Her breath hitched, grew faster. Her lips found his. Their tongues met.

Just what he'd been wanting.

He took her mouth even as she kept taking him. *Slow and deep.*

His spine prickled.

Her cream thickened and her body stiffened. He held onto his control with all his strength. Held on until he felt the tremors caressing the length of his cock. Those slow, clenching spasms told him Erin was coming for him.

And now he could come for her.

His hands flew to her hips. He drove up and held her as tight as he could.

Jude thrust hard. Once, twice. He bared his teeth even as a roar rose in his throat.

Erin kissed him, muffling the cry, and he climaxed, exploding in her hot depths and plunging as deep into her as he could go.

*Mate.*

Zane glanced at the closed door. His senses weren't as good as a shifter's, but they were a whole lot better than a human's.

And he'd heard that sound. A low groan.

His nostrils twitched.

Aw, hell.

No mistaking that particular scent in the air.

He shook his head. *Lucky bastard.*

The cute little redhead with the seriously cold shoulders marched toward him, a file in her hands.

Not really toward him so much as toward Erin's office . . .

He stepped in front of her. "Now isn't a good time."

Her jaw tightened. "Erin's due in court," she gritted. "She needs this—"

He plucked the file from her fingers. "And she'll get it. Thanks."

After a hard glare, and another temperature drop, she spun away from him.

"Ah, man, you owe me."

Erin stared at Jude, her heart rate slowing.

"Did I pass your test?"

Aftershocks had her sex squeezing around him.

"I'll take that as a yes."

He could take it any way he wanted. She swallowed, trying to ease her dry throat. Okay, jumping him like that really hadn't been her plan.

But she'd seen the heat in his eyes the minute he walked into her office.

She'd known what he wanted. She would have been an idiot not to know once he started sizing her up . . . and then glancing over at the chair like he'd been trying to figure out if they'd fit.

After a second's thought, Erin had realized she didn't want to wait on seduction.

And that she'd wanted to break some rules.

*Sex in the office.*

"Why?" he asked her and she could only stare back at him blankly.

*Slow and soft*—that's what she told him, but it wasn't what she'd wanted. Not really. She'd had slow and soft for too long. She'd wanted loud and wild. She hadn't wanted to worry about the others outside or—or about anything but Jude.

She'd just wanted him.

The truth was that she would have taken him any way she could get him.

But, yeah, she'd wondered if the sex would be different if she held her primal nature back. If it would be as good.

The answer was . . . um, *oh yeah.* She felt freaking great. Sex with Jude wasn't like being with other men. Never would be. Soft and slow—still wonderful. Wild and hard—*amazing.*

The guy was ruining her for everyone else. "Soft and slow with you," she finally managed, "is one hell of a lot better than the sex I had with other—"

"*Don't go there.*"

She blinked at the banked fury in his voice.

"I don't want to hear about other men, and I sure don't want to hear about them when I'm still *in* you." The edges of his teeth had sharpened and he was eyeing her neck with a little too much attention.

Erin scrambled back, rising off him in a rush and then managing to stand with shaky knees.

She clenched her thighs, aware of the sticky residue from their—

Jude jerked his zipper back up. He straightened his clothes fast, then rose, coming right at her.

Her panties were in his left fist. How had they gotten there?

Hmm . . . she'd really need those soon. She couldn't go to court without them. "Jude . . ."

"I'll take you any way I can get you, but I'll be damned if I share you with anyone."

Her eyes widened. "I wouldn't—"

His hand, the one without the panties, pressed against her chest. Right over her heart. "Talking about in here, sweetheart. When we're together, there's no room for anyone else."

This moment was important. The air was thick. His hand was warm against her, and her heart galloped away with that touch. "No one else is there." It was true.

She was in trouble.

He smiled at her and she thought about jumping him again. "Good," he rumbled and pressed a hot, fast kiss to her lips. "And, yeah, for the record, there had damn well better not be anyone else taking that sweet body."

She didn't want anyone else the way she wanted him. Never had.

"This insanity with the stalker is going to be ending soon," he told her. *Can't end soon enough.* "You won't need a hunter anymore."

She'd always need him. Not for protection or for his strength. She'd just . . . need him.

Erin hadn't needed anyone since her father died. No, she hadn't *let* herself need anyone.

*How had Jude gotten so close, so fast?*

He saw past the surface. He saw things that others didn't. Couldn't.

*He always looked at me as if he couldn't wait to get me naked. Always looked at me like I was a woman.*

Not a monster. Not the way Ben had looked at her hours before.

"I'm not gonna disappear from your life when he's gone." His hand was a warm, heavy weight. "And you're not gonna disappear from mine."

What the hell? The knot in her throat—what was that? Erin swallowed, shoving it down. "No, I'm not." She was done running.

And, maybe, she was ready to take a risk on someone.

With someone.

*Jude.*

*He can handle anything I throw at him.*

Even soft and easy. The tiger had held perfectly still and let her ride him. What a ride it had been.

She shifted from one foot to the other and realized she'd kicked off her pumps somewhere. Maybe near the chair.

His hand lifted. Her heart slowed.

Jude kneeled before her. He caught one foot in his hand and began to slide her panties back on.

*Strength and gentleness.* Hell of a combination. How was a woman supposed to resist?

He turned his attention to the other foot, and he eased the soft material over her toes and up her calf.

He pressed a kiss to her knee and lifted the silk even higher.

Erin gulped. She lifted her skirt up for him, aware of a quiver in her belly.

And in her sex.

*More, please.*

He pulled the panties up. The bikini design rode low on her hips. His mouth brushed her belly, then pressed against the crotch of her panties.

She tried to suck in enough air for her starving lungs. "J-Jude—"

One more kiss, then he pulled away. "This case is ending," he repeated and rose to his feet, "but *we* aren't."

Her skirt fell seamlessly back into place. The lust gnawed at her, burning and pumping through her.

She stared into his eyes, and there was only one answer to give. "No, we aren't." Because she wasn't an idiot. No way would she walk away from a man who could—

A rap at the door. "Uh . . . the DA is looking for you, Erin." Zane's expressionless voice.

Hell.

Jude licked his lips. "Later, we'll do things *our* way again."

Wild. Sounded great. She held his stare a moment longer and gave a fierce nod. That freaking knot in her throat was back so the nod was pretty much all she could manage.

"I have some leads to follow, but I'll pick you up tonight."

He eased away, headed for the door.

Erin scrambled for her shoes. The DA. *Court.* She toed into her pumps just as he yanked open the door. "Wait! Jude!"

He glanced back at her, and her breath caught. The man was really something.

"Wh-what kind of leads?"

"The kind that I hope will take me right to the stalker."

He'd told her the case would be ending soon. He'd meant those words, she realized. "Be careful."

"Always."

Zane was waiting for him. Jude bent toward the demon and she heard her shifter say, “I’m going to the den.”

Zane seemed to stiffen a bit at that.

Then Jude strode away. He didn’t look back, and Erin stared after him, feeling like she should say something, but having no idea what.

*It’s not over.*

No, it wasn’t.

# Chapter 17

An hour later, Jude entered hell.

From the outside, hell appeared pretty unassuming. It looked just like an old building, one with a few beat-up cars lining the broken lot. A drunk or two sprawled on the sidewalk outside the square, squat structure.

Appearances were so deceiving.

*Dammit, I fucking hate demons' dens.*

And he really did. Of all the shitholes in the world, the demons' dens were the worst. He hated them. Hated the stench. Hated the blood and booze. And Jude hated the drugged out demons who flocked to the dens looking for their next fix.

Demons. Talk about an addictive personality. He'd never come across supernaturals who were as hooked on drugs as demons. Some demons, all they lived for was their next hit.

They always had to get more. Had to get lost. To forget.

There were rumors that the demons *had* to turn to the

drugs. Especially if they were unlucky enough to have the whispered Dark Touch.

*The Dark Touch*. It was another name, a more fitting one, for the psychic powers that turned some demons into conduits for the dregs of human society—killers, rapists, child molesters.

Yeah, the rumors were that the drugs quieted or, in some cases, even severed that twisted link. But the problem was, once the demons started the drugs, it was a fast downward spiral.

Demons just got addicted too fast.

That addiction fear was one of the reasons Zane didn't so much as drink or smoke. Jude knew the demon had seen his father go down the drug path, with gruesome results.

Jude inhaled, caught the stench in the air, and knew he was in the right place.

Or maybe the wrong one.

The den waited for him. A hole in the middle of hell. Looked like a drug house, smelled like a drug house—because it *was* a drug house.

But the demons in there, they would talk. They'd tell him all he needed to know about Rogue wolves. Because if anybody knew about predators, it was those bastards.

It had been another grade A bastard who'd led him to this sour side of hell. Mickey had called him—yeah, somehow the bastard was already out on bail—and told him about the den. According to fast talking Mickey, Jude would find exactly what he needed in there.

The tip hadn't been free, of course. Nothing was free. He'd just have to wait and see what price Mickey demanded. Not that he'd actually pay the bastard.

Jude rapped hard on the old door. A demon with a giant rod shoved through his nose jerked it open. Jude flashed him a twenty.

The demon's gaze darted over him, then he smiled and eased back.

Erin's sweet scent clung to Jude's skin—he'd just had to claim her once more, couldn't resist that temptation, but the stench of the den wrapped around him as he crossed the threshold.

And he went deeper into the demons' den.

*Fuck. Fuck. Fuck.* Mickey McQueen rocked back and forth on his heels. He'd gotten out of jail—*finally*—and was ready to blow this city.

But first . . .

First he wanted his money.

He stood on the street corner, glancing to the left and to the right. He still couldn't believe his luck.

That tiger wouldn't know what hit him.

Mickey laughed.

But he choked back the sound when a long, black car pulled up to the curb.

*This was it.* His ticket to fast times.

He grabbed the door handle. Jumped inside.

"You told the hunter?"

Damn but it was hot in there. Didn't the guy know to turn on the fucking air in Louisiana? Mickey gave a grim nod. "Yeah, yeah, told him everything you said."

Mr. Money had approached him at his arraignment. Mr. Money—Mickey liked to call him that because the bastard was gonna be giving him a shitload of money. He figured the name fit. Mr. Money had paid his bail *in cash* and promised him a hell of a lot more.

All he had to do was just make one phone call.

Easiest job he'd ever done.

A soft snick of sound—the doors had locked. Must be one of those automatic deals.

Mickey rubbed his fingers together. "You got my money?" He already had it spent. New clothes. Fast ride. Good-bye cops.

The car eased away from the curb. "I've got it."

Fucking A. "So . . ." He had to know. "What's gonna happen to the tiger?" He hoped the bastard got torn up. Clawed from head to foot.

The car turned into an alley. Mr. Money glanced over at him, smiling with too-sharp teeth.

*What the hell?* The guy *couldn't* be a shifter.

"I'm going to rip him apart."

Mickey blinked. "Good. Good." He realized he was sweating. It was the teeth. His nostrils quivered. No, no shifter scent. But the guy couldn't be a vamp because—

"Just like I'm going to rip you open, Mickey."

"*What?*" Shit! Mickey scrambled, trying to jerk open the car door.

But it wouldn't budge. Stupid lock. If he tried hard enough, he'd be able to force it—

Claws came at him. He saw the attack coming from the corner of his eye and he twisted, trying to fight.

Too late.

The claws slashed right across his throat and the scream building in him never broke from his lips.

Blood splashed onto the front windshield.

The claws came at him again.

*I'm going to rip him apart.*

When he was done, he shoved the body—what was left of it—out of the car. Blood was everywhere. The scent surrounded him. Soaked his clothes.

Perfect.

He brought his fingers to his lips and licked away the sticky liquid. He loved that rich taste.

But the hyena had been too easy. No fight at all. Like killing a human. Really, he'd expected more.

The tiger wouldn't be such easy prey. He knew that and had prepared appropriately for Donovan.

After all, he liked to hunt. He liked to kill.

But he didn't believe in taking foolish chances with his own life.

The tiger would die. No question.

He'd be there for the end.

He yanked the car door closed and frowned at the windshield. That wouldn't do. The last thing he needed was for someone to see that wonderful blood.

Leaning over, he unlocked the glove box and pulled out the cloths he kept for just such an occasion.

Moments later, the glass was clean. He shoved the cloths back in the glove box and turned on the car. Then he took a deep breath, because he did love that sweet smell.

But he couldn't linger any longer. Not with the body just outside. The area was deserted, for now, but someone would be coming along soon. They always did.

With a flick of his fingers, he punched the button for the radio and the soft strains of Brahms floated to his ears.

A smile curved his lips. Now it was time to go.

Time for the next kill.

As he backed out of the alley, he couldn't help but wonder, *how long will the tiger fight?*

And when he died, would Donovan have time to scream? Or would he die like the hyena, choking on his own blood?

"Down there." The demon, eyes completely black, raised his hand and pointed down the twisting steps.

The first floor of the den had been completely deserted. No big surprise there. Jude knew the demons liked to be prepared, just in case there were any unexpected and unwanted—*usually human*—visitors.

So the real action was never up front in a den. No, it was always in the back, or in this case, below.

The faint drum of pounding music teased his ears. Jude deliberately relaxed his shoulders, ready for whatever hell he'd find waiting down there. He brushed by the demon, his nostrils flaring as he caught the stale odor of sweat and cigarettes.

Carefully, he eased down the creaking steps. What was this? A basement? Lower level?

The door behind him swung shut.

Jude stiffened.

Then he heard the sound of a bolt sliding into place. *Locking me in.*

No, locking *them* in—because he could hear voices from below. Laughter.

He shook his head. Like a lock was going to hold him in this den. When he was ready to leave, he'd just kick the door down. Easy.

His claws broke free, the brief pain making his heart surge. His canines burned as they lengthened, readying him for the fight to come. He'd go in as a man, but if the shit got too bad, he would go out as a tiger.

His claws scraped over the stair railing as he climbed down the rest of the steps. No rush. The bastards weren't going to get by him.

The room below was bigger than he'd thought. Not a room, more like three rooms. Thick with smoke, from the flickering flames of candles that were the only light and from hell knew what else. The scents in the air had his nose twitching and burning. How the demons could handle that crap . . .

"Hello, shifter." The voice was loud, mocking.

The rock music kept pounding in the background.

Jude jumped off the last step.

His gaze swept the area. Demons were lounging against the walls. Some were curled up on the floor. Maybe fifteen of them total. He eyed the dark shadows. More bodies could be in there.

*Maybe twenty.*

Demons and their addictions.

But the guy who'd called to him, *he* didn't have that blank, slack look on his face. No, that guy, the big bastard with his black demon eyes, was planted about fifteen feet away. His legs were braced a shoulder's length apart. His arms hung loosely at his sides, and the guy was smiling. A come-and-get-me grin.

Never a good sign.

The demon lifted his hand. The minions on the ground didn't move. Jude figured those guys weren't gonna be moving anytime soon. But the others, those against the walls and those hiding in the shadows, jerked forward, suddenly appearing way too alert and aware.

Jude rolled his neck, getting loose and ready, and the tiger snarled.

"We've been waiting for you," the demon said, that cocky-ass smile still on his face. "Haven't we, guys?"

A murmur swept through the group. Laughter.

*Mickey.* Payback would be a bitch. He raised his claws and caught the glint of a knife in the darkness.

Ready for him *and* armed.

Demons in a den were supposed to be so screwed up on the drugs they couldn't tell reality from—

"Always hated shifters," the bastard who had to be the leader muttered. "Fucking animals."

The demon was trying to piss him off now.

They started to close in, a sea of black eyes.

Stairs behind him. Demons to the front, left, and right. Running wasn't an option for him. Never had been.

"You're messing with the wrong guy," he warned, feeling the burn of the shift pulse through him. It would take a few moments to turn. Vulnerable moments. They'd attack when the shift started. The demons would catch him with their knives and do as much damage as they could.

But once he was in tiger form . . .

"Oh, no, you're the right guy, Jude Donovan." A snap of the demon's teeth. "You're the guy we're gonna carve apart."

Jude fell to the floor as his bones began to snap and crack.

The demons attacked, knives ready, blades flying. Slashing, stabbing, cutting too deep.

He opened his mouth to scream and the tiger roared.

"Your Honor, I object! This is pure hearsay, the witness has no way to confirm that—" Erin broke off, stumbling. The judge's face swam before her eyes.

"Ms. Jerome?" Judge Sally Chen called out. "Ms. Jerome, are you all right?"

Erin made a grab for the edge of the jury box. She barely managed to catch herself before she fell face-first onto the gleaming floor. "Ah, yes." She blinked. The judge's face sharpened before her, and Erin could see the firm chin and the dark green gaze again. She tried to straighten herself up.

And nearly hit the floor.

"Do you need a recess, ADA?"

She could only manage a faint nod.

"All right, folks. Look, it's close to quitting time anyway. Let's resume this case tomorrow morning, eight a.m." The gavel slammed down.

Erin took a deep breath. Her hand rubbed over her forehead. Her stomach was churning, her knees shaking.

*Not good.*

"You okay?" Zane's voice. The guy had followed her to court and plopped down in the front row.

Right then, she was *so* glad he was there. Erin shook her head. "No. No, something's wrong—"

*The courtroom disappeared.*

"Zane?" This couldn't be happening.

*Black walls. Laughter. Snarls.*

Erin jerked her head around, straining to see.

*A tiger, with blood matting its white body. Men attacking the beast, slashing and stabbing with knives.*

*The tiger fell before her. Its head hit the floor. A puddle of blood spread around the fallen animal.*

*The fur dissolved. Tanned flesh appeared. A man with blond hair, bloody flesh. Not moving. Not breathing.*

*More laughter.*

*"Too fucking easy."*

*"I thought he wanted the shifter bastard alive."*

*"Doesn't matter—we'll still get paid."*

*"We damn well better."*

*The man's eyes were open—blue and empty. Not like Jude's at all.*

*Not like Jude, not anymore.*

"Erin!" Her head snapped back. Zane shook her, hard. "Erin, what the hell? Can you hear me?"

She blinked, and the courtroom was back. She was on the floor. Zane's fingers dug into her arms, and he crouched above her, lines bracketing his mouth. "Jude."

"No—it's Zane." His head lifted and he called out, "Hey, I need some help over here!"

She grabbed his shirt front and jerked him toward her. "Where's Jude?" Her teeth wanted to chatter, so she clenched them.

*Death dreams*. She hated them.

*Jude.*

How long had she been out? "*Where is he?*" Close to a scream in a courtroom. Like she cared about the rules then.

"Ah . . ." He glanced down at her white-knuckled grip. "Your claws are cutting me."

"He's in trouble." Absolute certainty. *Too late. Always too late.* Lee was still in the hospital. Still in a coma because she'd been too late. And her father was in a grave because she'd been too late.

Damn dreams. Why, *why* did she have them if she couldn't stop death?

Not Jude. Not him.

"What?" The demon shook his head. "Look, you're confused. You fell hard." A wince. "I didn't catch you before you slammed your head on the floor. Give things a minute, you'll be fine."

No, she wouldn't be. "If you don't tell me where he is, Jude's dead."

Finally, *that* got his attention. She saw his Adam's apple bob. "You—you can't—"

"Psychic, remember?" No time to go into the twisted story of her particular talents.

"Jude's out hunting." He rose, jerked her to her feet, and ignored the scrape of her claws over his flesh.

"Hunting where?" *Hold on, Jude. Please, hold on.* She couldn't lose him.

Wouldn't.

*Always too late.*

Dammit.

Zane jerked out his cell phone and punched in a number. His jaw flexed as he waited. Waited.

Erin rocked forward on her heels. *He could be dying.*

"Dee! Dee—where's Jude? What? No, I don't have time—*just tell me which damn den!*" His eyes widened and Erin caught "Jamestown? You sure? Fuck." He ended the call, his fingers whitening around the small phone.

"Zane?" *There had been so much blood.*

*Won't. Lose. Him.*

"He's in a demons' den on Jamestown." He shook his head. "We can't go there. There's no way you can—"

*Jamestown.* Erin spun away from him and ran for the double doors.

"Wait! You won't find the den. You'll never be able to—"

She jerked open the courtroom door. Hesitated. *Demons' den.* Her neck craned as she glanced back at him. "You can find it."

His face paled.

"If you don't, he's dead."

"Dammit." His hands clenched. "Then let's go to hell."

"A demons' den is like a crack house." Zane stared at the dark building before them. "Only much, much worse."

Erin didn't really care how much worse the place was. Yeah, the place looked like some kind of hole in the wall, but if Jude was inside, she was bringing him out. "You sure this is the place?"

"Yeah, yeah. Dee said he was following a lead on your stalker."

Jude was going to die because of her. The thudding of her heartbeat filled her ears.

*No. Not for me.*

Erin jumped up the cracking steps.

"Wait. There'll be a guard, armed. Always is at a place like this. He'll—"

Erin kicked in the door. The wood exploded under her foot, shattering instantly. She barreled forward, ignoring the scrapes along her arms and face.

"*Hey, bitch, what the fu—*"

A big, lanky guy with pitch black eyes ran at her, spittle flying.

Erin caught him with her claws, right in the chest, and shoved the bastard back about ten feet. He hit the wall, sent plaster flying, and sank to the floor.

He didn't get up.

A long whistle behind her. "Yeah, you're scary," Zane said. "And someone is stalking *you*?"

Her gaze snapped to the left, then the right. Old furniture. Freaking rats running around. Enough dust to clog her nose and numb her sense of smell but *no Jude.* "Where is he? You said this was the right place! *Where is he*?" So she sounded hysterical. If there was ever a time for a freak-out, it was *now.*

Zane's stare swept the room. Then the floor. "What's that?"

Two deep grooves dug into the old wood. Erin stared at the markings. They'd started next to the far wall and they ended at the big, scarred chest on the other side of the room.

"Something's behind it, something's—"

Erin bounded across the room. The chest had to be seven feet high and maybe four feet wide. She rubbed her damp palms on her thighs. Then she grabbed one side of the chest and shoved.

The chest flew out of the way.

"Damn woman."

*A door.*

"They must have blocked it off. Doesn't figure, why would they—"

"Because Jude's down there!" Erin wrenched the knob. "And they didn't want him getting out." Not until they were finished with him.

Erin broke the lock and thrust the door open. A yawning black space stared back at her. The faint thud of drums reached her ears—or, hell, was that her heart? "*Jude!*"

"No, Erin, you've got to be careful," Zane's hushed voice. "If somebody's got Jude down there—"

Screw careful. He needed her.

And she damn well needed him. More than she'd realized.

*I didn't know—didn't understand—until I saw him die.*

Erin ran into the darkness.

*He'd better not be dead.*

# Chapter 18

Dim, sputtering candles lit the basement and revealed the massacre. A trail of broken, bloody bodies littered the floor. The moaning men had claw marks all over their flesh.

But all of the bastards weren't moaning heaps on the floor. More of the assholes were up and they were still fighting. Five, no six of them were on the tiger. They'd backed the beast up against the far wall and they were punching him, stabbing him—

*Killing him.*

One blade drove into his side, into the already red fur, and the tiger jerked back, a keening cry on his lips.

Erin growled.

"Oh, no, the hell they aren't—" Zane's snarl behind her.

No, *they weren't*. She attacked, with Zane charging at the same instant.

Erin grabbed the closest asshole and spun him around.

"What the hell?" Black eyes, darker than night, colder

than hell, stared down at her. *Demon.* They were all demons in this den. "Bitch, what do you want?"

Her claws slashed over his chest. His mouth dropped open as the blood soaked his shirt. He fell to his knees, screaming.

"I want you to get out of my way," she gritted and shoved him to the side.

*Next.* She lifted her claws up, ready to fight.

But Zane grabbed the next demon and broke the jerk's wrist when the asshole lifted his knife. Smiling, Zane punched him in the face. Blood squirted, there was a sickening squish, and then that demon went down, too.

A scream of pain ripped through the room. Erin's gaze jerked up. The tiger had caught one demon beneath him. Claws and teeth took him out in seconds.

Another demon launched toward her. Bald head. Soulless eyes and skin too pale. And like the others, this guy was armed. He grinned at her, then whispered, "Come play . . ."

Like she had to be asked twice. Taking a breath, tasting blood, Erin raced forward.

But this one was fast. In a breath's time, he'd attacked and the blade of his knife sliced down her arm. *Dammit*! Fiery pain burned her flesh.

The music pounded around her. Where was it coming from?

"I love to watch a woman bleed."

Her eyes narrowed. The guy's breath was a stale wind in her face. He towered over her, grinning and flashing yellowed teeth. Giant, oozing sores covered his face and arms. He looked like some kind of Meth head. Maybe he was.

"I'll slice you open, carve you up!" He lunged, but, this time, she was ready. When he came at her, her claws caught him, tearing flesh and muscle, cutting to the bone. His bloodshot eyes flared wide and a choked gasp broke from his lips.

"Or maybe I'll slice you," she whispered and tried really, really hard not to think about what she was doing. Not killing, no, she wasn't killing the demons. They were still alive, just out of commission.

*Fight.*

*Save Jude.*

*Fight.*

No, she wasn't killing them, but if it came to that in order to save Jude, she would.

Her claws jerked free. The demon groaned, then fell.

Another demon landed on top of him. This one was a broken, bleeding mess—courtesy of a knife-wielding Zane.

So many broken bodies surrounded them. And the tiger stood poised for a final attack. His powerful body bunched as his mouth opened over his prey.

"No, no!" Erin lunged for the tiger. "Zane, don't let him!"

Zane was already there. He grabbed the shuddering demon from the mouth of the tiger and hauled the bastard back by the scruff of his neck.

The attacking demons were done. The jerk that Zane held was the only one still conscious in the room.

Her breath caught as she looked at the tiger. *So many wounds*. Too many. He wouldn't be able to hold that form much longer. No way could he—

The transformation began. Fur melted before her eyes. Bones snapped. Scrambling, slipping in the blood that pooled on the floor, she went to him and held him tight. She could feel the slow thud of his heartbeat against her. "It's okay." Not a lie. It *would* be okay. They'd gotten there in time. "You're safe."

He shuddered against her and as she stroked him, her fingers skimming over his wounds. The deep cuts and slashes marked his sides, his back, his chest.

Erin swallowed. *No, he'd make it. Jude would live.*

"We've got to get him to a hospital." Her voice was cold, *she* was cold.

So was he. His skin had turned to ice.

Jude's blood poured on her, soaking her clothing.

In human form now, he seemed even weaker. She grabbed his face with her hands and forced him to look at her. "Jude? Jude, dammit—stay with me!" His blue eyes were dull. Faded, not bright like they should have been.

"No! You're stronger than this! *Fight*!" A scream of fury and fear. Blood burned her nostrils. Drums pounded. *Turn off the damn music.* "Stay with me." A whisper now.

Erin kissed him and tasted blood and man.

*Stay with me.*

His mouth didn't move against hers. Too slack. Too cold.

"What the hell happened down here?" A sharp, furious demand.

Erin lifted her lips from Jude's but didn't glance back. *Dee.* Zane had called her again on the way to the den, told her to come. *Armed.*

"It was a setup," Zane said, voice thundering. "When we got here, they were trying to slice him apart."

They'd almost succeeded.

"Jude." Still a whisper, but she thought she saw his eyelids flicker at the sound. "I know . . . I know you're weak." Her cheeks were damp. Blood or tears? Both? "But you've got to try and fight, okay? You can't stay human."

If he did, he'd bleed out before help arrived. She knew it. Wouldn't lie to herself.

Her lips wanted to tremble so she pressed them together. His eyes were open, on her. Did he hear her? Did he understand?

Her fingers smoothed over his face. "Try to change back." It was the only thing that would save him. The power of the shift. The beast could heal, the man couldn't.

Jude wouldn't be able to hold the tiger form long, she knew that. Probably only for a few seconds, but if he could just shift . . .

Some of the wounds would close. The healing powers would amp up and he'd survive.

*Maybe.*

No, no, he *would* survive.

The only reason he was still breathing now was because he'd shifted from beast to man. Every shift worked to mend his flesh. So if he could just transform one more time . . .

*There might be a chance for him.*

"Shift, Jude." Her arms wrapped around him, held tight. "*Shift!*"

His heart rate kicked up but his head fell forward.

She held him tighter.

A growl built in his throat.

"Get an ambulance!" Zane ordered.

The thunder of footsteps on the stairs as Dee ran for help.

If he didn't shift . . .

Soft, thick fur brushed against her skin.

Her eyes squeezed shut. Yeah, *tears.*

The crack of bones tormented her ears. Her hold never lessened. "Fight."

Faster, faster—his heartbeat thudded in a double-time beat.

Her eyes opened. She saw white fur and the long, lean body of the tiger.

"*Sonofabitch!*" Zane's cry. "I knew the bastard wouldn't go down easy."

No, not easy. Not her Jude.

He bucked against her, his body trembling. The shape of the tiger began to fade.

*Be enough.* Enough to let him live.

Moments passed. The tiger disappeared, leaving the broken man in his place.

"Jude?"

He slowly raised his head and stared at her with confusion clouding his eyes. "Erin?"

Her smile felt like it was going to break her face. Too big. Too wide. Too—ah, hell. Erin kissed him.

And he kissed her back. Moved his lips, his tongue.

*He was back.*

She pulled away, just a few inches. "Don't ever do that to me again, tiger." Not too late. For once, finally, not too late.

His mouth hitched into a half-smile. "Trust me, not . . . part of my . . . plans."

Her hands roved over his back. She could still feel the wounds, but they weren't as deep. The blood flow had eased. The shift had done its job.

Jude wouldn't die on her.

"You're one tough asshole, shifter." Zane whistled. "For a minute, I thought you were a corpse."

Jude winced. He was naked, his flesh rippling as he moved. "For a . . . minute there, I did . . . too."

So had she.

Dee's shoes pounded down the stairs. "Help's coming, just tell him to hold on—"

Erin glanced back at her in time to see the human stumble to a stop. Dee blinked twice, then smiled. "Shifter."

If he hadn't been, he would be dead.

Swallowing, Erin tried to ease back.

"Erin—wait, *you're hurt*!"

Yeah, but he didn't need to worry about her. The scratch

she had was nothing compared to the wounds still on his body. "I'll be okay."

"Can't you shift to heal?" Zane asked. The demon he'd hauled away lay bound near his feet. Good thing Zane carried his own cuffs—*Other* proof cuffs she'd glimpsed in the car. They were made out of some kind of special titanium. "You're losing a lot of blood."

She'd lost more blood than she would have liked, but her wound had already started to heal.

Jude caught her arm. Lifted it, turned it for better inspection. "You don't . . . have to shift." He sounded stronger. Good.

She shook her head. No, for her, the healing didn't depend on the shift. A lucky thing, because otherwise, she'd be very easy prey.

His gaze rose to hers. "I saw . . . what you did."

"I couldn't let them kill you." Her voice was rough and scratchy. She didn't want to think about what she'd done to those men. No, demons, not men. Not human.

"You're not . . . weak." His eyes widened and he sucked in a sharp breath. "You're the . . . next step, aren't you? Evolution of the whole damn . . . species. Why shift when you've got all the power . . . in human form . . ."

Her brow furrowed. Next step? The guy must still be weak. She wasn't anything special. Far from it.

"Donovan!" The door at the top of the stairs banged open. Voices shouted in the background, but Antonio's voice was clear as he demanded. "Donovan, dammit, you down there?"

"Help's arrived," Dee murmured.

"The cops? *Hell.*" Zane shook his head. "You called them, Dee? *Them?*"

"I called 911," she told him as Antonio flew down the stairs. It sounded like a dozen men were behind him. "Told them we had an officer down."

"He's not an officer," Zane said, rubbing a hand over his face and then staring at the demons littering the floor. "I fucking hate dens."

"Yeah, well, Jude's also not human, but I didn't tell them that, either."

"Donovan!" Antonio leapt over the last few steps. "What the hell happened here?"

Jude pushed up, staggering a bit as he rose to his feet. Erin wrapped her arms around him as she tried to steady him as much as possible.

"Ambush," Zane explained succinctly. "Who would've thought these drugged out assholes could even manage something like this?" Disgust was rich in his voice. No, not just disgust, almost . . . hatred.

"That . . . one." Jude lifted his hand and pointed to the bound demon. "He's not using."

"Aw, *Christ*, man, you're naked!" Antonio spun around. "You trying to make me go blind or something?"

There was a line of cops behind him. Men and women. A few EMTs were sprinkled in the bunch. Erin moved quickly, putting herself between Jude and the crowd. Not that Jude probably gave a rat's butt about his modesty, but she did.

"What happened to his clothes?" one of the officers called out.

Antonio's hands went to his hips. "This is a crack house—who knows what the drug heads were doing? Maybe they cut 'em off, thinking he was holding out on them."

The man was fast on his feet, and his explanation sounded like a good cover story to her. Especially since Jude's clothes were lying in a mangled pile to the right. "Dee," she called softly, trying to catch the other woman's attention. Dee worked with Jude. Did that mean she knew about his policy of keeping backup clothing in his vehicle?

"On it," the woman said immediately and headed back for

the stairs. "Uh, Tony, not to tell you how to handle your shit, but with all this *Other* stuff going on down here, don't you think you'd better clear the scene?"

He gave a grim nod then ordered, "Bishop and Peters—get over there and see what kind of damage the assholes did to Donovan. The rest of you—*upstairs*. Make sure the scene is secured. None of these pricks will be leaving the area until I'm done with them."

Dee brushed by him.

Antonio snagged her arm. "Next time, could you let me *know* what I'm walking into?"

"Wasn't time for that." One shoulder lifted, fell. "I thought he was dying." She glanced back at Jude. "He *was* dying, and I needed the cavalry to get its ass here as fast as possible." Then she jumped up the steps, hurrying her way to the top, right behind the line of retreating cops.

The EMTs moved toward Jude.

"No, no, I'll be okay. I don't need—"

"Stitch him up and then get the hell out of here," Antonio ordered.

The guy in the front, the one with the name tag reading John Bishop, gulped. "We—we're gonna need to take him to a hospital."

"No hospital," Jude's growl.

"You heard the man," Antonio said.

"He could have internal bleeding. Severe blood loss. He could have—"

"Get some thread and get a needle." Antonio glowered at him. "Stitch up any wound bigger than your hand, and don't worry about anything else."

Good advice. The cop obviously knew his *Other* business. Jude's internal wounds would already be healing and his body would be compensating for any blood loss. White tigers were amazing healers. If the stories were true, they were almost the fastest of the shifters when it came to wound repair.

The wounds on the surface would take the longest time to heal. Shifters recovered from the inside, out. Mother Nature's way of taking care of her priorities. Priorities like the heart and lungs and all the internal organs.

"You're a hell of a fighter, Erin." His voice was a soft rumble.

The EMTs went to work on him.

She forced a smile and stepped back, knowing she was in the way. "So are you." If he hadn't fought so hard, for so long, they never would have made it to him in time.

His gaze bored into hers. Not dull anymore. So very blue.

*Jude.* He was back. She could almost see the strength pouring into him.

"You had one of the . . . dreams, didn't you?"

Erin forced a nod. She'd never forget that vision. Until the day she died, Erin would always remember what it was like to see Jude murdered before her.

She took another step back.

"You weren't too . . . late this time."

No, not this time.

Jude didn't even wince when Bishop drove a two-inch needle into his shoulder. Probably not necessary, not like he could get an infection, but—

"Thanks for . . . saving my ass, sweetheart."

Her lips trembled into a smile. "You're welcome." And she slipped in the blood and fell on her ass.

Come nightfall, the demons would be making his delivery.

A bound and beaten tiger shifter—all ready for the kill.

He smiled as he stared into the swamp. Thick trees, lazy moss, muddy water.

When he was finished, he'd toss the body out here and let the alligators take care of Donovan. *What was left of him.*

The body would never be found. No evidence, no crime.

It'd be for the best that way. The shifter had too many friends. Too many hunters on his side.

Yes, it would be far better for the world if the bastard just vanished, and he would make certain that was exactly what the shifter did.

Erin would be all alone then. She'd think her lover had abandoned her.

All lost and alone—what would she do? *Turn to me.* He'd take her, of course, but not until she'd paid for bringing the tiger into their lives.

A little pain would be good for their relationship.

An alligator cruised past him, never slowing, never glancing his way.

"Dinner's coming," he whispered.

The woman was amazing—and she'd seriously saved his ass.

The EMTs were done. Done jerking on him. Done driving their needles into his flesh.

They'd stitched him up. A good thing because he needed the stitches. Until the healing was finished, the stitches would keep the wounds from worsening. When the skin mended, the stitches would fall away, and he wouldn't have to worry about leaving a trail of blood behind him when he hunted.

Because, hell, yeah, he was going hunting.

Dee tossed him a pair of jeans. His backup clothes. Jude jerked them on, managing not to wince at the pull from his injuries. Nudity didn't bother him a bit, but there were humans around, and they expected certain things.

Like clothing.

"Good job," Tony told the EMTs.

"He needs to be in a hospital." From Bishop, the chatty one. The other guy hadn't said a word the whole time he worked. When he'd first strode from the stairs, Jude had seen the way the fellow eyed the demons on the floor. Too much knowledge had been in his stare.

The guy knew they were in a den, the demon equivalent of a crack house, and he wanted out.

Was he a demon? Could be. Then again, he could be just about anything.

"I'll make sure he sees a doctor," Zane said. "Night Watch has a physician on staff."

Since when? The guy was a world class bullshitter.

The EMTs filed up the stairs. Most of the demons had already been hauled up to the upper level. Other paramedics had come to patch those lucky bastards. Tony had wanted them stitched, then shuttled to the jail, ASAP. The sooner the demons were off the street, the better for the rest of the city.

The door slammed behind the EMTs with a loud, hollow clang.

Jude rose, feeling every ache and pain in his body. He met Zane's stare, then Tony's. Yeah, most of the demons were gone—all but one, in fact.

The ringleader. Zane had gagged the asshole when the EMTs first went to work. A good precaution, that.

*Time for some payback.* Jude stalked toward him, with Zane and Tony right at his heels.

The demon's eyes widened and a high cry broke against the gag.

A smile curved Jude's lips. "Hey there, asshole. What? Did you think I'd forgotten you?" No way. This one, the guy who didn't reek of drugs and decay, was the ringleader. The one who'd set up his ambush.

The one who'd wanted him dead on the stinking floor.

Jude lifted his claws and put them right over the demon's chest. "I'm having a really bad night, as you can see . . ."

"*Jude.*" Erin's tense voice.

He stilled. This wasn't going to be pretty, but then, she'd already proved she could handle the hell that came in his life. He wouldn't tell her to leave because he knew the attack was tied to her. Had to be. He'd been hunting her stalker, only to become prey.

*Prey.*

Oh, yeah, the demon would pay.

He glanced back at her. "You don't have to see this." He'd told her about the darkness inside of him, but this could take it to a whole new level for her. Fighting to protect was one thing. Savaging a demon for information was another.

And it just might be something she couldn't accept.

Erin's gaze held his. "Yes, I-I think I do." She wet her lips. *Her kiss*. It had been like the woman's kiss had brought him back. "I'm not leaving you."

He sure wasn't leaving her. Jude managed a nod. *Don't fear me.*

Her eyes narrowed.

No choice. He turned back to his prey and jerked the gag loose with his left hand. "Tell me the name of the asshole who hired you to kill me, or I'll cut your heart out and fucking stuff it down your throat."

Erin sucked in a sharp breath. *I warned her.*

And he was really holding back with the asshole. If he'd had his way, Jude would have already been attacking because in his mind, he could still see the demon swarm going after *her.*

"I-I wasn't s-supposed to k-kill you!"

His claws dug in. "Erin, you sure you want to see—"

"*I* don't want to see this," Tony muttered. Jude glanced his way, but never lessened his hold on the prey. "And I *can't* see this! I'm a cop, I can't let you assault a—"

Zane punched Tony in the face. The cop went down, out cold. Zane shrugged. "Now he doesn't have to get all cop-worried on us. Clear conscience. Nice sleep."

"Fair enough," Jude said because it was, unfortunately, a routine they'd done before with Tony. The guy would wake up soon, pissed, but in the clear.

"Uh-oh." Dee dropped beside Tony. "I think he hit his head when he fell."

"I think his head just hit my fist."

She shoved Jude's mangled clothes beneath the cop's head. "No, that was his *face.*" Her fingers skated through his hair. "No bumps. No blood." She rose, brushing off her hands. "Next time, watch where he falls."

Because, unfortunately, there would be a next time. For them, there always was.

But now . . . Jude looked at the demon jerkoff. Now the focus was on the guy who was breathing hard and sweating and clogging Jude's nostrils with his stench. "Ready to die?" he asked the bastard.

"*No!*" The demon tried to jerk back, but his cuffs were locked tight to the chair. "H-he just wanted you hurt, w-weak—not dead."

"You would have killed him." Erin's voice. Cold and absolutely certain. "You wouldn't have just *hurt* him."

The hair on Jude's nape rose. Knowing that Erin had experienced one of those weird-ass death dreams about him made his stomach knot. *That close, huh?*

Killed in a demon's den, body torn apart and left on the stained floor.

Not exactly the way he wanted to leave this world. But

then, again, he didn't exactly have plans to be dying soon—death dreams or not.

"Th-thought it would be easier," the demon rasped.

The guy had just confessed to planning to kill him—surely that deserved a good, old-fashioned ass whooping. Jude's lips peeled away from his teeth. One good bite and he'd be able to—

"Never saw . . . the guy's face."

"Then how the hell did he contact you? How'd he arrange the attack?" Zane demanded. *Zane*. Being in the den had to be torture for the guy. All those memories. Dee didn't know about the demon's past, but Jude did. Zane had told him one night when the tequila had been drained in an empty Delaney's.

"He called me." The demon's fat tongue swiped over his bloody lip. "T-told me you'd be coming."

So the stalker had maneuvered everything. He'd moved them around like freaking pawns.

*Mickey.* Some tip. He couldn't wait to get his claws in that hyena.

"I-I was s-supposed to deliver you . . . to him . . . tonight."

Jude's hold eased, just a bit. "Were you now?" *This was it.* The chance he needed. "And he was going to pay you on delivery, right?"

A slow nod.

"How much?" What was the going rate for a shifter's life these days?

"T-ten grand."

Now he was just insulted. Ten grand?

"Damn, Jude, vamps are worth more than that," Dee said, and she would know. Vamps were her specialty, after all.

"These demons are addicts," Zane grated. "They'd kill their own mothers for ten grand. Hell, they probably have."

Jude didn't look away from his prey. "This one's not on drugs."

The demon spit out a tooth. "Just . . . wanted the money. Knew the others . . . would do anything . . . for some cash."

"Same as you." Not an addict, but a killer straight to the bone. "And you *will* do anything . . ."

"Uh-oh." Dee let out a loud sigh. "I think I know where the tiger's going with this."

"No, he's not that crazy." A pause from Zane. "Unless maybe the demons hit him too hard in the head. Could be he's not thinking straight, could be—"

Tony let out a long, loud groan. Then, "Fuckin' bastard. Knew what you were gonna do. Couldn't you have pulled it some?"

"No." Zane's immediate reply.

"Wh-what are you talking about?" the demon demanded.

Jude smiled at him and fully retracted his claws. After all, he didn't want to damage the demon. Especially now that he knew he needed the jerk. "You're gonna earn your money tonight."

"Wh-what'd I miss?" Tony asked, the words a bit thick.

"*Jude*." Erin's voice was sharp.

She wouldn't like the plan, but there was no option. The game was ending. He'd end it. "You're gonna deliver me to the asshole who contacted you—and you're gonna collect your money."

Erin's fingers dug into Jude's shoulder and she spun him around. Her eyes were blazing as she snapped, "The hell he is."

# Chapter 19

"This is a really stupid idea." Erin's stare could have burned a lesser man. As it was, Jude felt distinctly singed. "You're already weak. You can't seriously be considering going after this guy now."

*Weak.* Not a word he particularly enjoyed even though he still felt like he'd been hit by a truck. Or a dozen demons. "I'm getting stronger every minute." True. He'd always known he was lucky to be a white tiger. If he'd been a fox—hell, it would have taken *days* for him to recover. Simple shifter fact: The stronger and rarer you were, the quicker you healed. Kinda like survival of the fittest multiplied, and it was sweet old Mother Nature's way of making sure her once-in-a-blue-moon shifters didn't vanish from the earth completely.

When you were hard to kill, you got to live longer.

"*You. Can't. Do. This.*"

He'd never heard that particular guttural tone from her before. The lady was walking a fine edge of rage. So was he. "This is it, sweetheart. The chance to bag the bastard and take him out." The others were silent around them. Watching. Waiting. Even the demon prey had the sense to keep his mouth shut. "We finish this tonight, and there's no more running for you. No more fear."

"And if he kills you?" Her hands were small fists. Blood dripped onto the floor near her feet, and he knew that her claws were out, cutting her.

A rumble built in his throat and he crossed to her. Took her hands. Unfurled the fists. Her claws had dug deep. "Erin . . ."

She jerked away from him. "You almost died here." Her right hand lifted, waving toward the peeling walls and sputtering candles. Luckily, someone—he thought maybe Dee—had broken the radio and ended the blasting stream of drums and rock.

"Almost doesn't really count," he murmured, and knew when her eyes immediately slit that he'd said the wrong thing.

"I saw you on the floor." *Death dream.* "Blood around you. Your eyes wide open. *Dead.*" She shook her head, sending her hair flying around her. "Don't tell me that doesn't count."

"Uh? What did she see?" Tony asked. He was up and gingerly rubbing his jaw.

Zane shook his head. "I'll explain later, but, man, I really don't think you want to know."

Their voices drifted around Jude. *Erin.* He wanted, *needed* to hold her. But the others—

Ah, screw them.

He caught Erin and yanked her against his chest. He held fast when she fought him and when her head tipped back, he kissed her.

She bit him . . . then kissed him back. "Bastard," she whispered against his lips.

A tremble shook her.

Or maybe it shook him. Hard to say. Her mouth widened

and his tongue swept inside. This—*this* was what he needed. Her taste. Her flesh. His for the taking. His.

Always his.

"Uh, dude, seriously, if you two have sex, I'm outta here, fast," Dee said, her voice gruff.

His head lifted. Sex with Erin. Always something he was up for but—

But darkness would be falling soon and a killer waited.

"You're really going, aren't you?" Erin asked as her hands rose to lock around his arms.

A nod. For her. He'd stop the bastard, one way or another.

She absorbed that, then said, "Then I'm coming, too."

"The hell you are!" No, no way, she—

"My life, Jude." Her hold tightened on him. "He's been screwing with *my* life all this time. I'm not sitting on the sidelines anymore, and I'm sure not letting you go in alone with this freak waiting to tear you apart."

Her scent filled his nostrils, sending his cock surging to full, hard attention and making his heart race with a twisted mix of lust and need and fear. Lust and need—because he always wanted her, even when he'd just left death's cold door. Fear—the fear came because he didn't want to risk her. She could take down demons, but if the stalker shifted, she'd die. "You can't go with me." Giving her a straight order wouldn't work, but logic might sway her lawyer's mind. "Erin, he'd catch your scent long before we closed in and the bastard would run." Then they'd be back to square fucking one.

No. The game would end tonight.

"Uh . . . this really isn't police protocol," Tony pointed out.

"The police aren't gonna be handling this." Jude released Erin and stepped back. He thought maybe the move would help to ease the hunger he felt. No such luck. "Night Watch has priority. The shifter asshole is expecting me and the demon, and that's what he'll get."

"Ah . . . not quite." Zane cleared his throat. Jude glanced at him and saw the hunter's green eyes fade to pure black. "He's expecting you and he's going to get *two* demons. The asshole over there—and me." His smile held a cruel edge. "You freaking shifters think you can scent everything a mile away. Well, when he smells me, all he'll get is demon."

An answering grin stretched Jude's lips. Zane had always been there for him, ready to kick ass and walk right into the dark. He slanted a glance at Erin. "Between the two of us, the wolf will go down." The other shifter wouldn't be expecting the threat—from Zane or from him and that would be his downfall.

Erin was one hell of a fighter. She'd more than proved that tonight. But now, it was his turn. "This is what I do," he told her, his blood already heating. "It's time for me to finish this hunt."

The struggle was on her face. Fury and fear warring together. Yeah, he knew that mix well.

Jude turned to the demon who'd set him up to die. "What's your name?"

His lips thinned.

"Ah, does he want me to beat it out of him?" Dee asked. "If I can't go hunting with you, at least let me have some fun now."

"Kyler."

Jude grunted. "Okay, Kyler, this is how it's gonna work. You'll do *exactly* what I say or you'll find out what it's like to have a tiger rip you open."

The black eyes didn't blink.

"Got me?" Jude pushed.

A slow incline of his head.

"I'll be watching you, demon. *Every move.*" If it looked like the demon was going to sell him out, the bastard would feel a shifter's rage.

Erin was silent and stiff beside him. The fury and fear raged on her face and the combination seemed to come off her in waves, thickening the air.

"You hired me to do this job," he reminded her. "So let me do it.

Her golden eyes went glacial. "It's not just a job. It's your life!"

And her life. "This is what I do," he said again. What he had to do, for her. Protecting what you valued most was the way of his breed.

Nothing was more valuable to him than Erin.

Her nostrils flared. "You don't get so much as another scratch, you understand me? *Not a scratch.* You go in, stop the freak, and you come back to me."

He blew out a slow breath. "You know, sweetheart, it sure sounds like you care what happens to me—"

"Don't be an idiot." Her finger stabbed into his chest. "You know I—"

Oh, come on, she couldn't stop there.

"—I do." Soft. Sad. "So *don't* leave me, got it?"

Leave her? Not an option, now or damn ever. "Got it."

She crushed her mouth to his. Made him ache and need and lust.

Her mouth lifted. Their eyes met. "I'll be waiting for you."

Then she brushed past him. The lady climbed the steps with her head high and her shoulders straight. The metal door screeched open when she reached the top.

Jude realized he was holding his breath. *Talk about a woman with power.*

She could bring him to his knees so easily.

"Oh, damn." Zane sounded bemused, confused, not like his usual cocky self. "That lady is . . . something else. Man, did you *see* the way she fought?" Zane had always had a soft spot for a woman who could kick ass and ignore names.

"Yeah, I did." There had been no missing the way she'd fought to save him. A smart man held a woman who fought like that very close.

A smart man told her how he really felt, and he worked like hell to make her feel the same way.

"Uh, Jude . . ." Tony's voice was back to that drawling roll now, not dazed anymore. "Are you sure about this plan? You don't know what that asshole could have waiting for you."

"He doesn't know what's *coming* for him." No way was he backing down. "Don't worry, Tony, I'm not scared of the big, bad wolf." No, the wolf needed to be scared of *him.*

The sun was starting to set when Erin marched out of the den twenty minutes later. Red gold lights shot across the sky, looking weakly like trickles of blood.

Her hands fisted. "You'd better come back to me in one piece, Jude."

He stood behind her, just inside the entrance to the den. "Don't worry about me."

*Right.* "You almost died on me once today." *Not again.*

"I'll have backup."

The demon.

She stared up at the sky and tried to pretend she was in control. *I can handle this.*

If she were going with him, she'd be handling it a whole lot better. If she were watching his back . . .

But Erin knew he was right. The wolf would catch her scent instantly.

Straightening her shoulders, she took a step forward. Dee stood next to a gray SUV, waiting semi-patiently for her. Jude had told the human to stay with her until he returned from the hunt.

A human? For protection? Seriously, she could rip the woman apart in less than ten seconds.

If she were the ripping apart type.

"There's something you should know, sweetheart."

She hesitated but didn't glance back.

"I realized a few things in that filthy hole."

Yeah, she'd realized some damn important things too. When she'd seen him and he'd been so still, a jarring realization had come real quick. *Can't lose him.*

"You stopped being a case for me, hell, almost from day one."

She kept her shoulders straight and her hands loose at her sides.

"I fell for you fast," he told her.

*What?* No, no, he couldn't mean—

She swallowed and stared up at that bloody sky.

"I'm coming back from this case, and I'll be coming for you."

Her hands curled into small fists. "Good." And she looked back at him, standing so big and strong in that doorway. "Because if I don't see your sexy ass within three hours, I'll be coming for *you.*" He wasn't the only one who'd fallen.

And Erin wasn't about to lose the best thing that had ever happened to her. "Watch that ass, Donovan."

Their eyes held.

*I love you.*

The words stuck in her throat. She wanted to say them so badly but—

"You too, sweetheart," he murmured and her breath caught.

Then he was gone. Jude eased back into the den and she was left with the taste of fear on her tongue.

He watched his mate and fury iced his veins. Her face—her eyes—

*Fuck, no.*

This wasn't the way the game was played.

The other shifter—he was prey.

But Erin didn't look at the tiger as if he were prey.

No, not prey. So much more.

"Bitch," the word was a growl that broke from his mouth.

He'd done so much for her. Sacrificed and punished—and this was how she repaid him?

*Unworthy.*

They could have been perfect. Unstoppable. The next evolution for their race.

The tiger had ruined that for him.

Ruined every fucking thing.

"You really think this plan's going to work?" Erin stood on Jude's ramshackle porch, her skin cold even though the night was too warm. She stared up at the stars and wondered just how close Jude was to death.

Again.

Bastard.

*Be safe. Come back to me.*

Because if something happened again, she wasn't sure she'd get another vision. She'd sure never been able to control the dreams.

No, this time, she might not get a vision.

Just a body.

"I don't know if it will work." Dee stepped to her side,

moving almost as soundlessly as a shifter. A good hunter, for a human.

Dee's response wasn't the reassuring answer she'd wanted, but Erin was quickly coming to see that Dee wasn't exactly a reassuring kind of woman.

"You've been on a lot of hunts with him, haven't you?" Erin asked, but she didn't take her gaze off the swamp. The twisting trees, the gentle movement at the water's edge. This was where Jude ran wild. His sanctuary.

Dee hesitated. "Ah, usually Jude hunts alone."

Like he'd gone hunting at that den.

The human turned toward her. "He's the strongest shifter I've ever met," Dee told her. *Okay, that was reassuring.* Erin glanced at her as she continued, "And believe me, I've come across more than my share of shifters since I joined Night Watch fifteen years ago."

*Fifteen years?* But the woman barely looked thirty. Hell, more like twenty-five.

Dee laughed. "Don't worry, I was legal." A pause. "Barely. Jude took me under his wing. Taught me how to fight the supernaturals. How to survive. He'd only been in the Watch for a few years, but he'd already gotten a reputation."

She'd just bet he had.

"Jude always gets the job done," Dee said simply. "You can count on him."

Yeah, she could.

A soft peal rang out from the area of Dee's left side. She shoved a hand into the pocket of her jeans and dug out a cell phone. "Yo."

Erin tensed.

"What? You're kidding! *That's great!* Does he remember anything? What? Yeah, yeah, we're on our way."

She ended the call with a flick of her thumb. "Givens is awake. That was McCall, he's one of the hunters we stationed with Givens for protection. A few minutes ago, Givens woke up. McCall said the guy just opened his eyes and then he asked for his son, Tommy."

Erin's breath rushed out. *Alive.*

"The way I figure it," Dee said, "we can sit up here with our thumbs up our asses or we can hightail it to that hospital, arrive before the cops do, and maybe get some info out of Givens."

"I don't really like having a thumb up my ass," Erin muttered and jumped down the steps. "Let's go." Jude was already hunting, so the info might not be any good to him, but at least she'd be doing *something.*

Other than having a thumb up her ass.

They ran toward Dee's SUV.

"You sure this is the place?" Jude demanded.

Kyler gave a grudging nod. "Yeah, yeah, this is the address he gave me."

A cabin at the edge of the swamp. A place that looked way too much like his own home.

*Gotta get a new place for Erin.* Because a dump falling into the moss really wasn't going to cut it for her.

He had the cash. Sure, he liked to run in the swamp, but Erin needed something different.

And after the way the asshole had christened her home, she'd probably like a fresh start someplace else.

They could get that start together. Maybe another antebellum, one they could restore together. One with a lot of land for running . . .

*Later.*

"All right then," Jude said, testing the ropes that held his hands. Damn tight, cutting-off-his-circulation tight. Zane knew his knots, how to tie 'em and how to place 'em. Thanks to Zane, the knots were perfectly positioned next to his claws. A few slices, and he'd be free. "Time to get your payment."

A grunt came from the sweating demon. His black eyes darted from the left to the right. "This is a real assed-up plan."

Jude grunted. "Who asked you?"

Zane eyed him with raised brows. "Guess I get to be the one to drag your sorry butt inside, huh?"

"No . . . *he* gets the job." Because he didn't want Kyler's hands free for a minute.

"Fuck," Kyler snarled.

Good thing demons were strong.

"Let's get this shit started."

Dee's foot shoved the gas pedal to the floor. She took the curves and hidden twists with ease, her gaze never darting from the road.

At this rate, they'd be at the hospital in no time. The road was deserted. Dark and quiet. Well, quiet except for Dee's revving motor.

"Does Lee know he was attacked because of me?" Erin's fingers tapped against the side of the passenger door.

"No."

Ah, that would be a fun conversation.

"He doesn't know that you saved his butt yet, either."

Headlights flashed in the distance. *Maybe not so deserted.* "Saving him has to count for something, right?" Erin asked quietly. She sure hoped it did.

Zane kicked open the door of the cabin. "We're here!" He called out, pretty unnecessarily to Jude's way of thinking.

Kyler tossed him onto the floor. "Got the shifter bastard you wanted."

Jude didn't grunt at the impact. He didn't move at all.

Old floorboards squeaked around him as Zane and Kyler edged out in the room.

Jude's nostrils flared. He couldn't scent the wolf, but Erin *had* told him the guy could disguise his smell. So just because he couldn't smell him, well, that didn't mean the stalker wasn't there.

His ears twitched.

*Silence.*

Thick and heavy. Too much silence.

He slashed through his ropes and bounded to his feet. "Where the hell is the bastard?"

Kyler was creeping toward the door. Jude grabbed him and slammed his head against the wall. *Payback for the headfirst toss onto the floor.* The demon went down and didn't get back up.

Jude's gaze raked the cabin. *Not here.*

But if the wolf wasn't waiting to rip him apart, then where was the bastard?

"Yeah, saving the guy's life has to count for something," Dee said, her fingers tightening around the steering wheel. "It's not like you could help the fact that this creep after you tried to kill him."

The headlights were growing closer. The dark shadow of that other car—was it swerving a bit?

Erin licked her lips. "How many . . . other cabins are out this way?" She'd never seen another vehicle when she'd visited Jude before. The guy liked his solitude. Not real big into sharing property and—

Something big and black ran into the road.

*"What the hell?"* Dee slammed on the brakes.

But whatever *the hell* that was out there wasn't aiming for them.

*"Is that a fucking dog?"* Dee's breath jerked out with a hard rush.

Erin's breath was gone. *Not a dog.* The beast was heading right for the other vehicle. Running fast and hard. The beast never halted, never faltered, just ran straight for the other driver.

Animal and car hit. Brakes squealed. Metal shrieked. Glass shattered. And the vehicle, a big, black SUV—pretty damned similar to Dee's, just a different color—swerved off the road and plowed into a line of trees.

*"Shit!"* Dee jerked off her belt and sprang from the vehicle.

The air from Dee's open door wafted into the SUV, and Erin's eyes widened as she caught a distinct scent. *No.* "Dee! Dee, stop!" She clawed through her own seat belt and jumped out, her heart racing. "Don't get close, it's—"

*"Holy Christ!"*

She hadn't even known the woman was religious.

"You know, if he were awake, the guy would be a hell of a lot more useful." Zane eyed the demon on the floor, his face grim. "Maybe you should have waited to bash his head until *after* we got some more information."

There was no more information to get. "The wolf isn't here." He'd been played. *Played.*

And he'd left Erin alone.

He grabbed his cell phone. Punched in her number.

One ring.

Two.

Then . . . *damn* CALLER NOT AVAILABLE message.

His fingers crushed the phone. Shit. "Try to get Dee on the line," he growled, and his gaze raked the cabin. Minimal furnishings. A chair. A bed. *Too much like my place.*

Except for the framed picture of Erin.

*Bastard.*

"Ringing," Zane said, and Jude glanced back to see that the demon had his cell phone positioned at his ear.

"Tell her to get Erin inside my cabin and to lock the doors. We're on our way."

*That picture . . .*

He turned back around, slowly, and paced across the room.

Her hair was longer. She was smiling, walking in what looked like some kind of park.

"No answer."

Jude reached for the frame. He traced the busted glass. It looked like someone had shoved a fist into the picture.

"We've got a big problem." He looked up at Zane. *No answer.* Their eyes met. The broken glass bit into his hand, sending droplets of blood onto the picture.

Onto Erin.

Blood was in the air. Thick and strong and so sickeningly fresh.

"I think the bastard is dead!" Dee scrambled to a stop near the middle of the road, right before the prone body of the giant black wolf.

"Get back!" Erin screamed, running as fast as she could. An injured wolf was dangerous. *Any* wolf was dangerous, but an injured beast would rip and tear anything in its path.

With a burst of speed, she reached the human and jerked her back.

"Erin, stop! The wolf is barely breathing. It's over, you're—"

Erin shoved Dee away. A safe distance behind her. Then she fell to her knees beside the wolf. *So much blood.* A growl rumbled in the beast's throat and the creature bared its teeth.

"Easy," she whispered.

"Are you insane?" Dee blasted. "Get away from him! Let him die! Your life will be one hell of a lot better!"

Erin reached out a hand to the wolf. The too-sharp teeth snapped together, barely missing her fingertips.

*"Erin!"*

"It's going to be all right," she whispered, but the words were a lie. A tear trickled down her cheek. No, no, this wasn't the way things should have ended.

She ignored the teeth and the claws that tried to swipe at her. *An injured beast would rip and tear anything in its path.* Even if she was the one in the creature's path. Her fingers sank into the bloody fur. The wolf's hind legs were broken, no, shattered.

*Hold on.*

"Call for help," she ordered, never taking her eyes off the wolf.

"Yeah, I need to get help for whoever is in that SUV! But not for this mangy wolf and I—aw, hell, I left my cell in the car!"

A growl rose in Erin's throat.

She heard the soft fall of Dee's footsteps as the human stumbled back. "Erin, wh-what's up with you? I thought you . . . hated this guy." Suspicion now. Worry.

The wolf jerked its head against her and managed to let out a long, mournful howl. The beast's eyes jerked to the left, and it whimpered.

Such bright yellow eyes.

"This isn't the asshole who's after me." The shift began then. Fast, because the wolf was weak and so was the woman. "This is my mother."

And she was dying.

"Where the hell are they?" Jude's foot shoved down even harder on the gas pedal as the car lurched forward. The car was Zane's, but he'd borrowed it while the demon secured Kyler.

*The bastard likes to get up close and personal with his prey. That's how he makes the kills.* And why he'd given the order that Jude would be brought to him alive. If he'd come to the den, if he'd learned what happened . . .

Fuck.

Jude yanked the steering wheel to the left. Every instinct he had screamed the guy had gone running, but not out of the city. Instead, he'd gone—

To Erin.

For a sports car, Zane's "baby" sure wasn't going fast enough. He shifted hard and the engine roared. Zane would have to trail as fast as he could on the motorcycle they'd found at the cabin.

*Erin. Be safe, sweetheart.* His claws ripped through his fingertips.

"I got Antonio on the phone. He's sending help." Dee eased onto her knees beside Erin. "I-I found this in my SUV." She handed her a loose jacket.

Her mother lay on the ground, pale and unmoving. So much blood. It was the only covering she had.

Erin put the jacket over her.

"Can't she change? Like Jude did back at the den, can't she—"

"She's too weak." If Antonio didn't get there soon with the ambulance, she'd be dead. Erin brushed back a clump of her mother's hair. They really looked so much alike.

When she'd been a girl, her mother had combed her hair every night before bed, laughing as she stroked her—

Her mother's lashes lifted, so slowly. Yellow eyes, hazy with pain, tried to focus on Erin. "*R-run.*" Blood trickled from the corner of her mouth.

Goosebumps rose on her arms. "Mother?"

*"Run . . ."*

Her breath whispered out and her eyes closed.

"Oh, God!" From Dee. "Is she—"

Erin grabbed her arm. "Did you check on the other driver?"

"Yeah, yeah, it's a guy. He's fine, just has a little cut on his forehead."

Her fingers tightened. "Do you have your gun?" She'd seen it earlier. Dee always carried her gun. *Always.*

Dee brushed back her shirt, revealing the butt of her weapon.

A twig snapped. *Close*. Too close.

Her mother had almost killed herself? Why?

*Run.*

The wolf—her mother—had headed straight for that other SUV. Attacked it.

*To protect me.*

The night was too quiet then. No crickets. No croaking frogs. Just silence, smothering her.

The fingers of Dee's right hand hesitated over the gun butt. Erin held her stare and mouthed, *Get. It. Out.*

A growl—from the left.

They spun around. Dee brought up her gun.

Erin expected to see a wolf lunge at them.

Instead, she saw a man.

One she knew. *What the hell?*

Judge Lance Harper—*the freaking judge!*—walked from the brush, as calm as you please. Blood trickled down the side of his face. He smiled at her, revealing his fangs, and said, "Erin, beautiful Erin, I'm going to have to punish you."

And he lifted his claws toward her.

"Shoot him!" she screamed at Dee.

His smile vanished, and he lunged for her.

Dee fired. Once. Twice.

The deafening shots echoed in Erin's ears.

The judge froze. He looked down at his chest, at the blood soaking his shirt, and he shook his head. "Takes more than that to stop me."

She knew that, oh, dammit, but she knew—

He attacked.

# Chapter 20

Dee ran forward, her gun up, but the bastard moved too fast. His claws raked down her arm, then across her chest. The gun flew from her fingers and she screamed as his teeth caught her shoulder.

*"No!"* Dee didn't understand. Harper wasn't like other shifters. *He's like me.* In human form, he was nearly as strong as a fully transformed shifter.

And when he transformed—

*Hello, hell.*

"Let her go, asshole!" Erin sank her own claws into his side, and twisted.

He howled in fury and pain, and he tossed Dee into the air. When she came down, Dee hit the ground with a thud, and she didn't get up.

*Dee!*

His head turned, just a few inches, and Harper met Erin's stare. His brown eyes were muddy, so dark, and the grin on his face chilled her. "Always knew you liked the blood. Just like me."

"I'm nothing like you!" She jumped back, putting some frantic space between them.

She could really have used Jude right then! When Dee had called for backup, she'd called Night Watch and Antonio. Not Jude and Zane. Dee had thought they were in the middle of their trap. Thought they were catching the stalker.

But he'd come for her, instead.

Harper raised a hand to his side. His fingers touched the blood that pulsed and flowed so hotly. "Wanted to do this . . . in human form."

Her claws were up, ready. "Do what?" *Hot Harper? Lance Harper?* His name blasted through her head over and over again. She'd been in his courtroom so many times, been so close to him, and never suspected.

He'd tried to rape her. He'd killed. Tortured.

*The judge?*

She shook her head. No, no, this didn't make a bit of sense.

He watched her with those dark eyes, and his blood splattered on to the ground. He didn't seem to notice or even to care. "You disappointed me, mate."

*Mate.* "I'm *not* your mate."

The judge blinked at that, looking vaguely surprised. "Well, of course, you are. I recognized you the first moment you stepped into my courtroom." His smile had faded completely. "I divorced my third wife for you."

*Divorced my third wife.* Erin guessed she was lucky he hadn't killed the woman. "There's no way you could have known from one look that I was your mate." *Keep him talking.* Backup would arrive soon. Had to. Just how many bullets would the guy be able to take and keep standing? Because when Antonio arrived, she knew he'd unload on the asshole.

"I knew the second I caught your scent that you were mine."

Bullshit. She hoped. Her eyes narrowed. "So what? You decided to make my life *hell* because you liked the way I smelled?"

He jumped toward her. Harper closed the distance in less than a second. *Stronger than me. Faster than me.*

Dammit!

His fingers wrapped around her arms, and she felt the sting of his claws. His breath—*freaking minted breath*—blew in her face. "I gave you *everything* you wanted. I punished the fools who hurt you or got in your way. I made sure your life was perfect."

*Insane.* There was a reason for the whispers about wolves being psychotic. Some of them really were. "You *killed.* You murdered Donald Trent!"

The claws dug deeper. "Because you wanted him stopped." His teeth snapped together and a frown pulled his brows low, as if he truly didn't understand. "If I'd found him guilty in court, he would have been out in what? Two, three years?" He grunted. "Not good enough for you. You wanted more—so I gave you more! I stopped him, permanently."

"You buried him in the woods behind his kids' house!"

The right side of his mouth lifted. "Thought it was fitting."

No, it was insane.

"I just had to go and watch the cops dig him up. So fucking perfect."

Erin could only stare at him. Why hadn't she seen the madness before? Why hadn't the cops? All the other lawyers?

The insanity had hid so well behind his black robes.

His gaze swept over her face. "When you walked in that first day, I thought you were the most perfect thing I'd ever seen. Just like *her,* that same fire burning inside." He jerked Erin closer. "I knew when I saw you then, I *knew* why fate had put that bastard in Theresa's path so many years before."

*What?* Her heart iced. "H-how do you know my mother's name?" The mother who lay dying just a few feet away. She'd risked her life to save Erin from this bastard.

He blinked and, for an instant, almost seemed confused. "I thought she was mine." The words came, slow and stilted. "For years, I thought she was the one for me."

A choked moan rumbled from behind Erin. Her mother's pain-filled cry.

Erin stared into Harper's eyes and knew.

Theresa's voice drifted through her mind. "*Such dark, dark eyes that saw into me so well . . .*"

Hell.

Her mother's lover.

Erin jerked against him, hard, horror giving her strength as she stumbled back from his hold.

His lip curled with disgust as he grated, "When she went with that human, I couldn't pretend about her any more. She wasn't mine."

Erin sucked in oxygen as hard and as fast as she could. Not. Happening.

"I left the pack." His teeth snapped together. "I went on my own, and then you came to me."

No, no, she hadn't come to him. She'd just been in court, doing her job!

"The instant I saw you, I finally understood what fate had planned for me. I *knew* you were my reward, the mate I'd always wanted." A laugh then, rough and wild. "You look so much like her," he said, "but you're better, stronger, *mine.*"

"No, I'm not *yours.*" Never would be.

"You know what it's like to be different from the others. Not human. Not wolf. More powerful than both." He lifted his hand toward her, long and deadly claws out. "We were made for each other. Perfect halves."

She stared at that hand and remembered the sight of Bobby Burrows's bloody body. "We are nothing alike." She held her body perfectly still. Now wasn't the time for an attack. Not yet.

He closed the space between them. His right hand lifted and his fingers trailed down her cheek. "I had to bide my time and make sure there were no obstacles between us."

Yeah, he'd tried to *kill* all the obstacles. Erin barely breathed as she stood before him.

One sharp claw pressed against the side of her face. "Purebloods always thought they were so fucking superior. I had to show the animals how wrong they were. Every day, I had to fight and claw my way through the pack."

*Alpha.* Her mother had said her lover was the alpha of the pack. Alphas were the most bloodthirsty of the wolves. The most dangerous.

Shit.

"They never understood what we are!" he snarled. "Fucking idiots!"

She swallowed. "And what are we?"

The claw dug into her skin, broke the flesh. "The next evolution. We can be strong in our human flesh. We don't have to wait for the wolf. We can kill and we can conquer as we are. Hell, we can rule the world. We don't have to wait for the shift. We have the power every minute of every day."

Her chin lifted and she knew the liquid sliding down her face wasn't tears, it was blood. "I can't shift."

His gaze burned her. "I know—that's why you're so *perfect.*"

Great, of all the people in the world, *he* thought she was perfect.

Harper licked his thin lips. "Our children won't need to shift. They'll be born with power. Always have it."

*Their children?* "Got news for you," she managed. There'd been no sound from Dee—or from her mother—for several moments. *Be alive.* "I'm not planning on having any kids with you." That would be the last thing she'd ever do.

Whack job for a father? Hell, no. She and her mother had very different taste in men.

His breath rushed out. More mint. "It's that fucking tiger. I've been watching you. Always watching."

She knew that. She'd felt his eyes too many times.

"I'm good at hiding. I was close enough to touch you so many times and you never knew."

Goosebumps rose on her flesh.

"I changed my hair, used contacts, held the shift so that my face was different—" He broke off, giving a muffled laugh. "You never even knew!"

He'd held the shift? How was that even possible? *The next evolution.*

"I love to watch you," he whispered. "Love to see your face." His jaw clenched as his eyes turned arctic. "And I've seen your face when you look at that bastard!" Spittle flew at her. "*You've been screwing him*. Fucking around on me just like your whore of a mother!"

Her claws were out. Ready. His wounds were close. *Keep talking. Hold his attention. Stir his fury.*

Fury could make him weak.

Erin smiled. A slow, wide grin. "Yeah, I have."

"You, bit—"

She shoved her hands up between them. *Don't forget how strong I can be, asshole.*

His mistake—he'd stayed in human form. She could take the jerk in human form. Because she was as strong as he was that way, maybe even stronger. *Maybe*.

*Time to find out.*

She drove her claws into his bloody wounds and wrenched up as hard as she could.

His head slammed into hers and black spots danced before her eyes.

She stumbled back. He raised his claws above her—

Erin caught his right wrist, then the left, and she held him as tight as she could. Bones snapped beneath her grip.

"Perfect," he whispered and he crushed his mouth against hers.

She bit him, savaging his lips with her teeth and his blood flowed.

But the bastard just laughed.

Furious, scared as hell, she threw him back.

Harper didn't stumble or stagger. He landed on his feet. The bastard balanced perfectly and then swiped the back of his hand over his bleeding mouth. "I like the way you taste." His stare dropped to her body. "When you're with him . . . do you think of me?"

What? "*No!*"

More laughter. "I bet I'm in your head. Late at night, when you close your eyes, you think of me, don't you?"

She had, for so long. But not because she wanted him. Because . . . "You attacked me! Almost murdered Ben! You've terrorized me, so, hell, yes, I've thought about you!" Her teeth ached as they extended even more. Longer, sharper than they'd ever been. "I thought about how I'd like to *kill* you."

"You've got the blood thirst, just like me."

A broken groan broke the air.

Erin's gaze flew to the left. Not her mother this time, *Dee.* The hunter was trying to push herself up.

"Why do you care about them?" His stare followed hers. "They aren't even worth your notice."

No, *he* wasn't worth her notice.

He held out his hand to her once more, claws stained red. "Come with me, Erin, and I'll let your human live, for now."

*For now.* Code for later, he'd be back to slice her to ribbons.

"Why do you do it?" she whispered. "Why all the killings? Bobby Burrows—"

His hand waited in the air, but he answered her. Harper had always loved to hear himself talk. That was one of the many reasons why his court had always been torture for her. "Burrows made you look like a fool. He escaped on *your* watch."

Well, the cops' watch.

"And he was worthless trash, eating away at the world. He needed to be put down."

"That's not your call to make! You can't decide who lives or dies! You can't—"

His hand fell. "I've spent fifteen years of my life deciding who lives and dies. I damn well know what I'm doing."

Executing his own brand of justice and claiming to kill for her. "You're crazy," she whispered. Probably not the smartest thing to say to a killer, but what the hell?

"Wolves in packs don't become psychotic." His voice had chilled.

*He hadn't been in a pack for almost thirty years.*

"Mated wolves out of the pack retain their sanity."

*He wasn't mated. Did the guy even see where this was headed?*

"You're my mate. Since finding you, everything in my life has become crystal clear." His lips firmed and he took a step forward—

And he stumbled.

*The blood loss. It was finally hitting him.*

She'd hoped if she kept him talking, kept him focused—yes!

Harper slipped in his own blood and went down, hard.

"Erin . . ."

She shook her head. "I'm not your mate, asshole, and even if I was, I wouldn't spend a day of my life with you."

"The tiger . . ." His head fell down. His body shuddered. "Should have . . . killed him . . . beginning . . ."

*No.* "Jude isn't exactly easy to kill." One of his best traits.

His claws scraped over the pavement. "Saw the way . . . you . . . l-looked at him . . . Has to . . . die . . ."

"No, he doesn't. You're not going to hurt Jude."

He threw his head back then, and she saw his face. A wild combination of man and beast. "*You're mine!*" A barely human howl of fury.

The transformation ripped through his body and he jerked, almost convulsing on the ground.

Not a shift. *No.* He should have been too weak to transform. Should have been . . .

Bones snapped. Fur burst from his skin.

*"No!"* Erin flew at him, attacking, hoping to stop the shift before it was too late. *Before he was too strong.* Because if he shifted, he could heal—and he could kill her.

But his shift was fast. Faster than Jude's. Faster than any shifter she'd ever seen in her life. When her body fell against his, she sank her claws as deeply as she could into his side—not the side of a man, but the body of a wolf. She thrust her claws past the thick fur and right into the muscle.

The wolf howled, and his head—*long, thick muzzle, too-dark eyes*—turned toward her.

This was so not good. Erin stumbled back, sweat coating her body.

The wolf rose to his feet. His muscles vibrated and his fangs dripped saliva.

*Too strong.* The beast showed no signs of weakness.

*Hybrid.* The rules didn't apply to him. Or maybe they did.

He could obviously heal as fast as she could. *When he shifted anyway.* She could heal almost that fast without a shift.

The next evolution? Had he been right?

The wolf snarled, and she stopped thinking about old Darwin—and focused on the killing machine before her.

*Backup!* Where was Antonio?

She took a deep breath and attacked with all of her might, ripping, shredding muscle as—

He rolled and his hind legs came up, catching her in the stomach. The wolf kicked her into the air.

Erin landed on her ass but jumped back up as fast as she could. Dee was inching ever closer to her gun. *A fighter.* She could be a fighter, too. "Come on, judge. You want me so bad, huh? Then come and get me." She had to keep him away from Dee and her mother.

Erin held up her claws and bared her teeth.

And knew that he was about to kick her ass.

*Can't take him while he's in wolf form.* She just wasn't strong enough.

But she could give him one hell of a fight. And maybe, maybe Dee could get her gun and blast the jerk with more bullets.

*Maybe.*

She just had to hold him off long enough to—

The wolf lunged at her. His teeth sank into her forearm, gouging deep holes into her flesh and biting all the way to the bone. *"Sonofabitch!"*

His claws raked across her stomach and his teeth—they wouldn't let go!

Fire ate at her belly, but she took that pain and used it to feed the beast inside who could never get out.

"Not a good way to treat your *mate.*" She grabbed his jaw and had to pry the thing loose with hands that shook.

His eyes rolled. She caught the faintest sight of white in that darkness, and he twisted suddenly, shoving Erin and kicking into her legs.

*What? Why was he—*

The hum of a motor rumbled in the distance. The wolf must have heard it before she had.

*Backup.* Antonio.

The wolf's ears shot straight into the air. His head snapped in the direction of the approaching car, then he looked back at her.

His muscles bunched.

And damn if it didn't look like the beast *smiled.*

*Smiled*—with her mother lying there, dying. With Dee bleeding out.

When the wolf leapt forward, Erin launched herself at him. They hit, hard, and the wolf knocked her into the dirt near the side of the road, and then he locked his teeth on her shoulder, *in* her shoulder.

*Bad idea. So fucking bad.* Her claws flew up and gouged at his eyes.

The wolf leapt away.

*Yeah, asshole. My dad taught me that move, before he realized I could break the hands of any touchy-feely punks who crossed the line.*

*"Go for the eyes, girl. Don't be afraid to hurt him."*

She sure wasn't afraid to hurt the wolf.

"Erin . . ." Dee's weak voice.

She glanced to the left. Dee was on her knees, weaving a bit. Her white T-shirt was soaked red.

The wolf snarled, and she knew he'd seen Dee. His teeth snapped together.

*Prey. Weak and ready.*

The thought was hers, a sick instinct she'd always ignored, but it was Harper's, too. She knew it.

So when he ran for Dee, she lunged after him. Her claws sank into his hind legs, and he twisted back. His paws hit her, taking her down with one hard blow, and she fell with the heavy weight of his body smothering her.

"*Run!*" Her cry this time, not her mother's. "*Run, Dee!*"

Because the wolf was too strong for her. Too strong for Dee.

Maybe even too strong for the backup coming.

Two bullets hadn't slowed him. She hadn't slowed him.

Saliva dripped onto her face. That breath wasn't so minty fresh anymore.

Erin looked up and found his open mouth poised right over her.

*This was it.*

No dreams this time. No visions. Her death.

Hadn't seen this one coming.

*Sorry, Jude.*

She'd found him too late. A man who accepted her, wanted her, maybe even could love her—too late.

*So sorry.*

She wouldn't be healing from this.

With a snarl, those fangs went for her throat.

The roar came as she felt the first puncture. A roar that filled her ears and seemed to shake the street.

Then the wolf was knocked right off her. His teeth scraped over her neck, slicing the skin.

She rolled away, lifting a hand to her throat and touching the wet warmth of her blood.

*Jude.*

The tiger was there, quivering with fury. Fighting with claws and teeth. Driving his fangs into the wolf's body. Picking up the smaller beast and tossing him into the air.

*A match for a wolf.*

Wolves were strong, no doubt about it, but a tiger shifter was no one's bitch.

She managed to rise to her feet. The blood flow was already starting to ease up. The slice hadn't gone too deep, thanks to Jude. All of her wounds throbbed, but they were healing fast.

Growls and snarls filled the air. The tiger and the wolf attacked, rolled, roared, and howled.

Blood soaked their fur. Bones crunched.

The wolf sank his teeth into the tiger's back. Jude jerked away, swiping with his front paws.

*Have to help. Can't just stand here and watch!*

"Erin . . ." Dee's voice.

*The gun.*

Erin ran to her side and grabbed the gun. It slipped in her blood-soaked fingers.

"No, wait, you need—"

No more waiting. The wolf had just cut open Jude's side.

The tiger seemed to move in a fast blur, launching at the wolf, his giant mouth open.

She lifted the gun, aimed. *Move, Jude, move—just a bit. Give me a shot.* A chance to end the nightmare.

His mouth locked on the wolf's throat. Jude jerked the wolf up with his hold, and Erin had a perfect view of the beast's back.

Her finger squeezed the trigger.

The bullet thudded into the wolf.

The tiger's teeth clamped down harder.

One beat of time. Two. She fought to hold the gun steady. If she just didn't have so much blood on her hands . . .

The tiger dropped his prey. The wolf didn't move.

Jude threw back his head and roared his rage at the night.

*Over?* Please, be—

Jude jumped over the fallen body of the wolf. As he ran to her, the fur began to melt from his body. He fell before her as the bones snapped and shaped with sickening crunches. His fangs disappeared and a man's face formed from the tiger's.

Naked, strong, he knelt before her.

Then he looked up at her. Jude didn't speak. He just gazed at her.

Her hands fell on to his shoulders. *Over.* She stared into his eyes. Finally, the bastard was dead.

And Jude was alive and strong and right in front of her.

"Erin . . . are you all right?" Gruff, thick. Somewhere between the man's rumbles and the beast's growls.

She managed a nod. Too much blood on her, but . . . "I'm a fast healer."

His gaze tracked over her bloody form, then rose back to her face. "Just so we're clear," he told her, his voice growing stronger. "You aren't his mate. Never were."

She shook her head. "No, you—"

"You're *mine*, sweetheart. Have been from the beginning, just like I'm yours." His hands wrapped around her waist and he pulled her close.

Hers.

A tear slid down her cheek and splashed onto his shoulder. She wanted that to be true because she wanted him so much, but—

His head tipped back a bit more. "Mine," he said again, simply, softly.

And she echoed the word as she gazed down at him. "Mine."

Then he was rising up, holding her too tight and so right and his mouth was on hers and he kissed her the way he'd always kissed her—

With hunger and need and lust.

And love?

She wanted to sink into him, to push the world away, but there was too much pain around her. Too much blood.

She twisted back, pulling her mouth from his. "Jude, my mother . . ."

His nostrils flared. He glanced behind her and swore. Then they were moving together, rushing to Theresa's side.

Her mother's eyes were open, and she didn't look as pale as death anymore. No, no, a hint of color lined her cheeks. "Did you . . . do it?" she asked, her gaze on Jude's face.

Shifters—always so strong. Theresa's legs were still a twisted mess, but the gushing blood had stopped. Her mother just might pull through.

Relief had Erin's breath catching. She was crouched in front of Jude, shielding his naked form as best she could. Her mother could see his face, but, hopefully, not much else.

Not that shifters were really known for any sort of modesty.

Jude gave a nod and said, "I ripped the bastard's throat wide open."

Somehow, her mother managed a weak smile at that. "Good . . . what the b-bastard . . . d-deserved." Blood stained the corner of her mouth.

"Take it easy." Erin put a light hand on her mother's shoulder. "Help's coming."

That smile stayed on her bloody lips. "Don't worry . . . baby. Hard . . . to kill."

Yeah, she was, and Erin had never been happier to have a wolf for a mother. Actually, it might have been the first time she *was* happy about that fact.

Theresa's right hand lifted and clamped down on her shirt. "S-sorry . . ."

Erin looked into her eyes and understood. "How did you know he was coming after me?"

Her hand fell away. "S-saw him . . . in L-Lillian . . . *knew* . . . wolf h-hybrid . . . f-followed h-him . . ."

"You could have died." Anger there, the fear that wouldn't leave because her mother was still too close to death.

"Had . . . to s-save . . . you."

Erin choked back the damn sob that rose in her throat.

"*Who the hell . . . is he*?" Dee's strained voice. Erin glanced at her. She was up now, on her feet, wavering a bit as she inched toward the naked body.

The fur was gone. The beast always vanished in death.

Erin's hands fisted. "His name's Lance Harper. *Judge* Lance Harper."

"Well, fuck." Comprehension darkened Jude's voice. "The dick in the basement."

Yeah.

"Erin, I-I'm s-sorry . . ." Her mother's whisper.

Erin straightened her shoulders and turned her stare back to her mother. "It's not your fault. What he did—you had nothing to do with that." Theresa had loved the wrong man. The wrong, *psychotic* man. But her mother hadn't known. "It'll be okay, Mom, just stay with me."

Her mother swallowed, the gulp loud and painful. "Trying . . . Legs are a . . . m-mess . . . need sh-shift . . ."

But she wasn't strong enough for that, not yet.

"A judge?" Dee asked and the scent of her blood burned Erin's nose. She was still bleeding. *Human.* She'd scar from the wounds, they were too deep not to scar.

She could sure understand Dee's disbelief. Her stalker had been Lillian's citizen of the year for five years running. He'd sure been good at fooling the world.

"Huh. Never did care much for judges."

At that, Erin fired a look over her shoulder in time to see Dee toeing the judge's body with her right foot. The hunter had her gun against her hip, and she was painstakingly loading fresh bullets into the chamber.

Better late than never.

Jude's hand curled around Erin's shoulder. "Hey. You okay?"

She would be. *Finally*, she would be. Her eyes fell to Harper's still face. Handsome, even in death. Refined, almost—

His eyelids flew open.

*Oh, hell.*

Sick understanding burned through her. *The shift had saved him. He hadn't shifted to die, he'd shifted to live.*

"Dee!"

Too late. Harper lunged up and grabbed her, jerking Dee down onto his body and anchoring her against him. One hand rose to clutch her throat and his claws dug into her jugular.

"I can kill her with one slice." His voice was hoarse, guttural. Because Jude had nearly ripped out his throat. The wound was still there, still red and jagged and angry, but he'd healed enough, *just enough*.

Erin knew he wasn't bullshitting. He'd kill the hunter in a heartbeat of time. "Harper, let her go." She rose to her feet, deliberately keeping her mother behind her.

Jude's fingers tightened around her.

Harper's eyes narrowed at that small movement. "Touching her . . . always . . . *touching* her . . ." He licked his lips.

Dee didn't move. Her face was blank, her body tense. Her blood pulsed from her wounds.

Erin shrugged free of Jude's hold and took a step forward. Behind her, she heard the rumble of his fury. "Let her go," she repeated.

But Harper shook his head. "Bitch . . . could have been . . . perfect . . ."

"There's nowhere to go." Jude's hard voice. The guy hadn't stayed back. Now he stood beside her, naked and strong and more than ready to face down the devil with her.

Gotta love a man like that.

*Love.* Erin's breath caught.

"*Bitch!*" A scream from Harper. "Should have . . . been mine! *My mate, my—*"

"I'll never be yours." She shook her head. "And you should know there's no way you're leaving here alive tonight." Wouldn't happen.

Sirens screamed in the distance.

A cage wouldn't hold him.

But they *would* stop him. "Now let her go!" Erin demanded.

"*Mine,*" he whispered, but sounded broken, lost.

"No, asshole," Jude growled. "She's not."

Harper shook his head frantically.

Erin's stare jerked to Dee's face. The woman's lips moved, soundlessly. *Save her.*

Dammit, she was trying! Trying to save them all. Dee, her mother—

Dee's eyes tracked to the right. Her gaze landed on the gun she'd dropped when Harper grabbed her.

Again, her lips moved. No sound. *Save her.*

Dee had reloaded that gun just moments before and she'd—

*No.* Not *save her*. That wasn't what Dee was trying to say.

Once more, the human's lips formed words. One word, not two. *Silver.*

Jude tensed beside her. He'd seen and understood.

"I loved you," Harper whispered and his hand flexed.

Dee's head moved in the slightest of jerks, and Erin saw her body rock forward.

She'd have to move, fast. They both would.

Harper's face twisted with hate, not love, and she knew he was going for the kill. "For you," he said and the claws dug deep.

"*No!*" Erin lunged for the gun.

Dee twisted hard, jerking and squirming, and Jude was there, slashing with his claws and yanking her into his arms as he spun, attempting to shield Dee with his body.

Erin brought up the gun.

Harper smiled. "Just like me."

She fired. The bullet blasted into his chest.

Right into his heart.

Her father had taught her that, too. Shoot to kill. Kill to protect.

"No, bastard, I'm nothing like you."

Harper's eyes were wide open when he fell back. All the better to see death.

Her breath came out on a hard, ragged exhale.

Jude lowered his arms and turned back to glance at the body.

A grim smile curved Dee's lips. "And this time, you'll stay down, asshole."

Silver to the heart. According to the legends, a surefire way to kill a werewolf.

Or in this case, a hybrid wolf shifter.

Slowly, Erin stalked over to the judge. The gun was a solid weight in her hand as she gazed down at his face. Dee was right. The judge wouldn't be getting up from that one.

*Over.*

The wailing sirens were so loud now, screaming in her ears. Doors slammed nearby. Footsteps thudded. Voices rose. Men, women.

One was louder, angrier than the others. "All right . . . get the hell out of my way! Jude! Dee!"

Zane was there.

Erin dropped the gun. She spun around. "My mother!" Theresa's eyes were closed and she'd sagged back against the ground. Tear tracks stained her cheeks. Had she seen Erin kill Harper? "Mother!"

Two men with stethoscopes raced toward Theresa.

"Easy . . ." Antonio appeared before her. He grabbed her shoulders, holding her steady. "I need an EMT here, now! She's got severe injuries and blood loss!"

"I'm already healing," she whispered. "But you have to understand, my mother's not human."

A quick nod. "Samuels!" A female EMT scrambled from the back of an ambulance. "Take care of the female victim!" He jerked his thumb toward Erin's mother. "Then, Barlow, come over here and see about this bastard." His hand sliced toward Harper.

One of the male EMTs left her mother's side and hurried to the body.

"Not much they can do for him," Jude muttered.

"Ah, *hell*!" Antonio closed his eyes. "Clothes! Man, I'm so tired of seeing your naked ass!"

"Yo!" Zane tossed a pair of jeans toward Jude, then his gaze snapped to Dee. "Woman, what the hell happened to you?" Worry there.

A wan smile curved Dee's lips. "Wolf tried to play with me."

"Huh."

"Nothing I can do for him," Barlow said, rising. "He's gone."

To hell, she hoped.

Dee's right shoulder lifted, then fell. "He didn't know I like to keep silver bullets handy."

"And wooden stakes in your bag," Zane added.

The ambulance's siren wailed on. They were loading Theresa. "I-I need to go with her."

"You can't." Antonio's face was grim. "I've got at least half a dozen cops who just saw you shoot that bastard—*and I'm real damn glad he was in human form at the time.*" Yeah, that after-death shift would have been a hard one to explain. "You can't leave the scene, not yet."

Samuels climbed in after her mother's gurney, and the EMT yanked the doors closed.

"She'll be okay," Antonio told her. "Samuels has a lot of experience with your kind."

*Your kind.* Erin licked her lips and managed a nod.

"We've got to do this by the book." His voice barely floated in the air. "There are too many eyes here. Watch what you say, Jerome."

She would.

The ambulance pulled away. The swirling lights vanished into the darkness.

Not the same as before.

Her mother hadn't dropped her off without a word this time.

She'd sacrificed herself. *Almost died, for me.*

You didn't risk death unless there was a very, very good reason. *I'd always thought she didn't care.*

*Tonight, she'd cared enough to die for me.*

This time, her mother had chosen her.

"*Dammit.* Now who the hell is that?" Antonio's hands fisted on his hips as he craned his head. "Hey, dick, get out of here! You're not one of my guys so your ass needs to get lost!"

Erin followed his glare and stiffened her shoulders when she caught sight of a familiar figure, the dick in question. *Ben.*

He was trying to push his way through the cops. He had his badge out, and he shoved it at the officers as they fought to keep him away from the crime scene.

"Asshole, did you hear me? Get the fuck out!"

Erin's fingers touched Antonio's arm. "He's a cop from Lillian. He . . . knows the judge."

Antonio's brows flew up. "Uh, the judge?"

Jude, with his spare jeans on but his chest bare and still bleeding a bit from his battle, stalked up to them. "Yeah, the dead bastard was a judge."

And so much more. She'd tell Jude. Tell him everything when they were alone, but her mother's secrets weren't for all the others to hear.

Antonio's jaw locked. "Never. Easy."

Another ambulance sped away from the scene. Erin's attention jerked to Jude. "Dee?" She hoped the human was all right.

"She'll be okay. Zane threw her bleeding butt into the ambulance. He knows how weak humans can be, and the guy wanted to make sure Dee wasn't taking any chances."

Weak—Dee? Not likely. She'd fought with more spirit than most shifters.

A long sigh ripped from Antonio's lips. "Asshole! Get over here!"

The cops holding Ben back glanced at the captain with raised brows.

"His name's Ben," Erin told him. "Detective Ben Greer."

Another sigh. "Long-ass night, I know it's gonna be one long-ass . . ." He waved toward the uniforms. "Let Detective Greer pass!" Then, for her and Jude, " 'Cause we're probably gonna need him to help cover our asses."

Yeah, they probably would.

Ben stormed toward them, his face locked in hard lines of tension and his eyes blazing. "Erin?"

Jude wrapped his arm around her shoulders and pulled her back against the solid wall of his chest. "She stopped the killer."

Ben craned his neck to see around them. She knew immediately when he caught sight of the body because his eyes doubled in size and his jaw dropped. "*Holy Mother of Christ*—Judge Harper!"

Erin was pretty sure most of the citizens of Lillian would be having that reaction. "He killed Trent. He attacked you. Murdered another man named Bobby Burrows—"

"*Butchered him,*" Antonio threw in.

"He tried to rape me, and tonight, tonight, he would have killed me." And Dee and her mother.

Death had been the only way to stop him. Her mother would understand that more than anyone else.

Erin stared into Antonio's dark eyes. This part was for him and for the mess he'd have at the station. "He confessed. In front of me, Dee and my mother. They'll swear to what they saw and heard."

He yanked out his notebook. "And what else did they see, Jerome? I'm guessing some things I don't want on the record."

"He was a wolf shifter," Jude said, his hold never wavering. "That's one of the reasons he was so hard to kill, and why when your ME digs into him, he'll find a silver bullet lodged in his chest."

"*Harper?*" Ben still seemed stunned.

She'd been that way, too.

"Silver bullet." Antonio closed his eyes. "*Great.*"

"It kept him down," Jude said. "I'd already all but ripped his throat out—and he still got up. Trust me, Tony, we needed that bullet."

Some legends were based on a bit of truth.

Some weren't.

Jude pressed a kiss to her shoulder, then she felt the warm lap of his tongue as he licked lightly at her flesh. Shifters tended each other this way.

The way of their kind.

Her head tilted back against him and heat spread through her.

"Save it!" Antonio snapped. "Get a room later, but I don't need this crap now!"

One more swipe of Jude's tongue. The tending wasn't sexual—well, okay, *maybe* it was. But the soft strokes meant more than just a prelude to sex.

To a shifter, it was the way to express affection.

Maybe even love.

Erin turned toward him. She found Jude watching her with eyes that were so very blue.

"You scared the hell out of me," he whispered, and the others fell away to her.

Disappeared.

"When I came up and that bastard was over your throat . . ."

Not a moment she really wanted to relive.

"I didn't think I'd get to you in time."

But this was a moment that called for honesty. "Neither did I." And her last thought had been of him.

Her Jude.

Her tiger. With eyes that burned so very bright.

She touched his face. "You saved my life."

"Only fair, considering you'd already done the same for me."

And she'd do it again, any day. Because—because—

Antonio cleared his throat. Hard.

—because she was in love with her badass, wild tiger shifter.

*In love.* Absolutely, freaking, crazy, I'd-kill-to-protect him—and *had*—in love. For the first time in her life. Pity that it had taken almost dying to make her realize that fact.

But, better late than never.

# Chapter 21

"I'm sorry, Ms. Jerome, but your mother isn't here."

Erin's eyes widened as she stared at the emergency room desk clerk, sure the woman was wrong. She had to be wrong. "But she was brought in on an ambulance not even an hour ago."

The clerk, a short, balding man with a round face, flushed. "Ah, yes, um, I remember *that.*"

This wasn't going to be a good story.

"When the doors opened, the EMTs were there, but the patient—ah, she'd . . . already exited the vehicle."

Erin blinked. "Run that by me again."

His face a deeper red now, he said, "The EMTs said she jumped out when they slowed for a blocked intersection. She shoved right past them and managed to kick open the doors."

A smile lifted her lips. "Really?"

Sweat beaded his brow. "I assure you, this isn't normal routine, and the EMTs did everything they could to restrain her."

Her smile widened. "I guess she didn't feel like being restrained." If her mother was back in fighting and fleeing form, then she'd be all right.

And Erin knew she'd be seeing her again soon.

*Thank you, Theresa.*

Their life was far, far from perfect, but a mother who was willing to risk her life in order to get back into her daughter's good graces, well, that was a woman who deserved a second chance.

Erin would give her one.

Her nails tapped against the counter. "And what about Dee Daniels? How is she?"

Seriously, no human should be that shade of red. "*Dee.*" He said the name like it was a curse. Based on that telling response, Erin figured the guy had probably seen Dee in the ER a few times. With the way Dee fought, that sure made sense. "Dee, she's ah . . . in recovery. Not up to visitors yet."

"But she's okay?"

A weak nod. His Adam's apple bobbed.

Her shoulders relaxed. "Good." Better than good.

She'd come to the ER at Mercy General alone. Jude had stayed behind to keep answering all the million and one questions that the cops had.

She'd gone after her mother because she'd had to make certain she was all right.

If the woman was well enough to flee, then, yeah, she had to be on the mend.

Voices buzzed behind her. Machines beeped. Doctors rushed past.

She couldn't see Dee yet—

But there was someone else upstairs.

Erin shoved away from the counter.

"Ah, ma'am?" The desk clerk's strangled voice.

Erin walked toward the bank of elevators.

"Ma'am? You—you've got a lot of blood there . . ."

She glanced down. The shirt had dried, finally, but the blood made it thick and heavy. And her fingers, the ones she'd been tapping on the counter, were stained red. *Whoops.*

The elevator doors opened with a chime. She walked inside and turned back to face the clerk. "Don't worry," she told him. "Only half the blood's mine."

The doors slid shut, but not before she'd seen his face turn from red to a very dark purple.

The crime scene looked like chaos, but Jude knew Tony had everything under control.

The body had been tagged and bagged. The area had been sectioned off. Evidence collected. No detail would be overlooked under Tony's watch.

Erin wouldn't be charged. Hell, after she'd given her story, Tony had even gotten one of the cops to take her to the hospital. A police escort.

No, she wouldn't be charged, and good old Judge Harper would go down as a twisted freak who'd gotten too attached to one of the lawyers in his courtroom.

"When we start digging into his past," Tony said, coming to stand beside Jude and staring out into the darkness of the swamp, "I give you fifty to one odds"—*Tony loved to gamble*—"that we're gonna find out this wasn't the first time he got batshit crazy."

Jude grunted his agreement. No telling what skeletons were about to fall out of the judge's closet.

"This *isn't* his first time." Ben Greer paced toward them, his hands shoved deep into his pockets. He'd clipped his badge to the front of his shirt. Lines were etched across his pale face. "There have been some . . . killings in Lillian over the last few years."

Jude narrowed his eyes on the cop. "What kind of killings?"

"The kind that some cops don't care about." Ben's lips twisted. "A rapist had his throat slit two years ago and his body was tossed onto the steps of the PD. Before that, a guy who'd walked on a murder charge—a guy guilty as fucking sin, because everyone *knew* he'd killed his wife and her lover—ah, someone cut out his heart . . . and then sent the *package* to the guy's lawyer."

"You're saying that Harper did this?" Tony demanded. "If you knew about him, why the hell didn't you move on the guy?"

"Because I didn't have any proof." A shrug. "I still don't." He didn't look at the bagged body. "I remember though. Harper was the judge on those cases, and a few others where the defendants walked when they shouldn't have gotten off."

A pattern. "Like Donald Trent," Jude said quietly.

"Yeah, yeah, just like Trent. And just like him these other bastards all ended up dead within six months." Disgust had faint lines appearing around his mouth. "No evidence was left behind, except, on a few of the bodies, we found some damn dog hairs—" He broke off and gave a loud burst of laughter, the kind that sounded a little crazy and the kind that didn't have one ounce of humor. "*Dog hairs.* Guess that makes sense now, doesn't it?"

Jude just stared back at him.

The human shook his head. "Hell. I still don't have a bit of solid evidence, though, do I? It's not like I can go to my captain and tell him the judge was a *werewolf* who liked to get off on-on—"

"On handing out his own justice." Because Jude realized that was exactly what the judge had been doing, probably for *years.* If he'd been Lone all that time, battling a nature he couldn't control, he would have needed prey.

The criminals would have been perfect for him.

So, during the day, Harper had presided on his bench, looking all perfect for the humans. Then at night, he'd let the beast out, and he'd hunted his prey.

Until one fine day, Erin had walked into his courtroom.

Not prey, something more.

*Good thing the bastard's dead.* His jaw clenched.

"He . . . he left the bench after Erin disappeared," Ben spoke slowly now, as if putting all the puzzle pieces together. "He kept a house in Lillian, but he told everyone he wanted to do some traveling."

And he'd traveled to Lillian. The better to kill and to make Erin's life hell. "*Sonofabitch.*" Jude drove a hand through his hair. "That's why the woman acted so surprised to see him at the government building."

"Man, I don't know what the hell you're talking about," Tony said. "Slow it down. I'm the bastard you have to bring up to speed, remember?"

Jude crossed his arms over his chest. "When we were in Lillian, Erin and I stumbled across the bastard in the government basement. A woman was there, too, Lacy something. She was acting funny around the judge. I thought it was because they were screwing, but I guess she was just shocked to see the bastard there."

Ben pursed his lips and a glimmer of humor appeared in his eyes. "Actually, they were screwing, until the judge left the bench."

"The DA was focused on the Trent case, so he didn't say anything about the judge." But the puzzle pieces had all been there. Staring him right between the eyes.

"We're gonna need to search the judge's place in Lillian," Tony said, nodding his head. "No telling what we'll find there."

Those skeletons. Because somebody like Harper wasn't the kind to kill and forget. Wolf shifters never were.

There would be trophies. Keepsakes.

And Ben would get his evidence to hand in to his captain.

Case fucking closed.

Erin hesitated in front of the hospital room door. Her hand lifted and touched the wood. The door was already ajar. She could hear voices. A man's voice, raspy, weak.

A kid's voice, high with excitement.

Now probably wasn't the best time. She could see Lee later, talk to him and explain.

Footsteps padded quickly toward the door. Her breath caught and she eased back a step.

But it was too late.

A small hand pulled open the door, and a little boy with a mop of curls stared up at her. "My daddy's awake," he said, and a broad grin split his face, revealing one front tooth.

Erin swallowed. "Th-that's great." The door was fully open now. She could see Lee. Pale, bruised, and bandaged. He was propped up in bed, pillows all around him.

A woman stood beside him. She wasn't touching him. Just standing close. She had the same curly hair that the kid did, only darker.

"E-Erin . . . Jerome," Lee spoke with the rasp again. Probably from the tubes they'd shoved down his throat. Or maybe—maybe just from the whole near-dying thing.

A smile swept over the woman's face. "You're the one who found Lee! You saved him! I-I heard the cops talking . . ."

Oh, this wasn't going to be easy.

The brunette's stare dropped to rake down Erin's body. "Uh . . . are you—are you hurt?"

She'd managed to wash the blood off her hands and she'd traded in her bloody shirt for a scrub top. But Erin knew she still had to look like warm hell. "May I talk to Lee, alone?"

"But what—"

"It's ok . . . ay, M-Melis . . . sa . . ." His blood pressure and heart rate flashed on the monitor behind him. "Give us . . . a m-minute . . ."

The cute kid was still smiling up at her, and Erin shifted from one foot to the other. Then his mother was there, catching his hand and guiding him outside. "Thank you," she whispered and Erin had to look away.

She closed the door behind them and knotted her fingers behind her back.

Lee watched her. Both of his eyes had thick, dark shadows around them. "You . . . saved me . . ." He shook his head. "Don't . . . re-remember much. How—how did . . . you know . . . where I w-was?"

This was the hard part. Erin eased into the chair next to the bed. Okay. The guy had almost died. She figured he was owed the truth—the whole truth. He might not believe her. He might think she was certifiable, but she was going to tell him. What he did with the knowledge, well, that would be up to him. "Lee, I've got a story to tell you." She glanced at her small, oval nails. "One you might not believe at first, but I swear, every word of it's true."

The machines beeped quietly. *If he gets too crazy and starts screaming for help because there's a monster next to him, I can always blame his reaction on the drugs. Yeah, the orderlies would buy that.*

But maybe excuses wouldn't be needed. Erin took a deep breath. "You see, Lee, there's a whole lot more to this world than most people realize . . ."

Jude was waiting for her when she came out of the hospital room. He'd heard the soft whisper of her voice and been stunned by her words.

But probably not quite as stunned as Lee Givens had been to hear that Erin was a . . . sort of werewolf.

Her shoulders were slumped when she came out but her eyes seemed to lighten a bit when she saw him. Good sign. He caught her hand and led her to the elevator. It was nearing one a.m. now. A curly haired kid slept on his mom's lap in the waiting area. The mother brushed back his curls, humming softly and crying a bit with each slow movement of her hand.

Erin glanced at them, swallowed, and let him push her inside the elevator.

He waited until the doors closed before he spoke. "The guy seemed to take it well."

"H-his grandmother was a charmer. He already knew about the *Other*."

He'd caught that part of the conversation, but he let her talk anyway. He figured she needed to.

"I thought he'd . . . blame me."

The lights on the elevator wall blinked as they descended.

"He didn't." She shook her head. "He just . . . thanked me. He let me talk, let me tell him all about Harper—*and he thanked me*."

Maybe Lee wasn't as much of an asshole as he'd always thought.

"He said things would be different for him, that he had a second chance."

Second chances were damn rare.

The last light flashed on. They'd hit the ground floor. The doors opened with a whisper. Erin stepped forward, but hesitated. "I don't want to go home tonight. Not there, just . . . not tonight."

And he wouldn't take her back to his cabin. The police were still combing that road. She didn't need to see the death scene again so soon.

"Don't worry," he told her, catching her fingers and bringing them to his lips. *Alive. She was alive.* He kept having to remind himself of that very important fact because the image of the wolf with his fangs bared over her throat wouldn't stop playing in his mind. "Got it covered, sweetheart." He stared into her golden eyes. "I've got it covered."

When he shoved open the hotel's front door, Jude caught sight of the same punk kid he'd seen before at the front desk. Hell.

The kid's eyes widened and Jude knew he'd been recognized, too. Blue eyes darted to Erin's face, lingered for a bit. "Two rooms again?"

Smart-ass. Jude slapped the money down on the countertop. "One—with a king-size bed."

The acne hadn't cleared up a bit for the punk. "You sure you only want one room?" The question was directed at Erin.

Why did he have to put up with this ass? Hadn't his night been hard enough?

"One room." Her voice was husky and soft and sounded like pure sex.

The kid gulped and shoved a key card across the countertop.

Jude kept his hand around her lush curves and guided her toward the stairs.

"Lucky bastard." The kid probably thought he wouldn't hear that, and if he'd been human, maybe he wouldn't have caught the whisper.

Jude glanced back at him. "Yeah, I am." He was hoping like hell that his luck continued to hold. Because now that the danger was past, he didn't want to lose his lady.

The silence stretched between them as they traveled to

the room. Erin's steps were slow and heavy on the carpet. She had to be close to collapse after a night like this one.

He shoved the keycard into the lock. The light flashed green, and Erin grabbed the handle and opened the door.

Different room. Same layout.

Jude swallowed and tried to ignore the fact that his cock was fully erect, twitching with hunger, and that he was more than desperate for Erin.

*Considerate.* He could do that bit. For her. "You should . . . get some rest." The door clicked closed behind him.

Erin gave a nod and jerked the garish green shirt over her head. Her white bra was striped with red. So was her chest. "Shower first," she said, and turned away from him. He watched her, his eyes on the sleek line of her back. Then his stare dropped to the soft sway of her hips and her truly phenomenal ass.

He'd loved that ass from the beginning. When he'd watched her walk away from him on that hot, stinking street, he hadn't been able to look away from that sweet ass.

She paused at the bathroom door. Erin kicked off her shoes and shimmied out of her pants. "The shower's big enough for two, you know."

Not like he had to be told twice. He toed off the shoes Zane had dug up—*from hell knew where*—and stripped as he stalked to the bathroom.

The rush of water poured into the tub. Erin had already turned on the shower. Wisps of steam began to appear in the air. He hesitated as he watched her. She'd climbed into the small space, and a clear pane of glass separated them. The water hit her, pouring over her flesh, soaking her hair and sliding in rivulets down her body.

*Erin.*

She soaped her skin. Lathered her stomach. Smoothed her hands over her breasts.

His mouth went bone dry.

*Considerate*. He could do it. Maybe.

The glass began to fog and when he lost his million dollar view, Jude jerked to action.

He grabbed the shower door and wrenched it open.

The blood was gone from her body. She was all soft, smooth flesh now.

Naked woman.

He eased in behind her. No way was she going to miss the raging hard-on, but if she didn't mind it poking her in that gorgeous ass—

Erin turned toward him. The water beat down on them both. "Kiss me."

His lips took hers. Her tongue thrust into his mouth and stroked over his. Fuck considerate.

The vision of her on the ground, the wolf above her, flashed before his closed eyes, and he growled. His hands locked around her hips and he yanked her even closer.

His cock pressed against her. The feel of that smooth, wet skin was a stimulant that had him shaking.

Her nipples stabbed against his chest. He had to taste the tight, hard tips. Wanted them against his tongue. Jude ripped his mouth from hers. Lowering his head, he craned down and caught one sweet pink tip.

Her moan filled his ears even as his tongue stroked the peak. He'd never get enough of her rich taste. The scent of her cream filled his nostrils.

She wanted him. He was dying for her.

His fingers pushed between them. Erin parted her thighs for him and Jude found her creamy heat. He drove one finger into her. *Ready.* She was more than ready.

So was he.

The water was too hot. No, maybe that was him.

Screw it.

Another finger plunged inside her and she moaned, a deep, guttural sound.

His cock jerked. *Inside.*

He backed her up against the side of the shower. He freed her breast, after one more greedy suckle, and his head rose as he stared down at her. Such golden eyes—filled with lust and hunger.

His fingers pumped in her. Once. Twice. His thumb stroked her clit, just the way he knew she liked and when her breath panted, when her eyes flared, when he knew she was just about to come—

Jude dragged his hand away from her.

"Jude!"

Ah, that was what he liked. The sound of his name on her lips, grated with hunger, whispered with demand.

He lifted her up, positioning her so that he could see that perfect pink flesh.

Her back pressed against the tile. Her wet hair stuck to her face and neck.

*Beautiful.*

He drove his cock inside as deep as he could go—and she came at that first plunge, her sex squeezing him and milking his erection as her delicate muscles convulsed. Her eyes seemed to go blind for a moment and her mouth opened wide.

He kissed her and kept plunging. Ignoring the pounding drive of the water, he sank into the warmth of her sex. Over and over. Thrusting hard and plunging deep.

*Like nothing else. Nothing. Else.*

Her sex held him tight, the flesh a greedy squeeze on his cock. Tight. So tight.

In. Out.

His groans filled the air. Mixed with her moans. The driving water caught them both.

She'd come again, he knew she would, and he'd be with her.

Her fingers latched onto his shoulders. Her claws bit into the skin.

Deeper. Harder.

Her legs were clamped around his hips, her heels digging into his ass.

"Again, Jude, again!"

His thrusts were wild now as he shoved into that slick paradise. Again, again.

She bit him. Erin caught him at the curve of his shoulder and sank those sharp teeth into his flesh.

Jude erupted inside of her, coming on a wave of white-hot release that gutted him. His knees trembled, his spine prickled and his semen poured inside her.

*Mate.*

Her cry filled his ears and she came again, squeezing him so tightly with her legs and arms and sex. He loved that—loved the way she held him, loved the sounds of her pleasure, the hot clasp of her body.

Loved her.

And he didn't even realize he'd whispered the words until Erin's head snapped up and she clipped him in the chin. "*What?*"

Ben Greer stared up at the antebellum house on St. Charles Avenue. Erin wasn't there. He shouldn't have been surprised, really, but he'd thought he might be able to catch her.

And apologize for being an ass.

He exhaled and turned away from the house. She was probably with that other asshole, the one with the icy blue eyes. Eyes that only warmed when they were on her.

That guy—Jude—wasn't going to be letting Erin out of his life. And he wasn't going to be too keen on an ex-lover paying her a visit.

Too bad. Because he would see Erin again. The news she'd told him and the things he'd seen since then, yeah, they'd made his head spin and ache like a bitch, but he was trying to play catch-up, fast.

And trying to figure out just what else he'd been missing in this world.

His cell phone rang. He glanced at the number. Officer Langley. He answered the call even as he climbed into his car. "You got the clear on the Harper house?" He'd called his captain as soon as he'd gotten the go-ahead from Antonio. They'd needed to search the judge's house and see just what surprises were waiting for them.

"Captain Henderson's already inside." Disgust there, anger. "He didn't want to wait for you to get back."

No, Henderson wouldn't. The guy would want as much glory as he could get.

"You wouldn't believe this place!" Her voice rose with excitement. "The guy kept freaking diaries, journals of his kills."

*Kills*. The fingers of his left hand tightened around the steering wheel. "How many are we looking at?"

"Henderson says maybe ten, could be fifteen. The guys aren't even halfway through his place."

He exhaled. How had they missed this? For all these years?

The judge had been good at pretending, and, apparently, killing.

"When are you coming back? Henderson thinks we can close some old cases—"

Yeah, they'd probably be closing almost all of Lillian's unsolved crimes going back for the last twenty years, right to the date when good old Harper had first appeared in the city. "I'm on my way."

He'd have to pay a visit to Katherine. Let her know that she and the boys were safe.

Then there would be other families to visit. Explanations to be made.

Explanations that wouldn't include a story about a man who could shift into a wolf. Not that anyone would believe that, anyway, not without proof.

*Those dog hairs*. They'd been all over some of the vics. He'd never even suspected the truth about them.

"I'm on my way," he said again and ended the call.

His eyes darted once more to Erin's dark house. He'd be back. Erin had meant too much for him to just walk away with things shot to hell between them.

They wouldn't be together again. Donovan would see to that. And so would Erin. The way she'd watched the hunter—*never looked at me like that.*

The car's engine purred to life.

Maybe, maybe after this case, it would be time for his life to take a change. Maybe a new start. A new city.

Hell, maybe Antonio needed a new detective—one who was learning the real score.

*Werewolves.* Who the hell would have thought those bastards were real? And sitting on court benches?

She'd wrapped a towel around her body. After Jude's big confession, Erin had finally managed to snap her jaw back into place and now she paced next to the bed, trying to figure out what to say.

"Erin?"

Her gaze flew to him. He hadn't dressed. Ah, damn but he was sexy. Those broad shoulders. That chest with the rippling muscles and light covering of golden hair. Erin gulped as she stared helplessly at that flat stomach—and that huge cock. Already fully erect again and so close. Hers for the taking if she just would reach out and touch—

*Focus!*

She sucked in a deep breath. Okay, she'd killed the wolf shifter tonight. She could handle this. Right? *Right.* "Did you mean it?"

His hands were on his hips. His narrowed stare never left her face.

Okay. The knot she'd hooked between her breasts seemed to dig into her flesh. "You said you loved me." Sure, lots of men were known to get a little wild and chatty during sex, but Jude wasn't most men. "*Did you mean it?*"

He took one long, gliding step toward her. Another.

She didn't retreat, and in seconds, he was right before her. "Hell, yeah, sweetheart, I meant it."

And that lump in her throat—the one that appeared pretty often when he was near—came back with a vengeance.

"I think I've loved you since that first hellish night at your place." *Since then?* "You were standing there, with the blood on your walls, and your chin was up and you were holding onto your control as tight as you could with both your hands."

She swallowed so she could speak. "My first instinct was to call you that night."

"You knew you could count on me."

Should have been impossible. She wasn't the trusting sort, never had been, but, yes, she'd known he'd help her.

And he had.

Erin wet her lips. "There's something you . . . need to know about the judge."

He waited. Just waited with that steady gaze.

"He was my mother's lover. The man she left my father to

be with." The man who'd nearly killed them both. "I didn't know, not until tonight." Because the surprises just kept coming for her. But she'd been trying to make sense of things and maybe . . . "Maybe I wasn't his mate, maybe he just got everything twisted in his mind because we look alike, maybe—"

He pressed a fingertip against her lips. "He was a fucked up bastard, sweetheart. I don't give a shit what he thought. You were *never* his."

His finger lifted, and her breath left her lungs on a soft sigh.

His blue stare held her gaze. "Something *you* need to know. This stopped being a case for me a long time ago." He shook his head. "I'm never supposed to get personal with the clients, but with you, I didn't have a choice." His fingers lifted and skimmed the edge of her jaw. "*You* were the case, and I would have fucking killed to keep you safe."

He almost had.

"I don't care if you're human or wolf. You're mine, Erin. The woman I want. The only one I've ever loved."

Oh, hell, and he was hers.

"Forget the past. Forget that twisted bastard and start over again—with me. You might not love me yet, but give me a chance, sweetheart. The blood and hell are behind us. We can go slow now, date like humans, play normal."

Normal was losing its appeal. "That's not what I want anymore," she told him and her hand brushed against his abdomen.

Jude sucked in a sharp breath and his pupils flared. "Erin, we can do this, we can—"

"I tried 'normal.' That wasn't really for me." *Wished I'd realized that sooner.*

Silence for a beat, then, "What is for you?"

A man who wasn't afraid of the darkness inside her. A man who had a wild side to match her own.

A man who'd saved her from death.

A man who kissed her like she was his life.

"You are, Jude." She was taking a risk. One big-ass risk. But for him, for what they might have, she'd do it. "You're the man I want." More than a man. So much more. "The one I love."

That scar, the thin line on his lip that she always wanted to lick, rose as his lips curved. "You mean that? Be sure, very, very sure, because I'm not talking about a fling here. I'm talking about forever."

Forever with her tiger. Sounded pretty good. She leaned toward him and used her tongue to trace that line on his lip. Then she said, "So am I."

She'd never thought about spending all her days with someone else before. With so many secrets, she hadn't even come close to trusting another man with her life.

But Jude knew all of her secrets, and he didn't care about her past. He didn't think she was broken or weak. When he looked at her, he looked at her with lust and hunger and—

*I can see it now—should have seen it before.*

Love.

Maybe she had seen it, but she'd been afraid.

It was time to stop being afraid. Time to start living. Really living.

Her hand rose between their bodies and caught the knot of her towel. With one tug, she jerked it loose. The towel hit the floor.

His gaze brightened. Such a bright blue. The tiger was close.

Good. She liked the beast and loved the man.

Life wouldn't be perfect for them, she knew that.

But screw perfect. She'd take her tiger and she'd take her wild ride.

And she'd take the love she'd found, *forever.*

"Fucking beautiful, sweetheart, fucking beautiful." His mouth pressed against her neck.

Her head fell back and the hunger rose. *Jude.*

She let her claws out and got ready to take her lover.

A man with more than a bit of the animal inside.

The perfect man for her.

Turn up the heat with this excerpt from

The first book in Cynthia Eden's new series

BURN FOR ME

Available February 2014

# Chapter 1

The first time Eve Bradley saw Subject Thirteen, he was in chains.

She froze in front of the glass wall that separated her from him—a wall that, to Subject Thirteen, would look just like a mirror. The two-way mirror let the doctors and observers watch his every move. Not that the guy could do much moving when he was chained to the wall.

"I-I thought . . ." Eve tried to fight the tremble in her voice. She was supposed to look like she belonged here. Like she fit in with all the other researchers who were so eager to experiment on the test subjects. "I thought everyone was here voluntarily."

Dr. Richard Wyatt turned to face her, his white lab coat brushing against her. "The chains are for his safety." His tone implied she should have realized that obvious fact.

Yeah, right.

Was she really supposed to buy that line? Being chained up—that equaled safety in what mixed-up world?

"Dr. Bradley . . ." His dark eyebrows lifted as he studied her with an assessing gaze. "You do realize that all of the subjects here are far, far from human, correct?"

She knew the spiel. "Yes, of course, I do. They're supernaturals. Here to take part in experiments that will help the U.S. military." So all the fancy guys in suits had told the media when the Genesis Group started their recruitment program last Fall.

Not that she believed their story. It had taken her months, *months,* to set up this cover and get inside the research facility.

If she'd been on her own, she never would have passed clearance. But, luckily, Eve had managed to make a few powerful friends over the years.

Friends who wanted to know the truth about this place as much as she did. They all had an interest in Genesis.

Some reporters really could smell a story. Right now, Eve's nose was twitching.

She glanced back at Subject Thirteen. Everyone knew paranormals were out there, living in the midst of humans. About ten years ago, the first supernaturals had made themselves known. They'd come on out of their paranormal closets. And why not? Why should they have been forced to keep hiding? Always hiding in the shadows had to suck. Maybe they'd just gotten tired of living a lie and decided to force the humans to see what was right in front of them—or what was living right beside them.

Since the big revelation, things had changed for the paranormals. Now some were hunted. Some turned into instant celebrities. The reaction from the humans, well, that was mixed, too.

Some humans hated the supernaturals. Some feared them. Some really enjoyed fucking them.

Eve didn't necessarily fall into any of those categories.

Subject Thirteen was staring right at her. A small shiver slid over Eve's body. His eyes were dark, they looked almost black—as black as the thick hair that hung a little too long as it brushed over his broad shoulders. Thirteen was a handsome man, strong, muscled—*definitely muscled*—and with the sculpted bone structure that had probably caught plenty of attention from the ladies.

High cheeks. Square jaw. Lips that were hard, a little thin, but still sexy. Sexy, though she could have sworn that mouth held a cruel curve.

Her heartbeat began to pound faster because Thirteen's eyes . . . they were sweeping over her body. A slow, deliberate glance. "Can he—can he see through the mirror?" His gaze felt like a hot touch on her skin.

"Of course not," was Dr. Wyatt's instant response. The doc sounded annoyed with her.

Her shoulders relaxed.

Subject Thirteen smiled.

Damn. Her shoulders tensed right back up again.

Wyatt checked his notes and then told her, "Go check his vitals before we begin the procedure for today."

Right. Vitals check. Her job. Eve nodded. She'd done two years of med school before realizing the gig wasn't for her, so she could pass muster with these guys, no problem. Only part of her resume was faked.

The good part.

Eve walked slowly toward the metal door that was the only entrance and exit to Thirteen's holding room. A guard opened the door for her. An *armed* guard. Which brought up the next question. *Why did volunteers have to be guarded?*

Oh, jeez, but this place was creeping her out. *Volunteers, my ass.*

Sure, she'd seen a couple of other subjects during her time at the Genesis facility. Not many, though. Her clearance wasn't high enough to get her past level one. Or it hadn't been . . . until today.

Until she'd been told that Dr. Wyatt needed her services for his latest experiment. Dr. Richard Wyatt *was* Genesis. A former kid genius, the guy had a couple of fists full of degrees, and, currently, Wyatt was the leading expert in the field of paranormal genetics.

He was also a hard-ass who gave her the creeps when his cold green eyes locked on her. Sure, maybe he was a fairly attractive guy, but something about him made her blood ice.

The guard waved his hand, indicating that it was clear for Eve to proceed. When she walked into Thirteen's holding room, Eve saw the slight flare of the man's nostrils. Then his head turned toward her, slowly, the move almost like a snake's as he sized her up.

He didn't speak, but his powerful hands clenched.

Eve opened her small, black bag. "Hello." Her voice came out too high-pitched. She drew in a steadying breath. The guy was chained. It wasn't like anything could happen to her right then. She needed to get a grip and do her job. "I'm just here to run a few quick checks on you." No machines were hooked up to him. No monitors. Wyatt wanted these checks done the old-fashioned way—hell if she knew why. Eve pulled out her stethoscope and stopped just a foot away from Thirteen. "I-I'll need to listen to your heartbeat."

Still nothing. Okay. Eve swallowed and offered a weak smile. Obviously, she wasn't dealing with a chatty fellow.

Eve slid closer to him. Her gaze darted to the chains. They held his arms trapped at his sides. Even if he'd wanted to grab her—*don't grab me, don't!*—he couldn't move.

What if Wyatt was setting her up? The guy was chained and that had to mean he was dangerous, right? Those were some seriously thick chains. They looked like something right out of a medieval torture chamber.

"I won't hurt you."

She jumped at the sound of his voice; and what a dark, rumbling voice it was. When the big, bad wolf from that old fairy tale talked, Eve bet the beast had sounded just like Subject Thirteen.

She exhaled and hoped she didn't look rattled. "I didn't think you would."

His lips twisted in the faintest of smiles—one that called her a liar.

Eve put the stethoscope over his heart. She adjusted the equipment, listened, and glanced up at him in surprise. "Is your heartbeat always this fast?" Grabbing his chart, she scanned through the notes. No, fast, but not *this* fast. Right then, his heart was galloping like a racehorse.

Eve put her hand against his forehead and hissed out a breath. The guy was hot. Not warm, not feverish, *hot.*

And she was now so close to him that her breasts brushed his arm.

Subject Thirteen's heartbeat grew even faster.

Oh . . . just . . . *oh*. Hell. She hurried backward a bit.

"I need to draw a sample of your blood." She also wanted to take his temperature because the guy had to be scorching. Just what was he? Not a vampire, those guys could never heat up this much. A shifter? Maybe. She'd seen one of those subjects on her first day. But the shifter had been in a cozy dorm-type room.

He hadn't been shackled.

Eve put up the stethoscope and reached for a needle. She eased closer to Thirteen once more and rose onto her toes. The guy was big, at least six three, maybe six four, so she couldn't quite reach his ear as she whispered, "Are you here willingly?"

Eve began to draw his blood. Thirteen didn't even flinch as the needle slid into his arm.

But he did give a small, negative shake of his head.

Shit. She eased back down and tried to figure out just how she could help him.

"I'm Eve." She licked her lips. His gaze followed the movement. The darkness in his stare seemed to heat. Everything about the guy was hot. "I-I can help you."

He laughed then, and the sound chilled her. "No," he said in that deep rumble of a voice, "you can't."

Eve realized she was standing between his legs. His unsecured legs. His thighs brushed against hers, and Eve flinched.

The smile on his face was as cold as his laughter. She'd been correct before when she thought she saw a cruel edge to his lips. She could see that hardness right then. "You should be afraid," he told her.

Yes, she was definitely getting that clue.

Eve pulled out the needle. Swabbed some alcohol over a wound she couldn't even see.

Then she stepped back, as quickly as she could.

"Don't come back in here," he told her, eyes narrowing. A warning.

Or a threat?

Eve turned away.

"You smell like fucking candy . . ."

She stilled. Now her heartbeat was the one racing too fast.

"You make me . . ." His voice dropped, but she caught the ragged growl of "hungry."

And he made her afraid. Eve slammed her hand onto the metal door. "Guard!" Her own voice was too high. "We're done!"

The door opened and she all but fell out of the room. Even though she was afraid, Eve risked one last look back.

Thirteen was staring after her, his jaw locked tight. He did look hungry. Only not for food.

*For me.*

The door slid shut and she remembered how to breathe. She'd sucked in a deep breath as she looked up—right into Dr. Wyatt's too sharp green gaze.

"Problem?" He asked softly, the barest hint of a southern drawl sliding beneath his words. Since the Genesis facility was hidden away in the Blue Ridge Mountains, many of the folks there had a slight drawl that spoke of roots in the south.

The guards, anyway. Thirteen hadn't possessed any accent that she could hear.

Yanking back her control, Eve shook her head and pushed Thirteen's chart toward him. "No problem at all, sir."

*Liar, Liar.*

She could still feel Subject Thirteen's stare on her body. Worse, she could feel *him.*

"Good," Wyatt said, "because it's time to begin."

Uh, begin? She'd rather thought her job was done.

He motioned to the guard. She'd already learned that guy's name. Mitchell. Barnes Mitchell. As Eve watched, Mitchell pulled out his gun and checked the clip.

"The first shot shouldn't be to the heart," Wyatt instructed as he cocked his head to the side and pursed his lips. "We want a comparison shot. Wound him first," he said with a nod, "then go for the heart."

*What?*

But Barnes just nodded and headed back into Thirteen's room with his gun ready.

Eve lost the breath she'd taken as horror nearly choked her.

* * *

Cain O'Connor drew in a deep breath. The air smelled of her. A light, sweet scent. He could almost taste the woman—and he wanted more of her. So much more.

What were the bastards thinking? Sending in a little morsel like her. Didn't they know what he could do to her? What he wanted to do? After all these months . . .

Maybe they'd wanted to tempt him. He pulled on the chains, testing their strength. They weren't made of any metal he'd ever come across. Reinforced with who the hell knew what. The Genesis pricks thought they were so smart with their inventions. "Supernatural-proof" as that ass Wyatt had gloatingly told him when he'd asked about the chains.

The chains wouldn't hold him forever. This prison would end. *Their* nightmare would begin.

*Soon.*

The door of his cell opened. He caught a glimpse of her—Eve—as she glanced back at him. Her blue eyes were wide, afraid. She should be afraid. She should run as fast as she could from this place. Before it was too late for her.

It was already too late for the others. He'd marked them for death. Especially that bastard Wyatt. The doctor got off on torture.

*How will you like it when you're the one screaming, Wyatt? Will it be so much fun then?*

The guard stepped inside. He smelled of sweat, cigarettes. The door closed behind him. No more Eve.

But Cain could hear her footsteps. Hers and Wyatt's. His senses were far more acute than he'd let on. Why give the enemy any advantage?

Why give them any fucking thing at all?

The guard, a stocky bastard with shifty eyes and a definite taste for torture, had his weapon out. Cain's jaw locked. He knew what the gun meant. This time, they were going to try old-fashioned bullets.

Would they take a heart shot? Or a head? Maybe the guard would shoot him right between the eyes and blow his brains out.

"*What are you doing?*" Eve's voice. Drifting lightly to his ears like a whisper. They thought they'd sound proofed his room.

They were wrong. He couldn't hear the voices perfectly, but he caught the whispers. Knew so much more than the not-so-good doctor realized.

Cain glanced toward the mirror. He saw right through the reflection and into the room. All it took was a little focus, a slight push of power . . .

*There she was.*

Her dark hair was pinned at the base of her neck. Her face—so damn pretty. Glass sharp cheekbones, red, plump lips that made him think of sin and sheets.

And her eyes . . . Fucking lethal.

Perhaps one of the few things that could be lethal to him.

"*Why does the guard have his gun out?*" Eve demanded, and he heard the fear shaking in her words.

He didn't like the sound of fear in her voice. Didn't like the smell of it on her, either. When Eve had gotten close to him, she'd been afraid.

Poor Eve. She probably didn't know who she should fear more . . . him or Wyatt.

Cain looked at the gun that the guard, Barnes, held. "Hardly seems fair," Cain muttered, "shooting me when I'm chained."

"*You're gonna let the guard shoot him?*" Was Eve's immediate cry.

Ah, she was definitely not like the others. That could be a problem. When hell came calling, and it would be calling soon, he'd have to make sure she didn't get burned.

Not too much, anyway.

The intercom clicked on. "Proceed with the test," Wyatt's annoying drawl ordered as it drifted through the speakers and into Cain's cell.

Dammit. Cain tightened his muscles. He hated for the woman to watch this, but perhaps she needed to see just what these bastards were capable of doing. She'd signed on for this, so she should understand just how psychotic her "boss" truly was.

"He can't proceed—" Eve shouted, her words tumbling through the intercom—

Just as the guard fired.

The bullet drove right into Cain's side. Tore through flesh and muscle. Blood spattered. Agony had his body shuddering.

But he didn't make a sound. That was a pleasure he wouldn't give the sadistic bastard watching.

"Silver bullets can pierce the subject's flesh," Wyatt's cool voice rattled off, as if the guy were talking about the weather.

Cain's hands clenched into fists. The next shot would be to a vital organ. He knew the drill. Wyatt liked to play at first. *Torturing SOB—*

"Stop!"

Cain glanced up. Eve was pounding on the glass. The mirror was shaking beneath the force of her fists. "Guard, get away from him!" She yelled and the desperate words echoed through the intercom system. "Drop the weapon!"

*Not like the others.*

Wyatt grabbed her by the shoulders and pulled her back. Anger pulsed in Cain's blood. The doctor shouldn't be touching her.

"Proceed." Wyatt's order.

Eve shrieked and twisted in Wyatt's arms.

Cain saw her break away from the doctor. She ran for the cell door. Yanked it open.

"*Proceed.*" Ah, now Wyatt sounded pissed.

And Eve was rushing inside. "Get away from him!" She yelled at the guard. "Drop your weapon and just—"

The guard fired.

This time, the bullet drove right into Cain's heart. He heard the *thud* as it tunneled into his flesh. Felt the sharp tear as it ripped through his heart. One instant of time. Two.

His gaze met Eve's. Her eyes—so blue—widened and her lips parted in a scream he didn't hear.

Too late. Cain was already dead.

Blood bloomed on Thirteen's chest. The bullet had blasted right into him—straight into his heart.

Eve ran toward him, ignoring the gun that the guard was slowly lowering. *Fucking killer.* Shooting a chained man. Yeah, that was fair.

Thirteen's legs had given way but the chains had stopped him from crashing into the floor. His head sagged forward, hanging limply. Her hands slid under his jaw, and she tilted his head back. *Oh, damn.* His eyes were closed, his lashes casting heavy shadows on his cheeks. Her breath whispered over him. "I'm sorry." She should have moved faster. Knocked out the guard. Done *something* to save this man.

Instead, she'd just watched him die.

"You need to step away from the test subject, Dr. Bradley," Wyatt said, his voice not on the intercom, but coming from right behind her.

Eve stiffened. "You just murdered a man in cold blood." She'd never expected to discover this. Experiments were one thing. Murder was a whole damn other sin.

One that wouldn't be forgiven.

Her fingers brushed lightly through Thirteen's hair. She'd said she would help him.

"He's not a man." Now Wyatt sounded amused. "You know that. No humans are test subjects in this facility. Genesis only recruits paranormals."

Fury had her shaking. "Human or supernatural . . . you *killed* him." She glanced back at Wyatt and the guard. Both were standing a good ten feet away from her.

Wyatt shrugged. "It's part of the experiment."

*What?*

He huffed out a frustrated breath. "Now you really should step away. If you don't, well, I'm sorry, but I can't guarantee your safety."

Insane. The doc was a mental case and as soon as she got out of that joint, she'd blast her story loud and proud to every media outlet in the country. She'd shut down this hellhole if it was the last thing she ever did.

Sure, some folks were hesitant about the supernaturals, but no one was going to accept a killing facility. No one would—

Thirteen moved, just a bit, beneath her touch.

"*Step back, Doctor Bradley.*" Was that fear in Wyatt's voice?

Eve couldn't tell, and since she wasn't looking at him, there was no way to read the emotion that might be on his face. Her attention was on Thirteen because . . . she could've sworn that she'd just felt him take a breath.

Impossible.

Sure, vampires could survive an assortment of attacks, but this guy was no vampire. Eve would bet her life on that. She'd seen him *die*. It was—

His lashes lifted. His eyes locked on her. Only his eyes

weren't black anymore. They were red, burning like flames. Burning so bright—burning, *burning* . . .

Hard hands yanked Eve back. She fell onto the floor, dragging Wyatt and the guard down with her. *Their* hands were on her. They were the ones pulling her away from Thirteen.

But almost instantly, Wyatt and Mitchell were back on their feet, and hauling her across the room with them.

Eve let them drag her away, but she couldn't take her gaze off Thirteen. Smoke was rising from his flesh, as if he were burning from the inside. That gaze—it looked like she was staring straight into hell. A man's eyes shouldn't flicker with fire.

His did.

The smoke rising from his body began to thicken.

"Out!" Wyatt's bark. The guard grabbed one of her hands. Wyatt grabbed the other. They all stumbled out into the hallway. Wyatt closed the door and quickly punched in a security code to lock the room down.

Eve memorized that code. Because what locked a man in . . . might just be able to let him out.

Then they all were racing back to that two-way mirror. Because it wasn't just smoke rising from Thirteen's body any longer. Flames were covering him.

"Oh, my God," the stunned whisper slipped from her.

Thirteen's head turned. Through the flames, he gazed at her.

Every muscle in her body tightened with pure terror. She'd never seen anything like this before. How? How could he still be standing? And he was standing now. Not on his knees any longer. Not handing from the chains. *Standing.*

The flames slowly died. They'd melted his clothes away. Ash drifted around him. Thirteen stood there, naked, strong, his body absolutely perfect.

No sign of the bullet wound that had ended his life.

Only . . . his life hadn't really ended, and he was still watching her.

"Wh-what is he?" Eve managed to ask.

Thirteen pulled on the chains that still bound him. Chains that had to be impervious to fire.

"I don't know . . ." Wyatt told her, and there was no missing the excitement that hummed in his words, "but I'm going to find out."

Thirteen's gaze cut to the doctor.

*He sees us.* She didn't know how, but the man who should have been dead could see right through that protective glass.

"Another successful experiment." Wyatt turned away from the observation mirror and headed toward the corridor that lead back to his office. "Tomorrow, we'll try drowning. It will be interesting to see if the test subject's flames burn through the water . . ."

Eve didn't move. She couldn't.

*Tomorrow, we'll try drowning.*

Dr. Richard Wyatt was some kind of seriously messed-up Frankenstein scientist. She put her hand to the glass. She didn't know what Thirteen was, but she couldn't let Wyatt keep torturing him.

"I'll stop him," she whispered.

But Thirteen shook his head. Then he mouthed two simple words: *I will.*

Richard Wyatt glanced over his shoulder just in time to see Eve put her hand to the glass—as if she were trying to touch the test subject. She should have been terrified, desperate to get away after what she'd just witnessed.

The others had been.

But, no, she was still there, staring in fascination at Subject Thirteen. Just as the subject was staring back at her.

How absolutely perfect. The experiment had been even more productive than he could have hoped. This new development could open up a whole world of unexpected possibilities.

A perfect killing machine. An immortal assassin.

One that only he could control.

The experiment had been a definite success. He could hardly wait for tomorrow's show to start.

Those flames were so beautiful. Would they burn Eve's delicate skin? Or would Thirteen finally start to show his true strength?

For her sake, Thirteen had better hold onto his control. Because the lovely Eve wouldn't just be an observer for tomorrow's event.

She'd be a participant.

Don't miss a single misadventure
of the marvelous mistress of mystery—
as Miss Seeton...

witnesses a murder at the opera in PICTURE MISS SEETON . . . investigates a local witches' coven in WITCH MISS SEETON . . . assists Scotland Yard in MISS SEETON DRAWS THE LINE . . . mixes with a gang of European counterfeiters in MISS SEETON SINGS . . . dons diamonds and furs for a game of roulette in ODDS ON MISS SEETON . . . encounters trouble at a tennis match in ADVANTAGE MISS SEETON . . . visits Buckingham Palace in MISS SEETON BY APPOINTMENT . . . takes a cruise to the Mediterranean in MISS SEETON AT THE HELM . . . foils some roadside bandits in MISS SEETON CRACKS THE CASE . . . helps to solve a series of suspicious fires in MISS SEETON PAINTS THE TOWN . . . stumbles into a nest of crime in HANDS UP, MISS SEETON . . . helps to capture an art thief in MISS SEETON BY MOONLIGHT . . . calls on her maternal instincts to solve a crime in MISS SEETON ROCKS THE CRADLE . . . attends a cricket game in MISS SEETON GOES TO BAT . . . tends to her garden—and roots out a killer—in MISS SEETON PLANTS SUSPICION . . . plays a backstage role at the Plummergen Christmas pageant in STARRING MISS SEETON . . . and helps trap some murderous antique thieves in MISS SEETON UNDERCOVER.

Available from Berkley Prime Crime Books!